THE UNSEEN KING

THE CARTOGRAPHER'S WAR
BOOK THREE

ALLISON ANDERSON

Cover Design by Cauldron Press

Published by Oliver-Heber Books

0 9 8 7 6 5 4 3 2 1

For Jeff Wheeler
I really should call you Doctor Frankenstein
since you brought this book back to life.

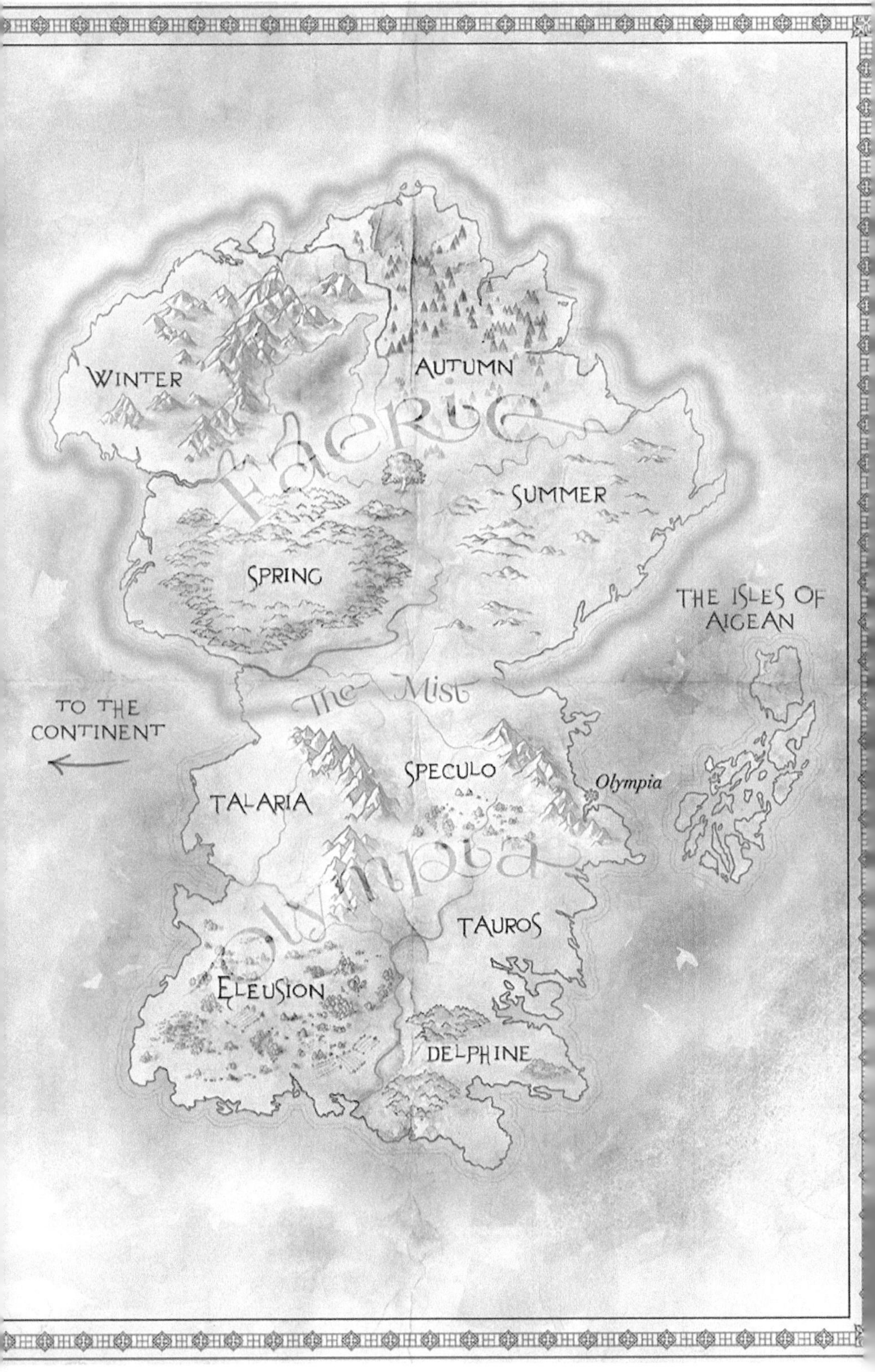

WINTER
AUTUMN
Faerie
SPRING
SUMMER
THE ISLES OF AIGEAN
The Mist
TO THE CONTINENT
TALARIA
SPECULO
Olympia
Olympia
TAUROS
ELEUSION
DELPHINE

1

AWAKE

Every inch of the ground was white. Snow powdered everything except the sky dressed in black and pinpricked with millions of stars frolicking through the velvet night. A howl rang in the distance, though not from any animal Aiden had ever heard. The sound sank into his very bones, into his erratically beating heart.

Then it vanished.

The white morphed into green and blue and pink. Pollen and wispy seeds pirouetted through the sun speckled air. Early notes of music wove through the greenery not far off. A group of goat-legged satyrs danced in a circle. Merriment filled their faces and Aiden's smile joined theirs. Penelope would have loved to see it.

Then they disappeared.

And there was only sand. It whipped up in dunes and sank under his feet like mounds of brown sugar. Forms flew across the sand a ways off, but he couldn't tell what they were. He took a step forward and the scene shifted again.

You are not ready for this.

Aiden whirled around. The voice in the dream—because this could only be called a dream—was not his own.

If you stay any longer, you will not be able to free yourself.

His forward step caught the edge of a cliff. A long line of snow-capped mountains spread in each direction. He could see the multiple colors of the land below him—all divided by sparkling rivers. Luscious green trees lined the frozen basin below him. Leaves the color of fire danced through the air toward dunes of golden sand. Like pieces of a crudely cut pie.

You must wake up.

Aiden's chest began to ache, the price of his magic making his heart slog in his chest. Whatever magic battled against his was taking a toll, but he couldn't understand why.

Now.

The voice turned hasty.

Before She consumes you.

Something pushed him from the cliff. Black shadows, not unlike the dark swirls of his own magic, crept into the corners of his vision. He fought to keep his consciousness with him. Something foreign within him fought as well.

They needed more.

They needed to see.

They needed to feel.

Open your eyes.

His eyelids stuck together, heavy. They split open slowly and he had to blink away the fog lingering from his dream. A pair of amber eyes reflected back at him. The color of Aiden's eyes were an oddity. He never remembered meeting anyone with a color anywhere near it. Penelope spoke about how interesting she thought them, but he thought they made him stand out.

The eyes blinked.

But Aiden hadn't blinked.

The brown-skinned face—one that was definitely not his own—broke into a wide grin, and Aiden felt unfamiliar hands resting on either side of his head. A lavender-colored brow lifted, and a deep chuckle rumbled through the hands cradling the sides of Aiden's face. "Good morning, cousin. Sleep well?"

Heart stuttering, Aiden brought his legs up and kicked the intruder off him. The stranger went sailing over the end of the bed. Wait. A bed? Shadows chased after, billowing off Aiden in waves toward the intruder. All drowsiness fled as Aiden leapt from the unfamiliar mattress to where the man he'd thrown was fighting off Aiden's shadows with his own.

He had shadows too?

Aiden reached for the sword that should've been strapped to his body but found none. The uniform he'd worn to Dion's wedding and every blade he'd tucked into it were gone. Instead, he wore a loose green tunic and a pair of leather trousers. Even his feet were bare, his boots and the knives sheathed in them, gone.

Useless. He needed a weapon or at least an avenue of escape.

Aiden took in the room. There was a door opposite the bed, likely leading to a washroom. An arched entry probably led to a dressing room. He turned and spotted the door leading out as he was tackled to the ground.

His body spun without thought and the heel of his hand went straight into the man's nose. Curses hissed through the man's lips as he fell back. Aiden slammed a fist into his jaw, knocking him unconscious.

Aiden yanked open the door leading to his freedom, only to watch his hasty escape plan go up in smoke.

A hulking man raced toward him, arms outstretched.

Aiden slammed the door and locked it before the hands crossed the threshold. A loud thump and a string of what had to be more curses rang from the other side.

Aiden's eyes roved over the walls. Murals painted every inch of the wood, and carpets covered the floors. He peeked through the other doors that led precisely to where he'd guessed—a washroom and a dressing room. There were no windows anywhere. He needed to get creative.

He turned back into the bedroom and bathed the entire space in shadow—quicker than he ever had before. Darkness billowed from him as he positioned himself where the door would meet the wall when it opened. If the giant got through, Aiden could use the few seconds it took the man to look around to slip out into the hallway.

The door swung open, but no footsteps came pounding into the room.

Aiden waited, holding his breath, and urging his slightly aching heart to stop its racing. His magic continued to sap his strength and weaken his heart as he tried to keep all of the shadows contained in the room. He needed to stay collected. He would get out of here. He had to.

The front of Aiden's tunic caught in someone's grip. He swung an arm down to dislodge it. The swing was swatted away, as if his hand were nothing but a pesky gnat. Aiden kicked off the wall behind him, using his strength to knock the assailant over. They both crashed to the floor. Aiden twisted out of the grasp but only made it onto his knees before being pinned to the ground. He bucked and turned under the heavy body holding him down. Shadows surged toward the attacker, but the behemoth didn't even flinch.

Aiden roared and used all his strength to push the monstrosity off him, but it was no use. His shadows pounded against the man's body, trying to provide Aiden the opportunity to dislodge his captor. The full view of the man only weakened Aiden's resolve.

Arms as thick and dark as pine tree trunks pinned Aiden's shoulders to the ground. A bandolier of sharp knives flashed at him from their places sheathed diagonally across the front of the assailant's body. The hilt of a sword peeked out over his shoulder.

Pointed ears stuck out of the long dreads hanging from his head.

Curses. Aiden fought against a full fae. His head thumped back against the floor beneath him in defeat.

"Wise choice," the fae said. The words came out clipped and hard between his teeth.

A moan floated over from the foot of the bed. The muffled words from the other stranger were indecipherable with his clogged nose and slight accent. Aiden looked over to see where the other man—the other *fae*—now stood, pinching the bridge of his nose between gold-ringed fingers. Blood oozed down his chin and amber eyes blinked back tears caused by the swelling under them. Unlike his comrade, this fae stood bedecked in finery. Studs of silver and gold glimmered along the edges of his pointed ears. Even his clothing was decorated with chains of precious metals, none of which Aiden could use as a reliable weapon. His hair ran straight down his back in the most vibrant shade of lavender Aiden had ever seen grow from a person's head.

Vibrations shook through every bit of Aiden's body, and it took him too long to realize the fae still holding him against the ground was laughing. Aiden looked back to see the wolfish grin spread across his face, his eyes on the other fae in the room. "Did he not appreciate you digging about in his dreams? Or was it your ugly mug he did not like?"

The other fae glared.

Aiden used the distraction to break the hold on his shoulders and flip the brute over, putting Aiden on top. He was on his feet one second then on the ground again in the next, this time with the ox of a male on his back.

A weak chortle was followed by a groan. A pair of finely polished boots came into view. "He is definitely family. No one else would be bold enough to fight this long."

Aiden was hoisted onto his feet. Well, almost his feet. The tips of his toes met the floor as the beast held him by the front of his shirt. Aiden's shadows zipped around his head when his eyes met the pale ones of the male in front of him.

"I am tired of playing games. I will not allow you to harm anyone in Crann Mòr. Is that clear?"

"No, it's not clear. I don't even know who you are or where I am!" He swung again, but his wild punch did no good. The brute easily blocked it.

His opponent huffed a sigh, blowing bits of shadow and dark hair from Aiden's eyes. "You will not win this fight," he bit out. "So I suggest you cease."

Before Aiden could respond, the fae shoved him out the door. The hallway looked as if someone had drilled a perfectly smooth hole into a tree. He noticed the wood itself framing a painting of a beach against the wall.

Or perhaps the tunnel grew that way.

I wonder if Penelope could do something like this. Where was she? She'd only stood a few paces from him before his sudden extraction from the wedding. He ran a hand through his unruly hair. Did they abduct anyone else? Dion was likely losing his mind. If Aiden didn't get back, would they be able to take care of Durant and the rest of the rebellion? The ache on the left side of his chest only grew.

Quiet footsteps followed behind them, the only sound in the vicinity. "Ugh, there is blood in my mouth." The lavender-haired fae spoke through a clogged nose. "I will be brushing my teeth for days just to get rid of the taste."

"Just do not expect me to wash it out for you."

"I would never allow you anywhere near my mouth, let alone to clean it." The purple-haired one's voice had already improved within the last few seconds. He trotted in front of them, nose already shifted back into place and the bruises yellowing. "And I do not believe *Màthair* will find your manners very hospitable. You did not even allow our new friend to get shoes."

Màthair. Aiden knew that term. Mother. The two were brothers then.

The brute grunted. "*Màthair* will not care, especially when she hears that the little imp broke your nose."

"I would not count on that." He gingerly prodded at his nose and hissed in pain. A glare flashed Aiden's way before those amber eyes returned to his brother. "You should have seen her fretting over the bedroom we put him in. Making a good impression on our new arrival is the only thing that matters to her at the moment. She will likely blame me for breaking my own nose and apologize to him because it was in his way."

So, their mother was in a position of influence. Did these two hold standing in this place? He glanced back over his shoulder at the glowering fighter following behind him. It would make sense that such a large ellylon would hold some kind of high ranking. No one grew that big without proper food.

The brute's light eyes narrowed in Aiden's direction, but he continued speaking with his brother. "I hope her fantasies of how she wants this meeting to go do not run away with her."

"I am more worried about what *Athair* will do. He has had many more dreams about this day than anyone else."

Their father as well then. They were likely taking him to their parents. More fae he would have to deal with. Aiden's shadows hadn't dissipated, twitching around him in reflection of his agitation. By the Goddess, he didn't have time for this. His fingers flexed. If he could get his hands on one of the blades strapped to the fae behind him...

A heavy hand clamped down on his shoulder. "Keep walking, Aedon. We do not have time for any more of your measly escape attempts."

Aiden bristled. The foreign sound of his name chaffed against his shoulder blades... and he would not refer to his attempts as *measly*. His shadows sharpened around him and the fingers cupping his shoulder tightened in warning. He took a deep breath. It would do him no good to attack when his opponent was expecting it.

His shadows continued swirling around the space, caressing every bit of the hallway. Aiden did his best to call them back, but not all of the black wisps returned. Almost as if there was too much for him to hold. His control and the blood pumping through his heart strained under the weight of them. He clenched his hands to keep his captors from seeing them shake.

The hallway ended at a flight of winding stairs, leading upward and out of sight. No handrails lined the edge, and the steps were simply flat planks of wood sticking out from the side of the wall. Thank the Goddess for his keen balance and affinity for heights. They made their way to the top and the steps opened up into a wider hallway.

Fae of every Court and station left no space uncovered. Furs, skins, and even wings in a rainbow of hues moved about the place.

Aiden was yanked back down the stairs before he could digest more than the single glance. The brute had taken hold of him again and turned on his brother. "Why are there so many folk? Do they not have better things to do than stand around talking?"

"Come now, Thaen," said the purple-haired one, in Olympian. "The crowds at Crann Mòr during the holidays are always such a delight."

Thaen. Finally, a name for the beastly fae.

"Perhaps for you," Thaen barked, "but if we take him through there, we will not get to the council room without causing a scene. No one is supposed to see his face until after the High Council speaks with him."

"I think we will have to brave the storm."

Thaen cursed under his breath, and Aiden pinched his lips together to keep from smiling. Thaen pushed past him to glance back down the stairs for an alternate route.

Aiden shoved the purple-haired brother down the stairs toward Thaen and raced in the other direction, not looking back. He zipped through the throng of fae, taking in every inch of the space and finding more than one door with folk coming in and out. He pulled the shadows around him and wove them into a haphazard cloak, hoping to give himself a portion of anonymity in the crowd.

He didn't allow his shoulders to brush against anyone and stayed near the wall. Everyone around him moved a few beats quicker than the people in Olympia, likely due to the superior strength and speed of the fae, but Aiden wasn't slow. He easily wound his way through the crowd. His steps followed the main flow of folk toward a tall archway, hopefully leading out of the bizarre, wooden building.

Only a dozen feet from the exit, strong hands pulled him into an offshoot of the hall. Aiden tried to twist free but was thrust into another room before he broke loose. A door clicked shut behind him. He spun around and Thaen's rough hands shoved him up against the wall. Aiden ripped a few of the knives from Thaen's chest and swiped at his face. Thaen reared and drew the sword from his shoulder. The black blade crackled with violet sparks and whirls of shadow. Aiden sidestepped a swing meant to send him flat on his back and sliced at the unguarded flesh of Thaen's bicep.

Before a drop of blood could fall from the wound, Aiden was on his back with Thaen's blade at his throat.

Thaen bared his teeth and roared, "Stop trying to fight me!"

Aiden's patience snapped. "I don't even know who you are!"

Thaen sheathed his sword and grabbed Aiden by the shirt

once again, bringing their faces to the same level. His pale eyes looked past Aiden's, as if looking into his very soul. "You want to know who I am? If you try something like that again, I am the one who will kill you whether Danu Herself permits it or not," he snarled. "Is that clear enough for you?"

2
NAMES AND PLACES

Dearest Penny,

The winter solstice celebrations in Winter were MAGICAL. I mean, besides having actual magic, there was such a spirit of joy in the air. I still have no idea what everyone was saying, but I could just feel the excitement buzzing about. There was so much food and drink and music and dancing I couldn't even partake in all of it! I was so sick the morning after, I can't even describe it. Devan's teasing was absolutely merciless, but I have no regrets. This was the way to do a winter solstice! I don't think I'll ever enjoy another in Olympia after experiencing it here.

We found out this morning that the Winter Court left the palace. We don't know where they went, but we hope it's nothing that will keep them away for *long. Devan has a good grasp of the language now, and he thinks if we continue to gain support here in Winter, we should be able to make some real progress in our negotiations—not that there has really been any negotiating thus far.*

Besides that, everything is going well. Winter (the actual season, that is) is in full force here. I can safely claim that I've lived through my first blizzard. I hardly slept, but when we finally woke up the next morning, the snow was astounding. Oh, Penny. I wish you were here. I know you have so much going on back home, but I wish you could have seen it. All of it! You would love this place and all of the magic and wonder it has to offer. By the Goddess, I'm going to bring you here someday if it kills me to do it.

Your Chilly Friend,
Angelica

PENNY'S FINGERS SANK INTO THE COOL SAND BENEATH HER PALMS. SHE spun back around to watch the swirling black portal disappear in a flash, leaving the glitter of the stars behind it as the only other witness. Even the Mist itself was nowhere to be seen.

"All right, Pen—*Nell.* All right, Nell."

My name is Nell.

Even if it sounded stupid the first time King Dion said it, my name is Nell.

Nell. Nell. Nell.

Maybe if she said it to herself enough times, she'd remember. She couldn't afford to use her given name. Not here where it could be used against her. Not in Faerie.

Penny wiped the granules of sand from her hands as she got to her feet. Faerie. She was in Faerie. Maybe slivers of wishes thought to never come true still made it to the Goddess's ears. Even after the exchange of letters with Angelica, she had never allowed herself even a hint of the dream. It had been impossible. A fantasy.

Yet here she stood.

Her gaze moved from where the portal had hovered. Dunes of sand stretched out in every direction, the grainy waves shifting in the light of the full moon hovering in the sky. The warmth of the sand fled without the sun's rays and Penny shivered.

Summer. The portal had spit her out in the Farraige Gaineamh to be exact. But where within the sandy sea was she precisely? It could be days before she found water if she went in the wrong direction. She looked up to the star-studded sky. If her memory was correct, the High Council met in Crann Mòr and would likely have taken Aiden directly there from the wedding. Faerie's capital was said to be in the very heart of the land, but she couldn't traverse miles of sand without some idea of where she was headed. It would be wise to either get to the coast and the oases Angelica had spoken of, or travel to Spring where there would be more water and food to forage.

Do not eat the fruit.

The Gray Man's last warning rang in her ears. What fruit? All fruit? Penny reflected on Angelica's letters, recalling something about avoiding fruits in Faerie, but not all of them. Which ones were fine for humans to eat?

A trio of barks pulled her gaze away from the horizon. Spot sprinted across the dunes, all three heads bobbing with delight. Something about the air in front of him caught Penny's attention. A face flashed in and out of the wisps of dust.

A sylph.

It glided over the sand, swirling up the golden grains into whirlwinds and sending them down the dunes for Spot to chase. The translucent body only showed up when the light hit it just right or if the sand caught onto its form. Penny's eyes followed, entranced. Sylphs never crossed through the Mist. The closest ecosystem to the wide-open spaces they loved were most found in Penny's duchy, and sylphs weren't the best for tending crops. They loved play more than anything.

The being of air couldn't harm Spot on its own, but if it led him back to its shimmer, the group of sylphs could trap him in a tornado or throw him high enough in the air to injure him with the fall.

"Spot!" Penny yelled, finally coming to her senses. "Spot, come back here!" Penny took a step toward the loping canine. A rumble shook the ground beneath her boots. She narrowly dodged the spontaneous burst of foliage as an entire tree erupted out of the ground. Penny fell on her rear in the sand— the pack on her back clanging in disapproval—and white daffodils burst up around her. A surprised scream tore from her throat. The flowers completely surrounded her. Her fingers reached out and brushed the smooth petals of a bloom. Three more daffodils popped up beside it.

"What on Gaia's—" She sprang up from the ground and more foliage sprouted where she stepped. Tall trees, bushes, colorful flowers; an expansive oasis exploded into life around her. Her eyes caught on the color of the leaves of the trees above her. The bluish tint called to her, and the white buds blossomed open—then turned gold. Just as they had in the mural at Barclay House, the one she'd slept under for weeks.

Penny looked back toward the horizon. The sun rose in the distance.

But it had barely been sundown when she'd left Olympia. After Aiden had been stolen right in front of her. When she'd gone to the gateway on the coast with Lady Alvis and Diana.

When she'd faced the Gray Man in the Mist and he'd asked for the one piece of her friend she'd had left. Penny's gloved hand wrapped around her wrist, naked without Sissy's ribbon tied there.

She shook her head. Not enough time had passed for it to be sunrise, had it?

Something fell over her shoulder, tearing a scream from her lungs. She shoved the thing off, only to find a vine had grown down from the tree above her. Penny's brow furrowed and she yanked a glove off one hand. Bright green blinded her, illuminating the plants cropping everywhere around her now that the first light of day barely peeked through. She pulled up her sleeve and gaped. The green light covered every inch of her skin from the tips of her fingers all the way to the crease of her elbow. The tell of her magic had never gone so far up her arm. The light throbbed as if to prove to her its odd behavior was real.

Penny closed her eyes, readying her magic to see through the growth around her. If she could find more plants, she could likely locate the way to the river that bordered Summer. The flora would need water after all. As soon as she called on her gift, it rushed into her, making her gasp aloud. Her mind flooded with images of plants that had to be miles away. An entire wall of life greeted her from the edge of the barren sand to the west of where she stood.

Penny went to shrug away the image, casting her gift off as she normally would, but it was as if the magic didn't want to let go. She fell to her knees and dragged her awareness back into her body with painstaking slowness. Why was it being so difficult? Panting, she opened her eyes and saw the world as it should be. She brushed a still glowing hand through her hair. By the Goddess, she hadn't had that hard of a time disconnecting since she'd been a small child.

The rumble of steps brought her back to her feet as Spot broke through the brush. His tail wagged excitedly behind him, and all three heads yipped. Praise the Goddess nothing had happened to him. Faerie presumably wasn't a place to chase after things.

Penny shook her head and grabbed the leather leash dragging on the ground beside him. "You can't run off like that. We don't know how dangerous this place is."

She checked him over for any injuries then proceeded to take stock of her supplies. Her daggers still winked at her from their sheaths as did the sword at her waist. A bit of sand stuck to the outside of her pack, but it didn't look like she'd lost anything going through the portal. She blew out a breath. Everything was going according to plan—at least as much as she could have planned in the scant amount of hours she'd had to prepare for this. Going from the wedding to the palace to the portal and through the Mist had all taken place in less than a day. When Angelica had been preparing for her and Devan's excursion, they'd planned for months. Penny prayed her haste wouldn't lead to her demise.

Penny led Spot back in the direction he'd bounded in from, but as they walked, the plants continued to shoot up around them. Penny took deep breaths, pulling as much of her magic back as she could, only growing more exhausted as she went. Sweet Gaia, it was like trying to hold water under the surface of the ocean. No matter which way she cupped her hands, it escaped between her fingers to dance around her. She recalled the exercises Mother had taught her...

Mother.

By the Goddess, what was Mother thinking now? Penny had fled Dion and Shaunie's interrupted coronation without a word. There hadn't been time. Besides, Mother would have tried to stop her from following Aiden. From following The Cartographer. From coming all this way to fight this rebellion. The unanswered questions of Mother's allegiances still swirled in Penny's mind. What was Mother doing without Penny?

And what was Aiden's operation doing without him?

They'd only just lost Hart—their sharpshooter and one of Aiden's closest friends. What would they do without Aiden? Rissa would be losing her mind. Penny knew there were protocols in place, knew that Rissa would be next to take charge in Aiden's absence, but it wouldn't be anything close to easy. The whole spy network had been in the midst of searching out The Cartographer's men—Adira's men.

Adira Durant. The one responsible for the High Queen's death. For Aiden's capture. For the rebellion back in Olympia. For all of this.

Penny's magic flared at the thought of the traitorous woman and more leafy ferns popped up from the ground around her. She took a deep breath.

Focus. She needed to focus.

The magic drew back to her. She tried to rub away the fatigue in her eyes as the green in her fingers flickered. It would have to do for now. Penny tugged the glove back on and looked down at Spot. All three heads moved about, sniffing and tasting the air, watching for trouble and exploring the new world around them.

Penny didn't know how long they walked through the Farraige Gaineamh. The sun rose higher until it beat down on them as they trod through the hills of sand. Penny ripped apart one of the extra shirts in the pack the MacGregor's had put together for her and tied strips of cloth around Spot's feet as the grains under them grew hotter.

Penny tried to remember exactly where her magic had reached the wall of plant life. She did her best to lead them in that direction. The plethora of vegetation could only be the border to Spring. If she could walk along the border, they could follow it all the way to Crann Mòr. She could do this.

Spot pulled at the leash, his nose up in the air. Penny looked up to see dark blotches against the shimmering horizon. She pulled Spot a few steps back down the dune they'd just crested and watched the shadows grow larger. Spot nestled in next to her in the hot sand as the forms sharpened and Penny watched the herd of centaurs shift, coming straight for them.

"We have to hide." She scrambled down the dune's incline, Spot sliding along next to her. Her gaze roved over the space, but there was nowhere to actually conceal themselves. The sand around them began to quiver, the centaurs coming up the other side.

Penny's hands began to shake, and she looked down to see green poke through the sand.

Praise the Goddess.

With a slow breath, Penny released the stranglehold on her magic. An entire circle of trees burst through the ground around her, nearly making her yelp. Vines tangled into her hair and more daffodils bloomed instantly around her boots. She heard shouts, followed by the crack of breaking branches and trampled stems. *Curses.* She drew the sword from the scabbard at her side. The centaurs were going to find them if they stayed there.

Penny urged Spot around, trying to keep them moving in the direction of Spring, but not wanting to risk an encounter with the herd. Centaurs were known for being mighty warriors during the Faerie Wars over two hundred years ago—the kind that trampled first and asked questions later.

Penny reined her magic back in, only slightly easier than the last time. A fine layer of sweat coated her back as the magic finally ceased. The quick beat of her heart chased away the price of her gift, and she whispered at Spot to be silent as they crept through the miniature forest. He may have gone chasing after sylphs, but he was smart enough to understand her order. *Clever dog.*

After about twenty minutes of weaving through the thick undergrowth, she spotted the golden sand peeking through the foliage. She didn't see any centaurs lingering around the edge and pushed Spot into a sprint to get as far from the area as they could.

She would get through Faerie. She would storm the halls of Crann Mòr and take back the man that had plagued her thoughts for the last two and a half years—who still followed her everywhere she went. Every thump of the heart in her chest beat with his name and her purpose.

Aiden. I'm coming Aiden.

3
AWARE

THAEN SHOVED AIDEN THROUGH THE DOUBLE DOORS HARD ENOUGH TO make him stumble. A sharp gasp echoed from across the room, and Aiden looked up to see a woman striding toward them. Every inch of her was tenebrious as onyx, from her hair and skin to the fabric of her dress. The only contrast to the dark colors were the whites of her eyes and the faint embellishments on her skirts.

"Bàsthaen," the woman snapped, "how dare you treat him like that!" She looked down at Aiden's feet. "And why is he not wearing any shoes?"

Thaen grabbed the back of Aiden's shirt. "He broke Dair's nose and knocked him unconscious before attempting to escape from his room. The shoes did not matter as much as getting him in here before he could attempt anything else."

The woman's eyes flicked over to the lavender-haired man —who must be Dair—and hissed at the fading bruises and the blood crusted around his nostrils. She looked back at Thaen. "He was likely caught off guard. You know how your brother gets sometimes. You have broken his nose once or twice as well."

Dair sauntered past them, a twinkle in his eyes and a fully

healed nose underneath. "I told you she would not blame him."

Thaen grumbled under his breath and drove Aiden toward the other side of the room. Aiden's bare feet slapped against the polished wood of the walkway that split the rows of chairs, leading up to a long table at the other end. Aiden recognized the fae seated at the table before him. They were the same ones who had taken him from Dion's wedding—who had taken him from Penelope.

His shadows thickened and dripped onto the floor like tar. The three pairs of eyes watched with interest. Aiden clenched his hands, but before he could do anything, Thaen shook him by the collar of his shirt. "If you want to go another round," he whispered, "I have nothing better to do than knock you senseless."

Aiden slowly relaxed his hands. He needed to be patient. Maybe there was another way to approach this. Thaen stepped back and strode toward where Dair had flung himself into a chair.

Dair's golden gaze turned to the woman. "Where is *Athair*?"

So, this was their mother? He looked between the two males and could see the resemblance, though Thaen looked the most like her with his similar coloring—with the exception of his eyes. Dair's pallor was fairer, more tawny than umber, but the regal air followed all three of them.

"He will be here any moment." Their mother turned to Aiden, and he noticed that the embellishments on her dress were embroidered constellations. She gave him a warm smile. "Come sit. No use standing there while we wait."

Aiden shook his head. "I'm fine standing."

The woman's smile dimmed a fraction. "All right. Whatever makes you most comfortable." She glided toward the seat beside the orange-robed man from the wedding. He sat next to the one in blue, whose lip curled up in disgust. Aiden glanced at the last one, the one clad in green.

"I am High Councilor of Spring," he said, as if reading the question Aiden hadn't yet asked. He gestured down the table. "You have met our High Councilor of Summer and of Autumn as well. Shirina, High Councilor of Winter, is the one who has been overseeing the needs of Winter alongside her husband."

Shirina, Thaen and Dair's mother, straightened. "Who should be here any—"

A side door opened with a *crash*. Another fae strode through, his eyes—his *amber* eyes—instantly homing in on Aiden standing in the center of the room. The fae staggered and Aiden felt his own legs wobble under him.

Shirina was at the newcomer's side in an instant. She wrapped a hand around his arm. "I know, my heart. He looks just like her."

Like her? Aiden's eyes remained glued to the new arrival as Shirina pulled him forward. Aiden looked just like *him*. His pale skin, the angles of his face, the width of his shoulders even. No one would be able to tell them apart except for the smile lines carved into the other male's face and the slight violet hue in his waist-length, black hair under the light. The mirror image stopped only a couple of steps from Aiden. By the Goddess, they were even the same height.

The newcomer let go of Shirina and laid a hand on Aiden's shoulder. Tears sprung up in the corners of his eyes. "I"—he took in a shaky breath and smiled—"I have waited twenty long years to look on your face. Welcome home, Little Shadow."

Aiden felt his brows pull together. His heartbeat sped up. His gaze flicked between him and Shirina. "Who are you?"

The male smiled. "I am Fiadh. I am your mother's cousin. We are your family."

Aiden stiffened.

No.

He took a step back, causing Fiadh's hand to fall from his

shoulder. No, he had a family. They were all back in Olympia. His brothers, his friends, his heart—all of it remained in Olympia. His eyes flicked around the room. He had to get out. He needed to convince them to let him leave.

He cleared his throat. "I'm sorry, but I have a family and they're back in Olympia."

Shirina stepped up next to him. "Of course you do. We are the other half, the half that you were kept from knowing."

Aiden shook his head. "While I'll admit the resemblance is striking, what evidence do you have that we're even related?"

He heard the whisper of fabric and Shirina and Fiadh moved to look at the other Councilors. The Autumn Councilor stood. "We know you are their family because you are the closest living relative to the late High Queen Rìanoch and are now the new High King."

"I'm not who you think I am."

"You are Prince Aedon of Olympia," the green-clad Councilor said. "You are the third son of King Horace and the first son of Queen Morana of Winter—Danu receive her."

Queen Morana is my mother?

The last queen of Winter had died twenty years ago. From what Aiden had learned growing up, she had been the younger sister of the High Queen. Queen Morana was said to have been a just ruler, though she'd had very little tolerance for traitors and helped her sister get on the faerie-glass throne. There were stories about how ruthless she'd been in the Faerie Wars, her magic a thing to be feared.

And they were claiming that she'd been his mother? He'd never even known who she was and now she was gone. But she had been from this place. Had lived here. Something fluttered in Aiden's chest, and it wasn't due to his overexcited magic.

He shook himself inwardly, casting away the seed of curiosity as quick as it had landed. "You have the wrong man. I'm none of those things." Perhaps if they believed he wasn't who they sought, he would have time to slip away and get back to his brothers. To Penelope. "I am Lou, a simple servant of Olympia. If you return me to my home, perhaps I can help you find who you are looking for."

Shock filled each one of their faces. Shirina gawked. "You can lie."

The Summer Councilor looked him over with a critical eye. "How can that be? He is at least half our kind, no matter that the other half is *mage*." He said the word as if it left a bad taste in his mouth. "It should have caused him a considerable amount of pain for even those few words."

"See?" Aiden agreed. "Perhaps you do have the wrong man."

Fiadh chuckled, pointing to the irises matching Aiden's almost perfectly. "You and I both know that is not true."

The scrape of a chair against the floor echoed through the hall. Everyone turned to where Dair sauntered around the table. "He is lying, by whatever miracle Danu has bestowed." He gave everyone a smirk. "The Land has claimed him already. That was why you could not wake him."

Aiden's eyes flew wide. "Couldn't wake me?"

"You were asleep for two weeks," said Shirina. "Nothing could rouse you."

Two weeks? His stomach sank. By the Goddess, what did his brothers think?

What did Penelope think?

Shirina glared back at the other Councilors. "Some thought your magic was going through some kind of stunned adjustment, but I called for Bruadair as soon as I could." She turned back to him. "I remembered your aunt speaking of dreams when she was first crowned High Queen. The bond with the Land can be quite an adjustment for the new High Ruler."

"I'm sorry, but I have to leave." Aiden's head swam. This was too much. It was all too much. "I have to go home."

Fiadh reached for him. "My boy, you are home."

Aiden dodged his touch. "*No!*" Shadows gushed from him.

Thaen took a step forward, but his father held up a hand to stop him, never taking his golden gaze from Aiden's.

Aiden had to shake his head. "This isn't my home. I'm not your king. I don't belong here. I have to leave."

Fiadh's eyes softened. "I am sorry, but that is not possible anymore."

Aiden took a step away from them. If he could make it to the door, he could lose them in the crowds. He just had to get to the border, and he could find Stone's gateway. Or he could sail to the Isles and send for Evan to come get him.

Dair blew out a dramatic sigh. "You cannot actually leave, Aedon." Aiden watched him out of the corner of his eye, but it must have been enough interest for him to continue. "If you leave, your bond to the Land will weaken, weakening you in the process." He patted Aiden on the head. "If you leave Faerie, you will die within a week."

They were toying with him. Trying to keep him here by feeding him lies. Aiden ducked away from Dair's hand. "Why should I believe anything any of you say? You appear uninvited at my brother's wedding, tell me I'm to be your *king*, then steal me away from the people I care about." His eyes narrowed at each of them. "Those are the actions of liars and thieves."

Shirina straightened, her demeanor shifting from matronly family member to stoic Councilor in an instant. "We cannot lie, and we would certainly not lie about this, even if we wanted to. You are our king."

A shudder ran through him. She was right. Dair had spoken just as plainly. From what Aiden could see, there was no way they could be twisting the truth. Unless that truth had been ingrained firmly into them, they couldn't be lying. Even attempting such a thing would have been impossible without causing them absolute torment. Even half-fae or quarter-fae could grow violently ill if they spoke a lie. Aiden often forgot because—as if he wasn't enough of an oddity—he, in fact, *could* lie.

And these full-blooded folk all claimed he was their king.

The thump of a staff on the hard floor drew every eye to where the Spring Councilor stood with the others. He watched Aiden warily, likely waiting to intervene if Aiden decided to run.

The thought still niggled at him.

"I would like to offer a proposal," said the green-swathed fae. "Since our sovereign is having a difficult time adjusting, perhaps it would be wise to allow him some time to come to terms with this new arrangement."

They were going to lock him up. It only made sense. He would do the same if he needed someone like him to cooperate.

Fiadh's brows puckered. "What are you suggesting?"

The Spring Councilor turned to the orange-clad one. A silent conversation passed between them before he nodded and turned his gaze back to them. "Take High King Aedon to Winter. Help him familiarize himself with his history, his family. Allow him to see what the Tuatha Dè Dannan have to offer him. We will reevaluate the situation at the equinox celebration."

The spring equinox? Was he mad? That was *months* away. And if the scant amount of maps he had of Faerie and the accounts he'd received from Devan were accurate, Winter was on the northern tip of the continent with the harshest climates and most treacherous terrain. It would take him ages to get to Olympia on his own.

Aiden needed to get home. Now.

He bolted for the side door Fiadh had come in through but felt Thaen's inescapable arms wrap around his torso. Thaen turned them around to where the Autumn Councilor wove a portal into the middle of the council room.

Aiden used every tactic he knew, every cursed trick he'd ever learned, to get out of Thaen's hold. He grappled with his hands and feet, hit every nerve point he could reach and clawed at every exposed piece of flesh he could see. His shadows flooded the entirety of the room, blinding everyone but him.

It wasn't enough.

Thaen held Aiden tightly to his chest as the portal swallowed them whole.

4
DANGER AND DECISIONS

Dearest Penny,

The letter I sent to you a few days ago has returned to my hands. They say the Mist is closed off and no one is going in or out. Devan was in an absolute panic and has gone to figure out what on Gaia's green earth is going on. Hopefully, this letter will make it to your hands.

Curses, Penny! I was waiting to hear back about Dion and Carnation's wedding. And the ball! You told me you had a surprise planned for Prince Aiden. How did it go? Was he surprised? I want all of the juicy details. I bet he kissed you. He better have kissed you.

By the Goddess, what am I going to do if we can't get letters back and forth? I'll die of *suspense! My parents are likely losing their minds. Why did they close it? What's going on?*

I suppose I'll simply continue writing these letters until I can send them. When they reach you, I expect every one of my questions to be answered. I want to know what's going on back home. I hope everything is all right.

If you can, check on my family for me. I send them letters, but they never share their worries with me. I certainly don't expect that to change now.

Your Friend That's Feeling a Bit Trapped,
Angelica

P.S. Devan just returned. PRINCE AIDEN IS AN FAERIE. Everyone is saying the High Queen was murdered, and he's the new High King. Sweet Gaia, what is happening?

A LINE OF TREES STRETCHED FROM ONE EDGE OF THE HORIZON TO THE other. The song of wildlife wove through the air, the melody sweet and enticing.

By the Goddess, they'd made it to the Spring border.

Penny turned a grin on Spot, who had all three tongues out, panting. She brushed a hand over every one of his heads. "We're going to find him, boy."

The emerald leaves of the plants grew more detailed, and Spot's ears perked at the same time Penny's did. The rush of water called and neither of them could deny it. Penny laughed as Spot pulled her in the direction of the sound and both of them collapsed at the edge of the wide river separating the two Courts. Spot took greedy laps of the water and Penny was almost jealous he could consume so much more than her. She drank until her belly sloshed then scooped the water to pour over her head, washing the gritty sand out of her hair.

Penny swiped wet tendrils of hair from her face and stood. Her magic hummed as she looked over at the forest across from her. She needed to find a way to get over the rushing water between them. The blue-leafed trees would give them better cover than the dunes as they traveled, not to mention cover up the footprints of magic she left in her wake. If she wasn't careful, she would lay down to rest and be trapped by plants in her sleep. It had happened when she was younger, and she didn't need a repeat of the experience.

Looking back at said footprints, she winced. If she attempted anything else with her gift, would it only end in disaster? The oasis she'd sprouted had been a risk, her magic being so volatile, but the volatility had saved them. Something that required a little more finesse would be an entirely different story.

The magic inside of her squirmed, ready for release, but Penny didn't so much as lift a finger. Not until she could come up with a way to get across.

Her gaze latched onto two sturdy-looking trunks across the river. Ivy and other crawling vines hung from their branches. Perhaps she could use her gift to weave a bridge across using the ropey plants. Then it would be easy to disassemble afterward.

She closed her eyes and brought her magic to the surface. Pieces of life and energy shot out from her before she was ready, absorbing into, not only the climbing plants, but the trees they clung to as well. The vines thickened around the bulging trunks, twisting as the branches burst above the forest canopy. The towering trees leaned in her direction, her intent for a bridge still working its way through the plants. The trees tumbled down, their leafy branches plunging into the water halfway across the river toward her.

A wave of water sprayed over the edge of the river, soaking Penny before she could leap to safety.

"Curses!" She wiped the water from her eyes and watched as the trees pulled free of the bank on the other side and floated downriver.

Spot splashed in the water next to her, drenching the ragged strips of fabric on his feet as he pranced about, bobbing his head in the water. Tiny, silver fish darted about, and Spot pounced into the water to catch them.

Penny sighed. "That certainly was not the plan." She called for Spot and raced north, following the trunks. The thought of the trees crashing into a boat or taking out a dock flashed through her mind. It had happened to the river harbor in Eleusion a few years ago, a flash flood bringing trees through and destroying the stilts of the docks.

Spot barked and nudged her hand with one of his heads. At his prodding, she spotted where the river narrowed ahead, the water raging around large boulders sticking out on either side of the bank. Had there been a bridge there once? The trees she'd knocked over bobbed in the water, the first tree slipping past, but the second caught on its large roots and lodged itself between the rocks.

The water built up quickly, trying to push the trunk along, but the roots kept it stuck in place. If she was careful, she could cross using the tree then use her magic to pull the tree from the river and allow the water through. They jogged over to where the large rocks held the tree in place. She attempted to be cautious but couldn't keep a smile from her face as Spot bit at the flashes of scales in the river.

Maybe they could still help her get across before dark. She didn't want to be out in the open at night and attacked by any nocturnal fae hidden in the trees. She also didn't want to risk swimming across. According to lore she'd heard growing up, it could be rife with danger. The Isles weren't the only places to home creatures with an affinity for water.

Penny made it to the bank, taking off her boots and wading in to touch the closest roots. She closed her eyes. Perhaps having a physical connection could help focus her magic. Her mind's eye connected with the vast rings of the trunk and the many tendrils of roots stretching out in front of her. She pushed a minuscule amount of magic out into the tree, using it to bend the roots. Sweet Gaia, maybe that would keep it from going too far. Warily, she opened her eyes to see what her enthusiastic magic had created.

Penny's shoulders sagged and she let out a tired chuckle. The roots had curved into a half-tunnel, open to the river, but still giving her and Spot plenty of walking room. She eagerly stepped onto the knobby platform, Spot jumping up next to her.

Her boots remained dangling off her shoulder, the water lapping at her ankles in the haphazard tunnel and the roots easier to grab with her toes. Spot eagerly passed her, getting to the other end and landing on the other bank in a spray of mud. He clambered up the embankment and shook the water and dirt from his coat, the droplets spraying in every direction.

Then his heads turned upriver, and he froze. Penny followed his gaze and stiffened as well. In the middle of the water stood a greenish-gray horse. Limp hair trailed down its face, mingling with the dripping chains hanging around its neck.

Púca.

Penny leapt for the edge of the tunnel. She had to get out of the water. She had to get into the trees so she could hide.

A scream punctured the air, and Spot began barking. Penny only looked up for an instant, but it was enough. The púca stood on its hind legs, a vision of a bloody death, and stamped its front feet back into the water. If it touched her, it would tether her to its back and drag her off to who knew where. Or she would stay on its back until she died of fear and exhaustion. Neither option was acceptable.

The tunnel ended and she splashed through the last stretch of water as quickly as she could and met Spot at the edge. Soggy clothes slowed her steps as she sprinted through the reeds thickening with her magic along the bank, heart galloping faster than her feet could manage. Spot charged ahead, leaving Penny with an easier path as they ran, but never leaving her sight. The screech of the púca came closer and Penny's steps took on a new burst of speed.

Hoofbeats pounded against the ground at the same rate as her heart. Penny could almost feel the humid breaths against her neck and the rattle of chains clanged in her ears. It took every ounce of willpower not to glance back at the terror chasing behind her.

Spot broke into a clearing ahead and veered left. Penny broke through a moment later and saw Spot turn around. When the púca charged through, Spot leapt and all three mouths bit down on the flesh of its hindquarters. The horse-like creature gave an angered scream and shook Spot off its back, but his distraction had done the job.

Penny allowed her magic to flood out of her once again, praying it followed her intention instead of doing whatever it wanted.

Roots shot out, binding the púca against the ground and squeezing. Even as it shapeshifted over and over again, morphing from a horse to a wild cat to a humanoid figure, the vines caged it and sank deeper into the ground. Penny covered her ears to block out the sound of the púca's wails as she ran out of the clearing, Spot on her heels.

The backs of her eyes burned with tears. What else could possibly go wrong?

When Penny stumbled over a root for the third time in five minutes, she finally called for Spot to stop. They hadn't met with any trace of another creature in the last hour and Penny would pass out if they continued on much longer. Her magic strained under her skin and the work she'd done during the daylight hours had left her energy drained.

Spot came loping up to her and rubbed his heads against her side. She nearly fell over before she could shrug the pack off her shoulders. Her supplies clattered onto the ground, vines reaching out to cushion the fall. Penny's lips pressed together, and she sent the vines away. She didn't need their unrequested assistance.

Her legs shook as she crouched next to the bag for her supplies. She found the maps, the notebooks, and a pouch of dried food. Soft moss spread over the stump she was about to sit on, and Penny begrudgingly sat. Her magic was driving her mad.

"All right," she began. Her voice boomed around the small clearing they rested in, and she winced. Lowering her voice, she said, "We need to come up with a viable plan to get Aiden out of Faerie and back into Olympia."

Spot gobbled up the last of the unrecognizable creature he'd caught for his meal.

Penny took it as a sign to continue. "With your help, it should be easy to find him in whatever building he's in. The only problem is getting into Crann Mòr without alerting anyone to our presence. Neither of us look like anything else here. While you could at least pass for some kind of fae creature, I don't think I could get away with looking like a fae." She pulled off her gloves and rolled up her sleeves to study the bright green shining from her arms. "Especially not like this."

Spot gave a chuff from one head while the other two bobbed up and down in agreement. Penny chuckled. He was certainly the most intelligent dog she'd ever encountered.

"We need to come up with a plan." She placed Aiden's quill

and the notebook in her lap and laid out one of the maps. "Our goal is to get to Crann Mòr, get inside, and get Aiden out."

But how?

Penny didn't know anything about the way the fair folk operated their lands. Aiden likely didn't go to the throne willingly. He could be locked up somewhere Penny would have a difficult time getting to or guarded by an entire legion of fae warriors. She needed allies.

Her eyes fell on the northernmost piece of the map. "What if we went to Winter first? We could find Angelica and Devan. They could help us at least get an audience with Aiden or those in charge." *Maybe.* Based on the letters Penny had received before she left Olympia, Angelica and her husband had a hard enough time getting an audience with the Winter Court. Would they be able to get into Crann Mòr to speak with Aiden? Penny folded up the map. Angelica would certainly be her best chance. It was a better idea than storming the capital, demanding they hand over their new High King.

Penny let out a breath. *High King Aiden.* Would he even want to return home after coming into such a title? A smile spread over Penny's face. The thought of Aiden staying away from Olympia sounded as ludicrous as keeping a root from water or a seed from sprouting in good soil. He would do everything in his power to get home.

Penny looked up at the stars peeking through the forest canopy. She prayed he just didn't get himself killed in the process.

5
ABOVE

AIDEN RIPPED ANOTHER STRIP OF CURTAIN AND BRAIDED IT INTO THE others coiled on the soft rug around where he sat. He'd already gone through the bedsheets and towels in the washroom and had moved on to the curtains hanging in the comfortable sitting room of his prison. Being seven floors up made it impossible to leap from the balcony attached to his bedroom, especially with the howling wind to blow away any shadow he used to cushion his fall, but if he could make enough rope, he could easily take the last two or three stories of his fall.

If he was discovered this time, Thaen was sure to throw him in the dungeon, as he'd threatened to the last time Aiden had made an attempt. Aiden yanked his new rope tight, checking for any loose pieces. *Curse Thaen.* If Aiden was lucky, the blasted fae would take a leap into the Mist. It would serve him right.

Aiden wrapped the end of his makeshift rope around the clawed foot of his elaborate bed. The thing was wide enough for four people; plenty heavy to hold him as he scaled the wall. He unwound the rope as he walked toward the balcony doors. He pushed them open, and the wind slapped the heavy glass against the wall. A flurry of snowflakes danced past his face.

It had snowed every day since he'd been put in this cursed room.

He couldn't help thinking of Rissa. She hated the snow and would often hide out with Heff and the dragonets during the coldest days of the year. She would despise being here.

Would Penelope? He shook his head. All his thoughts led to her and the quiet of this place didn't help him keep them tucked away. Was she all right? Had she gone back to Barclay Manor with her mother? Was Adam Cyrus knocking at her door?

Aiden's stomach burned and he shook himself. What a ridiculous thing to think. It wouldn't matter if the man was seeing her, Penelope was Aiden's. She'd said so herself. Aiden flung the end of his rope over the balcony's waist-high railing. She was likely holed up in the palace with Rissa and his brothers trying to figure out how to get him back.

Aiden chuckled. "Won't she be surprised when I come walking through the Underworld Gate."

"Who will be surprised?"

Aiden spun and found Thaen perched on the edge of the railing near the door. *Blast it all.* He let go of the rope. "How on Gaia's green earth did you even get up here?"

With a glare, Thaen hopped down and went to Aiden's side. He pointed over the side of the balcony rail. Aiden looked down and saw a shadow zip away but not before he could make out the silver moon shimmering on its surface. A flying carpet.

"You have a flying carpet?" Aiden asked.

Thaen shrugged then picked up the rope hanging over the balustrade and rubbed it between his fingers. "At least you know how to braid a good rope. I had hoped you would not be one of those helpless maidens that use bedsheets as an escape from their tower, but alas, Dair has won this bet." In a flash, he drew his sword and slashed through the woven cord.

Aiden reached for the severed piece, but it fluttered down to the ground below.

His hands clenched and he whirled on the fae. "You have no right to keep me here."

Thaen shrugged as if Aiden's anger were a minor concern to him. "When my king is in danger, I will do everything in my power to prevent his death—even if it would come about by his own stupidity."

"I wasn't going to kill myself climbing down the side of the palace." He looked back over the edge of the balcony.

That's where they had locked him up. A palace. On top of a mountain. As he looked out, he could see the lights of civilization on the dusk-soaked peaks of the mountains around him. Each peak was connected by long bridges, spanning six carriages wide if Aiden could trust what he saw in his dreams. Dair had said the visions in Aiden had in his sleep were the Land trying to connect with him, sharing bits and pieces of this insane kingdom. He didn't know what to believe. If only he could get out and see for himself. He hadn't actually been allowed down there. Hadn't been allowed anywhere but this cursed room since his first escape attempt.

Fiadh and Shirina had tried to give him a tour of his new "home" when they first arrived—and he'd stopped fighting with Thaen. The brute's skill with hand-to-hand combat far exceeded Aiden's, and he'd had to come up with some other plan of escape besides brute force. He'd jumped from a third-story window into the gardens. He hadn't even made it to the front gate of the palace before Thaen had tackled him into a fountain—which he'd certainly done on purpose. He'd hauled Aiden up the stairs by the collar of his shirt and thrown him in this room.

That had been two weeks ago.

If Aiden was High King, his *cousin* sure had a funny way of showing his respect. Aiden had tried to escape two other times, but neither of those had been fruitful either.

Aiden turned a glare back toward Thaen. The blackguard was everywhere.

But perhaps the blasted fae had just revealed his ticket to freedom. If there were flying carpets in the palace, Aiden would find them.

Thaen answered Aiden's glare with a smirk. "You may not have died climbing, but like I said, your stupidity would have killed you in the end."

Aiden felt himself bristle but took a deep breath. "I'm not as stupid as you think."

Thaen snorted, but before he could say anything else, a voice echoed out from Aiden's room. "If you are not stupid, then you must simply be deaf." Aiden frowned and strode to the open door of the balcony. Dair lay stretched out over Aiden's bed like a satisfied cat—or a lion. The fierce glint in his eyes reminded Aiden of the latter. His golden gaze narrowed. "We have warned you that leaving Faerie would bring your death."

Aiden threw up his hands. "That doesn't make any sense. Humans and fair folk alike walk back and forth through the Mist all the time."

Thaen stomped the snow off his boots outside. He huffed, shutting the door to keep the snow from taking over any more of Aiden's rooms and silently strode to the sitting room door. His steps didn't make a single sound. Actually, the only sounds he ever made were intentional.

Dair glanced down at the floor by Aiden's feet and followed behind Thaen with a chuckle. "You are not like most of the folk who go through the Fuath."

Aiden glanced down. A small puddle circled his boots. *Great.* He really did look like a bumbling fool in front of them. He stepped out of the melting snow and followed the brothers into the sitting room. Thaen had sunk down into the thickly stuffed sofa and Dair glided to one of the many windows, all made of faerie-glass from what Aiden could tell. For such an expensive material, the Winter Court sure used up a lot of it.

Aiden slouched into the chair he'd claimed as his in the sitting room. Thaen and Dair had been in here enough within the past week to make their own spaces in the room—Thaen usually finding a spot to lounge on the sofa, and Dair usually curling up in the chair next to Aiden's or the window seat. Or the floor. Or the arm of the sofa.

"I know I'm not like the rest of you. There aren't any mage-fae hybrids out there, but why does that matter when crossing the border?"

"You are the *High King*." Dair moved from the window to the chair next to Aiden and mumbled something under his breath. He did that a lot in Aiden's presence. "High. Rulers. Do. Not. Go. Past. The. Border."

Aiden blinked. "None? Ever?"

Thaen straightened. "It is not something we like to share, given that it could lead to a disadvantage on our side, but no. High Rulers cannot pass through the Fuath without meeting Danu at the door."

"Why?" Aiden asked.

"Because of your connection to the Land," Dair explained. "Your dreams—the ones we have been traversing together for the past several nights? They are only the start to the Land connecting with Her rightful ruler. If you leave, the connection will break, taking every bit of magic from you—even the magic that keeps your blood pumping and your lungs taking in fresh air."

Aiden's brows pulled together. The dreams he'd had since coming to Faerie had grown more vivid. That was how he knew about the bridges connecting the peaks. He could barely see them from his room in the palace, but his dreams had shown him every bit of the mountains around them and the frozen lake at their base. Dair had been explaining the lay of the land to him in his visions, using his magic over dreams to guide him back into consciousness if he slept too long.

"What do dreams have to do with the magic?"

"The dreams are only a taste of the connection the Land has with Her ruler. As High King, you should be able to see what is going on in any part of the kingdom and use the magic to aid in your rule." Dair shook his head. "There are many secrets even I do not know. In the past, the heir was usually taught by their predecessor, but even High Queen Rìanoch had not mastered all the gifts given upon deposing the previous rulers."

He knew Dair referred to the rulers during the Faerie Wars, the ones who enslaved mankind and acted as gods over everything. It had been their demise and the creation of the Mist that had ended those bloody times. And Aiden was to continue that legacy—if he couldn't get out of it somehow. Though that possibility seemed more impossible by the second.

Aiden's hands wrapped around the arms of his chair as he leaned forward. "So, no matter what, I'm linked to the land and if I attempt to leave, the separation will kill me."

Thaen shrugged. "Yes, that sounds about right."

The wooden arms of the chair beneath Aiden's hands creaked and it took effort to relax his hold before he snapped the delicate wood in half. He was trapped. He would never get back to Olympia. He would never see his brothers or Spot. He would never again hold Penelope's hand or see her smile. He would never be able to fulfill the promises he'd made her.

"Can I at least send a letter? Tell my brothers where I am?" *Tell Penelope how much I love her.*

Thaen and Dair shared a glance, but both shook their heads.

Of course not. Why would they let him? Shadows spun in the corners of his vision, but he paid them little mind. What was the use in keeping himself in check? It didn't matter considering he was going to be stuck on the top of this cursed mountain for the rest of his existence.

Well, until equinox. Then who knew what new torture they would implement. The rest of his days seemed bleak, and it would be a long time before he was given reprieve. Even half fae lived for centuries.

Something landed on his shoulder and his magic sharpened. He looked up to meet Dair's sorrowful, amber eyes as they twinged in pain. Aiden brought the magic back under control. Dair shook out his ringed fingers as if touching Aiden had stung him. It might have, for all Aiden knew. His gifts were doing all sorts of things without his permission lately.

"For what it is worth," Dair said, "I am sorry you were brought here without any warning. Without our High Ruler, the magic of the land would have run rampant looking for someone to attach to. We already have enough fae looking to wheedle their way into more power. Perhaps if you had been given the time you were supposed to have, it would have been easier."

"What time was I supposed to have?" Aiden asked.

"You were not set to inherit Winter until you were thirty," Thaen replied. "We were preparing to ask for your presence here when you turned twenty, but things did not go as planned."

Had Durant taken that from him too? The time to come to term with this? The time to get to know his family before they became the enemy? Aiden raked his fingers through his hair. It seemed her knowledge and influence had no bounds.

"What is done is done. Now it is time to decide. Do you want to doom your loved ones, or do you want to save them?"

Aiden pushed down the growl building in his throat. "What does that mean?" If these brutes were going to threaten his family—

"It means," Thaen cut in, "that someone murdered our

queen, and we believe it was the same force you have been battling in the mortal lands."

Aiden sat back in his chair, the feel of the leather under his fingers grounding him. "The Cartographer."

"A mapmaker?" Dair snorted. "What ridiculousness is this?"

Aiden shook his head. "Don't be so dismissive. She calls herself that as a statement. Her followers believe their cause will redraw the lines between the bronties and the gifted. They preach that they will create new maps of the continent and every piece of land—Faerie, Olympia, and the Isles—will be subjected to this new rule."

"You said 'she.'" Thaen leaned forward. "Who is this Cartographer?"

Durant's name came to his lips, but the geas he'd made as a child locked his tongue. He squirmed in his seat, thinking of a way to tell them within the bounds of his promise. "Duchess Durant." The words came out easily. The geas only applied to her identity as the last spymaster, not as the rebel leader.

Thaen cursed. Soundly.

Aiden looked between the brothers. "You know who I speak of?"

Dair nodded his head gravely. "We know much of Adira Durant and the facade she created using her husband. Even in Faerie, there are dark corners that whisper her name. We all prayed she was dead."

Aiden shook his head. "I can assure you, she's not. I saw her myself."

"And you knew it was the cursed woman for sure? That she is truly alive and leading this rebellion?" Thaen asked.

"I saw her nearly every day of my first fifteen years. Hers is not a face I would ever forget."

"I suppose being in the same palace as her would lend to seeing her regularly." Dair shuddered. "I cannot imagine running into her in the halls. They say she has the eyes of a demon and the face of nightmares."

The corner of Aiden's lip twitched, but he tamped down his amusement. He should not be smiling and joking with his captors. "I did more than run into her in the halls."

Dair met his eyes, a question swirling on his face.

"I did," Aiden affirmed. "I was her *protégé* after all. She practically raised me from the time I was seven until my father's death."

Dair's eyes widened, and he looked over at Thaen. "Did *Athair* tell you any such thing?"

Thaen's expression solidified the very air in the room. "He does not know. If he did, he would have done something."

Aiden's chest tightened. "What does your father have to do with it?"

"Aedon," Dair said, crouching next to Aiden's knee, "if he had known Adira Durant had been the one raising you during all that time, he would have swooped into Olympia and brought you back here before she could touch a single hair on your head."

"What?" Aiden's chest grew heavy, and a shadow skittered over his boot. "Why?"

Dair's eyes flashed under his brows. "Because she is the one who killed your mother."

The small bit of control Aiden held over his magic shattered into a thousand pieces.

6

MONSTERS AND REGRETS

The gulps of air Penny inhaled weren't enough. Her side ached with strain and her knees wobbled as her feet pounded against the dense vegetation under her boots. By the Goddess, would she ever stop running?

The pack of goblins behind her undoubtedly hoped she would. Hoots and screeches chased on her heels. Tiny, makeshift spears pierced the ground where she'd stepped a moment before. An array of cuts decorated the loose fabric of her trousers from the near misses. The mob crowed at every failure and gained speed with each of her labored steps.

A spear skinned her upper calf, making her jump. The horde cackled with glee.

A howl sounded off to her left.

Running water was near.

She put on another burst of speed, heading in the direction of the sound. If she could find somewhere to jump across, she could lose the little vermin and be on her way. The goblins jeered behind her at the transition. The cacophony grew louder, urging her forward.

The plants around her reacted to her distress but made it as hard for her to escape as it did for the goblins to chase her.

Trees bowed in front of her; vines tangled against her ankles; roots hit her as much as they knocked down her pursuers. It would have been better to avoid using the magic altogether if she had the choice.

The babble of water found her ears and she sought out the glitter of moonlight on its surface. Another howl rang through the trees and a loping shadow ran parallel with her. If she could get across the running water, she'd be safe.

For the moment, at least.

Penny broke through the line of trees, the chitter of angry goblins following close behind. Flecks of light shimmered over a thin stream, likely only knee deep, but it would do. Penny reached the edge and sprang over the water, her boots sinking into the viscous mud on the other side.

She spun and watched the front line of goblins careen into the water. The calf-high creatures flailed as the weak current pushed them downstream. If she remembered anything about goblins during her lessons on the little fae growing up, it had been that they hated running water.

The group left standing on the bank shook their tiny spears at her with knobby arms, their flat faces twisted with rage and their bat-like ears twitched about. A few even lobbed their weapons in her direction, but she took a few steps back and out of range. Their screeches fractured the calming air around the stream, their words clipped and chittering. Some bared their needle-sharp teeth at her when she made eye contact with them.

If Aiden could see her now, he'd laugh. He'd get that sparkle in his eye that told her he enjoyed being chased and there really was nothing to fear. What were a few pesky goblins to the infamous Lord of the Underworld after all? *By the Goddess, I hope he's all right.*

A moment later, the shadow that had been running with her bounded over the water and sank into the mud beside her. All three of Spot's tongues lolled out of his mouths and Penny scratched between his ears. "Good boy, Spot." She'd sent him ahead to find running water when the goblins had scurried out of their huts in the ground. Penny had thought the púca they'd seen bad enough, but being chased by the murderous, little beasties was just as terrifying. Was there nothing in this cursed land not out for her blood? It wasn't her fault her magic had destroyed their den when she'd been spooked by that bird. She couldn't help it.

Penny did her best to stomp off the mud caked to her boots as they walked into the next copse of trees. She checked her weapons again. All three blades and her quiver of arrows remained in their proper places, and her bow still hung from the pack bobbing against her back. A breath whooshed from her chest. *Praise the Goddess.*

Her muscles turned to jelly as she trudged through more of Spring's thick undergrowth. Spot led her through the trees, their branches only slightly reaching out to her, much shyer than their brethren earlier in the day. Penny could feel the breadth of her magic empty out, finally allowing her some peace from the constant spikes of power.

Sleep. Now she just needed sleep. Perhaps if she could rest, she'd have the power to control her magic. Penny rubbed her face with a gloved hand. Or perhaps the sleep would restore her magic and it would be even more out of control.

Spot's heads all turned to the right, his folded ears quivering with whatever foreign sound he'd caught. It must not have been too concerning, because he turned to look at her with his tail wagging. Penny's brows furrowed and she picked up the pace of her steps until she was walking right beside him. She didn't remember his shoulders being at the level of her ribs. Penny may have been a short person, but she didn't recall Spot being so... large. He bumped into her playfully, his tail cutting through the air as she set her hand on his back.

She shook her head. This place and her exhaustion were doing things to her mind.

Not even a full two days had passed since they fell from the portal, and she'd run into more creatures from Faerie War bedtime stories than any folk who could actually help her. Not that she could actually ask for help. A human trespasser in Faerie asking around after their new king? No, that wouldn't end well.

But it was still odd that she hadn't run into any other signs of civilization until the goblin nest. Where were the grand cities? There were the capitals of every season and Crann Mòr, but where did the rest of the fae live? The bwachod, she knew, lived differently than humans in that they used more natural-istic ways to house themselves, but the ellylon were somewhat similar. Where were their towns? Their people?

Spot pulled to the north, and it was all Penny could do to follow. The ground beneath her had never looked so inviting. If she was in the woods in Olympia, she wouldn't even pull out the cramped tent wedged into her pack.

But this forest is far from those woods.

Her eyes lingered on the trees with their blue leaves and their wide-petaled flowers. Perhaps it was because of the trees that she felt so comfortable at the thought of lying down right there in the underbrush. The mural in her room at Barclay House had to have been painted with these trees in mind. Even the way the artist was able to get the blooms to shift to gold with the rise and fall of the sun remained the same. Like painted magic and the real blooms were even more mystifying.

Spot gave a chuff and stopped at the base of a tree. He used his heavy paws to trample down a bed of leaves and curled up, his eyes on her.

"This looks as good a place to rest as anywhere," she said, thinking he was looking to her for approval. She must have been right because he folded his heads on the ground and closed his eyes a moment later.

Penny shrugged the pack off her shoulders and nearly fell over from the loss of weight. Why couldn't Paulo have supplied her with an enchanted bag that could've held everything and weighed nothing? Was that too much to ask?

She shook her head. By the Goddess, she sounded ungrateful.

Her arm reached all the way to her elbow as she scrounged through her supplies, looking for rope and the precious sacks of food the MacGregors had packed for her. Penny pulled out the note she'd found earlier from Mater, the twins' mother.

Do not quit. Keep going. There is hope just around the corner. Trust in the Goddess and believe that there will always be wonderful things to come.

Penny tucked the note back into one of the many pockets with a sigh. Penny wouldn't quit, but this wait for hope was looking far bleaker than she'd originally planned.

She missed Aiden. It may have only been a few days, but she missed him like a sprout misses the sun when it was cloudy. Her heart shriveled as the leaves would.

But she would be stronger. She would find that hope. She would find *him*.

Something screeched in the distance. The shadows grew longer.

No matter what monsters she faced.

7
AWAY

Aiden walked beside Dair to the dining hall. While he'd taken most of his meals in his rooms, he needed to get the family to believe he was willing to be civil. At least, until he could find the flying carpet.

"Who do you think Thaen is leaving for?" Dair asked.

Aiden's stomach did a little flip. "Thaen's leaving?"

It was like seeing the first rays of moonlight. Since Dair had revealed the history between Adira and Queen Morana, Aiden had thought of little else. She couldn't keep getting away with such crimes. Aiden had to stop her. He needed to get back to Olympia, help his brothers, help Penelope, he could figure out what to do about being Faerie King afterwards.

"Yes," Dair continued. "He told us his magic is calling him away at breakfast this morning—which you would have known if you had deigned to take a meal with us before tonight." Dair cast him a suspicious look. "Why did you decide to come this time if not to see Thaen off?"

"As apology, I suppose." Aiden bowed his head, tugging at the sleeve of the black jacket he wore. The cuff was embroidered with stars that slowly faded as they trailed up toward his elbow. It was one of the most ridiculous things he'd ever worn, but he thought it better to appease his captors by dressing appropriately for supper. "I've caused your family plenty of trouble and none of you are truly to blame."

Dair blinked. "You know, it is most unsettling to look at you and not know if you are lying or not."

Aiden kept walking even as his chest tightened. *Curses.* If Dair was already suspicious, there was no telling how the rest of the family would react to his sudden change in attitude. Thaen would certainly sniff it out.

It was as if the thought summoned him.

Thaen materialized in the hallway, his sword strapped across his back and his steps toward them purposeful.

"Are you not staying for supper?" Dair asked.

Thaen shook his head. "Danu has called, and I must answer. I have to gather my pack and then I will be off." He looked to Aiden. "Finally gracing the rest of us with your presence?"

Aiden held his mouth shut. He didn't need to rise to Thaen's bait. It wouldn't help him find what he needed. He scratched at his wrist where the embroidery rubbed against his skin. The sooner the blasted fae left, the better.

"Where are you headed this time?" Dair asked.

Thaen adjusted the strap of knives wrapped over his chest. "The Farraige Gaineamh. The Goddess has work there for me to do."

Dair grabbed Aiden's arm and waved over his shoulder. "Have a safe flight."

Aiden didn't allow himself to react and let Dair tow him toward the dining hall. If Thaen was flying, then he was certainly taking a carpet.

Perhaps the Goddess really did care.

Dair stopped at a pair of grand doors, looking back at Aiden. "If the jacket really is bothering you, there's time for you to switch it before supper is served."

Aiden stilled, not even having realized he was still fiddling with the sleeve. He looked back to where Thaen had just disappeared down the hall. "You know, I might." He took a step away and Dair followed.

"Dair," Shirina called from the other side of the door.

Dair frowned. "Fine but be quick about it. I will hunt you down if you make us wait."

Aiden didn't wait for Dair to turn away before he jogged back the way they'd come. When he heard the snick of the door behind him, he sent out small bits of shadow. All he needed was to figure out Thaen's location and follow behind.

The shadows swept through the palace, sending Aiden bits of information as they went. He couldn't see through them, but he could recognize the difference between dead things and living things. Almost like he could feel the souls. The magic swirling in them. He couldn't tell the difference between a book or a rock, but he could differentiate between a dog and a person.

His shadows found seven fae scattered throughout the palace in this wing. Aiden could tell one of them was near the royal wing, which meant Thaen was still packing.

Perfect.

Aiden raced up the stairs, tucking himself into shadows at every opportunity. At the end of the hall where his own rooms were situated, he ducked into an empty room. There were a few, since only three of them were occupied at the moment.

After a few minutes, Aiden heard the quiet click of a door. He held his breath, telling his heart to be silent so as not to alert Thaen to his presence. No footsteps echoed in the corridor, so Aiden counted instead. He reached thirty before he crept toward the door. He was glad he'd waited. Thaen had made it only halfway down the hall. The sword on his back crackled with magic.

Aiden stepped fully from the room on silent steps. He didn't close the door all the way behind him and followed after Thaen.

It wasn't far to the place where the carpet was kept. Thaen ducked into a room off the great hall and Aiden stopped outside it. The gap between the door and the floor was large enough for him to see. He pressed his cheek to the floor and watched the soles of Thaen's boots glide over the floor. There was a click of wood and moonlight swept into the space. Thaen's boots disappeared. A moment later, there was another click, and the moonlight retreated once more. Aiden jumped to his feet and slipped into the room.

While the room itself wasn't anything to gawk at, with its plain walls and hardwood floor, the carpets leaning against the far wall. Both carpets wiggled as he drew closer. They shifted but couldn't escape the wooden loops holding them firmly up against the wall. One was a dark purple that would shift to gray in the faint light. The other was all black, studded with pinpricks of silver, like the night sky brought to life.

He trailed a finger over the purple, which stiffened at his touch. When he did the same to the black, the carpet nearly danced. That gesture seemed more welcoming than the other. Aiden set to work unhooking the ring from the wall. There were no keyholes, but the ring remained fixed in place.

The carpet wiggled a bit more, the bottom of it tapping against the wooden board it stood up on. Aiden looked down and noticed the small lever next to the platform. He nudged it with the toe of his boot and the carpet slipped from its spot on the wall. The night sky unfurled near the floor as the carpet stretched, arching its middle like a cat.

Aiden had never seen anything like it. There were many magical artifacts he'd seen brought through the Mist, but nothing like this. It was almost sentient.

The carpet flattened out, hovering at Aiden's knee. He lifted a boot and stepped down, finding the surface the carpet provided completely stable. Carefully, he put all his weight on the woven threads and stood atop it. It didn't so much as twitch. A small laugh burst from Aiden's mouth, and he knelt down to get better situated. Once he was settled, the carpet moved again. It rose up and Aiden could see the shuttered opening in the ceiling above them. The carpet brought him close to it.

The crack of the door hitting the wall below made him jump. The carpet swayed as well, and Aiden had to grab the edges to keep from teetering off.

"Aedon! Stop!" Dair called from below him.

Cursed fae princes! Aiden didn't look for the mechanism to open the shutters. He sent his magic at the wooden barricade, blasting the doors apart.

The carpet didn't hesitate. It burst through the opening and out into the night.

Aiden shielded his eyes from the sun with his hand as he squinted at the darkness in front of them. The Mist stretched all the way across the horizon, the gray wall a stark contrast to the vibrant colors of Spring flying past beneath him. It had taken longer than he liked to get to the border. Faerie was much larger than he'd thought it would be, but the carpet had made it.

If he squinted, Aiden could make out the trees on the other side of the Mist.

He was nearly home.

He was nearly to Penelope.

Aiden couldn't help it. He held out his arms to the sky and laughed. The carpet dipped and did a flip, obviously effected by Aiden's good mood. He let out a *whoop* as they looped again.

The image of fire flashed into Aiden's thoughts.

His laugh fell away. Where had that come from?

The forest beneath him was engulfed in flames.

Aiden blinked and the image was gone, along with his breath.

The carpet beneath his legs turned gray, falling to pieces as the wind rushed past them.

Aiden shut his eyes and dug his fingers into his hair. "It's nothing." He opened them again and saw the carpet back to proper form. A breath slipped from his lips. They were almost to the Mist. He just had to get across. The carpet would get him across, and everything would be fine.

Screams rang in his ears.

Aiden slammed his palms on either side of his head, but it was no use. The screams were in his head. He roared, trying to cast the sound from his mind.

It quieted, only enough to let him hear the crackle of flames as he opened his eyes and saw the world on fire once again, only this time, the Mist was gone and everything on the Olympian side was aflame as well.

He covered his head with his hands and buried his face in the carpet.

"It's not real. None of this is real."

The noise silenced, though he could still feel the lick of heat against his skin.

This is what the future holds if you leave.

Aiden stiffened. He'd heard this voice before. Not Dair's but someone else. Some*thing* else.

Another thing keeping him from helping those he loved.

He pushed himself up and faced the silent flames ahead of him. "You cannot keep me!" he yelled.

The flames dispersed immediately.

You have always been mine.

The Mist rose up before him.

Before he could so much as cry out, the gray swallowed him whole.

8

ACCEPT

AIDEN KNEW HE WAS DREAMING.

And it wasn't the fact that he was dreaming that made his heart thump in his chest. It was the fact that he couldn't wake up.

Shadows surrounded him. Not the shadows he knew, but a suffocating darkness that stuck to his skin like ink. His breaths came out in panicked gasps. He felt like he was in his body, but he couldn't see his hands in front of his face.

"Where am I?"

He felt the presence near him before he heard the voice once more.

These are things which may yet come to pass.

The voice echoed in Aiden's head and images bloomed before him.

Miles of burnt trees, the ashes flaking off in the wind. Shaunie, staring blankly at the ceiling of her room as blood dribbled from her mouth and nose. An ellylon female, her face tear streaked as she reached for a child someone ripped from her grasp. Paulo MacGregor, screaming at the sky above him as he knelt next to the still form of a woman Aiden didn't recognize. The cliffs next to the Olympian Palace, the water below filled with bodies of water folk. Dion with a sword through his gut. Evan's still form surrounded by birds on the beach.

It was the flash of cinnamon-colored hair that brought him to his knees, his hands over his eyes.

"Stop! Why are you doing this?"

The visions faded.

So you understand.

Aiden threw his hands in the air. "What am I supposed to understand?"

What will happen if you leave.

Another vision burst into view. Aiden watched himself this time, his steps staggering as he pushed through the Underworld Gate. He stumbled up to the oak tree on the other side, his hands shaking and his skin cracking. No one saw him as he went to his knees, the shadows around him breaking apart before they could catch him. He watched as his body withered to nothing but dust.

"I die." A shudder rippled through him. Even if he made it to Olympia, he couldn't even get back to Faerie in time to stop this from happening. He couldn't stop Adira as his body decayed. He couldn't tell Penelope he loved her. Nothing. He would be nothing.

Now, you see.

The vision faded and Aiden blinked. The black was gone and instead a wispy gray hovered above him. Pieces of sounds swept past him. Whispered words, joyful laughter, screams of terror, flying past him before he could even react. He was in the Mist. It took him a moment to realize he was lying on his back, sharp rocks pressing into his back. When had he fallen from the carpet? With a deep breath, he pushed himself up.

A scream had him jumping to his feet. His heart skipped. Though he couldn't make out the words, it sounded like Penelope.

He swung around and ran in the direction he thought the noise came from. "Penelope!" He sent his shadows out, cutting through the Mist around him. How did she get here?

The Mist broke apart ahead of him, revealing what he could only describe as a monster.

Aiden skidded on the loose rock under his feet but stopped a few feet away. The creature's yellow eyes studied him as he slowly tilted his head.

"Hello, My Sovereign." The beast lifted a furry, gray fist to its chest and bowed. "I have been waiting for you."

Aiden took a step back, drawing his shadows to his back in a shield. "Who are you? Where is Penelope?"

An unnatural smile stretched across the creature's face. "I have not met anyone currently going by that name. Besides, time is a fickle thing. Perhaps whatever you heard happened weeks ago or has not yet come to pass."

A flutter of giggles swept past Aiden again. The sound of Penelope's scream had been so real, but he couldn't be sure. The Mist carried so many noises with it. He narrowed his eyes at the creature. "You must be the Gray Man."

The monster bowed. "In Faerie, I am called Am Fear Liath Mòr, though I have recently learned the Olympians refer to me by another name."

"You said you were waiting for me. Why?" Aiden glanced around. The gray was unceasing. Not even the sky above broke through. Aiden couldn't even guess how far it would be if he started walking to a break in the Mist. He needed to get out. He needed to...

He couldn't go into Olympia.

Am Fear Liath Mòr tucked his hands behind his back. "Come, My Sovereign. There is much to discuss." He turned and started walking.

Aiden waited for only a moment before following. The mysterious fae was likely the only way out of this place. The scene didn't change as they walked. Gray mist swirled past them, carrying sounds Aiden recognized and some he didn't. His boots crunched quietly over the loose rocks, but the creature next to him moved without sound. They traveled in silence for several minutes before Am Fear Liath Mòr spoke again.

"The Goddess cares about you, Aedon."

Aiden slowed. "Why does everyone here say my name that way?"

"It is the name your mother gave you."

The mother Durant had killed. Heat swept into Aiden's chest. It wasn't fair. The cursed woman was a plague on the world, and no one could seem to stop her before she committed atrocities. The loss of Hart still made his chest ache, and now this? Someone needed to stop her, but what could he do now that he was stuck in Faerie? "Did you know my mother?"

A rumble had Aiden's head whipping in Am Fear Liath Mòr's direction. The fae was chuckling. "Yes, I knew Queen Morana very well."

"I've heard things about her." Fiadh had shared tidbits with him, showing him all her favorite places in the palace. "Everyone in Winter seems to have loved her."

"The two of you are more similar than you likely know." Am Fear Liath Mòr stopped. "You have much to learn about where you are from, My Sovereign, before you are ready to face what comes next. I suggest you cease trying to return to the kingdom that carved you into the man you are and try to find your place in the kingdom of the fae that birthed you."

"How am I to do that?"

Am Fear Liath Mòr turned away from him. "Perhaps, you could give the family you have here a chance."

He stepped aside and revealed a break in the Mist. Thaen's familiar form stood right outside the reach of the gray border.

Thaen crossed his arms over his chest. "Has the Goddess finally knocked some sense into you?"

Aiden rubbed at the back of his neck, stepping from the Mist. "Perhaps." He turned back to offer his appreciation to Am Fear Liath Mòr, but the creature was already gone.

"Come," Thaen said. "It will be a long ride back to the palace."

9
GROWTH AND PAINS

Dearest Penny,

None of the methods we've tried have been able to get letters through the Mist. I'm still going to write these in the hopes that one of them will get to you. I'm so afraid for you. I can't stop thinking about it. How did Prince Aiden come to be in Faerie? Devan's contact in the Winter Palace was the one that first alerted him, and we've done our best to keep apprised of his situation. How did no one in Olympia know who he truly was?

And what are you doing about it? I know you, Penelope Barclay. I know you would not allow someone to take what you love from you. I only pray to the Goddess you are being safe.

I hate this. I have so many things I want

to talk to you about. So many things I have to tell you.

Devan has been trying his best to get in to see Aiden, but he claims the palace is practically a fortress. I don't know what this will mean for our trade proposals, but none of that matters until the border opens back up.

The only good thing going on is that the folk here have become even more friendly toward us. There wasn't so much veiled animosity as there had been in the Day Courts, but now that their High King is from Olympia, the neighbors have gotten very friendly. I'm doing my best to use it to my advantage. I even made a friend who works at the palace. Perhaps I can figure out what's going on and have some information for you when the Mist opens.

I'm going to become my own little spy.
Your Newest Recruit,
Angelica

Spot was growing. Of course, it wasn't abnormal for a dog to grow in their adolescence, but the rate at which he grew and since he was technically a full-grown dog, it made his new size... abnormal.

One of his heads bumped a low-hanging branch and he yipped in annoyance. The bog they'd entered had been difficult to navigate with Spot's new girth. Penny used her magic to push the branch upward and laid a hand on his side, which was now as tall as she was—not that her height was anything to brag about. However, it was apparently helpful to be her stature when tromping through a bog with bowing branches and plenty of other things to knock one's head on. Her magic zipped forward and readjusted the lower branches on the muggy path in front of them.

Praise the Goddess, Penny had finally wrangled her magic into some semblance of control. It still reacted violently when she was frightened, but her fear had ebbed in the last few days as they'd run into less creatures. A group of sprites had chased after them when Spot had hit their tree too hard with his wagging tail. They'd caught sight of another púca near a pond and had skirted around the water to avoid it. In fact, they had circumvented most of the large bodies of water because of the creatures and Penny was beginning to feel the effects of not washing after a full week of hiking through Faerie.

Spot's tail came whipping in her direction and Penny barely dodged it. "Hey! If you hit me with that thing, I'm going to have a concussion." His exuberance didn't ebb, and Penny stomped up toward his heads. "Seriously, what are you—"

A tiny spot of light swayed a dozen feet in front of them. It moved languidly, as if the thing found it difficult to remain still, but it never moved more than a foot in any direction.

A will-o-the-wisp.

Penny shook her head. "Oh no. We don't need any more trouble. Let's keep moving, Spot." Will-o-the-wisps were known for being mischievous. The little glowing guides had the ability to lead their pursuers to great fortune or devastating peril, depending on their whim of the moment.

But Spot didn't move. The only movement in the area was the wag of Spot's tail and the sway of the tiny floating form.

"Spot?"

He lunged.

His front feet slid deep into the mud where the wisp had just been floating. Spot's paws popped out of the ground, and he sniffed the area. A moment later, and the little fae creature reappeared again, several feet ahead of where Spot landed.

"Spot, no! We can't follow!"

Spot didn't seem to hear her. He leapt again with the same result. The wisp disappeared before he could reach it and materialized ahead.

Penny pushed against his side, not able to use the harness or leash he had grown out of days ago. It was like shoving at a wall. "Leave it! We don't know where it's trying to lead us."

Again and again, Spot pounced at the elusive light and every time it led him in opposite direction of their destination.

"We have to find Aiden!"

One of the three heads turned in her direction, but the others growled at the wisp ahead. Some kind of enchantment had been cast, one of predator versus prey.

But which was which?

Penny chased after him. Sweet Gaia, he could get them killed. They broke free of the marsh and onto more solid terrain, though the thickness of the trees didn't lessen. The *crack* of breaking branches and the excited yips gave away Spot's location. Every creature skittering around these woods would come out of their hidey-holes and attack them if Penny didn't get him to stop.

"Come on," Penny groaned as Spot took a bounding leap over a pit. Penny stopped at the edge and looked down into the somewhat deep ravine. The gap stretched farther than Penny could see and had to be more than a dozen feet across—too wide for Penny to jump.

"Spot!" she called.

Just ahead, the dog skidded to a stop and looked back at her. All three heads turned to the side, and he left the wisp, loping back toward the crag. *Praise the Goddess.* He leapt and landed in the soft dirt next to her. The weight of him shook the ground under their feet and Penny's footing slipped. She fell to the ground and all three of Spot's heads bent down to sniff at her.

"I'm fine, you big oaf." She pushed the prodding muzzles out of her face and narrowed her eyes at him. "Though, I'm not very happy about you running off."

Spot gave her an obviously repentant whine. Penny was getting better at reading him... slowly. The first few days had been an adjustment for sure. Spot wasn't like many other dogs. Yes, he did normal dog things like chasing fish and slobbering all over the place, but his social development was nothing like any dog Penny had known.

Her hands dusted off her trousers as she stood. "Come on. I think we need to head in—"

The ground gave way beneath them. Penny scrambled for the edge, but her fingers only met air. Heart in her throat, she plummeted. Her limbs automatically curled into a ball before she hit the bottom of the ravine on her side. Stars smattered her vision. Her lungs locked up and her chest couldn't take in any air for a few moments. When a breath finally slipped between her lips, the expansion of her rib cage had the stars in her vision twinkling against black. A groan escaped her, and she closed her eyes. The next breath hurt nearly as bad as the first, but she withheld a groan this time.

The vibration of the dirt against her cheek spoke of Spot's presence near her before she opened her eyes. His body sagged to the ground, all three of his giant heads pressing their wet noses to her.

"I'm still alive," she croaked. Short breaths were easier to handle than the deep ones. She slowly used her arms to prop herself up. Even the simplest movement sent breath hissing between her teeth. It took a minute, but she finally got to her feet. Stars still flickered at the edges, but they'd fade soon enough.

Her attention roved over the predicament she and Spot now found themselves in. The walls of the ravine were nearly sheer, their edges made up of stones and soft dirt. Penny alone would have a difficult time getting out. With Spot, it would be impossible. She didn't trust her magic enough not to hurt him if she used the roots to pull them out, and the ravine was too narrow to create a structure for them to climb—especially with Spot's new girth.

"We just have to find an area to climb out." Penny gently slid the pack from her shoulders. It fell from her back, and she staggered a moment from the sudden loss of the weight. That wasn't a good sign.

Her shaking fingers unbuckled the clasps, and she dug out one of the maps she'd taken from Aiden's office. From what he told her, this map was primarily made from details Devan had sent to him through Lord Hermen. One of Devan's assignments on this side of the Mist was to send accurate renditions of Faerie's layout. Penny had only added bits and pieces as they'd traveled, hoping to have something to bring back to Prince Dion—no, now it was *King* Dion. Great Gaia, what was going on at the capital without Aiden?

Penny shook her head and returned her attention to the parchment in her hands.

But there wasn't a ravine in Spring anywhere on it.

"Curses," Penny bit out. Looking over the map again, she found the area where the bog had been, about a day's journey to the capital, and guessed which way the will-o-the-wisp had led them. She reached into the pack once again and found Aiden's quill, the one charmed never to run out of ink. The tip of the pen scratched against the page as she marked where she believed they'd fallen.

"All right. If this goes in the same direction for a while, it should lead us somewhat closer to Crann Mòr. Maybe there will be a way out if we try to maintain a north-facing direction."

Spot sat up and his tail kicked up blades of grass on the ground behind him. Penny chuckled as the vibrations rumbled up her legs. That tail was going to decapitate someone.

She returned the items to her pack and stood to swing it onto her shoulders. She gasped when the weight of the pack bit into her ribs. The bag fell to the ground and her breaths came out in angry puffs. By the Goddess, it *hurt*.

"All right Pen—*Nell*. You can do this." She eyed the pack at her feet. "You can do this."

Her hands grasped the handles, and she swung the entire thing onto her back before she could think too much about it. Tears welled at the corners of her eyes, and once the straps settled on her shoulders, she let the breath out of her chest in a cry. Sweet Gaia, something was definitely wrong.

Penny shook off the thought. It didn't matter, even if she was injured. If they didn't get moving, something nasty would come along and finish them off. She would check on her ribs when they had a moment to rest. She had a few healing necessities in her bag, and she could at least wrap her torso if nothing else.

Her eyes fell on Spot. "Let's get out of here."

"Oh, sweet Gaia, thank you!" Penny nearly fell to her knees at the sight of the sloping embankment up ahead. Her steps picked up speed.

Night had descended on them hours ago, but neither Penny nor Spot had stopped to rest for more than a few minutes. Who knew what other horrible creatures were waiting around to snatch them from the hole?

The ravine had turned away from Crann Mòr a little over two hours before, and Penny's gut had been uneasy ever since. They were farther into Spring, but if they headed west, they should be able to get back on track and arrive at the Faerie capital by tomorrow evening—if her estimations were right. Something flickered in her chest and her lips curved upward.

Spot reached the embankment a beat before Penny, both of their chests heaving from weariness and anticipation. Spot clambered halfway up the side when shrill screams rang around them. All three of Spot's heads went on alert and Penny stopped in her tracks. The shrieks of what had to be dozens of creatures grew louder, drowning out any other noise. Penny scrambled to where Spot stood before the first fae popped into view. The rusty-red hat atop its gnarled head gave it away almost immediately.

Redcaps would be on them in an instant.

The bloodthirsty creatures would use their taloned fingers to shred Penny and Spot into bits. Redcaps were nothing to mess with, she knew that much. They would ravage any living thing they came across only to get enough blood to dip their crude little caps in.

"Run!" she shouted and skidded back down the embankment. Spot leaped down in front of her. Penny stumbled down the slope but kept her feet and followed after him. They dashed farther down the ravine. The screeching chased after them.

Penny's blood would *not* be dye for a hat. She absolutely refused.

She stopped and spun around. The swarm of bwachod scrambled over one another in waves, not a single one having concern over those they trampled into the dirt. Their rat-nosed faces screwed up in malintent and hunger as they surged toward her.

Before they could overrun her, she yanked off her gloves, dug her fingertips into the ground and prayed.

Thick roots burst from the sides of the ravine right in front of her, whipping out like snakes striking their prey. Penny's magic wove the roots into a cage, catching the wave of redcaps as it crashed into the dirt near her feet. One of them snapped their black, elongated teeth at her through the netting of roots. Penny wove the wood tighter together until it became an impenetrable wall between them.

Penny wiped the dust from her face with the back of her glowing hand and turned away from the wall, relieved. Spot waited for her several yards away, his hackles raised and a growl grumbling in his throats.

"I don't think they will be a prob—"

Thick netting shoved her to the ground. She didn't even have time to scream before she was dragged up the side of the ravine. She reached for her gift, but something blocked her magic from being used. She moved to grab the blade in her boot, but every limb was entangled in the twisted mesh.

"We caught her!" a man's voice hollered from above her.

Before long, she was heaved over the side of the ravine. Her body bucked as hands grappled with her and pushed her to the ground on her stomach. She heard Spot's deep barks as others called for something to trap him. Or kill him.

"*Run, Spot!*" Penny screamed. She didn't stop screaming until someone kicked her in the ribs, stealing every breath from her lungs. She choked on a few more breaths before one finally slipped through. The ache in her ribs had turned into a stabbing pain.

Spot could find Aiden, and Aiden would figure out someone brought him here. Spot couldn't die.

"Well!" a voice called out. "What a sight for sore eyes!"

Penny's whole body stiffened.

A pair of well-polished boots stepped into view. "Lift her up. We don't want our new guest lying about in the dirt all night."

Hands grabbed her and hoisted her to her knees. Netting cut into her cheeks as she looked up at the woman in front of her.

"Adira."

10

ANOTHER

 Dair said, "allow the magic to flow freely through you. The Land knows what She needs. Let Her take you."

Aiden closed his eyes. Not his real eyes, but the odd incorporeal ones he used in the dreams. He reached for the now-familiar magic mingling with the gift he'd grown up with. He couldn't shy away from it, even if it did remind him of Penelope's magic.

It was the strangest sensation. Whenever he looked at the magic, whenever he felt it brush against his, he thought of *her*. Penelope's magic was that of life, of energy. It made sense that it would resemble the Goddesses in that way.

It didn't mean Aiden appreciated the reminder of her. He would give up whatever magic he had if he could actually have her beside him.

Dair gave him a mental nudge. "Focus. You have to feel where She is taking you."

Aiden returned his attention to the task at hand. He pulled down the thin barricades he'd erected around himself and let in the Land's magic. The magic latched on, and he felt himself get pulled away from the snowy valley they'd been standing in.

Dair believed if Aiden could pull this off, tonight would be the last night they'd have to do this together. Praise the Goddess.

"Oh my," Dair breathed.

Aiden opened his eyes.

The magic had brought them to a beach somewhere on the coast in Summer. The moon glittered on the water before them, and the surf crashed against the sand.

But the sea wasn't the main attraction.

A herd of horses galloped in the waves, their hooves crashing into the sea foam. They nickered at one another, playing in the surf as they traveled, goading each other on and pushing their youngest members forward. Long manes of hundreds of hues flared out behind them. Each forehead boasted a long, curving horn.

The herd galloped down the beach, disappearing over a jetty a little way from where Aiden and Dair stood.

"Unicorns?" Aiden breathed. "I didn't think those still existed."

Dair shook his head, shock evident on his face. "Nor did I, until tonight." He turned to look at Aiden. "I am sure *Athair* will be pleased to hear there is still at least one herd running about. His prized mount before the wars had been a unicorn." He gave bereaved sigh. "He will probably bring out the miniature painting he still has of it when we tell him."

Aiden almost smiled.

Dair clapped his transparent hands together. No sound came from the action. "Well, I think we have reached the point where you can safely do this on your own, and I can finally get a solid night's sleep without dreaming."

"Wait, really?" Aiden hadn't really believed Dair when he'd said tonight could be the last night.

Dair shrugged. "There is not much I can actually teach you, cousin. This magic is not something widely spoken of. I trust you to know your limits and remember the things we have talked about."

Dair's confidence in him buoyed his spirit. Aiden stopped before he could utter a "thank you." Doing so could cause issues, the fae being known for their strict sense of balance. Even saying the words "thank you" could cause someone to find themselves indebted to the fae they said it to. He didn't think Dair would do such a thing, but it was a habit he'd have to build up sooner rather than later.

"I appreciate that," he said instead.

"Even if I didn't believe you to be ready, I am finished playing tutor." He smirked. "There are far more interesting dreams I can be traipsing about in right now."

Dair disappeared in a flash, leaving Aiden to watch the sunrise and pray he hadn't just been left stranded.

Aiden stared down at the floor of his sitting room, his breaths coming in gasps and sweat dripping off his nose onto the stones beneath his face. After thirty seconds, he bent at the elbows and started another set of pushups.

He'd pushed all the furniture against the walls, not wanting to damage anything as he worked through his exercises. He would return everything to the proper places before he had to go down for supper. First strength training, then agility. His forms meant nothing if they couldn't pack an appropriate punch. A smile touched his lips as he remembered how much Penelope groaned when he'd begun her strength training. She hated pushups.

When he completed his last set, he stood and settled into the first stance of *Cumadh*. His breaths evened out in time with the steps as he closed his eyes and let his memory do all the work. It was while performing these movements his head usually cleared.

His plans of escape began to twirl in his thoughts. After the incident in the Mist, he'd decided on a new tactic. Devan was somewhere in Winter. Aiden may not be able to leave Faerie, but he still needed to get word to everyone back in Olympia.

Especially Penelope.

His outstretched hand shook, and he moved into the next form, pulling it in and clenching it against his torso. He took a deep breath and let it out with the next move. Penelope needed to know he wasn't going to be coming back. He needed to release her from the oaths they'd made to each other that night under the oak tree.

He'd asked her to be his wife.

And she'd agreed.

Even as he stood on what felt like an entirely different world, that bond tugged at his heart. The desire to see the smatter of freckles on her face or a glimpse of her smile ached fiercely within him.

But he would need to let her go. She wouldn't survive in a place like this. She thrived in Olympia, with her friends and her family. He would never take her away from that.

A knock on the door slammed him back to reality—and complete darkness. He blinked a few times before realizing the dark didn't have to do with his vision, but the shadows filling the room. He clenched his hands and most of the magic disappeared. Some still curled around his arms, as if apologizing for being errant. He waved his hands through the air to dissipate them and strode to the door.

Expecting Thaen or Dair, he hadn't thrown his tunic back on, but the sight of Fiadh and Shirina in the hall had him regretting it. His hand rubbed the back of his neck as he cleared his throat. "Hello."

Shirina gave him a dazzling smile, a crescent moon against a night sky. "Hello, Aedon. Are you busy?"

Aiden held back the snort. "Not especially."

Fiadh quirked an eyebrow and glanced over Aiden's shoulder. "Are you sure we are not interrupting anything?"

Aiden glanced back at the piled-up furniture. "I was doing some exercises."

Shirina's grin didn't falter in the least. "Would you like to join us for a walk through the palace before supper? Our last tour was cut a bit short."

Her expression didn't change, but Fiadh gave him a knowing look. Their tour had been postponed because Aiden had tried to escape, and Thaen had tackled him into a fountain.

"I'd be honored." He looked down at his shirtless torso and then back to them. "May I have a moment to change?"

Fiadh nodded. "Of course. We will meet you down the hall in the family sitting room."

Aiden shut the door behind their retreating forms. He made it across his lavish prison to the oversized changing room they'd stocked for him. He'd shoved every article of clothing to one side except a few neutral-colored tunics and pants. His boots sat beneath them. Every other day or so, his soiled garments disappeared and two more items of clothing more suited to him appeared. He hadn't spotted what he guessed were the brownies who took care of his room, but he likely wouldn't even if he tried. The elusive bwachod were notoriously shy. He knew of a select few places in Olympia that had begun employing them after the treaty passed five years ago, but he'd never actually seen any of the little folk.

He tugged on a black tunic with silver embroidered cuffs. It was the only ornamented shirt he had on this side of the closet, having enough decoration to be appropriate for being seen with the ruling family. He didn't want to stand out too much as he walked with them and if anyone knew how to wear a disguise, it was Aiden.

He slipped his feet into his boots and left the dressing

room. When he made it to his sitting room, he sent his magic to straighten out the furniture, putting it all back exactly as he'd had it before his workout. When that finished, he slipped out of the room.

The family sitting room sat only a few doors down from Aiden's. He knew Thaen occupied the room across from him and Dair the ones beside it. Fiadh and Shirina shared rooms somewhere in the family wing, but he didn't know where. They hadn't taken over the king and queen suite in all the time they'd lived here. From what Dair claimed, no one had been inside except to clean since his mother died with Aiden himself technically being her heir.

His mother. By the Goddess, he was still reeling from the fact he knew who she was. He'd never truly realized how much the lack of information had left him hollow until it had filled the gaping hole in his chest. He didn't have the entire story. All he knew was that the Queen of Winter had gone to Olympia and had met Aiden's father there after Dion's mother died and Evan's had returned to the Isles.

And then Aiden's mother had died too. At the hands of the woman who had raised him.

The knowledge still stabbed at him. Dair had given Aiden the full account of her death, but it still hadn't fully sunk in. Durant had poisoned his mother before she left Olympia, after getting close to Aiden's father. Dair had said it was a rare poison from the continent—an emetic that didn't leave a trace after a certain amount of time and had the symptoms of a common illness that simply grows violent. However, the poison's work progressed through her body faster as she'd been with child. The fae healers found traces of the poison when her symptoms had grown extreme. Dair said they'd figured out it was Durant who had given her the poison. Fae pregnancies were already difficult, but with the added complications, the queen had been sequestered in her rooms until Aiden's birth... and her death.

Dair mentioned she'd kept a journal of the time she'd been ill, but Aiden couldn't stomach even the thought of looking at it. Not yet at least.

Aiden stepped through the open door of the family sitting room. It had a very different feel than the one he'd shared with his family in Olympia. Where Olympia's had been a barricaded fortress stuffed with fine rugs, leather sofas, and enough drink for Evan to swim in, this room seemed like a breath of fresh air. Floor to ceiling windows encased one wall, showcasing the three other peaks connecting Winter's capital, Eagallach, together.

All four parts of the city formed a misshapen square if looked at from above—the view him and Dair had seen in his dreams a few nights prior. The palace sat at the tip of the eastern peak, taking up the only habitable part of the mountain. The northern mountain held Danu's temple, shining from the highest peak. The western-most peak contained mostly markets and houses as well as the art district—the only colorful spot on the mountains of snow and stone. The southern peak's flat top held up mostly residences with odd shops scattered between the buildings.

Fiadh and Shirina stood from the sofa they'd occupied while waiting for him. Fiadh gave him a wide grin. "Excellent. I have been looking forward to this. Our family has been the proud stewards of this palace for many years. It will be nice to show it off."

Shirina eyed her husband with mirth. "You only wish to show it off so you can tell him about all of the changes you will make after the anointing."

"You know me too well, my love." Fiadh took her hand and placed it on his forearm. He guided her toward the door where Aiden had entered.

After Aiden's mother died, apparently the crown was supposed to have passed to Aiden on his thirtieth birthday. But because he was not of age, Fiadh had been acting as regent until Aiden could ascend the throne or abdicate. But where he could have passed the Winter throne off, the title of High Ruler was another matter entirely. With the magic of the land being involved, there was no simple way to pass it off unless Aiden wanted to become a villain or die an early death—neither of which appealed to him.

But with Aiden's ascension as High Ruler, Fiadh would become Winter's king after Aiden's anointing—the fae version of a coronation—at the equinox. With Aiden technically being the heir to both, a crown had to be on his head before he could abdicate and pass the role onto Fiadh.

If only Aiden could figure out a way to abdicate from both. He never wanted to be king. He'd rather find a remote hole somewhere in the mountains and live out the rest of his days in seclusion. The temptation to throw himself out the faerie-glass windows took form in the back of his mind as he trailed behind the couple. Maybe he could make it to the bridge this time before Thaen caught up to him.

"Now, where did we last leave off?" Fiadh tilted his head back and forth in feigned thought. "Ah, yes, I believe it was the fountain—"

"Fiadh, do not tease," Shirina admonished.

Fiadh smirked over his shoulder at Aiden. "Perhaps this time we can get a little further, hm?"

Aiden gave him a short nod even as he hunched his shoulders to keep them from sagging. He wouldn't risk another attempt to escape. A new purpose for this particular occasion materialized. If Thaen wouldn't allow him to write his family, perhaps he needed to ask someone with a little more authority. If he could show his willingness to adhere to their rules, he may be able to get what he wanted.

He followed the couple back toward the entrance closest to the fountain Thaen had pummeled him into, and Fiadh began his tour for the second time. They started in the North Hall,

Shirina pointing out the masterful art pieces and Fiadh adding odd family history to them.

"This tapestry depicts the War of Asphodel. Your great-great-grandfather cursed the plains in Summer, and they transformed into the Farraige Gaineamh." The woven cloth showed the land turning from thriving fields of thick grass into hills of sand. Aiden's ancestor had been powerful enough to turn fertile ground into wasteland. He stared at the tapestry, a bit awestruck, until Fiadh pulled him away.

They moved on to the Grand Hall, where most of the palace's large events took place.

Shirina pointed toward the ceiling. "The chandeliers are made of faerie-glass and diamonds mined from the very mountains making up our great city. The dwarves have found some of the greatest deposits of gemstones in these mountains and continue to find hidden wonders within Danu's land."

Aiden soaked it all in. The Grand Hall stood in the very center of the palace, the rest of the wings branching out over the peak. The Family Wing sat on the north side, as well as the formal gardens and the bridge leading toward another peak. Dair had named them in Aiden's dream, and he now regretted not listening when he should've. The only one he remembered was the one they stood on: Ulbhag.

From above, the Winter Palace spread out over the mountain like a large turtle cradling the peak under its belly. The Entry Hall filled the place of the head while the Grand Hall, the Throne Room and part of the Family Wing made up the torso. The rest of the palace spread out into its sturdy legs. The West Hall led toward the guard barracks, the servants' quarters, and the kitchens. South led to guest quarters and other public rooms while the East held the solarium, the library and many of the offices used by visiting nobility.

"We hope," said Shirina, leading them back into the Grand Hall, "you will be able to find comfort here, Aedon."

It was time to bring up the real purpose in why he'd taken the tour with them. "I'd feel more comfortable here if I was able to get word back to—" He stopped. He'd nearly said Penelope. By the Goddess, he hadn't meant to even think it. They couldn't know about her. "If I was able to get word back to *my family*."

Fiadh rubbed at the back of his neck. "Unfortunately, that is not possible at the moment."

Aiden's hands tensed and his magic slipped out of his sleeves before he reined it back in. "Everyone keeps saying that, but no one will explain why."

Shirina tutted at Fiadh. "Wind and snow, you males and your obtuse brains. There is absolutely no reason to be so vague." She shook her head and turned back to Aiden. "We are not keeping you from writing, Little Shadow. It is only that your letter will not reach the other side of the border. The High Council ordered the Fuath sealed after our return to Eagallach. Until we are able to apprehend the rebels trapped here, it will remain that way."

Aiden's shoulders sagged. Even if he'd tried on his own, there was no way to reach his family. He took a deep breath through his nose, doing his best to inflate the heart shrinking in his chest. Until he found Durant or figured out her plans, he would have no way to speak with those he loved.

"I am sorry." Fiadh reached out a hand in comfort, but Aiden stepped away. Fiadh sighed and rubbed at the back of his neck. "It was foolish not to explain, but with everything going on..." He waved a hand through the air as if Aiden should understand what "everything" meant. "Unless the rebels are caught or we can get you secured on the throne and out of harm's way, the border will not be opening anytime soon."

So, either Aiden had to discover where Durant was, or he had to cement his rule. A grimace tugged at his lips. The former plan sounded the most appealing, especially to his skill set.

"But," Fiadh continued, "it will not remain closed forever. I am certain you will prove your mettle as our new High King."

"When we can get back through," Shirina cut in, likely noticing Aiden's obvious discomfort, "is there anyone besides your brothers you would like to contact?"

Fiadh's eyes sharpened and Aiden reined in his emotions as quickly as he would in front of an opponent in a fight. They were digging.

"No," he replied. Even if they could hear his heart pound against his chest, their questions would only make shallow holes. "No one else."

11

ASPIRE

MAGIC FLUTTERED AGAINST THE CURTAINS OF AIDEN'S BEDROOM, stirring the fabric like a sleeping giant would with his snores. If only Aiden had been snoring, then perhaps he would feel a modicum of peace.

Sleep continued to elude him and, if he was being honest with himself, it mostly stemmed from the fact that he didn't wish to sleep. He didn't want to get swept away by the dreams of Faerie and the cursed magic that held him captive in this place. Falling in love with his prison was not part of the plan. Taking a flogging from Durant sounded more appealing.

The thump of someone's fist rattled the door to his rooms. Aiden's shadows darted back to him as he made his way out of his bedchamber and through the miniature sitting room. Out the window, stars still danced on the stage of the mountain peaks, but the light gray of the horizon told him it would be dawn soon enough. Aiden opened the door and found Thaen's broad form filling his doorway. A wide smile split through the shadows of the brute's face.

Aiden withheld the urge to punch him. "You do realize most people sleep at night, don't you?"

Thaen snorted. "Please, little cousin. Let us not pretend you have been doing any sleeping. I can hear your muttering across the hall." He turned and began striding away. "Come."

Aiden bristled at the command, stifling any mutters, and shut his door behind him. He had to play nice. For now.

Thaen led him out of the Family Wing. The Grand Hall stood quiet and empty at this time of the night. Not even Shirina with her odd waking hours was seen during this time. Moonlight filtered in from the skylights in the ceiling, pooling over the cool, black granite floor. They passed through the cavernous space and entered the southern section of the palace.

Thaen headed toward where Aiden recalled the guard barracks were. "What weapons are you proficient with?"

Aiden wanted to laugh. Like he would give Thaen an answer to that. The fae would likely use the information against him. "Enough of them."

Thaen cocked his head and turned down another hallway. "Do not be evasive. I would rather know now than have to figure it out myself."

Aiden shook his head. "I'm not going to make it easy for you." The brute certainly hadn't done the same for Aiden.

Thaen chuffed out a fraction of a laugh. Aiden hadn't actually heard his true laugh, only mockeries of one or quiet chuckles. It was like he didn't have a single thing to enjoy in life. Perhaps he really was as miserable as he seemed to be.

Thaen reached a set of double doors and opened them wide. The smell of metal and sweat swept over Aiden like a caress. If he closed his eyes, he could pretend he'd just walked into his headquarters in Olympia. If he tried hard enough, he could hear Hart and Rissa playfully bicker somewhere ahead.

The doors thumped closed behind him, banishing the figments with them.

Thaen glided into the middle of a moonlit ring. Sand

covered the floor and weapons glittered along the walls. Thaen turned and gestured toward the blades. "Grab one."

A shadow passed by Aiden's ear, flicking at the bit of hair that had grown past his earlobe within the past several weeks. He looked to the walls. Was this some sort of test? Thaen hadn't let him anywhere near a weapon, or anything that could be used as one, since his arrival.

Thaen waited patiently in the middle of the circle, not drawing any of the many weapons strapped to his leather armor.

Aiden took a step toward the wall. Then another—not taking his eyes from the fae. He let his magic sweep over the weapons rack, flinching away from ones he wouldn't want to use against a larger opponent and licking at others that would be wiser choices.

"Your control has improved since your first day here. It does not rush about as if you had recently grown out of the nursery."

Aiden didn't take the bait Thaen had thrown with the insult and settled on a longsword hanging on the wall. He snatched it from its hook and tested the weight. It wasn't nearly as balanced as one Heff could create, but it would do for a practice bout. He stepped into the sandy ring, testing his mobility with the blade, and getting a feel for it.

Thaen shifted and drew his own sword from his back. In the low light, it seemed to glow violet. Thaen took a stance. "It seems you may have an idea how to handle a blade, but let us see if an idea is all you—"

Aiden swung. He'd always been of the mind that it was best to simply strike at the first possible moment. Better to get the fight over with than let it drag on.

The sword crashed into the sand.

He looked down at his empty hand in disbelief, then back up to Thaen. The blasted fae gave him a cheeky grin and nodded to where Aiden's blade lay on the ground. "Go on then."

Aiden picked up the weapon once again and settled into position. He wouldn't be taken by surprise a second time.

Thaen's arm snaked out and his sword met Aiden's. The force of it rattled Aiden's hands as he held the blade up to block the blow. Thaen moved again and Aiden barely managed to guard his left side. The blows came quicker. Thaen struck like a viper, catching any piece of unguarded skin he could bite into. Every swing was precise, every swipe deadly. Aiden barely kept his feet, his defenses rushed and his blows feeble. Back and forth over the sand, the brute pushed, not letting up for a single moment of what seemed like an hour.

Aiden lost his sword a second then a third time. His jaw ached from how tight he held his frustration behind his teeth. Aiden had never fought the likes of Thaen before. He plucked the sword from where its tip dug into the sand and turned back to his opponent.

"You are slow, Aedon." Thaen swiped down and his blade collided with Aiden's again, making Aiden's arms shake. Thaen frowned. "We need to work on your upper body strength as well."

Aiden lashed out with his blade, but Thaen dodged it easily as if to prove his point. "You have trained too long with the humans. They have allowed you to become weak when you should have become strong."

Aiden growled. Even if Aiden was a tad weaker, Thaen had to be using magic. The brute smacked Aiden's thigh with the flat of his blade for what had to be the hundredth time and Aiden's temper snapped. He grabbed Thaen's forearm, his own skin blackening in stripes down to his wrists.

Souls flooded the space.

The most souls Aiden had ever summoned for a killer had been perhaps a dozen, but Thaen had triple, perhaps quadruple, that amount. Fair folk, water folk, and human alike all hovered around them.

"What are you doing, cousin?" Aiden looked up into Thaen's face, but the fae was looking down at his hand questioningly. "Do you really think your puny hand is going to stop me from knocking you senseless?"

The spirits around the room gave Aiden a knowing smile, but he couldn't begin to guess what was happening.

"What do you mean?" He used his free hand to gesture to the beings standing about the room. "Can't you see..." His brows furrowed as he continued to watch Thaen.

The brute finally realized Aiden had been doing something and squinted about the room. His eyes narrowed where the spirits settled about the space, but no recognition sparked in his gaze. The fae's pupils appeared hazy this close, and the color of his irises bleached out into the pale blue Aiden associated with him.

Brilliant clarity struck Aiden and his head fell back. His hand dropped away from Thaen's. The chuckling spirits disappeared, no longer necessary—or useful. Aiden sighed at his own idiocy. "You're blind."

"And they say you are some great spymaster in the mortal lands." Thaen took a step back, settling the flat of his sword on his shoulder. He looked about, obviously noticing the absence of the spirits even in his blind state. "What did you do? You used magic, but I could not see what it did."

Aiden swallowed, looking everywhere but at Thaen's face. "I, uh, summoned the spirits of those you've killed."

"Oh?" His voice came out blasé. "I suppose you were trying to pull something on me, hm? Thought to distract me?"

Aiden picked up the sword laying on the ground. "I certainly did." He turned toward the empty hook on the wall. This conversation had evolved from crossing blades. "I won't lie, I'm very intrigued. Why didn't you see them? For a blind man, you act as if you can see everything."

"Just because I do not see the way you do," he scoffed, "does not mean I am blind. Danu enacts a price for her *tiodhlacan an spioraid*—Her gifts. Mages are not the only ones who must pay for their magic."

Aiden's step faltered. "What?" he asked. And not just for the translation. He had always assumed the fair folk were simply gifted without any more repercussions than having to tell the truth. He never even thought about their individual gifts. Olympia had destroyed much information about the fae in those early days after the War. He had never truly realized how much.

Thaen grabbed the sword from Aiden's hand and placed it back in its spot on the weapon wall. "All Tuatha have gifts passed down from Danu through Her blood: glamours, quick-healing, animal affinity, immortality, voice manipulation. You know the list. The ellyllon are given *tiodhlacan an spioraid*, abilities unique to each fae. But like with all things, there is a price to be paid. I cannot see like you or the rest of the Tuatha can, but I see more than anyone else. Danu speaks to me, and I am Her messenger. I am the one who sees Her mark of death on the souls all around us and I am the one who will mete out Her judgment in this kingdom."

"What do you mean?" asked Aiden. "You can see Danu?"

"It is not so simple. Danu is *everywhere*." He spread out his arms. "She is life and light, shadow and death. Her hand is in all things and *that* is what I see. Your magic, for example, comes from Her. It is a part of Her essence and shows me what I need to see, though if I look closely, it has your unique signature as well." He prodded Aiden in the chest. "Even the spirit that lives within that body is Hers. I can see you just as well as I can see the stars glittering in the sky and the grains of sand beneath our feet. I simply cannot tell you what color your hair is or read what is written on a sheet of paper."

Aiden's boot ground into the sand Thaen claimed he could see. This fae, this member of Aiden's own family, paid a heavy price for a gift he used in the name of another. Most people would be resentful of such a thing, but when Thaen spoke of his goddess, it was with reverence. With love. He glanced back up at his cousin. "And you aren't angered by it?"

"No. This is what has been asked of me and I will not allow anger to take root where it should have no place to grow." He hesitated for a moment. "Though I am curious. How many were there?"

"How many what?"

"Souls, cousin. How many souls were you able to summon?"

"A few dozen?" Aiden couldn't help but allow the sentence to come out as a question. What was Thaen thinking? Was he so heartless that he didn't even know the number of people he'd killed?

"There should have been fifty-two at least."

"Fifty-two?" Aiden gaped. "*At least*?"

Thaen chuckled and sheathed his sword. "Yes. That should be the number of people I have killed."

Aiden took a step toward his blade. "Are you not afraid?"

Thaen gave him a questioning look. "What do I have to be afraid of?" He smirked. "You and your laggard swordplay?"

"Of course not!" The words came out before he could consider them. Thaen chuckled and Aiden rolled his eyes. "You know what I mean. Aren't you afraid of facing retribution for those you've killed?" The holy men in Olympia had often preached about the fires of Gaia's justice the monsters of the world would face. The Goddess was a goddess of justice, balance, and order.

"Do you fear facing retribution for those you have killed in the name of justice and honor? Are we to fear Danu's wrath for doing good? No, I do not fear that which has been asked of me."

The doors to the sparring room burst open and Dair sauntered in, his golden eyes flashing with mirth and a smirk playing on his face. "And why should he? He gets to gallivant all over the place, assassinating people for Goddess and glory while the not-so-special folk have to stay home and do boring things like fetch their relatives for meals."

Thaen glared at his brother—his *twin* brother, as Aiden had learned. "I do not *gallivant* anywhere. I simply dispose of the marked and work to protect our kingdom from those who would do it harm."

Aiden's stomach plummeted to the floor. "By the Goddess." Of course. His cousin, the only opponent he'd ever been absolutely pummeled by, was the blasted *Lòchran*—the legendary assassin. The creature of darkness and death.

"Now you see it, cousin." Dair laughed. "Do not fret. Our little Thaen only kills those he is supposed to. Well, unless he gets very annoyed." He paused. "I am honestly surprised you are not dead."

"I would not kill our king," Thaen said, indignant.

Dair waved a flippant hand, guiding them out of the training room. "Yes, yes. The new king must sit on the glass throne and save us all from our perils." He flicked his hair over his shoulder. Silver tinsel flashed between the colorful strands. "Now, *Màthair* has demanded we all sit down to break our fast together this morning before she retires. She is to call on one of the other council members this evening to apprise them of how Our Sovereign is adapting."

Aiden nearly rolled his eyes, following behind. If he didn't *adapt* and learn to outmatch Thaen, he wasn't going to get out of this palace anytime soon. He needed to gather more information, use his mind more than his might in order to escape and find Devan. Stone's son-in-law would have a network set up. Connections Aiden couldn't access here. It seemed there was much he didn't know about this land, and the time for learning would pass him by if he didn't take hold of it quickly.

"It is good to see you up and moving, My Sovereign," said the Autumn Councilor. The fiery red of his hair bled into the carrot color of his robes.

After breakfast, Shirina had insisted Aiden accompany her to meet with the High Councilor regarding his "health" that evening. They sat in a formal sitting room in the East Wing, the drapes and upholstery in several shades of black and silver—the colors of the Winter Court.

"You are kind to say so, Councilor," Aiden replied. "I'm feeling much more myself since we last spoke."

"No need for formalities. You may call me Sgiath." Sgiath's eyes flicked to Shirina before his mouth twitched with a smile directed at Aiden. "How are you enjoying your stay in Winter?"

Aiden withheld a snort. The fae asked it like he expected Aiden to admit it had been a holiday. "I've learned much since I arrived."

Sgiath's right brow lifted a fraction. "Have you come to terms with your situation then?"

Aiden opened his mouth, but he couldn't put together the words he wanted to say in a way that wouldn't be taken poorly.

Shirina stepped in. "We are not trying to rush you into anything, Aedon. We understand the predicament you have been put in, and we wish for you to see how much good you can do with your new situation."

"Though we would all like to hear of your acceptance sooner rather than later." Sgiath clasped his hands together. "We still wish to announce your participation in the capital's equinox celebrations in two months."

Two months. Had the time gone so quickly? He'd been in Winter for almost an entire month already and had nothing to show for it except the plethora of faint bruises from his practice bout this morning and his magic-plagued dreams.

"Have we heard back from the Isles about their attendance?" Shirina asked.

"Not yet. With the Fuath being closed, it has been difficult getting through to them. It seems as if our usual methods of communication are not working as they once did for some reason."

Shirina nodded, her expression thoughtful. "I will speak with Fiadh and see if there is anything else we can do."

"I am sure everything will work out." Sgiath cleared his throat and turned to Aiden. "Shirina has sent word that you wish to speak with the Olympian Court."

Aiden's gaze whipped to Shirina. "You told them?"

Shirina's eyebrows drew upward. "Was it a secret?"

"No. Not really. I'm only surprised." Shirina had listened to his request and even if she had seemed to ignore it, she'd actually taken the issue to the other Councilors. He turned back to Sgiath. "Yes, I would like to send word to my brothers." Since it had been six weeks since his capture without any contact, his brothers had likely begun to assume the worst. "Is that still not an option? If you can speak with the Aigeans, surely, I can reach out to my brothers."

"In the past, we have used a collection of enchanted conch shells given to the High Ruler and the High Council to communicate with the Isles, but they would not work as a way to reach the Olympians." Sgiath gave him an empathetic smile. "I understand your desire, My Sovereign, but after the murder of the High Queen—Danu receive her—we have blocked all access in or out of the Fuath, for your safety. We have not been able to apprehend the murderer, and if we reopen the way into Olympia, we fear we may lose them."

Well, there went another one of Aiden's wishes. "But why lock it down?" he asked. "Isn't the Gray Man there to monitor the Mist?"

"Am Fear Liath Mòr has some ability to see what goes in and out of the Fuath, but even he can be fooled by charms or magic. For the time being, it is simply safer to not allow anyone else through before we can root the rebels out. We plan to reevaluate in a few months, after your anointing."

A few months? Aiden couldn't wait that long. "But I thought there was only one safe passage through the Mist. Wouldn't it be simple to monitor that one area while we send a message through and then seal it back up again?"

Shirina laid a hand on his arm. "It is difficult to lock down. It took us a full day this time and it may take us longer the next. If any whisper of an opening were to spread, do you really believe the rebels would pass it by?"

No. Durant would never allow even a crumb of a possibility to escape her. And she had always been good at collecting crumbs. Even the ones no one remembered existed.

Sgiath leaned back in his chair. "Thankfully, Am Fear Liath Mòr reported only one other mortal passing through after the murder. He even said they came to our side through Olympia's portal."

Something in Aiden's chest caught. Only himself, his brothers, Stone's family, and Lady Alvis knew about the portal into Faerie. Had Stone sent someone through the portal to come after him?

Shirina's voice broke through his thoughts. "If we are to open the border, we cannot guarantee the murderer will not get away. I am sorry, Little Shadow."

"I understand," Aiden said. At least Durant was still holed up somewhere in Faerie. That was one mark in their favor. Aiden took a deep breath. "Has anyone seen the person who made it through before the Mist closed?"

Sgiath shook his head. "No. We learned the portal was set to let them out somewhere in Farraige Gaineamh, but we have not located them. The Mist can be somewhat fickle, and we cannot be sure where or when those who cross through will arrive. We sent a herd of centaurs to patrol the area the day the Fuath closed, but as of the report that came in this morning, they only reported a strange new oasis that had not been there before."

"I see." Aiden allowed the council members to move on to other topics, but his mind remained on the mysterious Olympian running about Faerie. By the Goddess, if there was someone else out there, where were they now?

12
CHARMS AND CHAINS

Dearest Penny,

I have never felt so trapped in my life. I'm losing my mind without knowing what's going on at home. There's a rebellion going on, for Gaia's sake! I worry for my family. I miss them so much. I want to talk with my mother, Penny. I need her right now.

Devan is still trying to get into the palace. He even leaves in the middle of the night for his attempts, though I have no idea what he's going to do in the dark. His hours have always been odd though. He could call himself a member of the Night Court for all of the activities he does during those hours.

That joke might have been a bit of a stretch, but I'm dying here! I'm half tempted to march right up to the Gray Man and demand to be let out myself.

But I won't. There must be a reason for all of this, I simply can't see it yet. The Goddess must have a plan, even if it feels like She's left us in the most impossible of situations.

Your Despondent Friend,
Angelica

CHARM-RIDDLED CHAINS CHAFED AGAINST PENNY'S ANKLES AS SHE kicked out at the darkling nipping at her feet. She would wrap the beast in vines if the charms surrounding them didn't suppress her magic. The creature hissed at her, and she hissed back. The scrawny bloodsucker would have to find his dinner elsewhere. Its red eyes turned toward the leprechaun hanging in the cage next to it. It licked its bloodless lips.

Sweet Gaia, Penny would likely start nibbling on a few toes herself if they kept only feeding her once a day.

After being caught by the rebels' nets, Penny had been dragged back to their camp in the middle of Gaia only knew where. Penny had woken with chains on her wrists and ankles, surrounded by fae creatures in a humongous tent somewhere. She hadn't been outside in what had to be a week, based on the sunlight that peeked through the slit forming the door. Though, she didn't know how long she'd slept when she'd first arrived.

Since then, rebels had come and gone with every fae creature in existence. Within the short amount of time she'd been there, she'd seen satyrs, pixies, hobgoblins, werewolves and werecats, hags, and even a young dwarf come into the tent and leave in chains. She had no idea what Adira was doing with them but didn't know if she wanted to find out.

The flap to the tent opened and the darkling screeched when the sunlight licked at its skin.

A wide shadow lumbered in and yanked on the darkling's chain. "Shut it!" The darkling scuttled back on its chain as the man turned on Penny. "Have you been able to make some new friends?" he asked sardonically.

Penny only repeated what she'd said the last several times anyone had come in. "Take me to The Cartographer."

Adira hadn't shown her face since Penny was taken, the men in charge of the captives claiming she had better things to do than speak with "filth" like her. But even with all their jeering and flimsy interrogations, Penny had only spoken those five words. She didn't know how long she would hold out if they grew truly violent, but she wouldn't let up for as long as she could withstand it.

"Well, little mage, today's your lucky day." The rebel seized the chain attached to her ankle and pulled. She held back a scream as her foot went up into the air and the rest of her body followed until only her head and shoulders touched the ground. The piercing pain in her ribs flared through her body. She aimed a kick at his head, but he blocked the lousy attempt easily and unlocked the cuff. Her body smacked against the ground, and she gasped when her spine hit the packed dirt.

"What are you laying around for?" the man asked, leering down at her. "I thought you wanted to see the boss."

Penny glared up at him and slowly sat back up. She'd been attempting to keep her strength up while chained inside the tent, but her knees still shook as she got to her feet. Adding lack of nourishment to the excruciating stabs of agony in her torso and being constantly surrounded by creatures that would likely kill her without a second thought, resulted in torturous days and sleepless nights.

The man sauntered toward the tent flap, not even watching his back. Like she wasn't even worth treating like a threat.

Were the other magic-wielders here in such a state? Unfortunately, Penny could do nothing but follow behind. As she got closer, her attention caught on the charms woven into the fabric walls making up her prison. It was no wonder she couldn't use her magic. They covered nearly every square inch of the fabric and were branded into the posts holding it up.

Sunlight seared her eyes as she walked out of the tent. Stumbling forward, she chased after the dark blot she guessed was the man in front of her as she blinked away the pain. When her vision finally returned, she gaped.

A swarm of tents spread out through a leveled field. The forest around them had been cleared, leaving space for hundreds of the temporary sleeping quarters. Dozens of men and women worked within sight; groups washing clothing; partners sparring; a line of soldiers with a red patch over their mismatched tunics hauling supplies; a rotation of armed pairs guarding the perimeter. Charms jingled overhead and stained every spare piece of canvas. The smell of humans and war permeated the air. The whole encampment stood within the confines of the fae forest. Like watching an army of strangling weeds overtake a flowering garden. When had Adira found the time to orchestrate such a thing? Something on this scale should have taken weeks. Months. And she shouldn't have been able to hide it from the fae long enough for it to have grown so large.

Yet here it was.

A city of tents and rebels.

Penny followed the rebel toward the tent in the middle of the swarm. The queen bee's dwelling then. The man really was taking her to Adira. He spoke with one of the armed men standing by the door and the guard gestured for Penny to come forward. "They're waiting for you."

"*They're* waiting?" she parroted.

The guard hauled her inside by her tunic before she could ask more. Her bare feet tripped over the thick rugs covering the ground and she fell to her knees. Her arms instantly went around her ribs, attempting to keep them steady as she breathed deeply through her nose. She would not cry.

Instead, she turned her attention to the room. Just as in the kitchens at *The Western Edge*, Adira's tent was immaculate. Thick rugs lay systematically on the ground, not allowing a sliver of the dirt beneath them to show. Chests sat in a perfect line along one wall, the polished metal locks gleaming. Even the bed at the edge of the room had tightly pulled sheets, not a wrinkle present.

"There she is." Adira and three others gathered around a table. The rebel leader spread her arms out before her. "Look what gift the Goddess has delivered to us. An Olympian mage who also happens to be the spy that took down so many of our comrades in Olympia."

The table of gawkers hissed.

"Though the scamp of a girl looks harmless, remember her face. She can do more harm to this camp than you'd expect. Though, trussed up like that, she looks rather unworthy of such praise." Adira flicked a hand and all the others stood from their places at the table.

Penny recognized one of them as the woman Penny had met, the one with salt and pepper hair who had given her and Aiden the assignment at the bakery... the place where Adira had put a crossbow bolt in Hart's chest. The bolt meant for Penny.

Once the crowd had all taken a turn sneering at her and the room emptied, Adira stood up and came around the table. "My, my. It was certainly a shock when I saw you hauled out of that pit, and I'm so rarely surprised that I can't help but find it a delight." She stopped in front of Penny and crouched down. "What are you doing here, Lady Penny?"

Penny flinched at the name. Apparently, Adira didn't care if the tricky fae likely hovering on the outskirts of her camp heard Penny's name. *Not like I should expect anything less.* Penny straightened under Adira's scrutiny. "I'm here to stop you." Her voice came out dry, the lack of water in her system taking a toll.

Adira threw her head back and laughed. "By the Goddess, you must be joking." She nudged Penny's shoulder. Penny held her muscles taut, doing her best not to give away her fatigue, but she still wobbled. Adira's smirk grew. "Did you honestly believe you could show up here and stop me? On your own? Oh, I forgot what it is to be so young and self-righteous." She laughed again. "My dear, we both know that was never going to happen. Look at you! Four days in and you're dead on your feet. If our dear prince had trained you correctly, you'd be able to live weeks without food and sleep, even with that little magic payment of yours." She stood and walked over to the table.

Heat crept up Penny's chest and she pulled herself to her feet. "You underestimate a great deal, Adira."

"Perhaps you're right." Adira tutted. "I certainly didn't expect you to come gallivanting through the Mist, though it does open up quite a few more possibilities for me." She turned a dazzling smile Penny's way and grabbed a water skin hanging off the back of her chair. With a toss, the filled skin landed near Penny's bare toes.

Penny's hands shook as she bent to retrieve it, but she withheld the urge to snatch the thing from the ground and guzzle the water until she threw it back up on Adira's pristine rugs. By the Goddess, she'd grown up as heir to the greatest duchess in Olympia. She could playact just as well as the old spymaster could.

The water skin felt wonderful in her hands, but she didn't open it. What little pride she still held demanded it. "Why are you in Faerie?"

Adira plopped back down in the chair she'd been sitting in when Penny had come in. "There were a few things that I needed to set into motion before taking the throne from Prince

Dion—oh excuse me, *King* Dion—namely, getting his younger brothers out of the way. Aiden needed to be taken out of the picture and making him High King of the blasted fae was the perfect way to do it. Prince Evan's departure from Olympia is in the works as we speak."

Penny took the seat across from Adira and could almost imagine they were sitting at the wobbly table in the kitchen of the Western Edge. "How did you know Aiden was in line to be king?"

"You're not daft, Penny, so don't start to act it now." Adira gave her a blank stare. "I've known who the boy was since he was dropped on Harry's doorstep as an infant. I have spies on every piece of this continent stretching through the Isles and reaching all the way to the land across the sea. The little wretch that sired our boy knew my king was the father and if one person knows it, I usually do too. I'd watched them when they were in Olympia. I'd seen them together. I poisoned her myself, but it didn't affect the pregnancy, unfortunately."

Penny took a sip of the water, the pad of her thumb rubbing over the cord wrapped around the mouth of the skin. She wiped her lips with her dirty sleeve. "Unfortunately?"

Adira's lips puckered shrewdly. "Yes. Most of the women my Harry paid *special* attention to died with the children still in their bellies. The mer-witch that birthed Prince Evan disappeared back into the sea before I could take care of her. Queen Morana of Winter made it to the very end and then the boy prince ended up becoming mine to raise. Such an interesting twist of fate, don't you think?"

The water in Penny's stomach swirled and she had to bite down on the inside of her cheek to keep from losing it. This woman was a monster. An absolute monster. Not only did she obsess over someone who did not belong to her, but punished those he chose over her. Poisoned them. She killed women and unborn children. By the Goddess, this woman...

She swallowed down the bile rising in her throat. A change

of subject. They needed a change of subject or Penny was going to launch herself at Adira and destroy whatever chance she had of making it out of this camp alive. "Aiden was the son you told me you lost. The one you claimed had died."

"Yes, and he's dead to me still," Adira stated, only a hint of the bite Penny had first heard when they'd spoken about Aiden's upbringing. "The moment he chose his traitorous brothers over me was the moment he died. I raised him as if he were my own blood. Cared for him. Taught him everything he ever needed to become the best and what did he do to repay my kindness? He stabbed the love of my life in the chest and came for me next. The cursed boy is dead to me."

Penny drained the last drops of the water, doing her best to keep it down in case she didn't see more after this conversation —whatever this conversation actually was. It still made little sense why she was there. Adira had been adamant about killing her the last time they'd seen each other. "So now Aiden is king, Dion is king, and you're still in Faerie. I thought The Cartographer's mission was to take down magic rule once and for all."

Adira kicked her polished boots up on the table, her thick trousers tucked neatly into the tops of them. "And it is—at least to all my very loyal followers. Once my plans come to fruition, magic will simply fade away until it's nothing more than bedside tales and superstitions."

Penny set her hands in her lap, fiddling with the cord attached to the water skin. "And how are you going to make that happen?"

"My dear, it's simple." Adira gave her a smug smile. "All I have to do is take down the Mist and the rest will all come tumbling down around Aiden in glorious destruction. I'll take his brother's crown, then I'll take his. I'll take his people, his family"—she gestured to Penny—"his love, everything he could tie a modicum of care to. I'll put it on a pyre where everyone on this continent can see and burn it all to the ground while he watches."

Penny's heart nearly pounded out of her already-broken ribs.

Adira leaned forward, the smile morphing into a sneer. "Then, when nothing but a broken husk remains of the boy, I'll take his head."

13
ALIGN

That was all Aiden felt before Thaen came twirling through the shadows, sword swinging right over his shoulder. Thaen had thought it a brilliant idea to make Aiden use his magic to darken the arena as well as fend off any attacks in the darkness. While his magic could sense what was around him, it was still like attempting to catch a fish with his hands. Yes, he could see it, but that didn't mean the thing wouldn't slip right out of his fingers if he wasn't careful.

Aiden sidestepped the swipe and brought his own sword up to deliver a blow. Thaen easily dodged the attempt and disappeared into the darkness again.

"Better!" called Dair through the darkness. "You were not taken completely by surprise that time."

Aiden almost rolled his eyes. Dair had become quite the commentator during the sparring sessions. Well, Dair was quite the commentator during everything. Aiden's cousin couldn't seem to keep his mouth shut, even for someone who had the fae compulsion to always tell the truth.

Straight ahead.

This time, Aiden met Thaen's blade with his own, the force

of the blow sending him back a step. Thaen disappeared once again.

"We must work on your strength," Dair said. "You are such a weakling for your size. That blow should not have moved you."

"Shut up, Dair!" Aiden and Thaen both snapped.

Aiden looked forward to these daily sparring sessions every time he woke up. The simple weight of the blade in his hand seemed to be one of the only things still familiar to him. And if he was honest with himself, the exercise helped him reach exhaustion. If he slept deeply enough, the dreams-that-weren't-dreams were never as strong.

Thaen came out of the dark again, this time with his own purple flecked shadows zipping toward Aiden's eyes and his sword lifted overhead. Aiden blocked the raw magic with the shadows floating about the room and avoided the blow. The twinge in his chest throbbed but dissipated almost as quickly.

"He almost had you," called Dair.

At that exact moment, Aiden thought of Penelope. He understood why she'd sent him flying up a tree during one of their earliest training sessions in Eleusion. The constant criticism wore down his control. Even as tired as he was, he sent a swirl of shadow to where he knew Dair sat on the edge of the arena. A muted thump and a curse hissed from that direction as the bench went flying out from under him.

Thaen's chuckle burst out from behind Aiden. He turned to meet Thaen's attack, but the fae was watching his brother pull himself off the floor, sword hanging listlessly by his side.

Aiden smirked and allowed the shadows to dissipate from around them. "Does that mean I win?"

Thaen's chuckle melted into a hum. "No, but it was a good distraction." He took up another offensive stance.

The doors to the sparring room thudded against the walls and all the shadow in the room swept up into the domed ceiling. Shirina stood in the doorway, hands on hips, as her magic effortlessly swept Aiden's into the rafters above them. "Wind and snow, you are all going to put me in an early grave sparring with real weapons."

"You are eight hundred and twenty-one years, *Màthair*," replied Dair from his place on the ground behind the bench, where Aiden's magic had dumped him. "I do not think that would be considered an early grave."

A black mass with specks of silver light sprung up behind him and whacked him on the back of the head.

"If eight hundred years makes me old, then perhaps your thirty-five means you should be sleeping in the nursery."

Dair cursed again and Thaen shook his head. "That was foolish, brother."

"At least you are aware of such foolishness, Bàsthaen." Her ire turned on him. "I was beginning to worry with all of your recklessness in the sparring ring that you had lost your sens-es." She looked to Aiden. "Are you injured?"

Aiden shook his head. "Nothing more than a few bruises."

Dair hissed and Thaen took a step away from Aiden. A grin grew on Aiden's face. Mentioning the bruises had been petty, but they deserved to feel a little uncomfortable every once in a while. Beating him to a pulp everyday was certainly not helping their already-inflated fae egos.

Shirina narrowed her eyes at her sons before returning her attention to him. "If you are up for it, I would like for you to join me for luncheon with the Court's noble families. It is about time they meet their High King."

Aiden's smile dropped. "Me?" And luncheon? Shirina didn't often host things during the day, having a preference for the night hours.

"I do not see any other High Kings here." She lifted an eyebrow. "Do you?"

Dair snickered from where he now stood a little behind Thaen.

Aiden decided to ignore them. Sweet Gaia, she wanted him

to mingle with the Court? So soon after arriving here? It had been several weeks since he'd been brought to the Winter Palace, but he still felt like a novice in the ways of the Tuatha Dè Dannan. Mingling with them did not hit the top of his list of priorities at the moment.

"Who will be in attendance?" he asked warily.

"The noble houses of Autumn and Winter. There are twenty-four, a dozen for each court. We invited their families as well, so I cannot give you an exact number."

That could be hundreds of people. A shudder worked its way down his spine. "I don't know if now is such a good time."

Shirina stepped into the practice ring. "It is likely the perfect time. The equinox is only a month and a half away. We do not have the luxury for you to ingratiate yourself into the Court slowly. There are many folk looking forward to speaking with you."

A shadow curled against his cheek, and he swatted it away. He didn't want to talk to any of these folk. He wanted to speak with someone he knew, someone he didn't have to worry about impressing.

Wait...

"All of the Night Court will be there? What about ambassadors?"

"We don't have any—oh! You mean the Olympians?"

Aiden nodded. Devan and his wife were in Winter last time he'd seen a report. If he could speak with Devan, perhaps they could figure out a way to get information through the Mist. Devan might even have something already.

And maybe Aiden would feel a tad more comfortable in front of all those folk. "Do you know if they're still in Winter?"

Thaen took a step forward. "They are. They have been peti-tioning for an audience more fervently since the border closed."

Aiden turned to Shirina with something like hope growing in his chest. Devan was still there. This was his chance. She must have seen it in his expression because hers softened. "If I invite the ambassadors, will you come to the luncheon?"

"Yes." The agreement came without hesitation. Aiden would go to every meeting for the rest of the year if she allowed Devan to attend—not that he was going to tell her that.

"Excellent. Then I will see all of you bathed and dressed in two hours in the reception hall off the solarium."

Thaen and Dair groaned from behind Aiden.

"You did not think the two of you would be off the hook so easily, did you?" Shirina whirled, her long skirts flaring out behind her as she strode toward the door.

Olympia's grandest hall did not compare to what Aiden saw.

Light poured down through the stained faerie glass above them, the colors pieced in a way to make the window look like a painting of the peaks making up Eagallach with the frozen waters of Lake Truaighe glittering beneath them. The colored light danced along the white marble floor, casting vibrant color on the already colorful folk. The room was large enough to accommodate the entire Night Court.

Aiden was just beginning to learn what that actually meant.

The highest houses in Winter and Autumn stood before him. An ellylon male with bright blue hair knelt on one knee to speak with a gnome wearing a pointed green cap. A group of winged darklings mingled with a few of the púca with their furry ears and twitching tails. Pixies hovered near a table, their gossamer wings sparkling, as a goat-legged satyr did his best to impress them. He must have told a joke because the group of tiny beings cackled at him as he grinned. There were so many creatures of all different shapes and sizes.

It was like a dream... or a nightmare.

Aiden shook himself. This was real. These creatures were real, and they were expecting a king. By the Goddess, he wasn't a king. He'd never been trained as one. He'd watched Dion's tutelage from afar, but he'd never even thought he'd be in a position like this. His becoming king in Olympia had been impossible. Now, he regretted not sneaking into Dion's lessons.

And he didn't want to be king. He just needed to find Durant and squash this rebellion. Once that was accomplished, he would figure out how to pass the crown to Fiadh—who would make a much better king than him.

He hadn't spotted Devan or his wife, Angelica, but he prayed they were in the room.

"So, are we actually going to go in or are you planning on standing out here in the hallway watching everyone else eat?"

Aiden flashed Dair a scowl over his shoulder and closed the sliver of an opening he'd been using to look into the room. Dair had changed out of the practice clothes he hadn't even used during their training and into his more decorated attire. A violet tunic lay open at his collar, accompanied by a short cloak made up of what looked like raven feathers. Silver glittered in his ears and around his fingers. He'd even added lines of kohl around his eyes, brightening the amber hue of his irises.

Thaen stood behind him, contrasting Dair's elaborate costume with his standard black leather armor and flickering sword strapped to his back. The twins could not possibly be any more different.

Aiden straightened the finely tailored jacket he wore. It was the closest thing he'd been given to what he would have worn in Olympia and had arrived in his closet the day before. The only difference from what he had worn back home was the elaborate silver trimming and the way it buttoned down the middle versus the sides.

The tips of his ears burned at being caught hiding in the hall. "I only wanted to take a look."

Thaen brushed past both of them and put his hand on the door handle. "You will get a better look if we go inside."

Before Aiden could protest, Thaen opened the door wide and Dair pushed Aiden forward.

"High King Aedon everybody," Dair announced proudly before leaving him to stand on his own at the edge of the room.

Every eye turned on him.

The palms of his hands slicked. It wasn't uncommon for eyes to find him, but what *was* uncommon were the many kinds of eyes now settled on him.

A rustle of fabric came from his right and Councilor Sgiath arrived at his side. The Councilor set a fist to his heart and folded into a bow. "My Sovereign."

The rest of the room followed suit. The dwarves held up their fists. The satyrs went down on one knee. The banshees bowed their heads so low their blackened hair nearly reached the ankle-length hems of their white dresses. The were-creatures laid on their bellies. Every fae in the room delivered their own variation of deference. It was as if they didn't even care about him being half Olympian, never having stepped foot into this kingdom. Aiden shifted awkwardly until Shirina saved him.

She took him by the arm and whispered, "You have to release them."

At least he was good at taking orders. Aiden cleared his throat. "Please rise and enjoy the wonderful food that has been provided." The moment the words left his mouth, the members of the Court straightened and began speaking amongst themselves again, excepting the few standing closest who watched him as if he were some kind of spectacle.

Well, I suppose having a half-fae-half-mage king who has only been around for a few weeks would be considered a spectacle.

Sgiath straightened at Aiden's side. "It is good to see you well, My Sovereign."

Aiden really needed to look into why everyone called him that. "I'm glad you could make it, Sgiath." There. He could be a good host.

"I am happy to see so many of our families have taken the journey to greet you. They all come from many different places within our Court. I pray you will have the chance to get to know them all."

His smile strained. Great Goddess, he could *not* be a good host.

Shirina patted his hand. "Our new king has not yet had something to eat. Let us allow him to fill his plate. I see they have brought out a fresh tray of *loukoumades*. Best get some before they grow soggy."

Sgiath's eyes roved over the tables. "Of course. We will speak more later." The Councilor left with a bow and hurried toward the arriving dish of honey-coated bread balls.

By the Goddess, Shirina had saved him yet again. "You are a marvel," he whispered.

Shirina squeezed his arm and led him to the buffet tables. "I did not envision such an entrance for you." She passed him a plate from a tall stack at the end of the table. "I should have expected something, but I do not think you need to worry. It will not be like this for long. The Night Court, while civil, does not stand on ceremony as often as we probably should. It happens when you have known everyone for a few centuries."

Aiden attempted a smile, but he could tell from her pitying expression it didn't fool her. He turned back to the array of foods and busied himself with loading his plate while also scanning the room. He spotted a head of short brown hair seated at one of the tables.

"Oh, good," said Shirina, spotting the same person Aiden had. "The Olympian was able to make it."

Aiden nodded and headed in Devan's direction. He searched for Angelica—whom he'd met a few times at her father's house, though usually under glamour—but he didn't see her. Devan's dark eyes met his and he stood, a wide smile on his face. Aiden felt his own smile stretch across his cheeks in answer.

"Your Majesty." Devan stood to greet him with a bow. "It's an honor to be here."

"Hello, Devan. I can't tell you how nice it is to see you." Aiden grabbed a chair from another table to move to join his comrade.

Thaen drew up on the other side of him, followed closely by the rest of Aiden's family. Almost on cue, the rest of the table's inhabitants vacated.

Devan's eyes grew wide as each of Aiden's cousins sat with smiles on their faces. He stood, but Shirina sat beside him and flashed a sparkling smile in his direction. "Sit. Sit. Just pretend we are not here." She turned to Fiadh who had seated himself beside her and Dair took up a one-sided conversation with Thaen.

Curses. Aiden would have to be very careful about how he spoke to Devan. He didn't need anyone to know he was still trying to contact his brothers, not if they were purposefully trying to keep him from receiving information.

Devan's brows furrowed as he hesitantly returned to his chair. He shook his head and leaned over to Aiden. "After nearly a year of attempting to get inside to meet the leaders of the Night Court, I find it a pleasant surprise to be in such close quarters with them all of a sudden."

Aiden grinned. "I'm glad I could do at least one nice thing for you while you're here. I haven't been put to the task of looking over any trade proposals quite yet, but I'll make sure Stone's is at the top of the pile if I do."

"I appreciate that, as would he." Devan leaned closer. "Though I don't know how much that will help with the border being closed. We have not been able to reach our contacts on the other side of the Mist since winter solstice."

Without looking at his family, he lowered his voice. "You haven't been able to speak to anyone?"

Devan shook his head. "Angelica has been quite frustrated by it." The look in his eyes told Aiden he was also frustrated by it. Without having contact with Olympia, they were isolated in a kingdom they only recently had come to a truce with. It could turn dangerous for them if they weren't careful. Aiden would have to talk to Fiadh and Shirina about making sure both Devan and Angelica were safe. He trusted them enough for that at least.

Aiden looked about. "Where is Angelica, if you don't mind me asking?" Penelope was likely frustrated by the lack of communication as well. She lived for Angelica's letters.

Something sparked in Devan's eyes. "She was not feeling up to coming. She's been a bit ill recently."

"I'm sorry to hear that. If there's anything she needs—"

Devan waved him off. "She's all right, but she's been worried about you."

Aiden's head tilted. "Me?"

"Of course. When we heard you'd been brought here, we almost couldn't believe it. It took a few days to figure out what actually happened—and even still I'm not sure what is true and what's gossip—but what was certain was that someone had killed the High Queen, and you were her heir." He lowered his voice even more. "I did my best to get into the palace after we found out, but it was to no avail."

A dark chuckle rumbled across the table and Thaen leaned in. "His attempts to rescue you were even lousier than your attempts to escape, cousin." Thaen leaned back into his chair to once again pretend to listen to Dair.

A look of chagrin passed over Devan's face and Aiden clapped a hand on his shoulder. "I don't blame you for failing. Not even I could get past the blasted Lòchran." Well, until he went to the Mist, but it didn't really count since Thaen had known what he was about.

All color leached from Devan's dark cheeks. His eyes flicked to Thaen and then back to Aiden.

"You didn't know who he was?" asked Aiden.

Devan shook his head and an amused smile spread over Thaen's face. Aiden glared at his cousin.

"Don't worry about him." He turned back to Devan. "I need your help."

Devan's curiosity pushed aside his worry. "Anything." He reached forward and set a hand on Aiden's shoulder. "I mean *anything.*"

Aiden could easily read what his friend insinuated. He would smuggle Aiden out of the palace if he asked. The offer was tempting. Very tempting. But Devan would break whatever tentative alliances he'd made to do so, making him and his wife a target in the process. Something in Aiden's throat stuck and he had to swallow a few times to clear it. "I appreciate that," he whispered, "but there's some information I need you to sniff out for me."

"All right." Devan nodded, but Aiden could still see the promise there, the unfailing loyalty.

He pushed aside his relief at not being so alone and put on an air of severity. Now that he knew Devan couldn't communicate with anyone in Olympia, they needed to focus on what they could do. "Someone came through the Mist after I did."

"Really?" Devan's eyebrows shot up. "We were under the impression the border closed the moment you came through."

Aiden's eyes slipped over to Thaen who shook his head. No, he couldn't tell his friend the Mist took longer to close down than most believed. "It happened quickly, but no one has found the Olympian who came through." He searched Devan's eyes for any sign that he knew about it, but confusion clouded his expression. "You haven't been contacted by anyone?"

Devan shook his head. "Not a soul from Olympia has reached out to us."

"And your contacts haven't heard anything?"

"Your Majesty, I haven't even heard of anyone coming across the border and we few humans on this side of the Mist talk frequently."

Which meant nothing had come through his growing network either. Aiden sagged in his chair. It must have been a rebel then if they haven't reached out to Devan's contacts. He rubbed the back of his neck.

"But," Devan said, "there may be a way of finding out anyway."

"What do you mean?"

Devan grimaced. "Since you're the new High King, you can try to speak with the Gray Man."

14
VILLAINS AND VENDETTAS

THE COLD WATER STRUCK PENNY'S FACE LIKE THOUSANDS OF TINY knives. She stood with her hands tied above her head to a pole, being brutally washed after Adira ordered someone to bathe her. Penny had begrudgingly agreed to the unorthodox cleaning as the smell had started to get to her as well.

She regretted agreeing to it now.

Another bucket of water was dumped over her head, running down her already drenched clothing and into the puddle surrounding her feet. Her toes curled in the viscous mud under her feet. She shut her eyes, searching for the cord of magic connecting her to the earth, but the connection remained cut off. Adira had charms hanging from every post and enough iron to bind hundreds of fae around camp. Penny's magic remained inaccessible, but at least now she was semi-clean.

Her hands came loose from the pole, finally. She hissed as blood rushed back down her arms and her ribs protested the movement. The two women charged with the humiliating washing grabbed her elbows and hauled her toward Adira's tent. The chain laying in the middle of the space once again swallowed her ankle with its jaws and the rebel women left without another word.

Adira sat at her scheming table, as usual, with a large conch shell in her hand—probably stolen from one of the many fae she'd abducted. She stood and locked it away in a chest before setting to tidying her desk. A pile of papers sat haphazardly on one corner and Adira fiddled with it until it looked almost straight. She didn't spare Penny a glance. "Glad to see you don't smell like filth any longer."

Penny bared her teeth in a smile. "I figured for a person who spent so much of her time in the underbellies of Olympia, you would enjoy the smell of rot."

"Such insults." Adira dipped a quill in an ink pot, not looking the least bit effected by Penny's words. "And here I thought you were above such things."

Penny gritted her teeth but said nothing. A shiver wracked her body as she huddled on the floor in her sodden clothes. The afternoons were warm enough, but the evenings held a chill that had Penny shuddering as it swept through the cracks of the canvas surrounding them.

The scratch of Adira's quill filled the silence between them. They'd played this game for five days already. Every night after a meager supper of whatever slop the prisoners were served, Adira summoned Penny into the tent where they'd have their little chats. Well, Adira would talk, and Penny would either make snide comments or not speak at all.

But tonight would be the beginning of Penny's new resolution. For the rest of the night, she would try to keep her mouth shut no matter what anger clawed up her throat.

Adira set the quill down and moved her paper aside. "You look like a drowned goblin."

"And you look like a psychotic warmonger." She sighed. *So much for keeping my mouth shut.*

"Oh, good. Just the look I was going for." Adira plunked the quill back into the ink pot. "It wouldn't do to have me look like a doddering old woman while I'm wreaking havoc, now would it?"

Penny gritted her teeth. There was no point in this constant back and forth. Penny was already losing. Playing this game only gave Adira satisfaction and no one could afford for Adira to win anything else.

The tent flap opened, and a guard stuck his head in. "They're ready, Your Grace."

Adira stood. "Excellent. We'll do it in here."

The guard looked to Penny for only a moment before slipping out. There was a rustle near the opening and the flap opened once more to let in two guards hauling a bedraggled ellylon between them and another man followed behind. He held a dark wooden box spanning the length of his forearm. A sinking feeling took root in Penny's stomach and her heart began to pound, though she couldn't really understand why.

"Penny," Adira said, "allow me to introduce my most favorite pet. She's the one who has made it so our little camp hasn't been discovered. Her gift with magic shields is absolutely remarkable."

Once they reached the center of the room, the guards dropped the fae. Adira crouched down and swept aside the fae's long mane of turquoise hair. Penny gasped when she saw the multitude of wounds riddling the female's neck and shoulders.

Adira held up a hand. "The box, Teagan."

The man that carried the box set it into her hands and took a step away. Penny studied him, trying to figure out if she recognized him. He had a thin face, with dark hair and ice-blue eyes. Those eyes flicked up and met her gaze. She barely suppressed a shudder.

Adira opened the box and the fae began to tremble.

Inside, a twisted mass of iron lay in a bed of red velvet. Adira drew it out and held it up. It wasn't some random mass, but a snake wrapped around a rod.

"Behold, Penny, the tool that will be our victory." She set the box down. "A horrible thing. Said to make it feel as if your very soul is burning. They call it *thoir agus gabh*. It gives—" she pressed the horrid thing to the fae's skin "—and it takes."

The fae's back arched and she opened her mouth in a soundless scream. Penny watched in horror as the iron tangle moved, the head of the snake twisting and latching its teeth onto the female's shoulder. Golden light rippled under the ellylon's skin, slowly fading as the snake gorged itself.

Penny covered her mouth with her hands.

The cursed thing was stealing the fae's magic.

This was how Adira was hiding the camp. She was stealing the magic from fae to shield herself.

After what felt like an eternity, Adira finally pulled the abomination from the female's skin. The fae sagged to the floor, her tremors heightened. Penny could only watch with blurred eyes as the guards dragged her back out of the tent. Adira tucked the horrible device back into its box and handed it back to her comrade.

"I'll have you know," Adira said, breaking the silence as the man slipped from the tent, "that fun little toy was very hard to find. It took me years to track it down after I learned about it. Turns out, a small group of fae had left Faerie some time ago and took that artifact with them. I had to kill half a dozen ellylon and a troll to get to it, but my, it was well worth it."

A tear fell on Penny's cheek. "Adira, that thing is evil."

"Many could say the same about you, my dear."

Penny ignored the jab. After what she'd just witnessed, she was done playing games. "What am I doing here? I assume that monstrous tool works on mages as well as fae. Am I to become another one of your *pets*?"

"I have enough options in my menagerie to choose from," she said, wiping the last blot of ink from her hand with a handkerchief. "No, you're here to help me get revenge."

"Yes, you've said that. Repeatedly." Penny adjusted her

foot, doing her best not to let the shackle around her ankle rub against her clammy skin while also avoiding moving her torso. "You also said you wanted to kill me for said 'revenge.' You're becoming a contradiction."

"And we'll get to your untimely demise eventually." She folded her hands together over the table. "But plans need to be flexible. It's one thing to ruin a prince, but another to destroy a king."

"Then why make him king in the first place?"

"I believed getting rid of the High Queen was the easiest way to get what I wanted while also hurting Aiden. Unfortunately, it was not so simple."

"You believed killing the queen would take down the Mist?"

"Indeed." Adira frowned. "I thought it was her magic holding it up and getting rid of her would get rid of the problem, but I've come to find out my sources were mistaken. Now, I have to find the fae responsible for the border magic and kill them as well. Then the Mist comes down and the rest of my men in Olympia can come assist in the demolition of the Faerie Courts. After that, we can begin spreading the fae and their magic throughout the rest of the continent and hopefully across the sea as well. I have some very interested investors that would love to get their hands on a few particularly gifted fae."

Penny shook her head. Adira's plans were beginning to resemble the knots Penny always created when she attempted embroidery. "You really are crazy."

"No," she chuckled. "Spiteful and maybe very angry, but never crazy." She stood and walked around the table.

"Perhaps *delusional* is a better term," Penny mumbled.

If Adira heard Penny, she ignored her. "I did receive word about where they've hidden our boy king."

Penny's spine stiffened and she withheld a moan. The pain in her ribs was going to be the death of her if Adira's ceaseless gloating didn't kill her first. "What do you mean?" she finally grunted.

"Oh, didn't you know? He isn't at Crann Mòr."

Curses. Penny had been working under the assumption that he was. Angelica had a few connections in the capital and Penny could have used those to get to him. "They didn't take him to the capital?"

Adira leaned against the table as if they were having a chat between friends. "They did at first, but he isn't there now. They've taken him to his family's house."

Penny blinked. "His family?"

"Yes. His mother's cousin is set to become Winter King when Aiden takes the faerie-glass throne. He's been regent over the Night Court since the Winter Queen's unfortunate death."

The death Adira herself had brought about. Did Aiden have any idea Adira was the one who had killed her? That she'd tried to kill him too?

Penny left those questions for later. "So where exactly is he?"

"They've taken him to the Winter Palace in Eagallach." Adira pursed her lips. "Unfortunately, we aren't in a position to lay siege to the mountain."

Penny's mind scrambled for where Eagallach lay. Devan had been thorough in his notes on the location along with the maps she'd had in her pack. The city sat in the mountains in the northwest corner of the Winter Court. If she could get away from Adira, she could make her way to Winter. She could get to him and tell him about Adira's plans.

The tent flap opened and one of the members of Adira's inner circle stomped in. The woman's cold gaze never met Penny's but swept past her as if she were simply part of the scenery. Penny's stomach hardened. Perhaps she was turning into just that.

"There's been an incident," the woman reported.

Voices moved closer to the tent until the shouts of anger and one cry of despair broke through the opening. A gathering of men and women surged through, dragging behind a man screaming for release.

"What happened?" Adira snapped, quieting the room.

One of the men stepped forward. "He's eaten the fruit."

Penny's attention zeroed in on the man. *The fruit?* The captured man's mouth was tinged blue, and he held something against his chest. Liquid the color of sapphires dripped from between his fingers.

Adira stormed over to the man. "Tell me you didn't, Justin."

A sob broke from between the man's lips. "I—I can't." His hands curled more tightly over whatever he was holding. "It wasn't my fault! It was the cursed fae. They tricked me! They tricked me."

Adira's head hung. "You know what must be done now."

"*Please,*" he begged. "Please don't."

Adira knelt next to the man, her face a portrait of regret and pity. "It doesn't matter that they tricked you. You ate the fruit. You are now bound to this wretched place and cannot lie or work against the magic here. You are as tainted as the cursed souls that call this land home." She gave a bone-weary sigh. "But you've been a good soldier, Justin. For that, I will show you mercy."

The man's shoulders sagged. "Oh, thank—"

A dagger stuck out from his chest, his life cut off as quickly as his words.

Penny gasped. By the Goddess, she hadn't even seen Adira move.

Adira pulled the knife from his chest and wiped it on his trousers. "Get this out of here," she ordered to no one in particular. Every person in the room scrambled to lug his still form out of the tent.

His lifeless arms flopped down as his still-warm body was lifted up and out of the space. Penny watched something drop onto the ground and roll toward the wall of the tent. She leaned forward, trying to figure out what the now dead man had thought so precious he couldn't let it go even in the face of death. Penny tried to scoot closer, but the rattle of her chain stopped her.

"What are you looking..." Adira's words trailed off as she walked toward the small lump. She hissed and pulled her sword from her sheath. She stabbed the mound and the thing squelched at the end of the sharp blade. Adira hoisted it in the air, as far from her as she could, and went to the opening, calling for a fire.

But as she opened the flap, the firelight glittered on the dark, cobalt flesh hanging from the end of her blade and Penny saw it for what it was.

A piece of blue pomegranate.

15
ALIGHT

AIDEN LAUGHED FROM HIS PERCH IN THE GOLDEN-LEAFED TREE AS A púca shifted from its terrifying water-horse form into a giant, pink fish that danced along the riverbank, delighting the pixies twirling through the air. The golden hues of the trees and the crisp air wrapped around Aiden. The map living somewhere within his soul told him he was in the heart of Autumn, in the forest outside Autumn's capital of Brònach.

The map had become clearer and more dynamic during his training with Dair—a breathing, moving thing inside him. Now, he could almost always tell exactly where he was when in this state. It wasn't really a dreamscape because what he saw was real. He'd proven as much to himself.

The first few times alone had been tumultuous. Even still, the magic sometimes moved him when he didn't wish to be moved. It was disorienting—and frankly disturbing—not having command of where he went. Now that he had more control, he could ask for things to see. The bond he had with the Land was a partnership, he'd learned. The Land was sentient. It felt things and did things because it needed to. Sometimes Aiden swore he heard it speaking to him, not through words, but through something deeper.

After he'd realized he could communicate with the Land in a way he still didn't quite understand, he'd had more mastery of movement. But even though he'd asked, he still hadn't found where Durant was hiding. The magic seemed confused by his request, hopping him around the kingdom as if searching itself. He'd also pushed to find the Olympian that had crossed through the Mist and had only been taken to the border over and over again.

One night, he'd asked to sneak in on Fiadh's family. That had not gone at all like he'd thought it would. Thaen slept in his room like the dead, not even his breaths making a sound, but Dair had sat up and cursed the moment Aiden had slipped into his room. Apparently, Dair could still see his presence in this incorporeal form as well as he could the body which still slept in Aiden's room.

Aiden had decided not to sneak about anywhere Dair might be in the future.

Which was why he was sitting in a tree, watching a púca shed forms like Shaunie—by the Goddess, Dion's *wife*—changed dresses for every hour of the day. Over and over, it took on a new face, a new body until finally settling into the two-legged, furry shape. According to Dair, this is what they were born as. Pointy ears twitched through thick hair on top of its head. Its small nose sat beneath two large, glowing eyes. Its long arms drooped down to its knees and a tail curled around its bare ankles.

Aiden watched the creature begin leaping about with the pixies, but his thoughts drifted to where he really wished to go. The magic picked up on his desires and whisked him from the forest.

He stood squarely on a piece of cracked earth, staring up at the wall of swirling fog before him. A swirl of gray magic looped around his outstretched fingers, like it was trying to grab onto him but couldn't find purchase. He looked down both sides, the expanse of the border reaching from horizon to horizon.

He yelled, knowing somehow that the creature within the Mist could hear him if he wished it. He yelled again, calling for Am Fear Liath Mòr to come to him, to answer his questions.

But his call only echoed back to him from the fog.

He took a step forward, but his form couldn't move more than a foot into the Mist without being pulled back out.

Aiden huffed. *How am I supposed to find the creature if he doesn't wish to be found?*

The magic inside of him remained silent, not quite ready to give up its secrets or simply not yet able to. Aiden sighed and rubbed a hand over his face. He would get all of this figured out. He would learn how to work with this new bond, learn as much as he could, and figure out how to stop Durant.

There was still so much of the Winter Palace to explore.

After the fruitless night search, Aiden had decided it was high time he become better acquainted with his world during the waking hours.

He peeked through another door, finding an opulent music room with a grand piano situated in the center next to a harp. A mandolin, a flute, and an array of other instruments hung on the walls or leaned against stands. He shut the door behind him and moved onto the next section.

Now that his family somewhat trusted him not to run off after he returned with Thaen after his escape, he was more or less free to wander. Yes, Fiadh and Shirina had shown him through the halls, pointing at the doors leading to this or that room. But it was an entirely different thing to look through all of them himself and he would consider himself a lousy spymaster if he didn't have a better picture of his surroundings.

The Winter Palace layout was vastly different from Olympia's palace. For one, it felt like there was an endless number of rooms and wings and hidden alcoves to discover. He'd been wandering for two hours and had yet to make it to the other side of the palace where he knew more of the offices and servants were located. He'd felt rather foolish this morning for not even starting off his network with the workers here. He was the Lord of the Underworld, for crying out loud! Building relationships and loyalty with those who were looked down upon was his modus operandi.

He turned a corner and stopped, his head tilting to the side. The familiar cadence of leather-clad steps met his ears and he quickly slipped back out of sight. The footsteps stopped at the other end of the short hallway.

"Aedon?"

Blast it. Aiden slipped from his hiding place to find Fiadh at the end of the hallway. Heat crept into the tips of his ears, as if he were a child caught sneaking into the kitchen for treats.

A warm smile broke over Fiadh's features. "There you are. I've been looking everywhere for you."

One of Aiden's brows rose. "You've been looking for me?"

"Yes." Fiadh gave a huff of feigned annoyance. "And let me tell you, this place is like a maze when trying to track someone down, even with help." He made it to Aiden's side. "What are you up to, Little Shadow?" Fiadh only referred to him—or on occasion, his sons—that way.

Aiden fell in step with him. "I was getting to know this *maze* of a palace. If I'm going to be..." He looked for a word besides *trapped.* "If I'm going to be staying here until the equinox, I'd like to get to know the layout for myself."

Aiden watched Fiadh's expression. A shadow of something

hovered in his eyes, but his smile diverted Aiden's attention from it. "This morning, I woke up with the feeling that I have been neglecting something."

"I certainly don't feel neglected." If anything, Fiadh and Shirina had been nothing but kind to him since he'd been brought here.

Their twin sons were another matter.

"I should have done this the day you arrived," Fiadh said, "but something stopped me. Perhaps it was my own cowardice or simply believing it was not the right time. But now I think it is."

They walked through the halls back toward the Family Wing—where Aiden had not yet snooped. Knowing Thaen would probably be close by, it made sense to scour those halls last. A few members of the Night Court crossed their path, bowing with fists over hearts as they passed by. Aiden answered with a fist over his own heart, but he didn't bow. He, the third son with no chance of becoming king, bowed to no one in this land except the Goddess. It had been a hard truth to come to terms with, but he understood that fighting certain protocols would make the folk in this place uncomfortable. He didn't wish to cause anyone discomfort. They weren't the ones who had put him in this position. They were innocent in the chaos his life had devolved into.

Fiadh stopped at a pair of ornate double doors. Silver shined deep from within the grooves of the carved wood. The night sky and all its constellations glittered across the dark stain. Fiadh pushed them open, breaking the heavens apart to reveal the wonder within.

Paintings. Dozens of paintings hung on the walls. Not only portraits, but beautiful landscapes and likenesses of mystical creatures.

Fiadh spread his arms wide. "Welcome to the Royal Gallery."

Aiden spun in a circle, trying to take it all in. Dozens of

pieces floated against the walls, reaching up to the gilded friezes circling the ceiling. Silver framed every image, the shining outlines stark against the black paint behind them. His mind flashed to when he'd taken Penelope to the gallery in Olympia. They'd nearly shared their first kiss in that room. He had been so angry with Dion for ruining that moment.

Movement broke through his recollections, and he watched Fiadh approach the eastern wall, the shadows Aiden had glimpsed earlier in his expression on full display. It was regret. Aiden could nearly taste it as the fae stopped at one particular frame. Aiden came up next to him, entranced by the deep emotion on his older cousin's face. What could have possibly turned this cheerful male into a somber husk?

Aiden's eyes took in the painting before them. Black hair, rich as ink, flowed down the canvas in waves. A pair of bright, amber eyes gleamed through the paint, set into a heart-shaped face with high cheekbones and a pert nose. Lips curled into a smile, hinting at a joke or some knowledge she held that the viewer didn't.

"Aedon," Fiadh finally said, his voice a hoarse whisper, "this is Queen Morana. Your mother."

Aiden could see the resemblance. Their hair was the exact same shade, not holding any of the violet hues Fiadh's did. They had the same high cheekbones, the same shaped eyes. Even the color of their skin nearly matched. She was the feminine version of him in every way.

Something in his chest broke open. He'd never looked like Father. Both of his brothers had taken after their paternal parent. Dion was a near perfect replica except the color of his eyes, and Evan had been mistaken for their elder brother more than once growing up. Aiden realized now he'd envied them for that. Penelope had been right when she'd said all his glamours looked like his siblings. They had, because somewhere deep down inside, he'd wanted to look like his family.

And he did. Just not the family he'd grown up with.

His fingers reached out toward Queen Morana's face. She looked so much like Fiadh they could have been twins rather than cousins. He turned toward to him and said as much.

Fiadh gave him a sad smile. "In all honesty, we were as close as siblings could be." He led Aiden toward the other end of the room. "Your mother and I were born only ten years apart. I know that may seem like a lot to you, but in Faerie a decade is nothing. Rìa—excuse me, High Queen Rìanoch was nearly two hundred years our senior and we rarely saw her when we were children." He stopped at another painting. Another pair of golden eyes stared out, but the owner of these looked very different than the last. Golden ringlets curled over one shoulder and haloed a crystal crown. A serious expression settled on the face that could have been pretty if the aura of the subject wasn't so striking. He could see the same shape around the brown eyes and the same full lips, but the resemblance ended there.

"The High Queen was a member of the Day Court—those with magic of light and creation—which did not allow for much of a relationship to grow between the three of us. My mother told me our fathers rarely spoke, theirs being a noble house in the Day Court and my father having married a member of the Night Court. It wasn't as taboo back then as it is now, but the families still had little to do with each other. Until Morana that is."

"I don't understand."

Fiadh began walking again. "Your grandparents lived in a very different time than even we do now. I remember my mother retelling memories of the Isles breaking away from Faerie rule and the separation of the Courts in your great-grandparents' time. Olympia is not the only kingdom that has fought a war over magic. We also faced a magical division in our land, only it was the base of our gifts that separated us."

He stopped next to a stunning landscape. The painting showed a beautiful glen, one half blanketed with snow against the backdrop of the night sky, the other swathed in green and cast in the brilliant light of day. Fiadh gestured toward the day-lit side. "When the mortals came to this land, those with the gifts of light and life saw how they reacted to those of us with the gifts of darkness and death. Humans have a different relationship with mortality than we do, they having more experiences with it. When they saw those of us with shadows at our fingertips, they cowered and turned toward those with light."

He pushed out a weary sigh. "The Tuatha Dè Dannan gifted with the powers of life decided they enjoyed playing gods to the mortals and became rulers over them. That was how everything began. The Andàn warned us of our pride, that it would lead to destruction, but it was too late."

"The Andàn?" Aiden asked.

Fiadh's attention returned to him. "Yes. I believe the humans refer to them as 'the Hags.'"

Aiden shivered. Yes, he'd heard of them. The three witches of Faerie, known to be blessed with the gift of prophecy, but at a steep cost. They were also said to be able to change a person's fate. It was blasphemous to say the least.

"What did the fae do?"

"They brushed aside the warnings, but one must never ignore the words of the Andàn." Fiadh's face turned grave. "They are the daughters of Danu herself, the last living of the first generation. They sacrificed their youth and beauty to live long lives and help the Tuatha Dè Dannan remember the path back to the Goddess's arms. Without them, we would have lost our way long ago—though they rarely show themselves now."

"Where do they live?"

"No one actually knows. It is written that they will walk the land until the end of the world, but they only show themselves when they are needed. I suspect they will be visiting here soon."

Aiden looked at him in surprise. "Really? Why?"

"Because they always come to deliver their telling of fate to the new High Rulers."

"When will they arrive?"

Fiadh looked up and gave a long sigh. "When you least want them to." His eyes suddenly flicked around the room. "But do not tell Shirina I said that."

16

INVITATIONS
AND BLACKMAIL

Dearest Penny,

Things here just got interesting.

There's going to be a revel at equinox!

And we aren't invited!

Only the fae—which I suppose is understandable since, you know, their queen was murdered by a human.

But still! What am I going to do? I'm trapped in the house all day right now, and all anyone can talk about is going to a revel I won't be attending. The short time we have until equinox will be the longest weeks of my life.

Devan finally did get in to see new King Aiden, praise the Goddess. He said he was all right—not that that means much. I think he was only taking stock of his physical wellbeing. Devan *also said King Aiden was surrounded by his family—and the Lochran is his cousin. Well, his mother's cousin's son. His second cousin? Here they just call any relation cousin since they are all rather closely related, being practically immortal and what have you.*

But he's alive. We've seen him. He's safe. He isn't alone. At least we've been given that assurance.

If only I could know the same about you.
Your Fretting Friend,
Angelica

PENNY'S CHIN BOUNCED AGAINST HER CHEST, AND SHE SPRUNG UP from where she sat on the ground of the prison tent. The darkling was gone, replaced last week by a were-cat that pretty much left her alone, praise the Goddess. The fae trapped in its feline form paced back and forth as far as its chain would allow. About four feet in each direction, the poor thing. Penny hadn't seen it shift with all the charms surrounding them, but she'd heard their jailer talk about what the creature was. The dark green coat of fur also gave it away.

Her head thumped back against the post she was chained to. After the pomegranate incident a few days ago, all the rebels had been on their guard around the camp—some of them not even bringing in the daily rations of food. They hadn't come with their serving of slop yet that day—which Penny couldn't decide whether to be grateful about or not. Her stomach knotted in on itself and she had to pick the latter in that moment.

She would never again be ungrateful to eat whatever

eclectic foods were served at the noble houses. She would eat anything and everything put on her plate for the rest of her life.

The snap of fabric turned Penny's head in the direction of the tent flap. One of Adira's regular guards waltzed in, keys swinging around her fingers. She crouched in front of Penny and unlocked the cursed irons around her ankles, not meeting the eyes of any of the creatures hungrily watching.

The manacles dropped to the ground and Penny stood. The ground swayed beneath her, and her vision blacked out for a moment. She needed something in her stomach.

"Come along," the guard ordered. "Can't keep Her Grace waiting."

A pang shot through Penny's chest. Mother? Mother was waiting—

Her thoughts halted. The guard spoke of Adira, the old Duchess Durant. Penny had nearly forgotten, and she shook her head of more than just the black spots dancing in her vision.

No. Mother was not there. Penny prayed she would not be there.

Penny stepped out of the tent and followed the guard. Was this what her life would be reduced to now? No magic, no food, no escape? The backs of her eyes burned, but she didn't have enough water in her body to create the tears. Besides, she refused to cry. By the Goddess, she was a spy! Spies did not cry.

A sad chuckle broke from her chest. *Perhaps better spies also wouldn't be in this mess in the first place.* She winced as her ribs protested her mirth.

Penny walked into Adira's tent, her hands hanging loosely by her sides. The guard grabbed the new set of manacles, attaching one after the other over Penny's bare ankles which had grown red and cracked after so long with the irons around them. Even if she did get loose, her body would likely give out before she could get far enough to truly escape.

Which was likely the point.

"Penny," Adira's voice called from her seat at her table, "so nice of you to join me this evening." Adira really had been a duchess in her previous life in Olympia. These nightly talks had proved it over and over.

Penny remained silent. It had taken a lot of control those first few days, but now the silence was more rewarding than the biting insults. Instead, she stared down at the gap that had been slowly growing between the rugs near the foot of Adira's table over the last several days. Penny had seen Adira adjust it more than once, but the last couple of days it had only grown wider.

Adira clucked her tongue. "You look like a miserable little thing this evening."

Nothing.

"What? You've deigned not to speak with me again tonight? Is this what our friendship has finally been reduced to?"

Penny nearly snorted. *Friendship.* As if the cursed woman even knew what that was. They would likely have been friends, if Alta had been real and Adira wasn't a murderous tyrant bent on destroying everything Penny loved.

A swallow stuck in her throat, and she had to shove it down. Oh, how she missed Aiden.

"Come now. Surely, you'd like to speak with someone other than those rabid creatures in the tent. It must get so lonely, sitting in there day after day, surrounded by so many, but not able to have a conversation with a single one because of their distaste for magekind."

Penny closed her eyes and leaned her head back against the post. Perhaps if she went to sleep, Adira would quit jabbering.

"Fine. Suit yourself." Adira sighed. "I did want to speak with someone about this fancy revel invitation I received."

Penny opened her eyes to see Adira waving a silver embossed envelope.

"Aren't you going to ask what it is?" A smirk settled on

Adira's face as she pulled out the black, glittering parchment from within. She brought it up to the light. "'You are invited to attend the Spring Equinox Revel celebrating our new ruler High King Aiden of the Night Court. The revel will begin following the anointing ceremony...' blah, blah, blah." Adira slipped it back into the envelope.

"Where did you get that?" Penny asked, her voice breaking over the words like rocks crashing down a hill. She had nothing to wet the back of her throat.

"So now you want to talk?" Adira set the glittering package on her desk. "A slippery new friend was able to infiltrate a Summer Court's noble house recently. This came in only a few days ago." Adira feigned a look of exasperation. "I simply can't decide what to wear. I'm thinking red though. It will cover up the blood soaking that ballroom floor. What do you think?"

"That's your big plan? Go to the party and kill everyone?" Penny felt the heat rise up in her chest. "Not very original."

Adira smiled. "Ah, but we've talked about that, haven't we? Clichés exist because they are effective, not simply because no one can come up with anymore ideas. Why would I plan some elaborate scheme when I can simply walk into a party and kill everyone?"

"Don't you think they'll have some kind of guard watching for you?" Penny gave her a flat look. "It's obvious to everyone the queen was murdered. Why would they let someone get to their new king?"

"Why wouldn't they allow one of their guests in?"

Penny rolled her eyes. "In case you haven't noticed, you're not fae. They'll see you coming a mile away."

"Perhaps, but do you think they'll go against the word of one of their own noble houses?"

Adira's eyes lifted to the door as a guard shoved a new prisoner in. Irons clanked around thin limbs and a tearful pair of fuchsia eyes met Penny's.

"A child?" she hissed, shooting to her feet. "You kidnapped a child to use for blackmail?"

"Kidnapped is such a nasty word." She gestured for the little girl to come to her. When the girl didn't move, the guard yanked on her chains. A soft cry slipped between her thin lips, and she shuffled over to Adira. Adira settled a hand around her shoulders. "We're simply watching her until after her lovely parents take me and a few of my followers to the revel as their attendants. Besides, you've met Aiden. You know how good I can be with children."

"Aiden is *not* the product of your design," Penny barked. "He's a good man."

Adira balked. "Penny, my dear, he isn't even a *man*. The fae refer to themselves as *male*, desiring not to attach themselves to any piece of mortality. He is fae."

"It doesn't matter what he looks like or where he comes from. He is a better man—a better *human* than you'll ever be."

Something sparked in Adira's eyes, but she turned away before Penny could truly see it. Adira thrust her hands into the little girl's curls and pulled her head back. The child cried out. Penny took a step forward, her hands reaching forward, as Adira yanked her knife from the sheath at her side and sliced through every rose gold strand of hair. Adira threw the pale hair to the ground and tilted the child's face until Penny could see the long, tapered ears on the side of her head.

"Don't you see?" Adira demanded. "They're not even remotely *human*! Even their very bodies attest to the difference."

But Penny saw no difference in the terror in the girl's eyes or the shaking of her hands. It didn't matter what she looked like; she was still a being, created by the Goddess. She was still just a child. "All right, Adira. I see it." Penny took a step back, holding out her hands as she would at a spooked horse. "Now let her go."

The anger instantly disappeared behind whatever steel

wall Adira constructed. She shoved the little girl toward the post next to Penny and the guard shackled their chains together.

"I know that I've sunk rather low in your esteem." Adira crouched in front of them, her eyes trained on Penny's. "I kill. I maim. I abduct. But whatever I've done, you all deserved it. I know that I'm right, that what I'm doing is right, and I'm ready to make the whole world see it. I am The Cartographer and I'm going to redraw the lines on the map to how they should be."

Penny remained still, not even looking at the girl as quiet sobs wracked her tiny body. "But is becoming the villain really the way to do that?"

Adira barked out a laugh. "Is that what you think I am? A villain?" She stood and walked back around the desk, settling her palms over the top. "This path may be dark, but I can easily see where it leads. I will be a savior to those who have yearned for something more, something miraculous." She sank back into her chair. "Hate me. That's fine. In the end, it won't matter. You're still going to die, and I will still get what I want."

17
ASCEND

...The Fae Isles took their independence, seceding from the Faerie Courts and creating a nation of their own: The Isles of Aigean. All water folk received citizenship upon the truce and took on a more critical part of their new government. It was also during this time that both the ellyllon and the bwbachod saw decline in fae births, resulting in a waning population...

Aiden sat up from where he was slumped in his chair. "*Ellyllon* and *bwbachod*. Is that supposed to be ellylon and bwachod?" Aiden vaguely remembered Thaen pronouncing the words differently as well. He flipped to the next page, only to find the same spellings there. Praise the Goddess he'd found a history book in the common tongue in the library the day before. Sitting in his rooms, waiting for a trio of ancient fae to drop in unannounced to decide his fate, made him twitchy.

Thaen huffed from his place on the sofa across from them. "No. Ellyllon and bwbachod is correct."

Aiden frowned. "What?"

Dair gave out a loud sigh from his position in the seat next to Aiden. "Olympians have been butchering the language. Just like everything else."

Aiden stared back down at the page. Humans had twisted

so much of the fae culture over the last two centuries. By the Goddess, how many times had he said it wrong in front of every fae here?

Dair folded backwards over the arm of the chair. "This is so *boring*."

"Then leave," Thaen grumbled. "You do not have to stay in here." He kept his eyes closed, content to sit in the room in silence.

Aiden peeked over the edge of his book at the both of them. He'd felt something brewing in the air the moment they'd followed him into the room after luncheon, but he hadn't wanted to bring it up. Blustering winds pounded against the glass leading out onto his wide balcony. Snow swirled on the wind, violent and sharp. The blizzard had been beating against the palace for two days already and Aiden worried it wouldn't let up any time soon. He'd been waiting to get back to this book after having searched for it for hours. Why did a kingdom that spoke the common tongue have so many volumes in so many different languages?

"But then what am I going to do?" Dair moaned. "We are not permitted to have anyone exciting over with Mister Important High King over here and the snowstorm is making it more than difficult to leave."

Thaen's eyes snapped open. "Why not take a dive off the balcony—"

"I am not going to go jump off the mountain just to entertain you, Thaen. No, we should all get out of this room and do something fun."

Aiden's interest thoroughly piqued.

"I know!" Dair sprang from his chair. "Let us play a game."

Thaen gave his brother a flat look. "No."

"Why not?" Dair shot back. "You love a little competition, even if it is not as bloody as a tournament or sparring."

Thaen tilted his head back and closed his eyes again. "I do not want to play."

"We could play *glam agus lorg*."

Thaen peeked out one eye. "Do you think *Athair* would really let us? Especially after what happened last time?"

Aiden set his book aside. "What kind of game is it? Why wouldn't your father approve?"

"Because we played once at Crann Mòr and I may have gone a little overboard." Dair's grin turned into an indignant pout as Thaen chuckled. "But I was only twenty-seven! Did they really expect me to stay out of Carthannach's room just because they told me to?"

"Yes," Thaen replied, but Aiden could see the glimmer of excitement on his face. The brute was going to agree to the game.

"How do we play, um, '*glam angus—*'"

"*Glam agus lorg*," Dair supplied. "I believe Olympians call their cheap version something like 'hide and seek.'"

Aiden tilted his head. "You want to play hide and seek? Isn't it a rather childish game?" He gestured at himself. "Especially for someone who's supposed to be king?"

"Not with the way the Tuatha Dè Dannan play." Thaen slapped his hands on his knees and stood. "I believe *Athair* is currently down the mountain until this evening when *Màthair* wakes. What they do not know will not harm them." Aiden watched Thaen walk to the door in shock. His cousin turned back with a savage grin on his face. "I never back down from a challenge."

"Then it is settled." Dair pushed Aiden toward the door. "The rules of the game are simple. One person glamours themselves and the rest of us have to find them. You cannot use magic unless you are the one with the glamour and you cannot let anyone in the palace onto what we are doing, unless, of course, they want to play. Once the glamoured fae is found, the finder takes their place and summons their own glamour."

"How do the other players know when it switches?"

"When they come across the last glamoured. And the last player is not permitted to tell who is now glamoured."

Aiden rubbed at the back of his neck. "This sounds nothing like hide and seek." *It sounds nearly impossible.*

"Well, hopefully you will catch on quickly," Dair said as he turned and skipped down the hall, "because Thaen has already glamoured himself and is off!"

It was like Aiden could smell them.

The atmosphere shifted when his cousins used their glamours. Aiden couldn't tell if it was the air or the sound or something else. Something inside of him just knew. Dair had been the one to find Thaen first, but when they'd traded places, Aiden had felt it. That switch being flipped and the magic coming to life.

He followed the feeling now, coming up to a plain wooden door and opening it to find a cleaning closet, most of the shelves at elbow height—for the brownies, he'd learned.

"Thaen, you are too wide to be a mop."

A pair of pale eyes opened against the back wall and the glamour fell from Thaen's body. Aiden had never met a fae powerful enough to use their glamour as complete camouflage, but Thaen could do it.

"It should not be this easy for you, cousin." The male bared his teeth. "You are up to something."

Aiden raised his hands in innocence. "I don't know how I'm doing it." *But I'm also not going to complain.*

Thaen grumbled as he trudged out of the closet to give Aiden the required two minutes to conceal himself.

Aiden remained behind, plotting what to do next. They had been playing for a little over two hours, all three having taken one if not two turns as the glamoured player. He'd been found pretending to be a random manservant by Dair—they didn't have any of them they didn't know personally. The second time, Thaen had spotted him glamoured as one of the librarians, whom he *had* met and knew worked in the palace. Aiden's shadows had been breaking through his glamour. His magic had flooded out the moment he'd drawn upon too much of it and had been too difficult to contain.

They only had an hour or so before Fiadh returned, and Shirina woke up with the moon. Creativity was key if he wanted to win. This time he needed to do something smaller, something that wouldn't cause his magic to be overeager and—

Got it.

He pushed a little magic into his hair, adding violet undertones and lengthening it. He then added a few aged lines near his eyes and mouth. He cleared his throat and spoke a few words, checking to make sure the accent sounded right. Then he added silver and black embellishments to his clothing, which weren't anything special. He straightened his shoulders and peeked out of the closet, listening for any traps. He'd learned to feel Thaen's stillness when he was near, but Aiden felt none of that waiting for him now. He quickly slipped from the closet and shut it behind him. He pulled a serene expression on his face as he wove through the halls. His body copied the way Fiadh stepped, the way he held his hands behind his back as he meandered and clenched them at his sides when he strode from one thing to the next, as if going off to battle. His head bobbed every time someone passed him with a "my lord" in the halls.

He turned down the hallway, heading for the massive library to hopefully find another book in Olympian. His step faltered slightly when he saw Thaen creep from the records room and head the opposite way.

Aiden pulled on a smile he'd seen on Fiadh's face when he'd looked at his sons. "What are you up to, Little Shadow?"

Aiden kept his shoulders loose and his steps easy. He'd had enough practice posing as other people, even in cases more nerve wracking than this.

Thaen froze and turned back. He tilted his head, looking Aiden over quizzically. "What are you doing back so early? I thought your meeting with the other lords went until nightfall."

Aiden held back the flinch. "We finished early, and I had some more work that needed done before the evening. Besides, the better question is, what are *you* doing?"

Thaen's eyes flicked back and forth, his brows pulling together. "Are you glamoured?"

Aiden narrowed his own eyes. Of course, Thaen could blasted see the glamours the whole time, the little cheat. And he though Aiden was breaking the rules! Aiden let out a light chuckle. "Yes, a small one. I got a stain on my tunic at luncheon and figured it would be better to hide it than look the fool in front of the others. I should go change."

Thaen shrugged. "Will we see you at dinner then?"

"Of course."

Thaen nodded and stepped aside to let Aiden pass as he went the other way. Aiden kept the languid steps up until he made it to the library. The door opened silently and clicked shut almost as quietly.

A laugh burst from his chest. Thaen had nearly caught him. If Aiden had added any more glamour to himself, Thaen would've known. The fae was such a cheat and Aiden bet Dair didn't even know.

But Aiden had gotten away with it.

Sweet Gaia, he'd gotten away.

The books called to him from their nests on the shelves, but only one foot made it toward them. This could be his chance. He could potentially escape out of the library if he wanted to. The room was only a few stories up. The jump would be easy.

His thoughts carried him to the window of the library. The

snow buffeted the faerie glass as Aiden set his hand against it and looked down. White powder swirled into drifts just below. Not a single fae walked among the mounds growing all over the lawn.

His fingers traced the tiny lock at the base of the glass. His heart raced and he watched the puffs of his breath fog the window in front of him.

Golden eyes reflected back at him from the glass—under Fiadh's deep brow. Aiden nearly jumped back, frightened he'd been caught, but realized he was still under glamour. He shed the magic quickly and stared back at himself in the glass, his chest heaving.

Something within him stirred. It wasn't the right time to be thinking of an escape.

His hand dropped back to his side.

Before regret could seep in, he pulled the thick, blue curtains closed. He needed to think.

He stepped away from the covered window and immersed himself in the stacks of books. All the spines were labeled in the strange characters he'd come to recognize as Faerie's old language. He'd never really thought he'd need to learn it, the common tongue everyone spoke now having become the most accepted language on their continent. The dead language still showed itself in Faerie's culture though. Aiden knew the names of all the cities and how to pronounce them correctly. But if he was going to be king of this place, perhaps he should take up a study of the older language so he could better grasp Faerie's long history.

His steps faltered. By the Goddess, what was he doing? He found a leather chair and sank into it. Had he really just been thinking about learning their old language, being their king? It was a betrayal to his family to even think it as much as he had already.

Something inside of him pulsed in his chest. *But is it, really?*

He looked down at the ground between his feet, catching

the vague outline of his reflection in the polished floor. He really did look like Fiadh. He looked like this part of his family.

He shot up from the chair and rubbed a hand through his ragged hair. His steps carried him back and forth in front of the seat. He couldn't be king. He couldn't begin feeling these things for this part of his family. He had responsibilities to his brothers, the family that had been with him his whole life. He owed his allegiance to them.

Right?

And Penelope. Great Goddess, he could never truly abandon her, could he? He needed her like he needed air or starlight or shadow. It had been months since he'd seen her, and the rawness of their separation never eased. He fell asleep every night with the vision of her fearful face at Dion's wedding. He dreamed of her under the oak tree, swathed in gold or white, depending on the night. Those dreams were often swept aside for the magic the Land foisted on him and he would grow all the more grieved at their separation.

His pacing turned frantic. He would never wish her here. There were plenty of whispers in Olympia and even more within these halls of the things that had happened to humans —and more so mages—within the Courts. He'd read accounts of how the fae treated mages during the wars. The public executions. The torture. While there were some laws against that now, that didn't mean there weren't other ways to hurt her. Even if most of the fae he'd met seemed somewhat reasonable, he would never subject her to their punishments or even their ridicule. But he wished he could kiss her, or even just hold her one more time.

If only he could help her. If he knew he had a way of keeping her safe and knowing she was happy, that would be enough for him.

Why can't you?

The pacing increased. His chest grew heavy again, the question settling and bringing ideas to life.

He could. If he actually became king, really took on the role instead of fighting it, perhaps he could use his influence against Durant from afar. She was still trapped in Faerie. He was nearly positive after hearing the report from Sgiath that only one other person had crossed through the Mist, and it had been *into* Faerie. There had also been rustlings of something in Spring which was one particular reason Fiadh had been meeting with other lords. A Spring delegation had come to Winter to look for aid from the other Courts, nervous about what was coming and hoping to have a word with the High King.

His pacing halted. *Me. They were hoping to have a word with me.* Some unseen force struck him between the ribs. *He* was the king. Why was he allowing his family to hide him from the duties that should technically be his? He fell back into the chair. He was a blasted fool. As king, there were things he could do that he couldn't as a prince. Yes, he had a responsibility to Olympia, but he knew Durant better than anyone, and while she was out attempting to bring down both of his kingdoms, he'd been keeping critical information to himself in hopes of possibly getting out and fighting the foe on his own. In hopes of impossibly getting back to the girl he loved.

Blasted fool.

He jumped up from his chair. This all needed to change. Aiden needed to change. He couldn't be Prince Aiden, Lord of the Underworld anymore. He couldn't be Dion and Evan's little brother. He couldn't be the Tyrant King's Bane. He couldn't be a thing that dwelled in alleyways and was whispered about in dimly lit corners. He wasn't a spymaster, a castoff prince, or a shadow lord anymore.

He was High King *Aedon* of Faerie, son of Queen Morana of the Night Court. He twirled raw magic at his fingertips and could connect with every part of his kingdom in his dreams. By the Goddess, he could likely access that bond in his waking hours if he actually tried. His aunt, the last High Queen of Faerie, had been able to.

He strode around a row of shelves and saw the long, blue curtains hanging in front of the window he'd looked through earlier. His fingers clenched the fabric, and he flung the drapes wide. The night sky glittered above him, shining over the peaks of Eagallach—of *home*.

Because he was High King *Aedon*.

Because he was a member of the Night Court.

Because this place was his home.

Because it was night.

Oh, sweet Gaia!

Aiden shoved the curtains closed once again and sprinted toward the door. Had he been in that library for so long? Thaen was going to kill him—and right after he'd decided to actually become king!

Curses.

Racing through the halls, Aiden listened for the sounds of his family. It wasn't until he reached the opening to the balcony over the Great Hall that he heard Fiadh's voice. His words were indecipherable from the distance, but the tone was accusatory.

Dair's groan came from below as Aiden made it out onto the balcony. He said something in return and Shirina snapped at him.

Aiden reached the stone balustrade and looked down at his family gathered below. They were so different from the family he'd grown up with. Had Father ever cared where he was the way Fiadh and Shirina did? Had Dion or Evan ever grown worried when he'd disappeared for hours or even days? Sometimes, it had almost seemed like they were more shocked when he was around.

He knew his brothers loved him. They cared for him, involved him in their lives. Great Goddess, Dion had been the first one to put a sword in Aiden's hand and had sat with him at night when he was little and had nightmares from what Durant had exposed him to. But he'd never had something like this; something so overwhelmingly simple as family dinners every night and someone who always said "good morning" to him. Of course, he'd found a family with his operatives in Olympia, but he'd still had to keep so much to himself. There had never been anyone who he'd been at least somewhat honest with.

Until Penelope.

Until them.

A smile bloomed across his cheeks as he watched the worry lines grow longer on Fiadh's forehead and a frown carve deeper onto Shirina's mouth as they debated.

He would ask for Court lessons from Shirina. His dreams would become a regular topic of conversation with Dair instead of a chore. He would take his sparring practice with Thaen more seriously. If Fiadh let him, Aiden would ask more about his mother.

Now, he would try. It was what he should have always done for his family.

He braced his hands on the rail in front of him and kicked his feet over the edge. The three story drop onto the floor of the Grand Hall was nothing and he landed on his feet. All four of his family members turned toward him, shock rippling across their features.

A real, joyful smile stretched across Aiden's cheeks. "Does this mean I won?"

18

CAPTIVES AND CANINES

PENNY TUCKED THE FRAYED EDGES OF THE GIRL'S SLEEVES BACK UNDER the cuffs to keep the already blistered skin of her wrists from burning on the iron. She'd done the same with the child's ankles, ripping the edges of her leggings to cover up the skin under the manacle.

At least she would be more comfortable, if only for a little while.

The sliver of light peeking through the tent canvas hinted at the day's closing. Hopefully, Spot was far, far away from the camp by now. Both Penny and the little girl had been bound together in Adira's tent for the past three days—Adira reasoning that she could keep a better eye on her two most prized prisoners better from her own room. Penny didn't dare take her word for it, but it was the only thing that made sense with her limited knowledge of what Adira had planned.

She settled the child's head in her lap, brushing her fingers through the short strands of rose gold hair. The ellylon child was beautiful, with or without her long locks of metallic hair. But Penny didn't want to mention it. Anytime the girl had reached up to touch her hair, she'd cried. She hadn't spoken to anyone since arriving, no matter how much Penny had tried to get her to.

"Perhaps I'll call you Rose," Penny mused quietly, "just until I learn what your name actually is. Well, not your *real* name. That wouldn't go over well with your parents I'd think." Having ultimate power over such a young thing wouldn't settle well on Penny's conscience. No one should have that kind of power over someone.

The child sighed as Penny held her. Penny prayed the girl at least found a modicum of comfort being with her. It would be crucial in the days to come.

Penny's plan was almost complete. Her goals hovered at the surface of her mind.

She needed to unchain herself and the girl. Adira herself carried the keys to their manacles now that Penny and Rose had become a permanent structure of the tent.

Then there were supplies. Adira's tent was a stock of information, but not a storehouse for food or gear. Penny mourned the loss of her maps and the many useful things the MacGregors had supplied her pack with, but she could be flexible.

Lastly, she needed the invitation to the revel. She couldn't allow Adira's plans to come to fruition. If the rebels gained access to all those folk... No. Penny wouldn't allow it. Not only would she steal the invitation so Adira couldn't use it, but Penny would take it in case she needed to use it herself. She would gather every possible tool to add to her arsenal.

After all of that, she would sneak from the camp with Rose in tow. They had to weave through the sea of tents, but it wouldn't be difficult with how many people there were. Gathering simple disguises from around camp should be enough to get lost in the hubbub. Once they broke out of the ring of charms, Penny could use her magic to trap the rebels in their own camp. If she got lucky, she could reach Aiden and warn him about Adira before the rebels had the chance to escape. If

Adira still found a way out, Penny would be far enough away the camp would be unable to catch up to them.

But how to execute such a thing.

Adira had her tent patrolled at all hours. Adira herself stayed in the tent for at least half of the day, going over plans and meeting with her cursed leadership team. It wouldn't be plausible to do anything while she was sleeping. Penny had already thought to test that, and Adira maintained the same rigid practices in her sleep as she did in her waking hours. Even the slightest jingle of chain had her eyes open and glaring at what Penny now called "Prisoner Post."

It had to happen while Adira was away. She worked a shift with the patrols once a week, but never on any sort of schedule. Penny wouldn't even know she was gone until the guards at the tent flap turned someone away or Adira herself had already returned. Even Penny could begrudgingly admit Adira wasn't foolish enough to give any leeway.

But she couldn't be perfect. No one could be, right?

Rose's breathing slowed and a small snore whistled out through her nose. Did fair folk actually snore? Penny almost smiled. She wouldn't have ever thought such a thing possible with their lithe forms and innocent-looking faces.

Perhaps if Penny could get her hands on a blade. Adira kept a chest of them by the foot of the bed but kept it locked. Penny glared at the offending keyhole. She was terrible at picking locks, and she would already waste too much time on the chains. She needed a key. The irons around her limbs seemed to tighten. She needed multiple keys.

Penny looked up to the peak of the tent as if she could see the heavens waiting on the other side. *Please show me how to get out of here.*

The back of Penny's head knocked against Prisoner Post, and she closed her eyes. It wasn't the first time she'd prayed for an avenue of escape, nor would it be the last it seemed. But no straight answers came, and only the faint instinct to wait remained.

Rose stiffened against Penny's leg.

Penny looked down to see the girl's eyes wide open and her breaths coming in short gasps as they did anytime someone came toward the tent. Moments later, the flap burst open, and Adira strode in as she always did—with a strong step and an air of righteous indignation.

"How are my favorite captives this lovely evening?" She walked toward the chest at the foot of her bed and opened it. Penny caught a glimpse of her own sword and one of the matching daggers, the red leather around their hilts the only vibrant color in the chest. Adira disarmed herself of all but her own short sword and a dagger Penny knew she had stashed in her boot. Leaving the chest open—whether in mockery of Penny's captivity or simply out of this new laziness she'd seemed to acquire—she then shed her outer coat and hung it on a peg sticking out from a post.

The key to Penny's chains hung from her waist. If only Adira would get close...

A plan began to form in her mind. When she'd trained with Rissa and Aiden in Olympia for those few months, one of the skills she'd begun to pick up was pickpocketing.

Adira sat at her desk, propping her feet up on the corner and causing a layer of tin plates to slough onto the floor. With a curse, Adira grabbed them up and haphazardly stacked them back up on the table—the state of which had devolved into complete and utter chaos. Penny could see the lines of stress deepen in her brow. Adira dug through the pile on the table, looking for whatever held the subject of her attention in that moment.

She frowned at Penny through the towers of dirty dishes and reports. "Enjoying the show?"

Penny withheld the eye roll and remained silent. She'd certainly grown better at keeping her mouth shut, much to

Adira's aggravation. Praise the Goddess. Penny would need to act as if absolutely nothing were amiss and keep Adira's focus elsewhere.

Rose shifted closer to Penny, nearly hiding behind her shoulder. Tremors ran through the fae girl's body at the sight of the insane woman. Penny settled a hand on her knee.

"So sweet! The scared fae child takes comfort from the young damsel trapped with her."

Penny only shrugged, deigning not to speak. The shrug always helped bring Adira a little closer to hysterics. The vein in Adira's forehead hadn't shown itself yet, but there were still plenty of hours left in the day.

Adira pursed her lips at the letter in front of her. "Perhaps you're getting too cozy with each other. Maybe I'll move her to a different tent so the two of you can't use one another as comfort."

Penny sighed and turned her gaze away from Adira, looking at the wall as if it held far more interest than Adira herself. That was usually the spark on the oil and Penny needed an inferno if she was going to pull this off.

Rose went rigid beside her. Adira's steps halted in front of them, and Penny did her best to keep her expression blank as Adira sank her fingers into Penny's chin and turned her head to look into the woman's eyes. Fury swirled in their green depths. "You will look at me when I'm speaking to you!" she snapped.

Penny widened her eyes in feigned horror. "Like this, Your Grace?"

The sound of Rose's scream registered before anything else.

Penny's head whipped to the side as her fingers wrapped around the iron key.

Pain bloomed across her cheek, but she covered up a wince with a smirk and hid her fists at her sides. She prodded the corner of her mouth with her tongue. It had cracked from the hit.

That had gone surprisingly well.

The key hadn't been hard to swipe. Adira likely hadn't even felt the leather string snap when Penny yanked on it. The punch to Penny's face had been the perfect cover for the sensation. *Adira hopefully won't notice its absence until it's too late.*

Adira paced at Penny's feet, her hands rubbing at her temples. "I have never met a young lady as insolent as you. My mother at least taught me to respect those in authority. It seems your education as a future duchess is sorely lacking."

Penny's smirk deepened. "I'll take that as a compliment, *Your Grace.*" It wasn't the first time Adira had subjected her to such vitriol. But it was the first time Adira had made physical contact. Penny's plan had paid off so far.

Rose still trembled at Penny's side, her head tucked fully behind Penny's arm. Tears wet the back of Penny's sleeve, but she couldn't reach over to comfort her. Not with the key wrapped firmly in her hand.

Adira gritted her teeth and stormed over to the desk, practically throwing herself into her chair. Penny read the signs as if Adira were an open book and Mother sat reading it to her. Being a member of nobility, Mother had been an expert at watching people and manipulating conversations to her benefit. She hadn't become the Domineering Duchess because of the way she glided around a dance floor. She'd taught Penny to read people as well as words and direct the story how she wanted.

The bags under Adira's eyes grew darker by the day. Her lack of self-control, the insults, the rumpled clothing, the restless nights. Even the tent itself was falling into disarray; the rugs folded on top of one another; copious amounts of dirty dishes and half eaten food littered the table; clothes lay scattered on every piece of furniture and the ground around them. Everything added up, telling Penny the story she so longed to hear.

Adira was growing restless which meant she was ready to make mistakes.

Getting close enough for Penny to take the key was the first one.

"I can't believe you made me do that, Penny." Adira grabbed up whatever paper she'd been looking at before she got up. The edge of the paper crinkled in her hand. "We were friends once. Friends don't goad other friends into hitting them."

Friends also don't lie or kidnap or hit one another. But she kept those thoughts to herself. She didn't want Adira coming close to her again. Penny only stared, her swollen cheek growing by the second.

Adira gave a long sigh and took up a different piece of parchment from her desk. Even those had become sparse as they'd been stuck in Faerie without help from the outside. Another thing for Adira to worry over.

Penny moved her arm to allow Rose to nestle into her side as they both settled in for the long night. Likely to be one of the longest Penny had experienced since she left the border of Olympia.

The sound of voices faded with the crackle of dying fires and still Adira sat at her desk. She hadn't said another word to either of them, and Rose had fallen into a distressed half-sleep. Her quiet whimpers cut through the still air every so often and Penny had to wake her enough to shush her. The poor thing.

Penny's palms had begun to sweat, the stale air in the tent not lending her any relief. Her cheek had well and truly swollen, the muscles in her face throbbing where Adira's knuckles had bruised her. Adira had forgotten about supper, but Penny couldn't risk drawing attention to herself by asking for food or water. Not now. Not when she held the very key to her freedom.

But she still needed a distraction. With Adira sitting there, eyes flicking up at them every half hour, there was no way she could accomplish what she needed. But what could she do? If she had her magic, she could easily keep Adira busy while they escaped. The plethora of charms around the tent laughed at the thought.

Rose's eyes shot open and a cry burst from her lips. She stood, screeching and yanking at the chains holding her. Terror ripped across her face, and she sobbed, still pulling at the chains and burning her fingers.

"What are you wailing about?" Adira demanded. "Penny, get her to shut up!"

Penny opened her mouth, but whatever words she could have summoned to calm Rose were swallowed up in a ferocious roar.

Adira was on her feet in an instant, pulling her sword around her waist and flying to the tent opening. "Blast it all!" Adira raced back to her open trunk at the foot of her bed and grabbed up her crossbow and a quiver of thick, ash-wood arrows. She bolted out of the tent, leaving the chest unlocked.

Hope bloomed in Penny's chest as the weapons shined from their haphazard pile in the open container.

Adira's second mistake.

Penny grabbed Rose with one arm, dragging her down beside her. "Shh. I need you to be very quiet," she whispered. She grabbed the manacle at Rose's wrist and flipped it over, exposing the keyhole.

"How did you—"

Penny set a hand over the girl's mouth to cut off the first words spoken by the child as she held up the iron key with the other.

Penny shoved the key into the keyhole and slowly turned. The telltale *click* brought tears to her eyes and she caught the cuff before it could make a racket. She gently settled it into the dirt beside Rose and went to work on the next. Rose watched the entire thing with widening eyes and her wobbling lip clenched between her teeth. Smart girl.

Rose was freed and Penny set to unlock her own manacles. Rose quietly caught the first cuff and set it in the dirt as Penny had. When her wrists were free, Penny reached for her ankles.

"How did you get out?"

Penny and Rose turned to a guard standing in the opening to the tent, the orange blaze of fire from outside lighting the side of his face. His eyes flicked back and forth between Penny and Rose.

Penny's mind stuttered back to life, and she finally moved. She reached down for the last two manacles around her ankles, dropping the key in the dirt between them. *Curses!* She had to take him out before he could call for back up. She reached for the key.

"Hey, wait—"

Penny looked up to see Rose flash toward him. Her enhanced speed took her from the open weapons chest to the guard in under a second. Her small arms raised Penny's beautiful short sword above her head, and with a fierce scream, she drove it into the guard's chest.

A breath whooshed out from his lips the same time it did Penny's. He fell, dead before he even hit the ground. The blade stuck through him, all the way to the hilt.

Rose stood to the side, her hands coming up to her mouth in shock. Tears glistened in her eyes as she stumbled back away from the body.

Penny hurried to unlock the last two manacles and raced over. She tucked the girl's head into her side, turning her away from the body. "I know you won't understand yet, but you did what you had to do." Penny leaned down and took the girl's face in her hands. She gave her a teary, grateful smile. "You saved us."

She wrapped her arms around Rose's shoulders and pulled her to the weapons chest. Penny dug through the arsenal, pulling out her dagger with its sheath, her bow with its quiver of arrows, and her scabbard for the short sword still sticking out of the guard's chest. Turning to Rose, she thrust the dagger into the small girl's hands. Rose took it hesitantly and pressed it to her chest as if simply holding it would save her from all of the problems they were about to face.

Leaving the chest open, Penny pounced on the piles of paper on the table. The missives fluttered up like doves taking flight as she grabbed the invitation and tucked it into her belt.

Penny pulled her sword from the man's chest, wiping it off on his tunic. Her stomach tightened at as she watched a pool of crimson leak out onto the dusty carpets. Leaving the body behind, she crept to the curtain, pushing it aside just enough to see outside. When she followed the line of running rebels toward their destination, she heard herself gasp.

"By the Goddess."

A troll stood as tall as the trees surrounding the wide clearing. One thick horn protruded from the top of its head, curling around the left side of its enormous skull. The other horn looked to have been ripped off somehow, blood pouring from the edges down onto its face. Thick jowls shook against its neck as it bellowed out another earth-shattering roar. It wielded a massive club, its blows breaking apart the ground as it smashed into the dozen or so rebels attempting to kill it from under its feet. The massive creature swung its club like a scythe, reaping the field of tents and rebels with a swipe. What had once been orderly lines of men and equipment were now thrown into complete disarray. Screams punctured the air. Bodies went flying and fire caught on the dry canvas now littering the ground.

Penny turned back to Rose. No wonder the child had been screaming. If Penny had known there was a troll coming, she likely would have been screaming too.

"This way," Penny whispered, gesturing back into the tent. They would run in the other direction until they got far enough away to get back on the path to Aiden. If she could get to him, she could explain who Rose was, get her back to her family and have all of them protected from Adira.

The sword in Penny's hand easily sliced through the thick canvas wall. She made the slit as tall as her and slid through, weapon at the ready. When she could safely say the coast was clear, she pulled Rose through, and the two of them ran through the rebel base.

They reached the perimeter of the tents and Penny pulled Rose down beside her. Her eyes scanned the tree line, waiting for some unseen patrolman to come rushing toward them. Penny gestured for Rose to stand.

Rose jumped up and grabbed onto her arm with a blood-curdling scream.

Penny's whole body jolted at the sound, and she was so stiff she nearly lost her footing as a huge, black shadow pounced just in front of them. Before her heart could start beating again, two wet tongues trailed up the sides of Penny's face.

Penny fell onto her rear and glared up at the looming crea-ture. "Curses, Spot!" She stood, her ribs protesting, and grabbed her sword. "You scared me half to death!" She looked up at him. The mouth that hadn't licked her held the troll's missing horn.

Penny nearly cried in disbelief. "Spot, you're a genius!" He'd brought the troll straight to Adira's camp.

Spot sat on the ground, his mouths panting far above her head. Sweet Gaia, he'd gotten bigger. His shoulders likely reached the troll's hip. He was taller than Aaron's sweet draft horse.

An idea struck. "Quick, lay down." Spot complied as she wrapped her hands around the waist of a still shaking Rose. She hoisted the slim girl onto Spot's shoulders and clambered up behind her. They straddled his middle neck, allowing the other two to keep them somewhat secure on his back.

"All right," Penny said. "Steady now."

Spot stood slowly. Rose squealed as he got to his feet, but they stayed on his back. Penny nearly cried with relief.

"North, Spot. We'll find Aiden in Winter."

The giant, three-headed dog ran into the trees, Penny and Rose clinging to his back and the roars of the troll fading in the distance.

19
ACCLIMATE

AIDEN'S EYES OPENED TO DARKNESS. WHEN THE MAGIC HAD WHISKED him into the ground, he had cut off his sight, afraid to watch himself be squashed against the earth. But he was still whole, even though it felt as if the top half of him was stuffed with pillow fluff and the bottom half stood in open air.

He crouched down. The bottom half *was* in open air. A tunnel, lit by some kind of bioluminescence, stretched through the rock in each direction. The space had obviously been carved out, the chiseled walls and the cleared path evident. He paused for a minute, catching the sound of knocking and crumbling rock from the left.

"Where have you taken me?"

He felt a spasm of anticipation not belonging to him. He'd come to recognize the difference between his emotions and the Land's.

He followed the nudge to go right, his bare feet meeting no resistance. The Land got impatient with him sometimes for walking and would whisk him where She wanted him to go. But this time, She allowed his excitement to bubble up alongside Hers.

New noises echoed down the passageway, the rough voices

of whatever beings ahead calling to him. The blue-tinged light on the ceiling gave way to the orange glow of fire. The tunnel stretched higher until he could stand straight without his head going through the rock. His pace picked up until he fully sprinted down the tunnel, laughing along with the magic inside him.

He turned a corner and skidded to a stop. The ground opened up in front of him. Houses built from wide stones ran alongside streets. The chatter of folk going about their business reverberated through the cavern. Aiden squinted at the residents of such a place. His eyes widened.

"It's a city."

Folk—dwarves, gwyllions, kobolds, and many others he couldn't name—raced back and forth from building to building, going about their evening, hollering at their neighbors across the street and singing songs around fires.

The Land connected to him... squealed? He was learning that the Land could do a great many things an incorporeal entity shouldn't be able to. She pushed him along, floating him above the streets as they went.

He tried to soak it all in but simply couldn't. There was so much to see. Children laughed and danced in the street. Mothers held tiny babes and kissed their stubby fingers. Fathers gathered together, tools in hand, marching toward the plethora of tunnels scattered around the outer edges of the small city. So much went on, it was impossible to grasp all of it.

Aiden looked up. Above the city, an odd formation of stalactites reached down toward the roofs of the buildings. The Land pulled him up, taking him closer until he realized they weren't rocks. They were *roots*.

"Are we under Crann Mòr?"

The Land gave the affirmative.

He reached out to touch the roots. His fingers passed through the physical flesh of the tree, but he quickly withdrew his hand when he felt the power surging through the wood. He reached out a second time and didn't pull away when the magic met him again.

Sweet Gaia, the tree itself was magic. He could see every creature held in its branches, every fae within its trunk. It pulled him even further out until he could easily see the land around it, feel every heartbeat and see every blade of grass.

He pulled his hand away again, recognition flaring inside of him. "This is *you*, isn't it? This is your center, your heart." It wasn't just magic, or the Land. It was the Tree too. Every part of this kingdom was linked to the Goddess's magic. It was life and death and shadow and light all hovering under the surface, reaching out and bringing magic to the folk who dwelled there.

The Land sent what felt like agreement.

His own heart latched onto the knowledge. It was no wonder the fair folk were so drawn to the Tree. It was the center of their world. Of everything.

"I want to see more," he whispered.

The magic pulled him skyward.

Past the roots and the trunk, past the folk scurrying about the city above the surface, he soared. He zipped by the great branches of the Tree and up into the night sky. He hadn't seen the whole of Faerie since the first dreams he'd experienced.

It was breathtaking.

The colors of the Courts stood out like a quartered rainbow. Even in the dark, Autumn blazed with the colors of fire; orange leaves twisting up with the flames coming from the blazing fires of Brònach. He could see the peaks of Eagallach, and Lake Truaighe's icy surface sparkling under the stars. The lights of Sona glittered through the forest in Spring. He looked out over the Farraige Gaineamh and saw a dark spot on its golden waves.

"What is that?"

Something new.

He jolted, his arms wheeling so far up in the sky. The words had come straight to his mind, but he couldn't process what She said with the revelation of the Land speaking to him. "What did you say?"

It is something new.

His brows pulled together, and She pulled him toward the dark splotch in the middle of the dunes. It wasn't until he was hovering right over it, he realized what it was. "It's an oasis."

It is new.

"You mean it wasn't here before? Where did it come from?"

Me.

"You created it?"

No.

"Then where did it come from?"

My gift.

He shook his head, not understanding. His feet finally touched down on the soft grass. Bits of moonlight caught on the ground around him. No, not moonlight. He crouched down and reached out for the bit of white peeking up over the grass. His fingers went through it, but he felt a physical pang in his chest when he realized what it was.

A white daffodil.

He remained there, staring at the white blossom as an ache spread against his ribs. Would everything always remind him of her? Would there ever be a day when she wasn't there, right at the forefront of his mind.

He took a deep breath. "Danu, please keep her safe."

The magic within him brightened. *I will.*

"So, the Night Court actually fought with the humans against the old rulers during the Faerie Wars?" Aiden looked down at the historical text on the table in front of him. One of the librarians had been kind enough to show him where the translated versions of the old books were kept when they'd arrived to help Aiden learn more about Faerie.

"Yes," Fiadh answered. "While there were many within the Court who did not agree, your mother was not one of them. After my *athair* passed into the Goddess's realm, Morana carried on his policies regarding not having slaves at the Winter Palace."

The history of this kingdom was vastly different than what he'd grown up hearing in Olympia. There had never been mention of any of the fae fighting alongside the humans, only that the residents of Faerie kept them as slaves. If what Fiadh told him—and what he was reading—was actually true, there was a completely different story.

When the humans rebelled against the fae, they'd hidden away a large group of mages in the southern part of Faerie—now known as Olympia. Then, it had been mostly the Day Court, their seasons taking up more land than the Night Court and thus becoming the leading Court in Faerie. The seasonal courts had bled down into that part of the continent before the Wars, but with the Mist cutting off access, the seasons had slowly normalized over the years until the land and weather functioned the same as the rest of the world. But with how large it had been, and how far from Crann Mòr, the rulers of Spring and Summer had grown lax. The mages gathered there and prepared to strike. With their magic, they freed many of the humans...

"What are 'brontannas?'" Aiden asked, staring down at the word on the paper in front of him.

"The gift-less," supplied Dair from the chair beside him. "Where do you think your people got the name 'bronties?'"

"It is an old fae term," Fiadh said, "carried over from before the common tongue came to our lands."

Was every piece of Olympia's culture tied to this place? Aiden sighed and turned back to the passage in front of him.

"So, the humans hid mages to basically even the odds against the ellyllon."

"Yes." Fiadh flipped the page of the book in his lap and turned it around so Aiden could see the picture. A scene of a brutal battle had been tattooed onto the pages. "They swept through Summer and Spring until they reached what is now the border, freeing the slaves as they went."

"What did the fae do in retaliation?"

"The old rulers continued to send troops down to stop them. Their arrogance led them to believe the threat could be easily squashed, but with every battalion that went out, a new wave of humans came closer to the capital."

The clip of footsteps preceded the arrival of Shirina. "How is it going?" she asked with a warm smile as she settled into the chair next to Fiadh's. With her addition, their small table in the corner of the library reached full occupancy.

"Aedon is doing just fine. We were just getting into how Rìan took the throne."

Aiden's brow puckered. "And how did High Queen Rìanoch come into the picture? She was a member of the Day Court, correct?"

"High Queen Rìanoch was the Queen of Summer before becoming High Ruler," Shirina answered. "Her Court did have slaves, but your mother was the one who talked her out of keeping them."

"And my mother was already Queen of Winter at this time, right?" Aiden ran a hand through his hair. "How did that come about? Wasn't your father the last king? Wouldn't you have taken Winter's throne instead of my mother?"

"The ruling laws of Faerie are a bit different than the ones in Olympia." Shirina gestured toward him. "While Danu chooses the High Ruler, the separate Court Rulers are actually appointed by the High Ruler and their Councilors. After my father died in the wars, your mother was chosen to take his place because she was the best suited to it."

"Did that upset you?" he asked Fiadh. *Dion would have lost his mind.* All Dion knew was becoming king. Having someone take that from him would have destroyed him.

Fiadh chuckled. "Not at all. I knew my path to becoming the Night Court's ruler was never really on the table. Once your mother arrived in Eagallach and we got to know each other, I greatly suspected she would be chosen."

"Having the Queen of Summer as her older sister was just icicles on the cake," Dair added.

Shirina gave him a confused look. "Who puts icicles on cake?"

"It is an Olympian idiom, I believe."

Not one Aiden had ever learned. He thought for a moment. "Don't you mean 'icing?'"

Dair sat up in his chair. "That makes so much more sense."

Shirina shook her head in exasperation. Aiden shared a smile with Fiadh before returning to the lesson. "So, my mother helped my aunt become High Queen?"

"No," Fiadh answered. "The magic of the Land detached from the previous rulers and bonded with High Queen Rìanoch."

"So, who became ruler over Summer?" Aiden grimaced. Shouldn't he know this? Perhaps if he hadn't been so bull-headed, he would be more involved in his new kingdom than he was now.

"King Comhachag."

"Summer," hissed Dair. "Nasty little buggers over there."

The corners of Aiden's mouth turned up. "Taking up Olympian slang now, are we?"

"Please," Shirina groaned, "this boy has been picking up demeaning terms since he learned to walk. He knew every curse word in our tongue and the Aigeans' by the time he was eight years."

Dair flashed a grin. "I know the ones from the continent

now too. Their delegation visited last year and were extremely insightful."

"Can we get back on task here?" Fiadh asked, bemused.

Aiden nodded. "So King Comhachag was the High Queen's husband?"

"Great skies, no!" Shirina said emphatically. "High Queen Rìanoch found her husband, Lord Graeme, soon after the war ended, and he became consort."

"Spouses do not generally rule with one another," Fiadh said.

Aiden sagged in his chair. "I'm never going to get this." Knowing the inner workings of the Courts was paramount to running this new kingdom Aiden found himself in charge of.

"I am sure the Courts will agree with you," Dair stated. He picked up a feathered quill from the table.

"Not helping." Shirina glared at her son before turning back to Aiden. "It can get a little confusing. Fiadh and I are a bit of an exception because I became High Councilor and now, he will be given Winter's crown as the High Councilors have decided."

Dair brushed his fingers over the edge of the feather in his hand. "Though, now that Aedon is High King, he could technically have *Athair* deposed."

Fiadh's coloring paled slightly. "Yes, I suppose you are correct."

Aiden leaned forward. "I wouldn't do that. If anything, I'll need the support when meeting with the rest of the Courts." Something he very much did *not* look forward to.

"You are doing wonderfully, Little Shadow," Shirina assured him.

"I'm just not sure how I'm going to remember all of this before the equinox." There was centuries of history to learn. He would have to study rigorously for the next few weeks if he ever wanted to come close to catching up.

"We could just leave you in here with all of the books until your brain is so full of our history it explodes," Dair suggested, echoing Aiden's thoughts. He casually swung his legs up onto the table.

Shirina flicked her wrist and a bolt of glittering shadow shoved Dair's feet back onto the floor. "We have plenty of time to teach you before the equinox. At least enough for you to get by. No one there will expect you to know everything you need to."

"Except King Comhachag," mumbled Dair.

Shirina waved her hand in the air, as if dissipating a bad smell. "No one gives a pixie's rear end what he thinks. He complains about anything and everything simply to get attention."

Aiden shook his head, but a chuckle bubbled in his chest.

The library door opened, and Thaen's head peeked into the room. "You are all here." He stepped fully into the room.

"What is going on?" Shirina asked as Thaen came up to their table.

"We received a message." He pulled what looked like a large moth from within his pocket.

Shirina gasped and clapped her hands in delight. "When will they be here?"

Thaen met Aiden's eyes. "The Andàn will arrive in three days."

20

LIGHT AND WINGS

 RUBBED her eyes and her face stretched in a weary yawn. She looked tiny atop Spot's broad shoulders, like a pixie riding a dog rather than the eleven-year-old girl she came across as. Actually, Penny couldn't tell how old the ellylon girl really was. Child development was different in Faerie.

"How old are you?" Penny asked.

"Fifteen." Nikki looked down at her through heavy lids. "How old are you, Penny?"

Penny cringed at the use of her name, but there was little she could do about it now. "I'm seventeen."

Nikki's eyes widened. "But you look so old!"

There had been no signs of pursuit within the last few hours. They'd spent the rest of the night and half of the next day getting as far as they could from Adira's encampment before turning north once again.

At least, what Penny hoped was north.

The dense foliage restricted her view of the sky. The forest had become overwhelming as she'd pushed her unused magic down as far as she could. Not having been able to use it during her imprisonment had filled her magical stores to near bursting. If she didn't use her gifts soon, the magic would overflow and wreak who knew what kind of havoc. She dared not use her gift in case something dwelled nearby and could see it. Especially other fair folk. It wouldn't look good for her to be traveling with the kidnapped daughter of one of their noble houses, but Penny couldn't simply let the child wander through the forest alone.

Besides, Nikki didn't seem to want to be parted with her at the moment either, and if Penny began showing off her gifts, that would likely change. Mages tended to stay out of Faerie for a reason.

Penny stumbled over a rock. Her knee cracked against the ground, and she hissed in pain. Spot stopped, all three heads turning. Nikki's drowsy eyes went wide, and she nimbly dismounted from Spot's back.

"Are you all right?"

Penny stood and dusted off her trousers. "I'm fine. Just tired." The shadows in the trees grew longer and the air turned crisp with the coming night. "Perhaps we should find somewhere to rest."

Spot's heads perked up and he charged forward into the trees. Nikki took Penny's hand and followed the trail Spot left behind in his wake, her quiet voice chiming in Penny's ears. The girl had grown more at ease the farther they got from the camp and the deeper they ventured into Spring.

Spot led them to a small clearing. He pranced right in and rolled over, scratching his back in the long grasses and stretching his legs high overhead.

Penny took a deep breath. She hadn't realized until that moment how much pressure the trees had been putting her under. With the trunks a few dozen yards away, the need to connect to them didn't scratch at her as deeply.

Nikki's laugh—the first one Penny had heard—rang through the meadow, clear as a bell. A strong breeze swept through, tossing up Nikki's skirts and prickling goosebumps up Penny's arms.

"We're going to need a fire."

Penny began collecting kindling, the grasses and the sticks littering the ground piling up in her arms. Nikki caught on to what she was doing and began clearing a space in the grass and collecting rocks. Penny told Spot to dig a small hole, clearing away the extra debris and giving them somewhere to put the kindling, before she sent him off in search of some kind of game for them to eat. Nikki placed rocks around the rim and Penny dumped her collection into the shallow pit. She was in the middle of stacking the kindling to light when the thought struck her. She had nothing to light it with. Her flint and steel remained in the pack she'd left behind in Adira's camp, along with all of her other supplies.

"It'll be all right," she told Nikki—though the words may have been for herself. "I have the dagger. I just need to find a rock that will get it started." None of the rocks around the fire pit gave off a single spark, so she stood to go in search of one.

"Is that how humans start a fire?" Nikki asked. "It seems so hard."

"Oh really?" Penny asked, intrigued but also teasing. "And how do fae start a fire?"

With a smile revealing a small gap between her two front teeth, Nikki crouched at the edge of the ring. She closed her eyes, thrusting her hands out toward the pit. Her face scrunched in concentration and her limbs began to shake.

Penny took a step forward but stopped when she saw the small bead of light blossom in the child's palms. Nikki opened her eyes and pushed the light from her palms in a beam toward the middle of the pit. Triumph stretched across the girl's face as a thin stream of smoke drifted into the air above them. The beam of light cut off and small flames licked up between the sticks.

A *whoop* burst from Penny's lips, and she grabbed Nikki up

in a hug. "Perhaps I shouldn't have nicknamed you Rose. Maybe *Sparks* would have been better suited." Penny set her down and met Nikki's adorable smile with one of her own.

They set out to look for more fuel, gathering sticks and breaking off large branches from dead trees within the clearing. Penny discreetly searched for the dried-out trees, hoping to prevent as much smoke from the fire as possible and avoid detection. The scant pieces of her gift she allowed shot around the clearing eagerly.

Spot returned with two rabbits in his mouth and dropped them at Penny's feet. Rose skipped around the clearing, scavenging random plants Penny wasn't sure she would be able to eat.

With the rabbits on a makeshift spit, and the fire warming her hands, Penny's shoulders relaxed a fraction. Yes, there were still rebels running through this forest and she had to get Nikki to someone who could take her home, but she was finally back on the path to finding Aiden.

The tips of her fingers skimmed over the pommel of her sword where the steel pomegranate reflected the fire's glow.

He was in Winter. He was with his family. At least it sounded like he was safe for the moment, even if Adira was bent on destroying him. Penny had until the equinox to get to him. She had time.

Nikki plopped onto the ground beside her, lips blue from whatever berries she'd found in the brush. Penny didn't know if there were any poisonous plants in the vicinity, but she also didn't know if they would even affect the fae. The only things she knew could kill them were iron and ash, a horrific accident, or very old age.

Nikki watched the rabbits turn on their spit, her magenta eyes gleaming with apprehension. The juices from the meat dripped onto the fire, the grease sizzling when it hit the burning coals beneath. Penny's stomach rumbled and Nikki giggled.

Penny chuckled. "Only a few more minutes, though I don't know if I'll make it." She feigned a swoon and Nikki's laugh grew louder. It was a lovely sound after the quiet that had been sinking its claws into Penny for the last two weeks.

Spot joined in with a symphony of yawns and stretched his paws out into the grass. He braided his heads over his paws and closed two sets of eyes, keeping one set alert and watchful. Penny had no idea how it worked, but all three heads seemed to work together and separately at the same time.

She pulled the rabbits off the fire, passing one to Nikki and blowing on hers. That didn't last long, however. The temptation was too great, and she tore a small piece off with her teeth, burning the inside of her mouth. They devoured their dinner in silence, the crack of the burning log in the fire the only sound. Penny stilled.

No other sound rang through the trees.

No insects. No birds. None of the nocturnal creatures she'd grown used to hearing over the last few hours.

The only noises were those of her companions and the fire. Penny's lips pursed and she let out a low whistle to Spot while getting to her feet. Spot's heads rose in alert and Penny pulled Nikki toward the thick trunk of one of the surrounding trees. If something was amiss, she could put Nikki in the branches with her magic and fight off whatever might be lurking in the area.

Nikki looked around with questions in her eyes. Penny nodded at the dagger strapped to Nikki's side and simply put a finger to her lips.

The short sword in Penny's hand slid out of the scabbard, silent as a whisper. The steel gleamed in the pinpricks of starlight coming through the branches above them. Her steps remained quiet as she crept around the trees, watching Spot and Nikki across the clearing for any signs of danger. Both of them had much better senses than she, but neither of them looked anything more than wary.

Penny shifted around a thinner tree than the one she'd

placed Nikki under and allowed her magic to shine through her hands. The green crept up her arms and she closed her eyes, focusing on the plants in the space around the clearing. She found the tree where Nikki stood, the girl's magic reaching out to the magic of the earth beneath their feet, similar to how Aiden's did in Eleusion, but Nikki's connection was much stronger.

Penny focused on where Spot's paws had crumpled the undergrowth. With the two of them centering her, she pushed out farther. The trees practically spoke to her, the magic running through their roots vibrant and alive. A tree held up a mass, the magic of the thing also connected with the earth like Nikki's. Penny withdrew her magic, eyes opening in the direction of the creature hiding in the tree above her.

Two, wide, yellow orbs met hers.

The creature moved, faster than a thing that size should be able. Wide wings spread out from its sides and the thing swooped down out of the tree right toward her.

Penny lifted her sword to block the flying thing from raking her with its talons. The creature screeched, shooting up into the trees just before the tip of Penny's blade sliced through its belly.

Penny spun and ran in the direction of her companions. "Spot! Get Nikki!"

Spot used his heads to scoop Nikki up onto his back. He loped toward Penny through the clearing. Penny sprinted along the line of trees, watching as the moonlight caught the flash of feathers weaving through the branches.

The ground shook, and Penny turned as a massive shadow smacked into the ground right in front of Spot, causing him to skid in the grass and eliciting a scream from Nikki. Dust flew up around the hulking mass and an earth-shattering roar blasted the air. Spot growled, barking at the thing to allow him to go around, but the creature blocked every escape. Enormous wings sprang from its back, effectively cutting Spot off from

Penny and revealing the violet-colored scales to the glittering moonlight.

A dracon.

Nikki screamed again and Penny's heart shot up into her throat.

"Get her out of here, Spot!"

Spot barked and the dracon moved to cut him off once again.

Green light tinged the corners of Penny's vision.

A wall of vines shot from the ground, weaving into a thick wall between the dracon and Spot. Penny ran toward them as she called for roots and vines to wrap around the dracon's legs.

The dracon opened its mouth and hot blue flame shot out toward the vine wall. The plants disintegrated, but only after Spot reached Penny's side. Nikki squirmed on Spot's back, shouting and gesturing toward the dracon fervently, but her words were lost in the cacophony.

"I know!" Penny called up to her. "We'll keep you safe. I promise."

Penny gestured for Spot to remain at her back as she charged toward the winged beast. Spouts of blue flame caught on the plants she used to tie it down and she did her best to replace them as fast as they burned. The trees likewise answered her call, surging forward from the edges of the clearing to grab the dracon's wings.

Only half a dozen feet from its tail, someone crashed on top of Penny. Penny fell, twisting so she could protect her ribs. The impact still stole the breath from her lungs and left her gasping in pain.

When she could finally see through the black fogging her vision, she saw Nikki scramble up from the ground next to her. The girl had been the one to pummel Penny.

Nikki grabbed Penny's face, tears streaming down her cheeks. "You are a mage!"

Penny couldn't pull enough air into her lungs to speak, and

before she could get back to her feet, Nikki took off toward the dracon. "Nikki, don't!" Penny finally screamed, scrambling to her feet.

The little girl's rose-gold hair shimmered from the dracon's fire as she ducked beneath its wings and climbed up onto its back. It was only then, with Nikki clambering up the spines that had gone still at her touch, that Penny saw the warrior astride the great beast.

"Oh, sweet Gaia." Penny felt the air leave her again.

There was only one fae in all of Faerie who rode a dracon, and she was a member of the Wild Hunt.

Penny lifted her sword, looking around the clearing. The Wild Hunt had forever been some of Faerie's most notorious occupants. Legends and myths surrounding the group exceeded that of any other creature. Penny grew up on those myths and she absolutely knew where there was one member of the Hunt, the other two were sure to follow.

The ellylon on the back of the dracon dismounted, scooping up an obviously excited Nikki in a one-armed hug and drawing a sword with the other. Hair the color of liquid gold sat plaited on her shoulder, her skin so richly bronze she looked forged of metal herself.

Nikki's magenta eyes stared at Penny's hands, the glowing green reflecting in their depths. The Huntress left Nikki next to the dracon and brought her fingers to her lips, letting out a whistle sharp enough to make Spot whine. Not two seconds later, a shadow burst above the trees and shot down to land at the ellylon's side. Two large, yellow eyes glared out from a woman's face. The head held up by her lithe neck tilted to the side, her sharp nose twitching at the air. The expression of interest, however, could only hold Penny's attention for a moment. A tunic covered the top half of the creature's torso, but the bottom half was feathered, running down curved legs that ended in taloned feet. Instead of arms, the creature had tall, brown wings stretching out from her torso, like a bird of prey.

Penny was almost too busy staring at the odd creature to hear the sound of pounding steps, but her eyes flicked over in time to see the female centaur burst into the clearing. A long sword came into the centaur's hands as she stared at Spot who was still growling behind Penny.

The ellylon took another step toward Penny, a threat plain in her stance and the narrow cut of her eyes. "What are you doing on this side of the Fuath, *mage*?"

Penny took a step back. Great Goddess, the *Hunt*? Could her luck be any worse? She kept her eyes on the group and her sword at the ready. Was she absolutely destined to fail in her quest to reach Aiden?

Nikki ran out, her small hands held out to stop the advancing fae. The ellylon scrambled to grab her and shield Nikki from Penny behind her back, but Nikki pushed forward. "You cannot kill her, Auntie. She helped me."

"Helped you?" the fae sneered.

All three of the Hunt stared at Penny as Nikki rapidly explained, gesturing in the direction they'd come. Nikki mentioned the troll attacking the camp and the Huntresses all turned to her.

Penny took a slow step back. If she could get into the trees, she may have a fighting chance. The flyers, at least, would have a difficult time getting through and it wasn't like Penny didn't have the magical stores to use the flora to her advantage. The magic practically begged her to be used. Yes, she could do it. Her and Spot could get to the trees, evade the Hunt, and get to Aiden.

And they would no longer have to worry about Nikki. If the dracon rider was her aunt, the Hunt would likely take the child back to her family. Even without the relation, they were the sworn protectors of Faerie. That was their job, right?

"How did the troll know where to find the camp?" asked

                    ALLISON ANDERSON

the centaur. "We had been looking for it for days and only found the ruins."

"Oh!" Nikki pointed to Spot. "The strange demon dog brought it somehow."

Curses. Penny turned and bolted for the trees. Spot loped at her side. A shout sounded from behind her, and the gallop of hooves followed after. Another whistle split the air and Spot was tackled by the dracon—the beast slightly bigger than him.

The centaur cut off Penny's path, sword and eyes blazing.

Penny ducked a swing from the female and swiped at her forelegs. The centaur outmaneuvered her and came back with another thrust. The blade skimmed just along the top of Penny's shoulder, the sting of the cut summoning a hiss against Penny's teeth.

Spot yelped and Penny looked to see him get back to his feet, the dracon and him circling one another.

The centaur swung again, this time nearly grazing Penny's neck. The pulse increased up to her throat, right where she would have been cut. A lock of hair brushed Penny's arm as it fell to the ground.

No more playing fair.

Penny let her magic flow free. The tall grasses tangled around the centaur's legs, hobbling her as she turned around to attack. Penny used the distraction to aid Spot by constructing a wall of trees between him and the dracon. It would give Spot a moment to regroup as the fire-breathing beast worked through the thick trunks.

Penny lifted her sword toward the charging centaur. The sound of Nikki's cry nearly broke Penny's concentration but praise the Goddess it didn't. The centaur, however, glanced toward the sound and Penny seized the moment. She leapt to the side and thrust her sword out toward the lower body of the centaur. Blood seeped from the centaur's side and the Huntswoman fell.

Penny scrambled back to her feet, but the back of her shirt

caught before she could take a step. She hung in the air, the momentum of the pull on her clothing spinning her until she came face to face with the ellylon.

"*What have you done, you filthy mage?*" the Huntress screamed.

Penny lifted her sword again, but before she could do anything, the ellylon shoved her away. Penny rolled to avoid landing on her face. She came up on her feet, but with the speed of a wasp, the ellylon whacked her on the head.

Penny's world was cast into darkness.

21
AFFIRM

Fiadh walked back and forth in front of the fireplace in the family sitting room... as he had for the previous two nights. With word from Spring about odd occurrences and a river blockage, not to mention the arrival of the Andàn at any moment, he'd been on edge. Shirina sat at the grand piano, plinking a tune Aiden had never heard. Thaen stood by the door, stiffening any time footsteps sounded on the other side. And Dair—well, Dair did whatever Dair always did.

Every night after supper, the family gathered and discussed what to expect once the Andàn arrived. Aiden's cousins had been in a tizzy over preparations for their arrival and now that the day had come, they didn't know what to do with themselves. The constant tension was driving Aiden mad.

Fiadh pursed his lips and turned to him. "Were you religious when you lived in Olympia?"

"Religious?" He cleared his throat. "I suppose. I attended services with my brothers and studied holy text in my youth."

"Yes, but what do you believe about our Goddess?"

"You mean Danu?"

"Danu. Gaia. We speak of the same Goddess."

Thaen had said as much before. "But why is She called different names?"

Fiadh stopped pacing, resting an arm on the mantle and looking back at Aiden. "Do you know how the race of mages was created?"

Aiden's brows pulled together as he thought, having difficulty keeping up with Fiadh's questions. "Wasn't it the same as all the others? Aren't we all created by Gaia's hand?"

"That is true, but there is a reason mages are looked down upon by the Tuatha Dè Dannan. Mages were made after Danu had created the humans and what they refer to as 'the fair folk.'" Fiadh finally sat in the chair next to Aiden. "We know that the first ellyllon and the first bwbachod were the literal sons and daughters of Danu, formed in her own womb and given life as a mother would her child. Human bodies were crafted from the earth and imbued with life alongside the other creatures of the land, but all precious to Danu as much as any of Her children.

"In the beginning, Danu freely walked among all Her children. She blessed them with gifts, taught them how to give back to the earth as they took magic from it. She showed us how to use the land to our benefit, growing food with our own hands or raising up livestock. She gave us this knowledge and the knowledge of where She is from and where we will all return after our time in this state."

"You said humans," Aiden cut in. "Are mages not considered human?"

"I was getting there," Fiadh said. "There was a faction of humans who did not believe it fair for them to not be given gifts as the Tuatha were. They desired access to the magic Danu had sewn into the very fabric of our world. So a movement formed, one that worked to find an answer to such a thing; a way to access Danu's power without a permanent sacrifice or the loss of their ability to lie. And in their search, they discovered Her name."

Aiden stood up straight, nearly sending Dair to the floor on his head. "You mean Her true name?" The concept of true names wasn't foreign to Aiden, but his only experience with them was that Adira had his. It is said the name is given by Danu, rather than by one's parents. Only the name holder and the Keepers in Faerie ever knew the names. Aiden had given his to Durant at a young age in a misguided attempt to earn her trust. It was still one of the greatest mistakes he'd ever made.

Fiadh nodded gravely. "They used it against her, entrapping her and demanding the magic She had so freely given Her children. But there are laws that not even Danu Herself can break. No gift is given freely."

Thaen cut in, "To access the magic, there must be a balance."

"Precisely," Fiadh continued. "Her children could not lie, so she cursed the new creatures She was forced to create. They may not have to pay a permanent price for their gifts as Her children do, but it would still cause them temporary pain, and ultimately death if not used with care. And though they can lie, She gave each one of them a mark, a *tell* of their magic when in use. The group that had controlled Her abused the magic, and in the end, it still cost them. A new race was born, but many of our kind believe our Goddess ultimately left the world because of the wickedness of those she had created."

Aiden slowly slumped back into the sofa. Was he inherently evil then? Was that why he was given such a terrible gift? Because the other part of him recognized it as something to be dreaded?

No. He couldn't believe that. He knew too many good mages. *Penelope is a mage and to the Mist with anyone who believes she could be anything but pure goodness.*

Heat crept up his neck. "So the Tuatha Dè Dannan believe mages are the creation of evil?"

Fiadh shook his head. "Not all of us. Danu is a being of

inherent goodness. She could not create something that was purely evil, even if it came about by such means."

"Then why do Her children shun mages?"

Shirina walked over and sat on the arm of Fiadh's chair. "The eldest ones blamed them for the Goddess's departure. Danu left with instructions for Her children to watch over the land and all Her creations. We were to be stewards over all of it and keep the magic flourishing, but there was too much anger within the factions of Her children."

Shirina sighed, the sound mournful and frustrated. "Eventually, there was a divide and then the centuries of wars. The one that ended two centuries ago was not the first, and unless something drastic changes, it will not be the last."

"So why hasn't she returned?" Aiden may not have been a parent, but even watching the division happening in his brother's kingdom caused him so much sorrow. "She easily could, right?"

Fiadh shrugged. "We do not know the true reason why She left. All we know is that we are to carry on with Her wishes and wait for the day when we leave this life and return to Her realm, as we were before."

Aiden's mind whirled with all the revelations. What the temple priests in Olympia always taught was not so detailed as this. Looking back, there were large chunks of reason left out of the knowledge they shared with the people. Could it be that without the fae's record and knowledge, they were missing their beginning, the truth of their religion?

Shirina stood from her perch near Fiadh's shoulder. Her eyes searched out through the tall window at the back of the room. "I am sure you have many more questions, but we will have to leave them for now." She made her way to the glass and looked down into what Aiden knew was the north courtyard. "In fact," she continued, "I think you are about to find yourself with many more questions." Her eyes glittered when she turned back. "They have arrived."

The Andàn were… unexpected.

All three ancient women descended on Shirina as soon as Aiden's family clambered into the Great Hall. Shirina had done her best to prepare him, but he felt anything but prepared for the intensity they unleashed into the room.

"I didn't realize they were so…" Aiden couldn't find the right word.

"Old?" Dair supplied.

Aiden winced but nodded.

Dair smirked as Fiadh came up next to him. "While they are old, it is not their age that gives them their haggard appearance, but their gift. It is said when Gaia blessed them with their gifts, the price was their youth and beauty. They have looked this ancient since the day they were gifted but have lived far longer than any other of the Goddess's first children."

"You mean they are actually *Her* daughters?"

"Carried in Danu's own womb as She left footsteps over our land."

Aiden studied the females—who were basically goddesses in their own right. There were three in all and each such a contrast to the next.

"You are looking mighty skinny, niece," said one, holding Shirina by her shoulders. Her skin was dark, marred with black crags of skin and dotted with large moles. One mole stood proudly on the tip of her nose, housing the only hair on the crone's body. She smacked her gums together. "Where is the kitchen? I will whip up something dense enough to put some meat on your bones."

Aiden leaned toward Thaen. "I didn't realize they were your mother's family."

Dair leaned in. "Great-great-great-great-aunts."

"Look how long your hair has gotten!" marveled another in an overly sweet voice. This one had bright blue hair gathered up in a nest of twigs and leaves atop her head. Large round spectacles sat on the end of her long, pointed nose, magnifying the bright carnelian irises of her eyes. Her smile stretched the already too thin skin of her face "You are such a beauty, even with all the stress you have been under. You must share your secret."

Shirina gave her a smile. "I learned how to handle it all from my favorite aunties."

The third one grunted, only going so far as to pat Shirina on the head with her large hand and move on to peruse the rest of the room. She was certainly the strangest to look at, her skin a reddish hue and her silvered hair shaved on the sides of a long braid swinging down past her waist. Her attention was the first to settle on Aiden with large, black eyes set over a wide, flat nose. Something within him balked, as if the fathomless gaze appraised his very soul.

Shirina cleared her throat and gestured toward him. "Aunties, this is High King Aiden. Morana's son." She turned her smile on Aiden. "My Sovereign, these are the Andàn: Snìomhadair, Alltadair, and Toirmisgte."

The blue-haired one stepped forward. "I don't think I've gone by Snìomhadair in the last century or two." She raised her pale, bony hand to her mouth as if to whisper a secret. "It is a mouthful, so just call me Auntie Niomi." She pointed toward the other two. "The mouthy one is Auntie Taddie, and the grumpy one is Auntie Tori."

Aiden nearly let out a sigh of relief. These were likely to be the easiest names he would have to pronounce in this kingdom. "I am pleased to meet all of you."

Auntie Taddie clicked her tongue. "We know you can lie, but there is no good reason to lie to us. Can see right through it."

Aiden's spine stiffened. Had he said something wrong?

He'd been dreading this meeting since he found out about it, but he thought he'd hidden it well.

Fiadh clapped him on the shoulder and laughed. "We are all simply apprehensive about your visit, Aunties. We know you did not simply come to chat and beat us all at Cruin."

A smile cracked over the face of Auntie Tori, the first expression of emotion from the heavy-set matriarch.

"We will not have a repeat of last solstice's shenanigans." Auntie Niomi wagged a finger at all of them.

Dair pushed past the group and wrapped her in an embrace. "You just want to avoid seeing yourself lose again."

Auntie Niomi pinched his face. "You have grown *cheekier* since I saw you last—if that is even possible."

Shirina pulled the other two crones toward the rest of the group. "We will have plenty of time for family reunions and Cruin later." Her eyes met Aiden's and gave him a comforting nod. "We have much more important things to do at present."

Auntie Taddie pulled up next to Aiden and hoisted a bag— one he hadn't even noticed within the many folds of her clothes—into his arms. "Come along, little king. Let us tell you what the future holds."

Aiden fidgeted in the middle of the floor in the family sitting room. Thaen and Dair pushed back the last of the furniture to clear enough space for all three of the Andàn to stand around him. Auntie Taddie had retrieved a stack of paper from within the bag Aiden had lugged up the stairs and set it on the table next to them. Niomi, Taddie, and Tori all stood before him, their magic swirling in mixtures of light and shadow around them.

Auntie Taddie leaned forward. "What you are about to hear are words only meant for you and your future. These words are to be applicable for your entire existence, not simply for the life you will live on this mortal plane. Some see this foretelling as a curse, but if we are to align our will with Our Mother's, we may view it as a blessing. Are you prepared to receive it?"

His palms began to sweat. Was he? What if they told him Durant was going to take over the kingdom? What if he was destined to bring ruin to this land? This could turn out worse than any of them could possibly imagine. He was a mage-gifted fae. He was a curse more than a blessing to anyone.

A steely sense of confidence flooded him. He closed his eyes as he felt the magic of the Land swirl within his own. It bolstered his spirit and held his spine straight. He swallowed down his trepidation. He was High King Aedon. A prophecy would not change who he was or what he knew he needed to do.

He nodded his head, praying it looked surer than he felt.

The Andàn closed their eyes, and their magic rolled over him as they all spoke as one voice. His eyes closed as well.

"We, the Andàn, do bestow this foretelling on Aedon, High King of Faerie and Lord of the Dead..."

A chill swept over him, but the unsettling feeling eased almost immediately, as if the words meant more than his mind could grasp.

"Aedon, first and foremost know that Danu is your Creator. Even before you were born, She has been with you. She knows you as no other, and she has full confidence in you and your abilities to use your gifts in the way She so desires."

Warmth flooded his chest. Everything else in the room disappeared as if he and the words of the Andàn were the only things in existence. He felt the magic inside of him surge to the surface, shadows curling through his hair, but it wasn't out of discomfort. More like a sense of belonging.

"You are the son of Olympia and Faerie, and you have been brought to your parents and this time for a reason. You will bring in an era of change as no one before. Have courage, Aedon. You will not

do this alone. There will be others to help you along the way. You will have the opportunity, Aedon, to find your other half, your chosen mate, and be bonded by the land and people you will both hold so dear—to be rulers of the Tuatha Dè Dannan and follow the Goddess's path laid out before you both."

His stomach sank. *Penelope.* He already assumed he would have to let her go, but to hear it so plainly pushed a wedge into his already cracking heart.

"There is much you have faced and there is still more you must endure. Evil will always find dark corners to dwell in and will step into the light in the name of good. Do not be deceived, Aedon. Danu will put the people you need in your path and assist you in whatever righteous endeavors you set out for. Know, Aedon, that everything happens for a reason. You have been given many gifts, gifts that you will be shunned and revered for, but know that Danu does not make mistakes. You are who you were always meant to become. Now go and do the Goddess's will."

Aiden let out a deep breath and opened his eyes. Tears he hadn't known waited at the corners of his lashes followed already wet tracks down his face. Auntie Tori offered him a clean handkerchief, which he thanked her for.

He wiped his tears and turned to face the rest of his family. Shirina's cheeks were wet, and Fiadh's eyes glimmered with unshed tears. Dair and Thaen stood and clapped Aiden on the back—Thaen with more strength than necessary.

Shirina and Fiadh came to embrace him next. Fiadh pulled back and met his eyes. "If only your mother could have been here. She must be so proud of you."

The tears Aiden had thought he'd gotten under control rose up once again. A part of him mourned the fact that she wasn't there, that he'd never get to meet her, but he could do nothing except praise the Goddess that the rest of his family surrounded him.

The aunties all gathered around and gave him hugs along with a sheet of paper. The words he'd just received stark against the parchment. He hugged the pages close to his chest. The words would guide him as he took his next steps forward —as a king and as a Tuatha Dè Dannan. There was still so much to do, but he had those he needed with him, and they would face the oncoming storm together.

Auntie Taddie clapped her hands together. "Now, I think it time we had some cake."

22

COURTS AND FLIGHTS

Dearest Penny,

By the Goddess, I am ready to be done with Winter! Of course, we have snow in Olympia, but it's nothing like this! Everything is constantly freezing and trudging through the cold, damp drifts every day is beginning to grate. If it wasn't for Devan and the few friends I've been able to make in this miserable place, I don't know what I'd do with myself.

Devan has been able to keep continuous contact with Prince Aiden. Nothing of great consequence has come up, but I wanted you to know he's fine. I know you won't see this for some time, but I feel like I needed to write it down. That you would need to know.

Because nothing feels fine.

There's so much I don't know. I feel like I'm in the dark most of the time. Devan is so supportive, of course, but there are things even he can't help me with.

Sweet Gaia, I miss you. When I see you again, I'm going to give you the biggest hug.
Your Lonely Friend,
Angelica

PENNY WATCHED THE SUN GO DOWN ON ANOTHER DAY SHE COULDN'T get to Aiden. The rays of reds, pinks, and oranges beamed through the leafy boughs above them, the light staining the leaves and turning them into a forest of brilliant fire.

Something raging and smoky burned at the back of Penny's throat.

Her flickering fingers clenched in the ropes around her wrists. The last time she'd used her magic, she'd been immobilized within seconds and her hands tied in front of her so the Huntresses could see her tell. If Penny were in any other situation, she undoubtedly would've been fascinated by the warriors—and perhaps she was. A little. They were the greatest force of justice sent out by the High Court. Like royal bounty hunters, they caught those causing trouble in the Courts, keeping the peace between the bwachod and the ellylon and taking down powerful beings when they became troublesome. The Hunt were almost as infamous as the Lòchran—the High Court assassin, the fae that was a whisper of shadow and dwelled in the nightmares of Faerie's enemies.

They were all fascinating in the best of circumstances.

Unfortunately, Penny was not in a position to be overly fascinated. Her ribs ached fiercely as her swollen feet stomped out every step. Even the large scratch on her shoulder from the centaur's sword had something to complain about.

A prisoner. Again.

By the Goddess, she was tired of being everyone's prisoner.

"Pick up the pace, Mage," the metallic fae—who Penny now referred to as 'Metal Woman'—called from ahead. The deep purple dracon the female sat upon marched between Penny and Spot and held up a drowsy Nikki. At least she was safe and comfortable.

Metal Woman turned around to face Penny. "I would like to eat before morning, if you do not mind."

Penny gritted her teeth but said nothing. If she replied, she, in all likelihood, wouldn't get food herself. But she did increase her walking speed.

Spot's heads bobbed up and down in front of the dracon, still watchful even as the Hunt guided their steps. If Penny found the chance, they would escape from the Huntresses and get back on the path to Winter.

Penny remained watchful, her eyes taking in every movement from the trio and picking up every word, whether she could actually hear it or not. There was much to glean from someone's expression and the language of their body when they spoke. Her eyes caught on the centaur. The bay hindquarters of the centaur's lower half dripped with sweat. The skin not covered by leather armor had turned pale rather than the sun-kissed gold it had been when they had fought in the meadow. Something was not right.

"I think we should stop," Penny called ahead.

"And why, for the love of every green tree," snapped Metal Woman, "would we listen to anything a *mage* would say?"

The centaur tripped over a root and collapsed.

That's why.

"Skies!" cried the winged woman—a harpy. Penny had learned what kind of bwachod she was from the snappish creature herself.

The harpy swooped down and landed at the centaur's side. She asked more questions, but the centaur only moaned. The harpy called to her dracon riding companion. Metal Woman hissed what sounded like a curse in response and leapt down from her mount.

The harpy hopped back, clearing the way for Metal Woman to examine the centaur's side. She pulled the large swath of bandages from the centaur's flesh and hissed.

Penny couldn't guess what they whispered to one another, but she could tell it was nothing good.

Metal Woman called to the dracon, and the beast answered with a swift grace that belied its humongous girth. Penny gaped as Metal Woman lifted the centaur—the *entire* centaur —onto the dracon's scaled back. Metal Woman rustled through her saddlebags and pulled out more rope. As she tied it around her companion, she began ordering everyone else around.

Her magenta-colored eyes, nearly the same color as Nikki's, met Penny's. "We are taking a detour. Tell the demon dog to follow." She mounted the dracon. "If you fight, I will tell her to drop you," she said over her shoulder.

Before Penny could ask what that meant, the dracon spread its wings and burst into the dusk painted sky. She looked over at Spot beside her, who was watching the dracon disappear into the sky. They'd left them there?

A short laugh slipped out from her lips. "Well, that was unexpe—"

Her torso was caught in a vice grip and her feet left the ground. Spot frantically barked as her body swung above the branches of the trees.

A scream finally burst from her caged lungs. By the Goddess, she was so high up. If she fell, she would shatter into a million pieces. All her hard work would be for nothing. The redcaps wouldn't even have the chance to stain their disgusting little hats, her body would pulverize on impact.

Something jostled her, cutting off her ragged screams and turning them into hisses as her still sore ribs protested. She looked up through teary eyes—whether from the whipping wind or her terror, she couldn't tell—and saw the broad, brown wings holding her aloft. The harpy smiled down at her with a sharp grin.

Now she understood what a rabbit felt like in the talons of a hawk.

The harpy swooped down a bit, causing Penny's stomach to flip and the wind to steal a squeal from her lips. Sweet Gaia, she'd nearly peed her trousers. Her eyes squeezed shut and she tried to calm her gasping breaths. The harpy called from above her—the cry something between an eagle's screech and a woman's holler—and Penny opened her eyes. They were gaining on the dracon and its load. Metal Woman gave the harpy some signals to which the harpy redirected her path.

A bark came up from the trees below. Penny's attention snapped down and saw the black shadow following beneath them. Her arms curled around her captured torso.

Spot.

A shaky laugh skittered across Penny's chest, making her swallow back another wave of fear. *Great Goddess, please don't let this winged woman drop me.*

Penny looked forward and her mouth dropped open.

A tree. *The* tree. Crann Mòr stretched beautiful limbs out like a swan gathering her cygnets to rest before the sun went down. They'd been even closer to the capital than Penny realized, Metal Woman conceivably planning on reaching the capital before midnight.

The trunk of the tree appeared comprised of what looked like many smaller trunks melded together and twisting upward toward the sky. The leafy bows drooped down, some of the branches even sinking into the ground. It looked similar to a yew or pomegranate tree, the odd-looking trunk and the way the branches hung down. She'd never seen a tree so gigantic.

Light glowed from within the trunk, the silver bark glittering. They swooped closer, the lights sharpening into doorways and windows, leading into the enormous trunk. Fae wove in and out of the openings, ants in their colony.

And where is their king?

Penny turned her attention north where it looked like someone had dumped confectioners' sugar over a quarter of the land, as if that part of Faerie were some kind of elegant dessert. Some of the powdery snow even dusted the top of the great tree. She could just see the tips of peaks surrounding the frozen lake that made up most of that Court.

More tears gathered in her eyes. She was so close. From that distance it would only take a few days to get across the icy lake and past those mountains to the capital of Winter—to *him.*

The harpy turned west and the fissure in Penny's chest ached. To be so close and not be able to get to him cracked something within her. She focused on the loping shape below them and sucked in a lungful of air.

"*SPOT!*" she screamed and kicked. Maybe Spot could get to him, protect him until Penny could escape. "*SPOT! GO TO HIM!*"

The harpy tilted with a shriek, Penny's thrashing causing her to lose her balance. She squawked, shaking Penny to get her to stop. But she wouldn't. If Spot could keep up with the Hunt, he could get there quickly. "*GO NORTH! PROTECT HIM!*"

The harpy shook her again, this time rough enough for Penny to bite her tongue. The pain in her ribs flared excruciatingly.

Tear-filled eyes found Spot again and watched him veer off toward the snowy stretch of Faerie. Her body sagged in relief.

Find him. Find our boy.

The harpy didn't complain for the rest of their long flight, Penny giving her nothing to be angry about. She was the perfect... dead mouse. By the Goddess, dangling from the talons of a giant bird woman, she felt like a dead mouse. But she would be a good dead mouse. Spot didn't need her to fall to her death before she escaped and got to Aiden. That would help no one.

The harpy stayed close to the dracon as the ground changed from white to moonlit gray. Skeletal trees stretched out before them, patches of leaves hanging to the branches by thin petioles.

Autumn.

A bubble of anticipation grew in Penny's chest. Angelica had spent the most of her time in this Court. They seemed the friendliest to humans, according to her letters. Perhaps Penny could find help here.

The Hunt sped over the drowsy trees and what looked like several abandoned villages, the increased pace exposing their eagerness to get to whatever destination they had in mind. That eagerness fed Penny's own. The dracon banked left in front of them, heading toward a patch of light shining through the tall trees. Penny's stomach flopped at the sensation of their descent. Praise the Goddess she hadn't eaten in several hours. The harpy should be grateful for that.

The dracon spread its wings wide, circling the small city below them. The harpy followed the dracon's flight path, giving Penny a decent view. Houses of varying shapes and sizes spread out in a wagon wheel shape from the center of the city where a large, orange orb—*Sweet Gaia, is that a pumpkin?*—squatted on a tall pedestal.

The dracon circumvented the humongous pumpkin, heading for the outskirts of the town where Penny could see a crooked hut leaned against a tree, smoke billowing out of the chimney. Their group headed for the open plain as close to the front door as a dracon and a harpy with a twenty-foot wing-span could.

The harpy dipped and the ground came rushing at Penny's face. She didn't have time to scream before the harpy unceremoniously dumped her on the ground. Her magic reacted, the grasses growing longer to cushion her fall. Penny rolled, the softened foliage taking the brunt of the pain, but she cried out as her ribs still took in the shock of the fall. Air seemed to elude her as she lay in the grass, sucking in short breaths as the bones in her torso screamed in anguish.

Black speckled her vision, and her ears rang for a few moments before her senses settled, her body finding its equilibrium even through the pain. Rage washed away a portion of the ache. If she hadn't been taken by the Hunt, she would be closer to Aiden, not further away. She looked up at the stars, attempting to gauge where she was in relation to Winter's capital.

Voices cascaded over the grass, out of view. Penny couldn't bring herself to care at the moment. Her lungs had just begun cooperating and she took as deep of breaths as they would permit. But the voices drew closer, one the voice of the Metal Woman and another Penny almost recognized. Her brows furrowed as she heard the crunch of their steps. Green flickered from her hands, her magic responding before she did.

Hair the color of polished gold came into view just before the familiar white braid did. A pair of deep, brown eyes widened at the sight of Penny laying on the ground.

Penny gasped. "Farrah?"

Farrah's cheeks stretched in a wide grin. "Hello, my girl."

Metal Woman's head swiveled back and forth between them. "You know this mage?"

Farrah reached down and grabbed Penny's hands, eyebrows furrowing at the now bleeding cut on her shoulder. "Indeed. This is—"

"Nell!" Penny burst out. "I'm Nell."

Farrah nodded, playing right along. "Yes, my dear friend Nell." She frowned down at Penny's hands. "Who shouldn't be trussed up like a cursed criminal."

Metal Woman whipped out a knife, pointing it at Penny. "This *Nell* was involved in the kidnapping of my youngest niece, intending to use her as a hostage to get into the High King's Anointing Revel."

Farrah's brow curved up at the blade and she deftly plucked it from the Huntress's hand. "The Nell I know would never do such a thing." She sliced the rope from Penny's hands with expert precision.

Penny gasped as the blood returned to her fingers and she rubbed vigorously at her aching wrists. Her arms still shined green, casting a ghastly glow on Metal Woman's fierce expression.

"*Someone* kidnapped my niece right from her bed. I then find this *mage* in possession of my niece. It was obvious what was going on."

Farrah looked back to Penny. "Did you kidnap Fearg's niece?"

Fearg must be the Huntress's name. And they must have been referring to Nikki. Penny shook her head. "No, I rescued her. If you ask her, she will tell you what happened."

The Huntress took a step toward her. "*I* rescued her. The child is simply confused."

Farrah set a hand on the Huntress's shoulder, but her eyes remained on Penny. "Who did you save her from?"

Penny licked her lips. She didn't know how much these folk knew about the war brewing in Olympia. The safest answer seemed best. "The Cartographer."

Farrah sucked in a breath. "You've seen her?" She looked about as if rebels would pop out of the grass like weasels. "You both need to come inside." She gestured for them to follow. Penny trudged behind the Huntress, not willing to put the fae at her back.

Farrah burst through the front door of the leaning cottage and hollered into the house. "Mama?" A muffled response rang out from within, and Farrah raced toward the noise.

Penny made it to the threshold and stood in the doorway, soaking in the view. A warm fire crackled from a wide mouthed fireplace on the far wall. A table sat near it, the base growing straight up from the wooden floor. A number of jars stood scattered over the entirety of its top. Labels stuck out from their sides, some capped with corks and lids while others waited to be filled, mouths open wide. Herbs, gems, and glass hung along the walls in neat rows, labels clipped to their edges by wooden clothespins or tied on with twine. The smell of the space cascaded over Penny, the smell of camphor and lavender, rich and calming.

It smelled just like Farrah's hut in Eleusion.

Penny's eyes burned and she blinked back the gathering moisture. *I really should have no tears left after everything I've already been through.* One trailed down her cheek, proving her wrong.

She shuffled toward the inviting fireplace but stopped when she saw Nikki. The child lay close to the fire, snuggly cocooned in a blanket. Fear spiked through Penny at how close the flames flickered near her sleeping form. Penny took a step forward, but a whimper stopped her short. Nikki's magenta eyes were hidden behind her eyelids, but Penny watched them twitch and the girl's mouth turn down in a frown. Penny wouldn't be the only one plagued by Adira in her nightmares.

Before Penny could move to wake her, Farrah burst back into the room, followed by another... well, another *Farrah*. The other woman looked exactly the same, her white hair swinging in a braid and her brown eyes warmly taking Penny in. The only difference was the slightly sharper angles of her face, and the faint smile lines around her mouth.

"Mama, I'd like to introduce you to Nell, my friend from Olympia."

The copy of Farrah nodded, wiping her bloodied hands on a rag tied to her apron.

The Huntress, *Fearg*, as Farrah had called her, stepped forward, eyes trembling with questions. Her gaze flicking from the Older Farrah's bloodied hands to her the door behind the older woman.

Older Farrah stepped aside. "You can see her now."

Fearg raced from the room, closing the door behind her.

Two pairs of brown eyes then moved to Penny. "Well, Nell," said Older Farrah, "my daughter tells me you have quite a story to tell." She looked her up and down, taking in what Penny guessed was her very disheveled appearance. "Though we should sit and get something warm in your stomach."

Penny swallowed. "Your daughter may be right, but more importantly I have an important task I need to ——"

Older Farrah held up a red speckled hand. "If you tell us your story, we will do everything in our power to help you, but a mage arriving in Faerie does bring up cause for concern. You will need to tell us exactly what is going on before we offer any aid."

"Oh, do not be such a numpty, Annalysa," called a voice from above.

Penny looked up and saw *another* Farrah, though this one even older than the two standing next to her. With agility belying her age, the Elder Farrah skipped down the steps and stood next to the Older. Penny blinked a few times, trying to take the image in, but her brain couldn't quite compute.

Farrah laughed. "Nell, meet my grandmother, Nonnie, and my mother, Annalysa." She waved a hand around the space. "My father isn't here, so it's just the three of us for the evening."

"Hello, my girl," said Nonnie with a little wave.

Penny bobbed her head and turned back to Annalysa who had finally wiped all of the blood from her fingers. Guilt clogged her throat. "Will the centaur be all right?"

"With a few days of rest and a good meal or two, she will be right back to sprinting through the Spring Wood. Dìoghaltas is a fierce female." Her brows rose. "There best be a good reason for her injury."

"Story time!" cheered Nonnie. She grabbed Penny's hand and cleared a spot on the table with her arm. Penny settled into a proffered chair.

Annalysa sat with a cup of hot tea and pushed it toward Penny. "From the beginning if you will. Then we will decide what to do about you."

The beginning. Where would she even start?

Penny cleared her throat. "I was sixteen when I first met the mysterious, amber-eyed fae..."

23
ACCOMPLICE

Aiden set the quill in his fingers back into the ink pot. He missed his enchanted quill. Dion had given it to him for his seventeenth birthday. It had been three days late, but it was the thought that counted. Aiden looked at his brother's name staring back at him from the top of the page. He waited for this new letter to dry before adding it to the growing pile within the writing desk in his sitting room. He didn't know if he'd ever get the chance to send any of them.

A knock on the door broke the quiet air around him and he glanced at the window. The sun was just setting over the mountain, the last rays reflecting off the snow-covered peaks in pinks and oranges. He stood and walked toward the door to greet whoever waited on the other side. *Hopefully, Dair with summons for supper.*

He opened the door and held back his surprise to see Shirina there. She generally waited in the dining room and sent someone else to fetch him for supper, her having just woken up.

"Is something the matter?" He looked up and down the hallway.

Shirina's smile curved up. "Not at all. I would simply be honored if you would accompany me to supper this evening."

With the door open, he could smell the tantalizing aroma of foods wafting up the steps. His brows furrowed. Supper usually took place in the dining room. Halfway across the palace. "Are we having supper in the drawing room this evening?"

Something flashed across Shirina's face, but she hid it before he could identify it. Her long fingers wrapped around his elbow, and she drew him out of his rooms. "What makes you ask that?"

Aiden tapped his nose. "I can't usually smell it all the way up here."

Shirina bit her lip. "Yes, well I had hoped to make it a surprise, but supper will be served a bit differently this evening."

Aiden thought back on the day and what had gone on around the palace. No one had mentioned any events taking place that evening. In fact, he'd barely seen anyone all day. The twins had come to spar before breakfast as usual—Aiden still had a nasty bruise on his thigh from it—but had disappeared right after. Fiadh hadn't come to the library during Aiden's regular study time and the servants had bustled about the place all day. Aiden had decided to stay in his rooms after lunch, out of the way, but now it was obvious that hadn't been the wisest choice.

He narrowed his eyes down at her. "What's going on, Shirina?"

"You will just have to wait and see." Her grip on his elbow tightened as she towed him down the stairs.

They made it to the ground floor where Fiadh stood peeking through a crack in the nearly closed doors leading to the Grand Hall. He clicked it shut and spun toward them, a delighted grin on his face. "Everything is ready."

Shirina attempted to shush him, but it only piqued Aiden's interest more. "What on earth is going on, you two?"

Fiadh attached himself to Aiden's other arm. "Just come and see."

Shirina sent magic swirling toward the door. The silver sparks running through the shadow of her magic reflected the sky outside. The magic curled around the handles and light poured through the opening.

Aiden balked at the sight, his steps halting completely before he could be pulled into the beam of light waiting in the doorway. He swallowed, hard, as he looked into the room at the creatures only spoken about in children's bedtime stories and Olympia's history books. Dwarves stomped about, the gems in their beards catching the lights hovering above them. Banshees glided over the floor, their white robes hanging down and their black hair floating around their faces. A pixie zipped by the opening, followed closely by a purple wisp. Aiden could even see a troll standing in one corner, holding up a bowl of what looked like some kind of punch.

He wasn't going in there. He already didn't appreciate crowds, but a crowd full of folk who would bow and scrape everywhere he went? The luncheon where he'd spoken with Devan had been one thing, but this was a party. A big party.

No. He wasn't going in there.

Fiadh leaned his head down next to his ear. "These are your people, Aiden. They are excited to meet you."

Magic twitched at his fingertips, but he clenched his hands to keep the shadows from drifting off. "What are they all doing here?"

Shirina stepped in front of him. "They came to celebrate with you." Her eyes glistened with emotion. "We have spent twenty years without celebrating your birth. I know it is quite late, but I could not wait for the next one."

Aiden stilled. "You threw me a birthday party?" Never in his wildest dreams would he have thought they would do something like this. No one ever did anything like this for his birthday—*except Penelope.* His chest ached at the thought.

Something must have come across his expression because Shirina's mouth tilted down. "Do you not want—"

"*No!*" Aiden took a deep breath. "No—I mean *yes.*" He'd faced worse. He could handle this. "This is great. It just came as a surprise. My birthday feels like a lifetime ago." It was closer to Penelope's birthday than it was to his. He'd had so many plans formulating for that day, but none of that would happen now.

Fiadh wrapped an arm around him and squeezed. "Well then, let us not keep the good folk waiting." He pulled Aiden forward.

Aiden held his breath. His boot hit the beam of light and all the fae in the room turned—every unique set of eyes trained on him. For a moment they were silent, until someone in the crowd gave out a holler. Aiden staggered back a step as a riot of cheers went up.

The breath he was holding slipped out slowly. He could handle this. He'd been to parties before. It was just like being back home. *Just avoid being touched and stick to the outer wall and you'll be fine.*

Dair came gliding through the crowd and took Shirina's place at Aiden's side. "Smile, cousin. You look like you are going to slit everyone's throats. We already have Thaen tromping around, death glaring everyone."

Aiden pushed a smile on his face.

Dair recoiled. "Perhaps we should stick with the death glare."

The false smile fell from Aiden's lips, and he allowed Dair and Fiadh to drag him further into the room. Any folk they passed bowed low and moved back a few steps from him. He attempted to make eye contact whenever he could, remembering the few things he'd caught from Dion's lessons on being king, and nodded at those he could acknowledge. Whispers bounded about the room until Shirina clapped her hands above her head and music wove through the air. Several members of the crowd migrated toward the center of the hall, swaying with the alluring sound and allowing the music to sweep them away.

Fiadh and Dair pulled him toward the buffet tables piled high with delicacies Aiden could easily identify and others he couldn't even guess at.

Dair immediately pounced on a tray of what appeared to be *saganaki*. The crisp crust of golden cheese pulled away as Dair bit through it. He handed one to Aiden. "Grab as much dairy as you can. Mother said we will have to begin rationing it since the border is closed."

Aiden looked at the plate of flambéed cheese. "You do not have cows or goats here?"

Dair shook his head. "We have tried to maintain herds within Spring, but it never ends well. If some of the livestock do survive the transition to such rich grazing, they eventually get picked off by the bwbachod. Some of them simply cannot help themselves. The fresh meat is too enticing, even if the milk is good too." He stuffed another piece into his mouth.

Aiden looked about at the platters with more appreciation. Dishes filled with honeycomb and milk mixed with platters of raw vegetables and several crocks of stew. But there were also jars of smoke and plates of raw meat. It seemed there were many different appetites to be filled. He picked up a bowl of fruit and frowned at the small, blue beads sprinkled over the top.

He picked up a fork and poked at one. The tines poked a hole into the outer layer and juice dripped from it, revealing a small white seed within.

Aiden's eyes widened. A pomegranate seed. Something in his chest snagged and he had to take another deep breath. How long had it been since he'd seen Penelope? Since he held her in his arms? The months felt like years, and he only had years without her to look forward to.

A vision of shadow and stars sidled up next to him, peering over his bowl. "I see you've discovered the *toradh na beatha*," Shirina said.

"The pomegranate seed?" He pointed with his fork.

Shirina nodded. "It is what mortals refer to as 'Faerie fruit.'" A blue-haired fae with twirling horns took a bowl from the other side of the table and popped the fruit into her mouth with a smile. Shirina picked up her own bowl and plucked out a seed. "Though it resembles a pomegranate, it can be very dangerous for mortals to eat. This fruit grows on the summer side of Crann Mòr and was given to us by Danu to strengthen our magic and our bond with Her." She placed the seed in her mouth and bit down.

Aiden looked again at the tiny seed in his bowl. "Can I eat it?"

Shirina chuckled warmly. "You have already been accepted by this Land and Her magic. I do not think you will come to any harm."

Aiden speared a forkful of fruit, the little bits of blue clinging to the larger pieces of what looked like melon and stuck it in his mouth. The tiny pods burst with sweetness and something deep in his very soul clicked into place. His eyes closed and he felt his magic settle in his bones. He hadn't even realized how much pressure had built up inside of him until it eased.

Shirina laughed and Aiden opened his eyes to see her glittering smile. "You can see why we serve it at parties. It does more good for our spirits than any drink or any other food."

He took another bite before speaking again. "I can easily see why."

Once he finished that bowl and Shirina had plied him with a cup of punch and a plate piled with Faerie delicacies, he found a spot along the wall to lean against. Anyone who passed by gave him a deferential nod or bow, but no one got close, and no one invaded his privacy. It was... nice.

He finished off the several items that featured the blue pomegranates in them and stood to look for a place to put his plate. His gaze swept over every inch of the room, and he could not find a single discarded dish anywhere. His brows furrowed as he took a step forward.

"I'll take the plate, My Sovereign," said a small voice.

Aiden startled and looked down to see a creature standing no higher than his knee. Bat-like ears drooped down off the side of its face and a round little nose sat beneath two large, brown eyes. A plain, black cap covered the top of its head, but tight, red curls fell down the tiny creature's back, reaching nearly to the hem of its dress. One spindly arm stretched up, its four fingers spread out to reach for the plate Aiden held.

A brownie.

"O-of course," Aiden stammered, passing the plate. He stopped himself before he blurted out a 'thank you.' "You are too kind."

It disappeared with his dish.

Aiden stood there, mystified. Brownies weren't known for revealing themselves, let alone speaking to anyone. His eyes scanned the room, but he didn't see hide nor hair of another of the mysterious little folk.

"Ah, there you are," said Dair, coming up next to him. "Enjoying yourself?"

"Actually, yes." And he was surprised to find his words true. This was the first event he'd ever attended where the guests didn't overtly stare or crowd him. In Olympia, he'd never gone to a single party without someone bumping into him or his shoes meeting something sticky. Here, not even the ladies' vibrant dresses rubbed against his legs and none of them swooned if he got too close.

Dair laughed before being invited to dance by a group of banshees. He left Aiden to watch.

Dancers flooded the middle of the room. From where he stood, Aiden could see where the musicians, a band of multiple variations of fae and just as many instruments, played in the far corner. There were groups of Tuatha chatting along the edges of the room as well as a few wandering off to find entertainment in the gardens or the game rooms Aiden overheard were somewhere in the halls.

Lights somewhat similar to magelights floated in the air around them. He hadn't paid much attention to them before, but the sheer amount of them hovering above the crowd drew his eye.

Fiadh came out of the crowd in time for Aiden to ask, "What do you call those?"

Fiadh looked up. "The wisps?"

Aiden's brow furrowed, but as he watched, he realized the lights *were* will-o-the-wisps. They moved slower than the ones near the floor, doing their best to stay still and provide light to the room.

"Do you often use wisps as a form of light?"

"It is mostly for aesthetic." Dair returned to his side, his cheeks slightly flushed from the dance with the banshees who were now circling a pair of satyrs. "*Màthair* appreciates the color they add to a party. She is one of few, besides the púca, who can get them to do anything she wants."

"Why is that?"

The two shared a look. "She is the most powerful Tuatha in the Night Court," Fiadh stated. "Your mother was the only one who could ever outmatch her magically and it was only because of their differences in *tiodhlacan an spioraid*."

Aiden recalled Thaen using those words and wracked his brain for the translation. He shook his head. "What does that mean again?"

"Their gifts. Their special abilities were very different." Fiadh watched his wife mingling in the crowd with a warm smile. "Shirina has power over the night sky. She can extend the night for as long as she wants, can move the stars about, or even cause an eclipse."

Aiden's eyes flew wide. "I cannot even imagine the price of such a gift."

Fiadh laughed. "It is silly really. She cannot rest in the dark. If she is to sleep, she must do so during the day."

Aiden shook his head. The way magic worked in Faerie boggled his mind. "And my mother?"

Fiadh grinned. "She could manipulate time."

"She could do what?"

Dair laughed. "Yes, Auntie Morana could mess with time. Who do you think helped create the Fuath?"

Aiden held out his hands. "Wait. Are you telling me my mother was the one who created the border? I thought it was the High Queen."

"High Queen Rìanoch placed Am Fear Liath Mòr to guard the Fuath," said Dair, "but she did not make it. And Auntie Morana was not its sole creator either. There were two."

"How could there be two creators?"

"The same way the mages combine their powers," said Fiadh. "When there is such a strong connection between two magic wielders, like parents and children, husbands and wives, or even siblings, they can use their bond to combine or enhance their magic. I know in Olympia you usually only see it in families with the same gift, though there have been accounts of married couples accessing each other's magic. It is easier to do as Tuatha, especially within the same Courts. Once a connection is made, the two magic users can easily access each other's magic."

"But I thought my mother never married." At least no one had told her she had.

"She did not," Fiadh answered.

"Then who helped her?"

Fiadh lifted a hand and gray mist swirled around his palm. "I did."

24
HEALING AND TIME

Dearest Penny,

I feel as if these letters continue to grow shorter and shorter. I'm finding myself with less and less time to think about them. Time is such an odd thing when we are given things to measure it by.

My last letter was a bit morose, so I've decided to write only about happy things for this one.

Devan and I had the opportunity to walk around Eagallach yesterday. The city is beautiful at night, the stars glittering and the people out enjoying the scenery. We found the most adorable little shopping center. We learned about all the best places to go to market. I figure if we're going to be here for the long haul, we should adapt.

I was able to collect a group of women to talk to. Devan has been helping me meet more people and between everyone in the group, we have a rather put together gossip vine. It's only getting better and I'm beginning to feel a bit more centered. No one can replace you though.

That's all for now. I'm looking forward to the day I can return home. I have so much I want to share with you that I feel I can't in these letters.

Your Newly Optimistic Friend,
Angelica

PENNY'S PACKING GREW DISTRACTED BY THE CENTAUR RACING OUTSIDE the window, scanning the horizon for the other two huntresses. They'd gone to take Nikki—whose name Penny learned but could not pronounce to save her life—to report to the Fae High Council on their way back to her home in Spring.

Dìoghaltas, the centaur, had recovered in the short three days they'd been staying with Farrah's family. Penny marveled as the centaur charged through the open field only days after her injury. Annalysa had also fixed the large cut on her shoulder and her cracked ribs. Only a small scar was left on her shoulder that was supposed to fade and the ache in her torso was nearly gone. Penny hadn't asked for aid, wishing to get to Aiden as soon as possible, but when Farrah had noticed her wincing, that argument had done little good. The healing was miraculous to say the least, even after having experienced her own quick healing after Adira had shot her with the crossbow in Olympia.

It felt like years had passed since that first healing. Since she woke up to Aiden's hand in hers. Since they'd shared their first kiss. By the Goddess, she missed him. A shadow hovered over her heart—the sun hidden behind a cloud, shriveling up the beating drum inside her chest.

A sigh slipped out from between her lips. She couldn't be thinking such things. It would swallow her whole. She grabbed another pouch of dried meat and placed it at the bottom of her pack. The plan began its almost constant repetition in her mind once again.

Have Farrah portal her to Winter.

Find Angelica somewhere in Eagallach.

Get a meeting with Aiden.

Make sure Spot had found him.

Stop Adira from attacking at the revel.

The invitation sat among the things she needed to pack, the glittering parchment inviting yet intimidating. Going to a *fae only* revel would not be in the cards for her. Getting to Aiden before the revel was crucial. She'd need to speak with Angelica about getting a dress. Penny's borrowed tunic hung to her knees and the rolled-up leggings she wore underneath could not be considered proper attire for any kind of Court appearance. All of Farrah's other clothing either wouldn't fit over her hips or pooled around her feet. And all of it was much more casual than she would've believed, considering how much color and style the fae in Olympia's Court had always flaunted. However, even if the Courts dressed more informally this time, she would stick out like a corn stalk in a barley field if she went to the Winter Court in anything Farrah—or the two older copies of her—owned.

No, she would find Angelica, gather everything she needed for an audience with the Winter Court, and then get to Aiden. She stuffed another tunic in with the rest of her supplies. There was plenty of time left until the equinox. She would accomplish her tasks with time to spare. And who knew? Maybe they could take down Adira at the party and this whole thing could be over in a night. Penny could stay to help round up the rest of the rebels with Aiden and Spot, then return to Olympia.

Her fingers fiddled with the strap of her pack. *I hope Spot's all right.* Had he reached Eagallach yet? What would Aiden think, seeing him? She prayed he would at least find some comfort in having his companion by his side. At least, until she could reach him.

"What are you sighing about over there?" Nonnie thumped her cane as she walked toward Penny. "It can't be over our new little king, now can it?"

Penny felt her cheeks burn, Nonnie hitting it right on the mark. Farrah's grandmother was always around, waiting for a story. Or a good joke, depending on whichever struck her fancy right then.

"I'm ready to get moving," Penny confessed, not willing to admit she was pining.

"Do you have everything you need?"

Penny looked over her pack and the few other items left to add. "I believe so." Her borrowed cloak would go on top, easily accessible for when they reached Winter's capital. She pushed it aside and picked up the invitation. The words curled around one another, jots and tittles swirling in the thick brush strokes of the letters.

Nonnie gently took the parchment from Penny's fingers. "It was fortunate you retrieved this. It is a very valuable thing to be in possession of." She tucked the pristine paper carefully into the sack. "It is always interesting that the tools we need always come from the most troubling of situations."

"How do you mean?"

Her hand patted the pack where she'd tucked the invitation. "If you had not been imprisoned by that cursed woman, you would not have gained this key to thwart her." She looked out the window. "The Goddess often has plans for us, but we are not always able to see them when our vision is clouded with the pain of the moment." She turned back to Penny, settling a hand on her cheek. "I think it is often in those moments that we not only receive the keys to our freedom, but also keys for ourselves. Should we have to endure such hardship? Maybe not, but I appreciate that our Great Mother gives blessings in spite of others' best efforts to frustrate them."

Penny took a shuddering breath as Nonnie's hand retreated. She looked up at the older woman. "Are you sure you don't have a gift? Maybe it's seeing through others' muddled thoughts." When speaking with the matrons of the family, Penny had discovered Nonnie had not been given any kind of unique gift of her own. Only the typical ellylon abilities. She did have an affinity to use rune stones and watch patterns to make guesses about the weather and things, but Penny knew of multiple humans in Olympia that could do the same.

"I have all the gifts I need," Nonnie chuckled. "That particular attribute is simply the wisdom of living a long life and seeing the ends of many roads." She settled her hands on her waist. "When do you and my granddaughter leave?"

Penny knew whom she referred to. "Farrah and I are planning to portal tomorrow afternoon if we can. Annalysa says my ribs won't be completely healed until morning at the earliest."

"Well, my daughter certainly knows best." Nonnie gave Penny an exaggerated wink.

Annalysa stepped into the room. "What do I know best about?"

Nonnie looked at Penny with a knowing twinkle in her eye. She'd obviously been aware her daughter was around the corner. "Oh, nothing. Are we ready for luncheon?"

Farrah came bustling in, a steaming pot dangling from a cloth in her hands. "It's just here!" She walked toward them, but in her haste, she ran into the edge of the table, sending the pot flying into the air. It smacked on the floor at Annalysa's feet, spewing its contents up her skirts.

"Mama!" Farrah yelped and ran to her mother with a cloth snatched from the table. "Step back before it burns."

Annalysa took a step back, her slippered feet popping out of the sticky pudding. Steam wafted from the substance. Farrah hissed when she got some on the back of her hand and hastily wiped it off. She helped Annalysa clean it from her legs, leaving behind red welts.

Farrah turned to Penny. "Can you go with Nonnie and get the burn cream? We'd best get it on as quick as we can."

Annalysa rolled her eyes. "Farrah, my child, it will sit until after we get this cleaned up. You know I cannot feel it anyways."

Penny had learned that the price for Annalysa's healing touch was the loss of the sensation of touch itself. With the amount of magic she'd used to heal Penny and the centaur, it would likely be days before she would recover.

Farrah frowned up at her mother. "Just because you can't feel it doesn't mean you're not hurt."

"We will fetch it." Nonnie stood from beside Penny. "Come, Nell."

Penny followed Nonnie into the healing room near the front of the house. A clean table stood in the middle; a crisp, white sheet draped over its sides. An array of cupboards lined the walls, housing a variety of jars and boxes with labels Penny couldn't decipher. Nonnie shuffled around the room, poking through the shelves until her gnarled fingers grasped a jar and she handed it to Penny. "Here," she said with a chuckle, "run this out to Farrah before Anna can bite her."

Penny plucked the jar from Nonnie's outstretched hand and jogged back to the dining room. Annalysa sat on the bench next to the table as Farrah used a mop to wipe up the sticky mess. When Penny reached Annalysa's side, Farrah set the mop against the wall and began lathering the concoction on her mother's legs.

"Sorry about the food," said Farrah when Nonnie returned

to the room. "We have some cold cuts in the ice box, and I can climb into the cellar for some carrots and apples."

"Good idea, little one," said Nonnie. "Nell and I will get the rest of this cleaned up while your *màthair* lets that cream soak in."

Farrah nodded and sprang out the door like a rabbit. Penny heard her call out to Dìoghaltas in the field, though the words were in the old tongue.

Penny passed Nonnie the mop and went to the kitchen for another rag. The wind blew through the open window above the washbasin, rustling a paper tacked to the wall. It looked like a calendar, but the dates were all wrong. She slung the rag onto her shoulder and untacked the paper.

Her eyes attempted to decipher the words written, but none of it made sense. Her thoughts carried her back into the dining room where she lifted the parchment to show Annalysa and Nonnie. "Do you follow the same calendar as they do in Olympia?"

"My girl," replied Annalysa, "where do you think they got it?"

Penny flipped it around so she could see the marks crossing off the days. "But it's the wrong date."

Nonnie's head tilted. "What do you mean?"

Farrah walked back into the room with more food. "What's going on?"

Penny waved the small calendar in the air. "This says we're in the third month, but we should barely be in the second month of the year."

All three women met each other's eyes. Annalysa shifted on the bench. "How long have you been in Faerie, Nell?"

Penny thought back. "A little over a month. It's been five and a half weeks since the winter solstice and I went through the portal the day after. The day Prince—*King* Aiden was brought here."

"Winter solstice?" Annalysa asked. "I think perhaps the

true timeline slipped past us when you were regaling us with the tale of your journey here."

Penny had told them the short version, doing her best to get through as much as possible as quickly as she could to convince them to help her. Had she not mentioned the dates to them? She was sure she had.

Maybe.

Farrah set her hand on Penny's arm. "Pe—*Nell*, it has been longer than a month since King Aedon arrived."

Penny felt her brows furrow deeper. "No, I've been in Faerie only five weeks at the most."

Nonnie wrapped an arm around her. "How long were you in the Fuath?"

"The what?"

"The Mist," Farrah translated. "How long were you trapped in the Mist?"

Great Goddess, that had been so long ago. "Uh, maybe an hour or two? It wasn't more than a day, that's for certain."

Nonnie led her over to the table. "I do not know how much the Olympians on the other side are aware of the magic of our border, but the flow of time is disrupted within the Fuath."

Penny nodded. "Yes, we've had people come out older, younger, or the same age they had been when they went in, but they'd been gone years before their return."

"That is the magic of the Fuath. There are ways to cross it without being affected, but only the High Council knows. When they allow anyone to cross, one of them is there to negate the effects."

Penny couldn't get any air into her lungs. No one had been there to greet her. She'd gone through without permission.

"Child, I am sorry to be the bearer of bad news," Annalysa cut in, "but winter solstice was nearly three months ago."

Penny's heart beat against her rib cage, the pain nearly making her believe she'd broken her ribs again. "What? That can't be right. It can't."

Nonnie slipped the paper out of Penny's hand and pointed to a line of written words in a square on the page. "We celebrate spring equinox in ten days."

25
ABRUPT

Auntie Tori would drain the Winter Court's coffers. Aiden was sure of it.

Well, if they had coffers. Aiden didn't even know what Faerie's coffers looked like or if he had any access to them. It would make sense that the royal household would have some kind of income. Most fair folk had money when they came into Olympia. He would have to talk to Shirina if he had his own household accounts and what he needed to do to access them —especially if Auntie Tori was going to bleed everyone dry.

A scarlet hand full of cards smacked against the table. Three crowns and a queen.

Dair groaned and sank back into his chair. "Just take my money already!"

Auntie Tori scooped up the pile and deposited the coin into her pouch so quickly Aiden would've thought it hadn't existed if he didn't feel the lightness of his own borrowed coin purse. Fiadh had been generous enough to offer one before their afternoon game had begun.

As if summoned by Aiden's thoughts, Fiadh stepped through the sitting room doors, followed closely by Aunties

Niomi and Taddie. Unease creased the male's face and the two ancient women bickered back and forth like children.

"What is it, *Athair*?" Thaen asked from his seat by the door.

Fiadh glanced over at Aiden, his throat bobbing. "I hope this does not come out wrong, but Shirina has made an appointment for you this evening. She left me a note to tell you about it, since she wouldn't have the chance until she woke up."

Aiden straightened. "Has something happened?"

"Yes, do not keep us in suspense." Dair leaned forward in his chair, his obliterating loss quickly forgotten. "What has Mother put on your plate so she would not have to do it herself?"

All the aunties chuckled and shook their heads in mirth. Shirina did this to Fiadh often. Anything from entertaining guests to signing off on important matters, if Shirina didn't want to do it, it fell to Fiadh. Shirina never seriously shirked her duties, and it didn't seem as if Fiadh was ever hurt by it, but there had been more than one occasion when Fiadh was informed of something he had to do while Shirina was indisposed with something else—fabricated or otherwise.

Fiadh scratched the back of his neck and came to stand near the table. "It seems my sweetheart has decided that you need a sweetheart of your own."

Aiden felt the blood drain from his face and his stomach churned. "What does that mean?"

"It means she is playing *matchmaker* again." Dair kicked his boots up on the table. Fiadh glared until he removed them from the tabletop.

So, it was as Aiden suspected. "I don't know if that is such a—"

Auntie Niomi came up beside him. "Shirina has ideas about how a ruler needs their other half. Someone they can have beside them to help carry the weight. We attempted to dissuade her, but something about your foretelling stirred something in her and we could not talk her out of it."

"Best to simply go along with it," Dair advised, patting him on the shoulder empathetically.

Aiden's heart shriveled in his chest, almost like it did when he'd used up too much magic speaking with the dead. The very idea of even looking at another female the way he'd looked at Penelope had his soul balking. It wasn't right, and it certainly wasn't right *right now*.

"Tell her I appreciate her thinking of me, but I simply cannot accept. There is so much going on at present and I cannot afford to be distracted." He wouldn't tell them about Penelope. Not yet.

Fiadh winced. "See, the thing is... well..."

"The lass is already on her way, hm?" Dair asked.

"She's just arrived."

Aiden groaned and thumped his forehead on the table, scattering his losing hand of cards.

"Stop fidgeting, Little Shadow," chided Shirina. She sent a wisp of shadow to brush hair out of his eyes as he straightened his tunic for the third time since they'd left his rooms. "It is unbecoming of a High King."

"Please do not make me do this." He even clasped his hands together for effect. "I will do anything to get out of this."

Shirina clicked her tongue. "Meeting a female is not the same thing as walking to your death, Aiden. Besides, her family will take it as a slight if you do not appear for supper."

Aiden groaned for what felt like the millionth time that day and strode past her. "I do not want to be meeting any *females*. I actually plan to rule the rest of my days alone and pass the crown onto one of Thaen's children—Goddess grant that he has some."

Shirina paused behind him. "I do hope you are not serious."

Aiden turned around, his eyes on the floor. "I cannot imagine it, Shirina. I cannot imagine anyone at my side." *Anyone but Penelope.* Sweet Gaia, how his chest ached just thinking of her.

Shirina took his face in her hands, raising it up to meet her onyx eyes. "No one should have to live the rest of their life alone, especially someone with so much life left to them. A hundred years is a long time to be alone, and there will be many hundreds in your future if Fiadh and I have anything to say about it." She patted his cheek. "Just meet her. Maybe you will be surprised."

He wouldn't be surprised, he was sure. But if he knew he wasn't going to be surprised, he couldn't be harmed by it, right? It would do more harm to deny Shirina's request than it would for him to have one evening where he had to play king.

"For you," Aiden said. "I will do it for you."

Shirina gave him a brilliant grin. "That is all I can ask for."

He allowed her to loop their arms together and lead him on toward the more formal dining hall reserved for guest visits. Fiadh waited for them at the door, nodding consolingly in Aiden's direction. Shirina gave his arm one last squeeze before taking Fiadh's and walking inside.

Aiden took another fortifying breath. It looked like he would just have to suffer through the evening. He could be cordial. Perhaps he could at least make another ally.

He pushed open the door, everyone rising from their seats at his entrance. A grimace nearly surfaced before he walled it behind a courtly mask. He still wasn't used to all of the pomp and ceremony.

"Deòir," Shirina spoke to the male seated across from her at the table, "may I introduce High King Aedon."

The male bowed in deference as Aiden made it to the head of the table—the place he least wanted to be at that moment. Aiden nodded and the green-haired male straightened. "It is an honor to meet you, My Sovereign." He gestured to his right. "This is my daughter, Saranae."

Aiden took in the curtsying lady at his left. Hair the color of mint cascaded in waves down her back. Skin the color of gingerbread made at winter solstice glowed in the candlelight from the plethora of lit flames around the room. She rose from her curtsy and met his eye. A dazzling smile stretched across her face. "Good evening, My Sovereign."

Dion and Evan would have already begun drooling. All Aiden could think was how his brothers would be trailing after this female like lovesick puppies. She was beautiful, even Aiden could admit that.

But she wasn't Penelope. Not one bit.

"A pleasure, Lady Saranae. You and your father are most gracious for joining us this evening." He gestured to everyone around the table. "Please, sit."

The hushed rustle of fine clothing and shifting chairs distracted everyone from Aiden for a moment, giving him a short reprieve. Why had Shirina chosen this girl? Did she have something to offer the Crown? Their meeting was rather sudden, giving Aiden the impression they may have approached Shirina themselves. Fiadh had told him Deòir was a member of the Summer Court. Perhaps Shirina was looking for a more political match for him than anything else.

Servants bustled into the room, platters balanced on shoulders or held up by large hands. The Winter Palace employed any and all types of fae, from the smallest pixie to the tallest troll. Bowls of some kind of creamy soup were placed in front of each dinner guest. Chicken floated about in the lemony-scented broth. Before he could grab his soup spoon, a hand settled on his forearm. He looked up to see Lady Saranae coyly smiling up at him.

"I must insist you call me Ranae." Her hand gave his arm a light squeeze and she didn't remove it from his sleeve.

He stared, even catching the tendril of his magic that shot across her fingers. He glanced up, everyone else watching him from the corner of their eyes. They were all waiting on him to take the first bite, as was custom, and this girl was keeping them from eating. He slowly pulled his arm away, looking at the arrangement of silverware around his bowl rather than at her reaction to his rebuff. But what else could he do? And why on earth did she *touch him*? Aiden lifted his spoon and took a bite, hurrying to allow the others at the table to do so as well. He glanced over at Lady Saranae, who didn't look as if his small rejection had affected her whatsoever.

Shirina cleared her throat. "Saranae, I hear you have recently been accepted for an apprenticeship."

"Indeed," the girl chirped. "The masters have been so welcoming and I am so looking forward to a more formal training."

Thaen had recently told Aiden about the magical apprenticeships the ellyllon undertook when their *tiodhlacan an spioraid* manifested. It happened later in their lives than it did for mages, considering their increased lifespan. Thaen had received his gift at fifteen, which was considered very young. Dair had been gifted at twenty-four. There were many gifts, and many were similar enough that at least one other Tuatha could assist in the transition. With the permanent prices of their magic, sometimes it took extra support for a newly gifted ellyllon to adapt.

What was her gift? Aiden turned to Fiadh, the question in his eyes. He didn't want to come across as impertinent, but if Fiadh could guess what he wanted to ask, he could do it without insulting someone.

Fiadh winked and turned to Lady Saranae. "Your gift is plant magic, is it not? A rare gift these days."

Aiden's spoon slipped from his fingers and clattered to the floor. Stars, was Danu trying to torture him? Really?

Every eye turned to him, and heat prickled the tips of his ears. "Excuse me." He reached down to grab the spoon and found it had disappeared, replaced with a clean one in its original spot on the table. *Bless the brownies.*

He straightened in his chair and took up his new spoon. A flicker of star-studded shadow slipped over his wrist, and he looked up to meet Shirina's questioning gaze. He shook his head surreptitiously.

Lady Saranae cleared her throat. "Why, yes. I am one of only three others with the gift, and I am the most proficient. I have just begun my training under the Green Man."

Shirina looked away from Aiden, surprise replacing the inquisitive expression. "The Green Man? How impressive!"

Lady Saranae leaned toward him. "Do you know of The Green Man, My Sovereign?"

He held his ground, though he did narrow his eyes at the way she crowded into his space and the slightly condescending way she asked. Perhaps the rest of his family hadn't picked up on it, but he'd learned more than enough about subtleties in communication—especially as an infamous prince.

"No, I do not know of The Green Man."

The female went on to explain about the ancient being trusted with the guardianship of Crann Mòr. It was said that this being was tasked with maintaining the architecture and watching for any disease.

Penelope would love to learn about this.

He shook his head of the intrusive thought. Penelope would never know about such things or even need to know. She was in Olympia, being taken care of by the other members of the Underworld.

He tried his best to return to the conversation.

"...and as I did have the highest rank of all of the other candidates, of course I was given first pick."

"I do not doubt it," Dair drawled from the other end of the table. A bit of silver-lined shadow tugged at his ear and Shirina sent him a disapproving glare.

But Lady Saranae turned her calculating smile on Aiden. "Have you considered applying for an apprenticeship, My Sovereign? Being so young and so new to the kingdom, I would assume it would be beneficial to you."

He saw his shadows stirring near the feet of his chair and pulled them back in. "Do they have an apprenticeship for High Kings who are also half-mage? I would love to request such a thing if available."

Lady Saranae went speechless and Dair had to cover up a snort at the other end of the table.

Honestly, what fair folk would ever train the likes of him? His magic worked the way the mages did, not the fair folk. He was High King of a people he was not raised with. There really wasn't anyone to properly train him for any of this.

Thaen straightened in his chair as the next course was brought out. "Actually, *Ranae*, King Aedon has been training under my watch and will not be looking for any other masters."

Aiden met his cousin's gaze—well, as much as one could meet Thaen's gaze—with gratitude. Thaen was right. Thaen and the rest of the family had done so much for him. It would be ungracious of him to forget that. He stuffed half of a roll into his mouth, the soft bread practically melting in his mouth and bringing the smile he had tried to suppress to his face.

Lady Saranae perked up, interest oozing from her. "Oh, I didn't realize you had similar gifts. How exciting! Everyone knows Thaen's gifts are rare. Are yours like his?"

His smile vanished and he choked down the bread in his mouth. "No."

The three of them had experimented multiple times with it. Thaen could barely make out the forms still and claimed all of them looked the same. Dair could see them if he touched

Aiden, but not without the contact. Even though they were all slightly similar in some way, Aiden's was still not accessible by anyone else but him.

"Perhaps you are not with the right master then. I know most of them personally. I would be happy to introduce you to one who had gifts more similar to yours."

A chuckle rang out from the other end of the table. "Yeah, that is not going to happen," said Dair. "There are no masters who can do what Aedon can."

Lady Saranae's father turned into the conversation. "Since we are already on the topic, what magic do you have, My Sovereign?"

A bit of shadow flicked past his ear. He bit his lips together between his teeth. No one asked about his magic. He'd been taught not to tell anyone. It was an oddity, one these somewhat important ellyllon would gossip about. He glanced at Shirina for help but found her gaze flicking between him and the nosy female next to him, not even noticing his plea.

Fine. He met the eyes of the pestering girl. "I don't go around bragging about the gifts the Goddess has given me."

That took the eager expressions off their faces, praise the Goddess. Saranae's father nodded, contemplation curving in the line of his brow. Disappointment flashed on Lady Saranae's face before being replaced with a mask of flirtatiousness. She laid another hand on his arm. "We simply have to get to know one another better."

After this disaster of a conversation? Not likely. He opened his mouth, ready to snub her a second time if he had to, when the doors slammed open.

All heads turned in the direction of the High Councilors at the door.

"My Sovereign"—the Spring Councilor bowed—"we must speak with you immediately."

Shirina stood. "What has happened?"

"They have attacked!" the blue-clad Councilor wailed. "They have attacked Flùranach!"

Aiden wracked his brain for where that was. Flùranach was Summer's capital if he remembered right. "Who has attacked?" he asked.

"The Isles of Aigean, My Sovereign," Sgiath replied. "And they have come in the name of The Cartographer."

Thaen spread the map of the entire continent and the Isles over the table. Dair danced about, fetching placeholders to keep the corners from curling up.

"They hit directly from the water." Deireadh pointed at the eastern coast where the capital of Summer nestled into its cove. "There are safeguards on the city, but the folk on the beach had no chance to escape. An entire legion came up on the waves and slaughtered anyone on the sand. The watchman that reported to us said there were multiple elite members of the Trident at the head of the force. They ransacked the city."

"Where are the rest of the citizens?" asked Aiden.

Sgiath frowned. "A number of them made it out, but we cannot say how many. The ones that could fly have already arrived in Crann Mòr ahead of the host moving through the Farraige Gaineamh. We do not yet know how many more escaped."

Aiden looked over the map. The Isles lay to the southeast of Flùranach. Summer's capital was a flourishing oasis on a land that stood mostly barren. The water folk would have had to bypass miles of Olympian coastline to attack them. And why attack Summer? There was little to be conquered there, the Farraige Gaineamh making the Court nearly inhospitable. In order to make a push into the heart of Faerie, the water folk would have to move across the dunes.

"And they only attacked from the water?" Aiden asked. "Where are The Cartographer's men?"

Deireadh shook his head. "We do not know. All we were able to gather is that the Aigeans attacked in the name of the rebels."

That did not bode well. Durant was not one for staying out of a fight. What was her plan here?

"It is not to be born!" the Summer Councilor thundered. "The Isles have no reason to attack us!"

The door to the study banged open and Farrah rushed in. "They've sent a message."

The Summer Councilor attempted to snatch it from her, but she skirted him and set it in Aiden's hand. "It is addressed to you, My Sovereign."

Aiden broke the seal and read through the message quickly. "They claim to have joined with The Cartographer and now declare themselves enemies to Faerie and all Tuatha Dè Dannan. They demand we hand over the faerie-glass throne and surrender the kingdom to the rebels. If we don't adhere to the demands, they claim they will flood all of Summer within the fortnight." The people still traversing the dunes would be washed out as well.

"The wretches! The worms!" cried the Summer Councilor. "How dare they attempt to threaten us. We are far superior to those maggots!"

"Peace," Aiden commanded. "There is no room for that kind of talk here. We must look at this from a logical standpoint."

"I agree, My Sovereign," the Spring Councilor said. "There must be a reason as to why the Isles have agreed to such a thing."

"I know Queen Bestia would not agree unless there was a logical explanation." Evan had called the queen a shrewd ruler more than once. Rissa claimed the ruler of the water folk was cynical and a bit intense, but never foolish. "We do not have the whole picture yet."

"Perhaps we should treat with the queen," Sgiath suggested.

Aiden waved the message in his hand. "This was signed and sealed by the queen herself. I do not think there is much merit to that idea." There was not even a request to negotiate. Only the bold demand of their surrender.

"What would you have us do?" Shirina asked him.

Wind and snow, what should he have them do? He rubbed a hand down his face, looking down at the map. "We need to figure out where The Cartographer and her men are. I do not know if this is meant to be a distraction or an actual attack, but knowing who leads the rebels, it is likely both. We also need to get the refugees to safety before these threats come to pass. What kind of militia is there in Summer?"

"Militia, My Sovereign?" The Summer Councilor asked.

"Yes. Is there a base somewhere in Flùranach where the local military is trained?"

"Summer does not have any military."

Aiden straightened. "Is there a collective force of fae that act as a military power then?"

"The closest thing Summer has to an army is the guard-house in the capital and the protections the noble families hire against thieves and the sort. There is not need for much else."

"What about the rest of Summer?" He gestured to the miles of land from river to river bordering the season. "Who metes out justice among the Court? How do the ruling families take care of all their people."

Shirina set a hand on his arm. "Aedon, besides Flùranach, there are not any cities in Summer. Stars, there are not more than a dozen small villages, and most are governed by the bwbachod and monitored by the Wild Hunt when needed. There has not been need of fighters for over two hundred years."

Aiden staggered back. "Are you telling me Summer has no kind of protection? No way for us to fight against the Aigeans encroaching across the Land?"

She shook her head in dismay.

He whirled to the Spring Councilor. "What about Spring? We could send out some of the folk from there to help the refugees out of the dunes."

"My Sovereign, while we will send as many folk as we can, there may not be enough."

Aiden blinked. He blinked again. "I need numbers. Right now, how many folk do we have capable of fighting in Spring?"

"There are one thousand seasoned warriors in Spring."

Aiden fell into a chair. "In Autumn?"

"There are around five thousand," Sgiath responded.

"Winter has seven," Shirina added without provocation.

"And... And how many did we lose in Summer?"

Sgiath gave a heavy sigh. "We do not know."

His thoughts spun. The Aigean Trident had an elite force of one thousand members alone. Evan had reported at the beginning of last year after a visit to his mother that the Aigean Navy had a total of ten thousand active water folk in training and another twenty thousand inactive—not to mention the guard, the island militias, and the local law enforcers. If what the council told him was true, Faerie had less than twenty thousand folk who could fight.

And if the Aigeans were working in conjunction with Durant, who had all the rebels in Olympia and the battalion already here...

We are all going to die.

Thaen must have felt Aiden's tension because he was in front of him in the next instant. "Breath, little cousin. Do not give up hope so quickly."

Shadows pooled around Aiden's feet. "Why? Why are there so few? Why do we not have folk who can fight?"

The Spring Councilor joined them. "That is a rather long story."

"Not so long," Shirina tutted. "It is because of the wars."

"The Faerie Wars?" Aiden asked.

Shirina nodded. "Before High Queen Rìanoch took the faerie-glass throne, our people had been at war with the humans off and on for over fifty years. During that time, many of the fae lost their lives. While humans have been blessed with easy procreation, the fae are not. During the wars, the humans continued to reproduce, each family blessed with multiple children who grew quickly and became warriors in their own right. Even the mage population expanded, though their gifts diminished as their ties to the Land dwindled. But while those families grew, the fae did not. The ellyllon especially. Bwbachod have an easier time, most blessed with children every decade or so. The ellyllon, on the other hand, are fortunate if they are blessed with half a dozen in their lifetime. It is one of the reasons so many have connected with the humans, their desire for posterity driving their actions. Children are such a sacred gift that Danu has given us."

"So, while the humans grew and replenished their armies, the fae did not."

"Precisely. When High Queen Rìanoch was able to dethrone the old rulers, she realized that, if the fighting continued, Faerie's population would be demolished, leaving us completely vulnerable to invasion."

"And so," Fiadh swooped into the conversation, "Morana and I saved the day."

"Indeed you did, my love," Shirina said to Fiadh. She turned back to Aiden. "Your mother and Fiadh built the Fuath to guard our land from invasion in order for it to recover. We gave the humans what is now called Olympia and cut ourselves off from the rest of the continent to recover."

"How many fae were killed in the Faerie Wars?"

"Two hundred thirty thousand fae including the children," answered Sgiath.

The number devastated him. "And how many have been born in the years since?"

"One thousand two hundred eleven have been born on this side of the Fuath since the end of the Faerie Wars," the Spring Councilor said. "And there are two more expected at the end of the year. A pair of dwarf sisters living in the city under Eagallach are lucky enough to be expecting within a few weeks of one another."

The Faerie Wars had nearly killed off the fae race. "That's why there's practically no one living outside of the capitals," Aiden mumbled. He had traveled all over Faerie through his connection to the Land and not once had he seen anything larger than what could be labeled a small village besides the capitals of each season and Crann Mòr. The goblins had nests of a few hundred or so scattered about; there were twenty active centaur herds of two dozen or so; a flock of harpies lived on a peak at the border of Winter and Spring; a shimmer of sylphs dwelled in the Farraige Gaineamh. But there hadn't ever been a group larger than one or two thousand outside the capitals.

"Do we have a census of how many fae are even in Faerie?"

A few papers shuffled along the tabletop as Sgiath withdrew a thick sheet of parchment from a stack. "The total we have on record is six hundred fifty-three thousand and eight. Of those, about six hundred thousand are bwbachod and only about fifty thousand are ellyllon. We were the ones targeted most in the war because of our *tiodhlacan an spioraid* and have the hardest time bearing children."

"By the Goddess," Aiden gasped. Olympia's capital itself housed at least six hundred thousand alone.

"You understand now why the Fuath had to go up," the Summer Councilor said solemnly. "Why we do not have a fighting force."

Aiden stood and stared at the map, the dark line cutting across the bottom edge of the page. "I understand why the Fuath was created, what I don't understand was how you could neglect to provide protection for the folk left."

"We did have protection," he argued. "We had the Fuath. We had our High Queen. There were only a few left after the battles and no one believed there would be anymore fighting—at least not until we recovered. It was painful to drudge up our losses. Better to look toward peace and healing."

"Your savior of a High Queen is dead!" Aiden snapped. "We have an army within our borders and folk are dying because none of you saw fit to prepare them for another fight because you were concerned about how it would hurt them to remember." He bared his teeth. "Do you think losing their homes and their families now was worth the so-called peace?"

"You do not understand—"

"You are absolutely right. I *don't* understand how you could believe this would not happen again as the people you had fought for so long grew and advanced while you tried not to dwell on your hardships."

"We hoped we would not see war for another millennia," the Spring Councilor said, his voice empty of the conviction he so often carried.

Aiden couldn't take anymore. He shrugged off Shirina's hand and made his way to the door.

"Well, you were wrong, and everyone is about to pay the price for your misplaced hope."

And he slammed the door behind him.

26
FAREWELLS AND HISTORY

FARRAH SLUNG A PACK OVER HER SHOULDER AND KISSED NONNIE ON the cheek. "Take care of Mama while I'm gone."

Nonnie swatted her arm playfully. "You know she is the one who has to take care of me, little one."

Penny smiled, but an ache settled in her chest. Who was watching over Mother now that Penny was in Faerie? Did the Underworld still have her monitored? She had enough friends in the capital she could rely on, but was she only creating more havoc under the name of the rebellion? Was she even part of the rebellion?

Penny crept past Farrah's family, stepping in front of the centaur standing in the doorway of the front room. The Huntresses had yet to return for their comrade, but they expected them back anytime. She gave the fierce Huntress a chagrined smile. "I'm sorry about your injury."

The centaur grinned. "Facing off with a mage was a new experience for me. I shall wear this scar with pride."

Farrah pulled Penny along the line and leaned close to her

ear. "Centaurs have this weird obsession with scars anyway. She'll likely brag about it everywhere she goes. You'll be famous before summer settles."

Penny grimaced and gave the centaur a hasty wave goodbye. Next, she stopped in front of Nonnie who swept her up into a hug.

"Never lose that spirit of adventure, my girl."

Penny pulled back, staring at the older woman as an echo of this moment flashed through her thoughts. The same smell of herbs and crisp leaves sang in her lungs, but she'd been standing in front of a tapestry of Faerie hanging in the window of Farrah's shop almost a year ago.

Nonnie gave her a smile that Penny couldn't label. The elder female remained a mystery to be certain.

Penny stepped to where they'd cleared a spot for the portal. Farrah took in a deep breath and stretched out her hands. Tendrils of black spilled from her palms and spun in the air in front of her. Penny caught flickers of red in the black mass as it shifted into the portal. She hadn't noticed them in the previous portals Farrah had pulled her through.

Farrah's hands fell to her side, and she turned to Penny. "Are you ready?"

The familiar crawling sensation crept up her neck, but it stopped before reaching her heart. Working with Aiden had certainly diminished her fear of the dark, but it still caught her in its claws every so often.

She nodded, not trusting herself to speak.

Annalysa came through the door. "You know where you are going, right?" she asked her daughter.

Farrah rolled her eyes. "Yes, Mama. There's no need to fret. I'll have us to the Olympian embassy before nightfall."

"You have your map?"

Farrah patted the pack on her shoulder. "Packed it with all the unnecessary supplies you made me take. You know I can get things in Eagallach."

Annalysa's eyes narrowed. "I will not have you go without supplies because of your foolish pride. You may be sixty-three, but you are still young enough for me to worry over you."

Farrah kissed her mother on the cheek. "We'll be fine." She wrapped her in a hug and stepped away.

Penny gave both older women a smile. "I can't express how grateful I am for all that you've done for me."

Nonnie clucked her tongue. "Now, now. Do not go flinging words like that around here. Worse folk will take advantage of a thing like that, hoping to collect favors and such. In Faerie, everything comes at a price." Penny winced, forgetting the rules about owing favors. Nonnie gave her a toothy grin. "But we are Goddess fearing folk in this house, and we do good in Her name."

"Then you are better than most," replied Penny, "and I will pray the Goddess blesses your home. I certainly won't forget everything I've learned while under your roof."

Annalysa leaned in and kissed Penny's forehead, the first sign of affection she'd seen the woman give anyone but her family. "Go, Little Nell, and save our king."

Penny tightened the straps on her shoulders and followed Farrah into the portal.

Eagallach was...

By the Goddess, there weren't words to describe it. Penny's eyes soaked it all in. The snow dusted rooftops. The shimmering icicles dangling from every overhang. The sun glittering off the ice of the frozen lake. Farrah had said its name, but Penny couldn't remember or pronounce it properly. Perhaps Devan would be willing to teach her pieces of the old tongue when he and Angelica returned to Olympia.

"Where's that *blasted map*?"

Farrah emptied the contents of her bag for the third time, still not finding the elusive map she'd sworn she packed with the rest of her stuff.

"Should we go back to get it?"

Farrah pushed out an exaggerated laugh. "And allow my mother the honor of saying 'I told you so?'" She shook her head. "Great gourds, no. I'd never hear the end of it."

Penny looked about, noticing the people milling about on the shoveled streets. *How many times a week do they have to do clear the snow?*

Farrah harrumphed and stuffed a jingling bag of coin back into the pack. "The embassy is somewhere on the eastern peak if Mama remembered right." She pointed toward the towers in the distance. "We just have to follow the main road."

Penny looked about, not seeing any heavy traffic on the road they were on. "And where is the main road?"

Farrah bit her bottom lip, her eyes flicking about as if looking for directions but not finding any. "Let's follow this one for a bit. I'm pretty sure it goes there."

"You're pretty sure?"

Farrah fiddled with the strap of her bag for a moment. Penny could see something hiding in the flick of her lashes and the tap of her boots on the icy cobblestones. She blew out a breath. "I may have a teensy confession I need to make."

Penny quirked a brow but waited for Farrah to continue.

Farrah gave her a pained smile. "I have a slightly difficult time with directions."

Penny blinked. "What does that mean, exactly?"

"That the price of my gift, the portals, means I'm at a complete loss when it comes to knowing where I'm going. I get lost easily and frequently."

Realization brought a groan to Penny's throat. "Hence the map."

"Yes." Farrah rubbed a hand down her face. "Without it, I have no idea where we are or how to get to the embassy."

"Why couldn't you have taken us right to the embassy?"

"I've never actually been to that peak before, and it can be difficult to navigate portals anywhere I haven't been. I could have accidentally portalled us fifty feet above the city or right in the middle of the mountain and we would have been smashed in the rocks. It's much easier if I've been there and seen a wall where I don't have to worry about my portal hurting anyone."

Penny settled her hands on her hips and looked about. "Well, I suppose you can ask for directions, right?" If someone else was able to tell them where to go, it shouldn't be difficult to figure out.

Farrah nodded and took a step onto the street. "I'll just have to give them to you so you can do the navigating."

Penny followed closely behind. "So how does it work exactly? Have you always had trouble with directions or only when you use your magic?"

"The Tuatha Dè Dannan do not pay for magic the same way mages do. We are similar in how we do not receive our gifts at birth but are given them after we've grown into our other powers. I didn't receive mine until I was twenty-four.

"However, mages only pay as much as they need to use their gift at one time and then they either must refill their magic by paying that price or they empty the well of magic within them and die. Fair folk are given a permanent price and a permanent limit on how much we can do. Because I can portal wherever I want, I struggle with directions, though my father also uses portals but has paid for his magic with the inability to move at more than a walking pace." Penny laughed and Farrah elbowed her. "It may sound funny until you're running late, and your father can't walk down the stairs at more than a stroll. Or he can't outrun a predator without portalling away."

Penny hadn't thought of it like that. And what about

Farrah's other parent. "So, your mother can't only not feel when she uses her gifts, but she can't feel *at all*?"

Farrah nodded. "The ellyllon—those of us with the power to access Danu's unique gifts—"

"The *ellyllon*?" Penny interrupted.

Farrah snorted. "The humans twisted more than just our religion."

Penny's stomach sank. "I've been saying it wrong this entire time?"

"That and *bwbachod*. But anyway, the ellyllon have to pay for their gifts. Permanently."

Penny allowed the information to seep in as they walked. She knew the fae had more enhanced abilities than the mages in Olympia, she'd simply never realized how steep the price for them was. Even Aiden's heart damage seemed minor in comparison. At least his fast healing could counteract it. A permanent price would have him dead, his heart a dormant husk in his chest.

They continued down the avenue. Farrah stopped a few times, asking if anyone knew where the Olympian embassy was located, but few actually even knew it existed. Farrah spoke with one gentleman for several minutes before returning to Penny's side. "He claims there isn't a real embassy here since none of the humans have ever shown any interest in visiting until recently. He did suggest we go through the market to get to the eastern bridge and ask around. There was mention of a human man over there who went to the palace not so long ago. Word carried about that he was friends with the High King."

"It must have been Devan, Angelica's husband." He was a spy for Aiden after all. It made sense that Aiden would've reached out to him. Gratitude warmed Penny's chest. Perhaps he hadn't been alone this whole time.

"The nice male said he's seen a few humans at the other marketplace on the other peak as well. We just have to get to the bridge."

"Bridge?"

"Eagallach is made up of four peaks, all connected by a series of humongous bridges. We have to go northeast."

Penny looked up at the stars. Praise the Goddess there weren't any clouds. She looked down the street going eastward. "That way."

Humongous hadn't been far off.

Penny matched Farrah's gait as they reached the edge of the stone bridge. The structure spanned half a mile from one peak to the next and spread wide enough for a team of horses to turn around and not get stuck on either side. Walls a few feet above Penny's head blocked the wind from knocking anyone over the side, though barred windows allowed a view into the valley below.

Cold blew through Penny's thick coat as they stepped down the stairs leading onto the next peak. She'd heard things about Eagallach—mostly from Lord Hermen who had visited right after the treaty had been signed. But nothing could have prepared her for the market.

Penny drank it all in, a fatigued root getting her first drops of water. Wonder awoke within her as she watched the folk mill about, hawking wares and garnering attention toward their stalls. Penny had watched a few fae work their magic on Eleusia's market street but watching them here was an entirely different spectacle. Trinkets hung from stalls and foodstuffs sat packed in crates, ready to be bought or traded. Magic flew through the air. Shadows and lights skittered over the street, catching eyes and guiding hands toward the sellers.

And the patrons were just as riveting. The faces differed as vastly as the merchandise—greens, blues, and purples mixing with the more human skin tones, but the colors were all deeper somehow. Horns, tails, snouts, furs, and fangs even decorated the vibrant folk.

A group of children jumped through the snow piles sitting along the streets in front of Penny, shadows curling over their fingers as their parents called after them. It didn't matter that Penny couldn't pick out the words they hollered. She still understood the language here. The language of life and magic and love.

Farrah pulled her through the crowd until they popped out into a vast square and began making a circuit of the outer edge. Penny looked at every face in the crowd, watching for the radiant smile and the riot of curls she associated with her friend while also getting more glimpses of the wonderful square.

"Isn't it magical, Penny?"

Penny pulled her closer. "Keep your voice down."

Farrah gave her a strange look. "Why?"

"I don't need any folk using my name against me."

Confusion whirled in Farrah's eyes until clarity broke through. "Is that why you didn't use your real name at my house?" She threw her head back and laughed. "And here I thought you were simply trying to be sneaky."

Farrah had thought she was being *sneaky*? What did that even mean? "I'm confused," Penny admitted.

"That superstition only affects fae," Farrah explained. "Names are important in our culture, but we can't use them to harm humans. Yes, the fae have true names, but those are the names Danu has given us. We don't have any kind of power over names." Farrah gave her a playful nudge and laughed aloud. "Does everyone in Olympia believe that?"

Penny shook her head with a laugh to match Farrah's. It was such a silly thing, such a silly rule. It made sense now why people thought names would have power. It just showed what happened when a piece of truth got lost in translation.

Penny looked up to find dark, brown eyes studying her. "What?"

"I just haven't seen that Penny in a while. I liked it."

Penny felt her nose scrunch up. "What 'Penny?'"

A soft smile spread over Farrah's mouth. "The Penny that sees magic in everything, even in something as simple as names. My girl, you've grown up in the months since I've seen you."

Penny's steps slowed and Farrah pulled ahead of her. Had Penny changed so much in such a short time? It felt like yesterday she'd walked into Farrah's shop in Eleusia and studied the tapestry of Faerie hanging in her shop's window.

Is that tapestry even still there?

So much had changed. The rebellion had planted itself in her lands. They'd burned her house down around her. Mother had nearly been charged with being The Cartographer. Penny had learned about Adira Durant and moved into the palace in Olympia. She'd learned how to be a spy for the Crown.

She'd met Aiden.

He'd completely changed her life in a single year. She never would have imagined herself standing on one of the peaks of Eagallach in the heart of the Winter Court when she'd been gazing at the strings of that tapestry a year ago. Yet here she was, and it was because of him.

It was all because of him.

She caught back up to Farrah. "You said the palace is on the eastern peak, but are the lord's and lady's houses on the northern one?"

Farrah thought for a moment. "The Courts here aren't the same as the ones in Olympia. We don't have hundreds of noble families running amok. There are a select few in each Court, making up about twelve altogether, including each ruling family in each Court. Most of them are connected to the ruling families in some way at least. However, Winter is slightly different."

"How so?"

"All of the ruling family has always lived in the palace. Cousins, sons, nieces, and nephews. They stay and work together in the palace. Those that don't generally find their own houses somewhere in the city, wanting to be close, but wanting their own space."

"So, Angelica could be anywhere."

Farrah winced. "Yes, but my father told my mother where they were, him being all important and what not, and my mother had marked it on the map."

"The map we don't have."

Farrah swatted at her. "Don't get pessimistic on me now. Yes, the map we don't have. But I know she marked somewhere on Thiodhlaiceadh's peak—"

"Whose peak?"

"Thiodhlaiceadh is the name of the western peak, the one we are standing on." She opened her arms wide, gesturing to the mountain they stood on. "Anyway," she continued, "Mama marked their residence on this peak so all we have to do is ask around."

Penny looked back into the bustling crowd and her attention snagged on a tall, serious man standing in the center of the square. But her eyes drifted to the radiant woman standing next to him and staring directly at her in shock. Penny felt the tears gather and fall from the corner of her eyes. She took a step in their direction.

Angelica took a matching step, her eyes pulling even wider. "Penny?"

27
ARRIVE

"WHAT NEWS DO YOU HAVE FOR ME?" AIDEN ASKED AS THAEN STRODE into the parlor. The rest of the family had yet to arrive before supper was served in the formal dining room.

Thaen had gone to Crann Mòr with the other High Councilors while Aiden had stayed in Winter—against his better judgement. The High Councilors believed he could be in danger if he left Eagallach. Until they could account for everyone and check for any of Durant's men in the group coming through the Farraige Gaineamh, staying out of harm's way was their best solution.

Aiden prayed Thaen had arrived with a good enough picture of what was happening at Crann Mòr. Being so separated from the action didn't suit him—nor did he feel right allowing his folk to suffer without him there. If he could just figure this out...

Thaen handed him a piece of paper, numbers covering it in neat rows. "The Aigeans have captured fifteen hundred fae and are holding them in the city. The ones that escaped made it through the Farraige Gaineamh with a total of about five thousand. There are three hundred wounded and ninety died of injuries on the rough journey to the capital."

Aiden took in every blow those numbers delivered. "And where are they now?"

"We have housed a good number of them in the Tree as well as the city. Many had houses in the capital and the ones who didn't have been given sufficient places to rest."

A breath puffed between Aiden's lips. "I worry about so many of them being there. It will cause so much havoc, especially with the anointing happening so soon."

Thaen agreed. "We need to speak with the High Councilors about our next steps."

The rest of the dinner guests arrived only a few minutes later. The High Councilors had portalled back with Thaen, returning to discuss the equinox as well as the refugees. Aiden pocketed the missive, deciding to share the news with Fiadh and Shirina after supper. He prayed it could at least wait until then. The last several days had been chaos enough and he could see the strain in the set of everyone's shoulders.

Aiden sat at the head of the table. Again.

Perhaps he could simply ban rectangular tables. Insist they can only use round ones like the one in the family dining room. He was High King. No one would question it.

The High Councilors sat to the left of him, chatting about the coming weeks as Aiden's family shifted in their seats. Not only would Aiden need to return to Crann Mòr to deal with the attack on Summer, but the equinox was next week. Their time for family bonding was coming to an end.

"We are eager to proceed with the anointing," spoke the Spring High Councilor. "We are glad to see your progress and your quick acclimation to our history and culture. It is a testament to your family's character for certain." He gave Fiadh and Shirina a warm smile.

"You would think it a miracle if you saw how he acted those first few weeks," Dair said. "He nearly broke his neck trying to use his bedsheets as a rope to scale the palace wall."

All three eyes turned to Aiden's cousin then back to him.

Aiden sent a bit of shadow that bit into the back of Dair's calf. Dair jumped in his seat, but when Shirina asked if he was well, he simply waved her off.

Thaen met Aiden's eyes and they shared a smirk.

"It is obvious Our Sovereign needs to return to the capital," said the Spring High Councilor. "There is much that needs to happen, and he needs to cement his rule to the folk in these tumultuous times. Is Our Sovereign ready to take his rightful place?"

Fiadh leaned forward. "You can certainly ask him yourself since we are not the ones to answer such a question. But if the last few days has shown me anything, it is that Aedon will make a wonderful High King, should he choose to fully embrace what Danu has given him."

Aiden straightened as the eyes at the table met his. This was what he'd been preparing for. It had always been coming —no matter how much he wished it wouldn't have come so soon.

His eyes fell on the faces of his family around him. They had been such a support to him even in his first days when he was nothing but a curse on their household. They loved him unconditionally. Would the rest of Faerie be so welcoming? Looking back at the Councilors, he wasn't sure. But the magic coursing within his body had chosen him and that had to be enough.

He took a steadying breath.

The doors to the dining room burst open and everyone turned away from him.

Not again. Please don't come in here with more bad news.

A pair of guards escorted a young satyr into the room. The clop of the fawn's hooves echoed across the hardwood floor.

The trio bowed at the end of the table. Aiden watched them for a moment before remembering to release them from their show of respect. One of the guards stepped forward. "My

Sovereign, we have come to report an odd occurrence at the front gate."

The guard nudged the fawn forward and the horned head nodded. "Yes, yes. There was a creature sitting in the road, My Sovereign."

"What kind of creature?" Sgiath asked, intrigued.

The satyr shook his head. "I cannot say exactly, but it looks like some sort of canine."

"You have interrupted this meal for a dog lying in the road?" Summer's High Councilor boomed, the jowls hanging against his neck shaking.

The satyr shook but cleared his throat. "Of course not. The dog followed me into the courtyard outside. If it was just a normal dog, I would not have dared bring it to your attention, but this thing is nothing I have ever seen before."

Aiden tilted his head, a buzzing beginning to stir in his chest. "What does this dog look like?"

"He's gigantic, My Sovereign. Biggest dog I've ever seen, but that is not the odd part."

"Spit it out, fawn!" Dair whined.

"It's his head—well, his *heads*."

Aiden was out of his chair and running toward the door, his family calling his name from behind him.

It couldn't be. Could it?

Thaen caught up to him just as he reached the front doors leading out. "Let me go first. We do not know what this crea-ture wants. This could be some kind of ploy from the rebels."

Aiden shoved past him and pushed open the doors. He stopped on the top step, eyes widening at the gigantic creature sitting in the arch of the front gate. But those three, spotted heads and those lolling tongues were unmistakable.

"Spot!" he hollered and jumped down the steps. Thaen followed a beat behind.

All three of Spot's mouths took up a bark and he jumped up and down, his weight vibrating the ground.

Aiden threw himself at his dog, his arms that used to be able to somewhat wrap around all three necks barely wrapped around one. "My good boy." Tears welled up in his eyes as he hugged each neck. He took a step back, wiping the emotion from his cheeks. "What happened to you?"

"Aedon?" Shirina's voice sounded from the front door and Aiden turned to look back at the same time that Spot licked his head. Aiden groaned and tried to wipe the copious amount of saliva from his neck and hair. Spot slobbered a lot when he was normal size. Aiden would have to carry a towel and a bucket around everywhere he went from then on.

The rest of his family joined him. Fiadh looked up at Spot. "Do you know this creature?"

Aiden laughed, a real laugh that hurt his belly, but he couldn't help it. "This is my dog."

"Your dog?" Dair echoed. "This is what dogs look like in Olympia?"

Aiden shook his head. "Great Goddess, absolutely not. Spot is kind of a special case." He smiled at all of them and slung an arm around one of his necks. "Just like me."

"How did you care for such a huge animal?" Shirina asked, circling Spot as if seeing a miracle. Well, Spot could probably be considered one.

"He was not this big the last time I saw him. In fact, his shoulders barely came to my waist."

Thaen stepped forward. "It is the magic. I can see it moving through him, around his bones. It has sparked something inside of him, increasing whatever it was. Same as your magic did when you arrived here."

Aiden looked up at Spot. "I suppose it has something to do with the enchantment I was working with when his mother was carrying him. He's the only pup of the litter that made it."

Shirina laid out a hand which Spot eagerly sniffed and licked. The drool soaked her arm all the way up to her elbow.

Shirina gave him a scratch between the ears and the other two heads bobbed forward for attention.

Aiden laughed and Thaen made his own circle around the dog. "The question I have," he said critically, "is how did he get here?"

"Spot isn't just an oddity on the outside, but the inside as well. He was the easiest pup to train and thinks almost as well as you or I would."

"But that still does not explain his appearance," Fiadh stated. "He would still have to cross the Mist."

Aiden considered Spot again. "How did you get here?"

Spot wagged his tail and barked, all three heads speaking at once, bobbing up and down. He hopped to his feet and ran back toward the open gate, stopping under the arch to wait for Aiden to follow.

"Are you sure he understands you?" Dair asked skeptically.

Aiden gave him a shove. "Just because he understands me does not mean he can speak." He gestured toward Spot. "He can take me to whoever brought him."

Thaen laid a hand on his shoulder. "It is unwise for you to follow."

"But what if he came with whoever crossed the Fuath before it was locked down? He could lead us right to them."

"If he came with someone," Shirina said, softly, "why are they not with him now?"

Aiden's spirits dropped. "Do you think something happened to them?"

"We have not been able to find anyone," Fiadh said. "It would make sense if they did not make it far from the border. There are still those in this land that do not take kindly to humans."

Aiden looked over at Spot and called him back. Spot took a step toward him and then bounced back, obviously trying to get him to follow.

"What if they're in trouble?"

Thaen folded his arms over his chest. "Then *I* will investigate. Not you. You have other things to worry about." He tilted his head back toward the palace where the High Councilors stood waiting on the top step.

"I suppose you're right." He whistled for Spot, calling him back into the courtyard.

Spot took a few steps before all three heads whipped up, zeroing in on something above the palace.

Aiden looked up and the breath he was about to let out caught in his chest. A pair of wings and a flash of purple scales descended over the towers of the palace and swooped down toward the courtyard. Thaen pushed Aiden behind him, but Shirina took a step forward, a grin on her face. The scaled beast landed with a thump, its glittering eyes staring behind Aiden's group at Spot as if the creature had a bad taste in its mouth.

A dracon. A real dracon was glaring at his dog.

The dracon folded its webbed wings, revealing the two ellyllon clinging to its back. The older one, a female seemingly molded of precious metal, swung down from the dracon's back and reached up for the smaller ellyllon. A child by the looks of her.

Shirina met them at the dracon's feet. "Fearg? We were not expecting you this evening."

The older of the pair, likely Fearg, stepped forward with the child's hand in hers. "I went to Crann Mòr to report to the Council only to learn they were here. In light of the attack on Flùranach, our message could not wait. We rushed here as fast as we could."

The three other Councilors came around the dracon. "What is the meaning of this?" the Spring Councilor asked, though more curious than demanding.

Fearg turned to them. "I have come with reports of rebels within our kingdom." Everyone crowded around them then.

"You should have reported to the Council at Crann Mòr, as you have been charged to do," the Summer Councilor huffed indignantly and looked at Aiden. "This is not an appropriate time."

"Perhaps, but none of you were at the capital and this news is urgent."

The Spring Councilor opened his mouth, but Shirina held up a hand before anyone else could speak. "We will all go inside and get these two something to eat before they tell us anything." She took the child's hand in her own, whispering to her as she led them inside.

The crowd bustled after them.

"What do you think the Hunt found?" Dair whispered.

"We know the rebels have been hiding somewhere," Thaen responded, his hands clenching at his sides. "Let us pray they have discovered exactly where, so we can catch them before they do any more damage."

Shirina led all of them to a larger sitting room, calling for their dinner to be transformed into an informal buffet within the space. Food materialized along tables and one of the brownies, the one Aiden had met at his party, winked at him before disappearing from the room.

Once both the new arrivals had plates in their hands, Shirina permitted them to speak. Fearg began her tale. Her young niece's kidnapping. Her brother calling on her to bring her back before he had to betray their new king. The discovery of the trail left by her kidnappers.

"We followed a set of odd tracks to the ruins of a *brontanna's* camp. The body of a troll had been left behind, but Nikki's trail continued in the other direction from the main group that had vacated the ruins. I decided to chase her first and go after the mortals later." She then moved on to tracking her niece through the forests of Spring, finding it difficult because of a mage's interference.

"I thought you said they were *brontanna*," Dair commented. "Are there rebel mages?"

The child, Nikki, piped in. "She was not a rebel. She was chained up with me in the horrible lady's tent."

"What horrible lady?" Thaen asked.

"I do not know what her name was, but she was not kind." Her thin fingers reached up to her hair and tears gathered in her eyes. "She cut my hair."

Aiden's eyes closed, rage and sorrow swirling in his gut. *Durant.* It couldn't have been anyone else.

"And the mage?" Shirina asked, a note of fear on her face. "She helped you escape?"

Nikki looked troubled. "I did not even know she was a mage until Auntie Fearg came."

Thaen turned back to Fearg. "How did her magic interfere with your tracking?"

"There were no tracks. And from what her gift was, she was obviously erasing them."

Thaen tapped nervously on the knives strapped to his chest. "What kind of gift?"

"She could make plants come shooting out of the ground!" Nikki exclaimed.

Aiden's heart stopped. Right then, he couldn't feel a pulse anywhere in his body. Even his lungs seized, and his muscles froze.

Then sensation came screaming back. Intense joy and absolute terror surged through his veins and across his body until he was on his knees before the little fae girl. "What did she look like?"

Nikki's eyes widened. "She had reddish brown hair and green eyes, almost as green as emeralds. She was also very short." The girl giggled. "She barely made it to Auntie Fearg's shoulder."

Fearg set a hand on her niece's shorn hair. "The dog in the courtyard was with her. He traveled with us before she told him to go when we took her to Autumn. They were looking for someone, though I don't know who. We left her in Autumn with another Huntress before seeking you out to report on the mortals."

"Was she hurt?" he asked, desperately. "Did she need help? Why did you leave her behind?"

Fearg tilted her head. "She had some broken ribs, but nothing life threatening. Unlike our Huntress that she attempted to skewer," she said with a grumble. "I sent Eud, our other sister, to check in at the house and bring the both of them to Crann Mòr to see the Council." She nodded at him. "Though now, I suppose, they will be brought in front of you."

Aiden let out a shuddering breath. By the Goddess, *she* was there. In Faerie. She'd been the one to cross through the Mist. She'd come.

For him.

Great Goddess, she was so close. He would get to see her. Hold her. Even if it couldn't last forever, he could at least say goodbye to her. Tell her everything he'd never been able to. He could at least have that.

He felt a hand on his back and looked over his shoulder to meet Fiadh's gaze. "Aedon, do you know who they are talking about?"

Aiden swallowed down the emotion and shook his head, not willing to tell them. Not yet. Not when he knew how the fae regarded mages. The rest of the family turned to listen to the Huntress as he pressed the heel of his hand to his heart, hoping to stop its frantic thumping against his rib cage.

The name he thought he'd never hear again bloomed across his lips in a silent prayer.

Penelope.

28

FRIENDS AND CONFESSIONS

Penny ran to her friend and collided with her in a messy tangle of laughter and tears. By the Goddess, it felt good to hold a friend in her arms. Someone who could actually understand her in this bizarre, foreign place.

Though the rather large cushion between them was new.

Penny pulled away and looked down at her friend's stomach. Her eyes widened. "Are you…"

Angelica's brilliant grin shined brighter than the blazing sun above them. "I'm pregnant!" she squealed. "I know it's so soon after we married and me only being twenty will be a bit of a shock to my mother when she finds out, but it was kind of expected once Devan and I married last year." She wrapped a hand around Devan's arm. Then she hit Penny's. "But we can get into that later. What on Gaia's green earth are you doing here, Penelope Barclay?"

Angelica's tone made Penny wince, still not completely comfortable with everyone knowing who she was, even if the name itself couldn't affect her. She ducked her head and stepped closer to Angelica. "I came for Aiden."

"Of course you did," Angelica said it as if it were an already stated fact. "But how did you even get here? And what are you wearing?"

Devan shook his head. "Perhaps we could have this conversation somewhere more private, my dear."

"Oh, bother." She rolled her eyes. "It's been over a year since I saw my friend and you want me to wait? You know how many letters I've written her these past several months. There is so much we need to talk about."

"Then, perhaps," Farrah said, looking about at the fae beginning to glance their direction, "this conversation could happen behind closed doors rather than out here on the street."

Penny nodded. "Yes. Good idea."

Penny and Devan both took one of Angelica's arms as Farrah followed behind. They wove their way out of the market and into the streets. The small businesses quickly transformed into residential buildings. Colorful townhouses and flats piled neatly atop one another, somehow less cramped than the ones on Olympia's streets. Coniferous trees grew between the lots, giving the streets a hint of color in the swaths of snow and ice. Angelica mentioned the art district close by and how they would have to explore it while Penny was here.

If Penny could accomplish what she came to do first.

She knew her friend was being kind, and while Eagallach was beautiful, Penny didn't care to take a tour. The reason she came had nothing to do with taking in the magical scenery. In fact, she knew if she stayed that it could reflect badly on Angelica. The folk would not be too kind to find she was best friends with a mage.

Angelica waved at a number of fair folk as they walked, calling out greetings and receiving smiles at every turn. Penny clung tighter to her friend. It had always been like that with Angelica. No one could ever resist her charm.

Devan led them toward the steps of a quaint town house on a less busy street. The trees around it dripped with sparkling icicles and the house glittered with fresh snow. The yard looked like a garden frozen in time, colorful blooms and manicured shrubs layered over with frost.

"The flowers are actually preserved under the frost," Angelica said, noticing where Penny's attention had turned. "The week of summer solstice, this peak will actually thaw for a few days and the flowers will get to soak in the sun before it snows again the next week."

"I can't imagine living in a place where it snows year-round," Penny commented.

Angelica shrugged. "I suppose you would get used to it, or at least vacation to another Court if it gets too monotonous."

Devan unlocked the front door and herded them inside. He took everyone's cloaks and delivered them to the coat closet while Angelica led them to the parlor. The house was modest, the furnishings inviting shades of blue and gold—likely in respect for Olympia's royal family—and the other decorations made the house feel like a piece of home. Penny nearly threw herself onto the settee against the far wall, only noticing the roaring fire in the fireplace after she'd passed by it.

Angelica gestured to the chairs scattered around the room as she made her way toward one of the thickly cushioned sofas. "Make yourselves at home. I'm sure Devan will send up tea and join us momentarily."

Farrah took up a chair close by the fire, holding out her hands to soak up the warmth.

Penny sat on the sofa next to Angelica. "I need help."

"Obviously, dearest." She gestured around the room. "Look where we are! By the Goddess, you're in Faerie, Penny! Now that we are in the house, what are you doing here? How did you even get here? Where does your mother think you are? Does anyone besides those of us in this house know your location? Have you eaten any of the fruit? Sweet Gaia, you better not have eaten any of the fruit."

Penny held out her hands. "I will explain everything."

And she did. She started with what happened at Dion and Carnation's wedding, what she greatly suspected The Cartographer had done to the previous Queen, and her decision to follow Aiden to Faerie. It all came out in a rush and Penny felt tears begin to track down her face. This retelling wasn't at all like the one she'd given Farrah's family. She shared the details of her time with Adira.

Devan spoke up from where he'd appeared in a chair across from them during Penny's story. "Do you remember where she was?" A quill scratched against the pad of paper in his hand. "Could you give an accurate accounting of your journey there and out?"

Penny nodded and laid it out, first speaking of the ravine where she and Spot had run into the redcaps and then the path they took to escape. Unlike Farrah, Penny happened to be excellent with directions. Praise the Goddess.

"Then what happened?" Angelica asked, practically bouncing in her seat.

Penny continued on. She spoke of the Hunt and Farrah's family.

"And now, here you are," Angelica mused. She cackled. "By the Goddess, when everyone back home hears about this, there will be so many people hounding you for your attention that you'll be considered a legend before you reach your twentieth year! Clarice will eat her heart out!"

Penny swallowed. By the Goddess, she'd be eighteen next week. She hadn't thought of it until that moment. She pushed the thought aside before it distracted her. "The struggle I have now is getting into the palace to see Aiden. I have to warn him about Adira's plans and try to help him get back to his brothers if I can. Olympia needs him." She turned to Devan. "Have you heard anything?"

Devan's eyes flicked around the room surreptitiously. "I was able to see him a few weeks ago."

Something in Penny's chest lightened. "How did he look?

Was he hurt? Did he ask you for help? Have you come up with some kind of escape plan?"

He looked at his wife and took a deep breath, then let it out in a weary chuckle. "I attempted to get to him right after I found out about his abduction through the channels I've made here. He actually reached out to me first and got me access to the palace. The only thing he asked me to do was find out who came through the Mist." He gestured to Penny. "I've completed that particular mission and have only to report back."

Angelica's head swiveled between the two of them. "Devan, what do you mean that you 'attempted to get to him?' And what channels? What is going on here?"

Penny met Devan's gaze and found a glimmer of mirth and a load of resignation there. IIe turned back to his wife. "My dear, I have something to confess."

Angelica's eyes pulled wide and then narrowed. "Devan Elie, so help me, if you confess to me right this second that you have been a spy this entire time..."

Devan took his hand in hers. "Angelica, I've been a spy this entire time."

Angelica withdrew from him and threw her hands up in the air. "How didn't I *blasted* see it? How? I mean, it only makes absolute, logical sense!" She slumped back onto the sofa, tears gathering in her eyes. "I had all the signs. The assignment to Faerie, all of the incorporating ourselves into the Courts, the way you nearly gutted our neighbors in Autumn. By the Goddess, I'm a terrible wife!"

Devan knelt down on the ground next to her and Penny stood to leave. They obviously needed to have a moment to speak to one another.

"Don't you dare try to get out of this conversation, Penny." Angelica pointed an accusatory finger at Penny. "How long have you known?"

Penny grimaced. "Before Barclay Manor."

"Oh, Sweet Gaia! And why didn't either of you think to share this very vital piece of information with me?"

"Because you would have crowed it from the rooftops," said Penny.

"You can't withhold that kind of juicy gossip," Devan said at the same time.

Angelica stood, hands on hips. "Oh really? Well, for your information, I've been sitting on the fact that Ròs next door has a daughter who works at the palace, and she saw the High Council there yesterday. She told me she overheard them making plans to leave for the Crann Mòr today and no one even knows!"

Penny felt every ounce of relief she'd gained since arriving here evaporate in an instant.

"What?" Devan whispered. He jumped up from his chair, striding for the door. "I'll be right back."

Angelica stood there, chest heaving, until her eyes widened, and she plopped back into her seat. "Curses."

Penny's breath fogged the glass as she watched out the window for Devan's tall frame. She could barely make out the spires of the palace from where she sat in the window seat of the second-story study.

Aiden couldn't be gone. She'd just made it here. She stood on the same soil as him, breathed the same frozen air he did.

She was so close.

The door to the study opened and Angelica swept in, a tea tray in her hands. Farrah had followed her out a few minutes ago to find somewhere to sleep, though Penny hadn't really been paying close attention as to where. Angelica delivered a chagrined smile and set the tray on a desk across the room. "I apologize for my attitude earlier. I'd planned on sharing the information about Aiden the moment I saw you, but in all the excitement... I should've done it right when you walked through my door instead of letting it burst out like that. By the Goddess, being pregnant does weird things to my brain."

Penny held out a hand. Angelica took it, joining her at the window. Penny squeezed her friend's fingers. "I already forgave you. I just pray I'm not too late." She turned to look at Angelica. "I can't imagine what Adira has planned, but if I can't warn Aiden before he returns to Crann Mòr, I don't know what I'll do."

Angelica tapped the glass. "There he is."

Penny looked out to see a shadow loping down the street toward the house. Penny pulled Angelica down the stairs and met Devan at the front step.

Sweat dripped down the sides of his face and his breath came out in frozen puffs. He shook his head. "I was too late. They've already left for Crann Mòr." He stepped into the house. "Though the guard at the gate told me the most fantastical story about a giant three-headed dog showing up. He said the king left it in the stables."

Penny's chest eased a fraction. "At least Spot made it." She could focus more on Aiden knowing Spot was all right.

Devan's head whipped toward her. He held his hand to his waist in measurement. "Spot?"

Penny nodded.

Angelica clapped her hands together. "All right, then, we have some mission planning to do." She swept past them, her chin raised in the picture of superiority.

Devan and Penny shared a look. Devan followed Angelica up the stairs and Penny watched them, her chest still aching in the same place it had for what had apparently been months now.

"All right." She swallowed down her trepidation. "Plan A it is."

29
ASSEMBLE

AIDEN'S FAMILY FLANKED HIM AS HE STRODE DOWN THE MAGICAL wooden hallway toward the High Council chamber once again. His eyes took in new details. The light practically permeated the walls—courtesy of the Day Court, he'd learned. The images molded into the walls all showcased the different Seasonal Courts, going so far as to feature the city beneath the tree itself. There was so much, and walking through the halls of Crann Mòr was decidedly different than having the Land whispering to Aiden in his dreams. He could feel the magic pooling under his feet, following every step he took through Her smooth trunk.

The magic kept him grounded. It was the only reason he'd been able to get through the last couple of days.

The Aigeans had fully taken Flùranach and were gathering more troops on the beach every day. They had sent another missive, demanding Aiden's surrender. And there was still no sign of Durant anywhere.

Penelope was here. In Faerie. That was what Spot had been trying to tell him. She had brought him through the Mist. She had come to find him.

Sgiath had left from the Winter Palace to speak with his

family in Autumn about Penelope, and Aiden had come to Crann Mòr. He'd told Aiden he would report back when he found her.

That had been two days ago.

Where was she now? Little Nikki had claimed Penny had been injured during her captivity and had been with Durant longer than the child had. How long had Durant had her? It had been months since the Fuath had been blockaded, since he'd heard someone was spotted by Am Fear Liath Mòr. What had Durant done to her? Penelope had escaped, though it seemed as if it hadn't been a simple thing. The child had cried recalling it.

And Penny had sent Spot to him without her. What did that mean? She knew Spot's capabilities. Had she planned to meet up with him in Winter somehow?

Would Sgiath find her at his home? Was she already on her way to Winter? They'd decided it best that she be taken to the Winter Palace where she would be safe. Nobody knew how the rest of the Courts would react to having a mage in their midst.

Shirina came up beside him. "You seem troubled."

Aiden shoved the thoughts of Penelope deep down. "Only a little nervous." He'd told them nothing about Penelope. He trusted his family, but he couldn't tell them about her, about *them*. His heart simply wouldn't allow it. Not yet. Not when he didn't know where she was. He didn't need to add to Fiadh and Shirina's plates, and he certainly didn't want his family to start hunting for her. The Hunt had reported on the things Penelope had done to protect herself. He couldn't send Thaen to apprehend her, especially when he'd gotten that glint in his eye when they'd said she was a mage over plants. Aiden still hadn't identified what the look had been, but he knew he wouldn't risk Penelope's life because of it.

"This will be quite different from the first time," Shirina said, cutting off his thoughts once more.

"I know."

"It will not only be the High Councilors," she said, "but also the Court monarchs as well. Many will be frightened after what has happened in Flùranach."

"You have said as much, Shirina." Not that it had settled him much the first time either.

"You only have to talk about the threat and what we are going to do about it. You do not have to fall into anyone's traps to start up debate. This is your first interaction with them, and they will be sniffing out weakness like darklings seeking blood."

They reached the staircase where he'd pushed Thaen after his abduction. "I understand."

She blew out a breath as Fiadh appeared at her side. "He will be fine, my love. We must trust our Little Shadow to become his own High King." He took Shirina's hand and led her up the winding staircase.

"Or at least spice things up a bit, hm?" Dair flicked his long, lavender braid, interwoven with black metal, back over his shoulder. Black spikes ran up along the tips of his ears, similar to the dracon that had landed in the courtyard in Winter. Dark lines of kohl circled his eyes, and he even had a few blades strapped to his wrists. He looked ready for some kind of battle —though the impracticality of his wardrobe didn't really give Aiden a hint as to what kind.

Thaen also bristled with weaponry, his title as Lòchran on full display. The broadsword at his back flickered with purple sparks. Even Shirina and Fiadh had donned armor-like attire. They were ready to battle these folk if necessary.

Aiden looked down at his own clothing. He'd worn only a simple tunic and matching black trousers—though Thaen had supplied him with a new sword, and he had a dagger tucked into his boot. He looked like a shadow himself. Perhaps if he needed to, he could disappear. He looked up the staircase at the brilliantly lit walls.

If there are any shadows to tuck into.

Dair ruffled Aiden's hair—which he'd finally cut earlier that morning. "I cannot wait to see what those brats in Day think about our king. And if any of them start anything..." He put up his ringed fists in a defensive stance. "Thaen will surely put them in their place."

Thaen grunted something from behind them that sounded like obvious approval but held a hint of annoyance for his brother.

"I do not think there will be much trouble," said Fiadh. "If I know anything about Courts, they will be more focused on the revel at the end of the week rather than anything we have to say. Some of them have lived in ignorance for so long they do not know anything else."

"You best pray that is the case," Dair replied.

"I still think we should cancel the party," Aiden argued. The High Council had decided to go forward with the revel after the anointing even with the attack along the coast. With so much turmoil, they wanted to put on a good face and show the rest of the folk how well Aiden was going into his reign. The Councilors thought it best for the citizens to have a moment's peace, in light of all of the destruction they were about to face.

Aiden thought it a load of garbage. While it was imperative to keep morale up, they could have at least postponed it. Having a party didn't feel right at the moment. The folk needed trained. The cities needed shored up with defenses and supplies for a siege. They needed weapons forged and defenses manned.

But he had been vetoed and the party would go on.

Aiden stepped up the final steps and found himself once again in the cavernous main hallway. The ceiling looked taller than when he'd been there last. The most significant change was that it stood empty.

"Why is no one here?"

Shirina took his arm. "When you arrived, everyone was still

around for the solstice and Queen Rìanoch's funeral." She waved to the empty space. "Crann Mòr is generally less populated during the regular times of the year, the Courts attending to their own lands and what not. The refugees are also in the lower levels and taking most of the attention away from the rest of the Tree."

They strode to a large set of ornate doors. Aiden hadn't paid much attention the first time, but he noticed the carvings decorating the surface now. It seemed every fae creature found a space on these doors, some having gone extinct long ago and others still walking on the land that very day.

Thaen reached out and pushed them inward.

The noise was overwhelming.

Ellyllon and bwbachod were on their feet, shouting toward the two Councilors at the head of the room. Sgiath remained absent. The other two Councilors saw him walk in and went on one knee, hands pressed to their hearts and heads bowed. The rest of the crowd turned, their voices quieting and eyes widening, and followed suit. There were several without bowed heads, openly staring at him.

"Oh, good show, Seirbhiseach," Dair applauded. He got into the face of one of the ellyllon staring up at Aiden. "Perhaps if you continue staring at him, he will turn to dust as your wife did after that curse you 'accidentally' put on her."

Aiden kept his own eyes from going wide, trusting Shirina to intervene if it proved necessary, but she swept past without a glance toward the male and took her place with the Councilors.

Red faced, and not just from the pinkish hue of his skin, the Tuatha bowed his head.

Dair patted him on the head. "Good boy." He found a seat in the crowd and sat, the others still on their knees.

A few murmurs began circulating and Aiden remembered his place.

"Rise," he commanded. His voice came out quiet, but

everyone in the room must have heard because they all got to their feet.

Aiden looked back to where Shirina stood and saw her gesture toward the empty chair between her and Summer's Councilor. Thaen and Fiadh walked just behind him until he stopped in the center of the room. He turned back to the crowd and saw the Huntress he'd met, Fearg, standing next to a harpy and a centaur, the other two members of her trio. His attention snagged on the only other familiar faces, those of Lady Saranae and her father. The female gave him a flirtatious wink and blew him a kiss.

Aiden mustered up every ounce of willpower not to react. It would not do for him to offend her in front of the entire kingdom. That rejection would certainly take some more finesse. He took a deep breath. "You may be seated."

The waiting crowd sat, albeit slowly, and kept their attention trained on him.

Once everyone found a chair, he began. "I am glad everyone could join me. I know there is much turmoil in the Courts at this time, and I appreciate you taking the time to meet with me to discuss the threat to our lands. I have asked High Councilor Shirina to deliver the report on Summer."

Shirina came to stand at the center of the room and read the numbers Thaen had delivered to them. The kings and queens gasped in horror as she apprised them of what had happened.

"Those Aigean scum could not leave well enough alone?" howled one of the werewolves. "What do they think will happen when these rebels are done with Faerie?"

"And where are the rebels anyway?" spoke up one of the ellyllon. By the crown of roses on his head and the robes flowing onto the floor, Aiden guessed him to be King Falaichte of Spring.

Aiden gestured to the Huntresses. "Would you please share with the rest of the Courts your report?"

The Huntresses stood, taking the attention of the gathering from Aiden. Praise the Goddess. They shared their tale, sparing no details about discovering the troll-raided camp and the child's kidnapping.

"So a few measly humans kidnap one lass and we immediately call it a threat to the kingdom?" said a dwarf. "I say we send a few redcaps and a herd of púca to take care of them and leave it at that." A few of her companions hollered in agreement.

"You think 'a few measly humans' could simply steal my daughter out from under my nose?" an ellyllon male cried out. Magenta eyes flashed with fury as he shook a fist at the dwarves. Aiden noticed the similarities to Nikki at once. He remembered Shirina mentioning her father was advisor to the Spring King.

"I do not think it would be too hard," replied another, this male bedecked in the orange and browns of Autumn's Court, "since you cannot see over that tipped up nose of yours anyhow." He tilted his face up, mimicking the stingy look of a prideful courtier.

The crowd around the Autumn fae snickered, even the crowned female next to him. He hadn't met Queen Arae, but the male who had spoken up would likely be her consort if he was here, since Aiden knew she had a female advisor. Likely the fiery-skinned lady next to her.

Summer's High Councilor pounded the ground with his staff. "We will not have any flak from you Unseelie if you want to remain in this room."

Unseelie. That had been a word he'd learned before coming to this kingdom. The Seelie and Unseelie were old terms for the Night and Day Courts. Aiden couldn't remember where the names originated, but he did know the use of Unseelie was *not* a compliment.

The right half of the room visibly bristled at the insult.

But only the right half.

The left half, bedecked in lightweight, more vibrantly colored clothing all smirked.

Aiden looked between the two sides. The Day Court and the Night Court were completely separated from one another.

Aiden whirled on the High Councilor. "I do not believe offending your High King's family Court is the best way into his good graces, Councilor." He kept his court mask up, but he let the threat drip from his voice.

The Councilor nodded, albeit begrudgingly, and took back up his seat.

Aiden returned his attention to the crowd. "The threat is very real, I assure you. It has taken root in Olympia and has its sights set on Faerie. It was their leader who killed my mother and who has most recently killed your High Queen. They were the ones who orchestrated the attack on Summer, and we should anticipate more to come."

"So we round up the humans and dispose of them quickly," quipped someone from the crowd. "The Isles will not attack if they have no allies here. Problem solved."

Spring's High Councilor thumped his staff on the ground. "Except it seems they are nowhere to be found. It was a coincidence the troll even discovered the encampment. We found evidence of multiple wards and even our own glamours within the space. They are using magic to evade us."

A gnome skittered out from behind the seats of the monarchs. "And what about the mage?"

Aiden's heart seized. "What mage?"

The gnome gave a short bow, nervousness etched in his features after being addressed by Aiden. "Well, My Sovereign, there was a mage tromping through the forest as well. Her dark magic blocked the river along the Summer border and even destroyed an entire goblin nest in Spring."

The crowd stirred.

"Now this rebellion is using cursed mages?"

"That mage will wreak havoc everywhere!"

"Best to rid of it first then go after the *brontannas*."

"Yes! Kill the mage!"

"Down with the mage!"

Aiden saw black.

Shadows rushed from under his skin, coating the walls in darkness. The Land's magic swelled within him as well, hearing his internal rage and answering it with Her own. The room flooded and light shone from under Aiden's skin, highlighting the thick, black veins snaking down his arms. His connection with the Land's magic showed him the whole tree going dark.

His eyes scanned the crowd, all of them cowering back in their chairs. All except his family.

Dair stood, his chair falling back to land on the foot of the werewolf seated behind him. Thaen stood at Aiden's side, his sword drawn and sparking. Fiadh and Shirina flanked them.

Fear and disgust sat in every fae's eyes.

Just as the people of Olympia had looked at Father.

Aiden withdrew the magic. His heart stuttered at the strain but picked up a regular beat quickly.

He met the eye of every member of the crowd. "I hope, in the future, that you all do not forget that your king is also a mage. If that thought disgusts you so much, perhaps surrendering yourselves to the mercy of the Isles that have attacked your shores would suit you far better."

He took a deep breath, the blackened veins finally receding as his quick healing did its job. "Listen well. We will not be killing *any* mages. We will *not* be throwing blame on a person who was reported as not being involved in the rebellion that even now works its way through our lands. There is too much at stake to allow old hatreds to cloud our judgment and deviate our course." He took a step toward them. "What we *will* do is find those who are the true threat. Then we will take care of the problem. We have plans execute, and refugees that need relocating. That should be our priority."

The Night Court side nodded in acceptance, at least placated for the time being. The Day Court only stared, not accepting or denying Aiden's words. Aiden blew out a breath. It already seemed impossible to rally together enough of a force to combat the Aigeans. If they couldn't even be in the same room, how would they work together in a war? They had made plans to relocate the refugees through the Night Court and into Spring, but with how the Day Court had reacted, he didn't know how they would make that work without causing problems. How would Aiden get them to cooperate when he was so new in his rule, and they had such prejudices working against him? Already, Aiden could see how hopeless it all could turn out to be.

He clenched his hand to keep from raking his fingers through his hair. If nothing else, at least he'd diverted the threat to Penelope. He faced the Courts once more. "The High Councilors will go over the plans we have constructed to help relocate the refugees."

Knees weak, he turned toward his seat at the table but was stopped by Shirina. Her eyes narrowed in his direction. She surreptitiously grabbed his wrist and pulled him down so her mouth was at his ear.

"After a display like that, we need to have a talk about this mage girl."

30
SPATS AND PORTALS

PENNY'S EYES SCANNED THE SHEET OF PARCHMENT STRETCHED OVER the table. "Show me again."

"Here, here, and here." Devan's finger jabbed three separate spots on the hand-drawn map of the wall surrounding Crann Mòr. The gigantic tree took up the length of the paper, not even including the leafy top.

"And tell me again how you came to know about the guard rotations and hidden entrances?" Angelica asked, wiping crumbs of pumpkin tart from her fingers with a laced kerchief. "Oh, yes. Silly of me to forget the outrageous secret you've been keeping our entire marriage."

"Angelica," Devan groaned.

"If you keep torturing him like this, he'll be in no state of mind to complete this mission." Penny smirked. "At least he didn't conceal his identity from you and then pretend you didn't exist after you found out."

Angelica opened her mouth with a retort but swallowed it back and gave a long sighed. "Fine, fine, fine. I'll admit, it was not *nearly* as dramatic as Prince—"

"*King!*" called Farrah from the window seat.

"Pardon me," replied Angelica. "It was not as dramatic as *King* Aiden's reveal."

A *king*. Penny had forgotten as well. Aiden wasn't a prince in this land or a spymaster. He was High King, sitting at the tippy top of the throne pyramid making up the Faerie Courts. Sweet Gaia, everything had grown so much bigger than just the two of them now.

"I suppose I could let the subject lie." Angelica gave Devan a mischievous smirk. "For now."

Devan blew out a breath and turned back to the page. "All three of these gates will be heavily guarded. We weren't even invited for the celebrations. If they look too closely, they will arrest you. They'll be watching for humans not bonded to the Land because of what happened to the High Queen."

"Bonded?" Penny asked. "What do you mean bonded?"

"It's what the fruit does," supplied Angelica. "The blue pomegranates—the Faerie fruit? It bonds humans to the Land. After they eat it, they're nearly bound as much as the fae. They can't lie and they can do nothing to physically harm the kingdom itself. It's like an adoption made by the Land."

"What about the fae?" Penny asked.

"The fae use it to stabilize their magic," Devan said. "It helps feed the natural magic of the Land while also helping the folk connect to their well of gifts. They can do marvelous feats of magic when they've eaten the fruit, unlike anything in Olympia."

"My mother suspects that's why the magic in Olympia is dying," Farrah said. "She believes that without the natural give and take that the fruit and the land provide us, magic will dwindle to nothing. Without access to the fruit and without giving a portion of your magic back into the land to cultivate it, Olympia's magic will eventually die off."

"What about mages?" Penny pointed to herself. "What happens if a mage eats the fruit?"

Farrah shrugged. "No one knows. Mages haven't been

given the chance since the fair folk don't have a good opinion of them. Even the simplest bwbachod would not offer it to a mage, knowing it would be like blasphemy."

Penny grimaced. Hearing that she could be considered blasphemous for simply eating some fruit rang wrong in her for some reason. She decided to return to their original subject.

"So, I need to sneak in first and then pretend to be a member of one of the Courts." Penny chewed at her bottom lip. "Are you sure sneaking in during the revel is the only option? I can't go beforehand?"

Devan shook his head. "Not if you want to keep your head. The folk are spooked. You need to get in on revel night. When everyone will be too distracted celebrating that they won't notice you slip in and out."

"But Adira was going to do the same thing," she protested. "She might beat me to him."

"She was working under the assumption that she'd have one of these." He waved Penny's stolen invitation in the air. "This event is going to be more than secure since the king presumably found out about the abduction and Adira's going to be more cautious because she suspects they've heard about their encampment by now."

Penny blew out a breath. There were too many ways this plan could go wrong. She gestured toward the north entrance to the tree. "So, I can circumvent that gate by using the frozen river and the ice bridge?"

"Yes, though it's going to be rough terrain. Luckily, the snow hasn't melted yet. It should be sturdy enough to hold you."

Penny's fingers trailed over the thin line representing the frozen bridge. "And the water leads to the base of the tree where the main entrance is?"

"Precisely."

"And why isn't the ice bridge guarded?" Angelica asked.

"I never said it wasn't."

Penny frowned. "Why is that way better than the gates?"

"Because the gates are watched by the regular tree guard. The bridge is guarded by a troll."

"*A troll?*" Both Penny and Angelica screeched.

Penny shook her head vehemently and took a step back from the table. No. No way was she facing down a troll. Not after she saw the one tear into Adira's camp like it was nothing but wheat stalks.

Devan raised his hands placatingly. "The troll guards it, but as long as you have the password, you can get past."

"What password?" Penny asked warily, her mouth dry.

Devan grinned. "The one I learned from the traders while I was there. He shared it with me when we were trying to get in to see the queen before she died. The password is *tòimhseachan*?"

"It's what?"

"*Tòimhseachan,*" he repeated. "It means something like 'riddle' or 'puzzle.'"

How on Gaia's green earth would she even learn how to say such a word correctly, let alone remember it? "Great Goddess, I'm going to die."

Farrah hopped down from her perch in the window. "Sometimes it's a good thing to come face to face with your own mortality." She plucked an apple from a bowl on the corner of the table and rubbed its green, speckled skin against her tunic. "However, I don't think this will be the thing that kills you. I'll help you with the password on the trip there." She took a large bite out of the apple, wiping the juice from her face with her sleeve.

"Are you sure you can't just portal me in?" Penny entreated.

Farrah gave her a flat look. "I already told you, unless you want to risk cutting one of the hundreds of people that will be there in half or alerting most of the tree with all of the magical alarms stashed around the place, you're going to have to walk in on your own, two feet." She spun and returned to her seat in the window.

Penny slouched into the chair closest to the table. "At least we can portal nearby." She grimaced and turned to Angelica. "I hope it doesn't make you too ill."

"Unfortunately, I'll live," Angelica moaned. "My stomach can't handle it on a good day, let alone while carrying this little bundle of joy." She rubbed at her round stomach, her face greening at the thought of the intense travel.

Penny blew out a breath. "I can't let you stay here. I need someone to watch my back." She smirked. "And Devan won't dare to leave you behind anymore."

"By the Goddess," Devan groaned.

But Angelica grinned. "He'd best not. I won't be missing out on any more adventures."

"Until the baby comes," Devan and Penny said at once.

"Until the baby comes." Angelica rolled her eyes. A smirk spread across her lips. "Then I'll have my own little spy to train."

"Goddess, save me," Devan mumbled.

Penny sat back up in her chair. "So, the dress should be finished by tomorrow, giving us plenty of time to get to the capital before the revel in three days."

"Yes. We have all the fun spy tools that I finally get to play with." Angelica stood from her seat and went to the corner, where their supplies were laid out, and pulled out a sleeve of lock picks. "I would have given all of my jewels to have a set of these when I was younger."

"*All* of your jewels?" Devan asked.

"Perhaps not *all* of them, but at least a handful. I could have pulled so many more pranks on my brothers."

Penny couldn't help but smile. *Like father, like daughter.*

Devan rose and went to his wife. "You can have your own set," he said, taking the picks, "after we get Penny to the king."

"Can mine be rose gold instead of iron?"

Penny was about to remark on the absurdity of such a question—not only for durability but also for the obvious aesthetic—when Farrah jumped from her seat.

"By every gold leaf in the forest! He's here!"

Penny and Angelica both scrambled to the window. "Who's here?" they asked as one.

"My father!" Farrah shouted, whirling into the room. "We have to leave. *Now*."

Both Penny and Angelica pressed their faces to the glass. A fae male wrapped in orange robes with vibrant, red hair strolled leisurely down the road toward the house. His right hand wrapped around a long staff, topped with a sizable gemstone. His gait reflected idleness, but his expression oozed frustration.

Penny turned back to Farrah. "Could he take us to Aiden?"

Farrah stuffed supplies into her bag. "Unlikely, at least, not until after the anointing. The High Council won't want anything distracting from the ceremony. They need someone on the throne, and they will wait until after to address what you're doing here. They'll probably stash you somewhere until they decide to tell Aiden about you."

"Couldn't the Hunt have reported to them already and then reported to Aiden?" Angelica asked from the window.

"And distract Aiden from his responsibilities as king?" Farrah shook her head. "Not a chance. I'll bet good coin that they've not even told them about the rebels here."

"That doesn't sound like something King Aiden would be all right with," said Devan.

Farrah cinched the bag closed. "I'm sure you're right, but I know the way things work here better than you do. Most of the fae won't give a fig that a small band of rebels are here. They'll say that the Land or even some of the bwbachod will take care of it."

Her hands began to move, shadows swirling in the air before her. "The Hunt will have reported to the High Council, and they would withhold all of the information until they have the new High King out in front of the people and anointed at the tree."

Penny reached for a pack herself.

"But what about the dress?" Angelica protested.

"I'll send Farrah back tonight to tell you where we've gone," Penny said, tying off the top of her pack. "Just bring the dress with you. If you have to leave before Farrah can come, try to meet me on the bridge of the Tine River." She pointed at the map of Faerie on their wall, drawing their eyes to the river separating Winter and Autumn. "I'll be there at noon the day before the revel."

"It's the *Teine* River," Devan corrected.

Angelica swatted at him and wrapped Penny up in a hug. "You better meet me there, or you'll be in big trouble, young lady."

A knock on the door made them all jump.

"I'll hold him off as long as I can." Devan bolted toward the front entrance.

Angelica took Penny's hand and gave it a firm squeeze. "I'll go help him to avoid suspicion. Be safe, Dearest Penny."

Penny swallowed back the lump in her throat as Angelica let go and raced after Devan.

Farrah's portal hovered in the air behind her. She turned to look around for anything they missed, but the front door closed, and voices made their way down the short hall. Her gaze met Farrah's fearful one and they both jumped through the portal before they were discovered.

The swirling darkness was more bearable than it had been the first time, but Penny still fell to her knees when the portal spat her back out. Her head spun and she took a few gasping breaths before opening her eyes. She gawked at the world around her.

From above, Crann Mòr had simply looked like a humongous, glowing tree, but from down below, it appeared as a city stretching into the sky. Buildings reached up toward the silver branches. Bridges met the limbs and went over the many streams feeding the massive trunk. Leaves floated down, spinning lazily until a flying fae caught it or it was swept up by the wind. The sheer amount of folk on the street in front of her tripled what she saw in Eagallach. The vibrancy of the place hummed within her, vibrating under her skin.

A hand wrapped around her bicep and Farrah hoisted her from the ground of the alley they'd appeared in. "We'd best get moving before my father attempts to track my portal here."

Penny blinked, reluctantly pulling her gaze away from the magical tree. "He can do that?"

Farrah nodded and took a step onto the street.

Penny followed but stopped. "The map!" The picture of the tree Devan had written notes on still lay on the table back in Winter. If they didn't have that to help them get around, there was no way Penny could get through the capital. She might be able to find something close in one of the shops, but the time it would take to even find a mapmaker was more than they could spare.

Farrah smiled and pulled a few pieces of paper from her pocket. "I wasn't going to forget it this time."

31
ADMIT

AIDEN SAGGED BACK INTO HIS CHAIR SITUATED AWKWARDLY IN THE middle of the lavish sitting room.

Fiadh shut the door softly behind the last visitor and turned to Aiden. "It certainly could have been worse."

Aiden groaned and massaged his fingers into the strained muscles at the back of his neck. It had been a full day of visitors and meetings; all prep work for the celebration in three days and helping the refugees with whatever they needed. Aiden let out a chuckle. Going on like this, he probably wouldn't last until the anointing.

Shirina used her shadows to propel a chair next to his. Dair had stretched himself across a sofa during one of the longer conversations with a Spring fae earlier but turned and crossed his arms over the back of the seat, setting his chin atop them. Thaen unceremoniously dragged a chair over, and Fiadh stood behind his wife.

"What else is on the agenda for the day?" Aiden asked no one in particular.

Fiadh chuckled and stepped over to lay a hand on Aiden's shoulder. "Now, your family gets an audience."

"Oh?" Aiden quipped. He had felt the interrogation coming ever since Shirina had said what she did in the Council Hall two days ago. He had just prayed it wouldn't happen until after the anointing and the revel.

Shirina leaned forward. "Who is the mage?"

Aiden's gaze flicked from face to face. A myriad of expressions ranging from curiosity—mostly from Dair—to fear stretched across their faces. Even Thaen looked mildly uneasy. Aiden prayed. He couldn't live with it, his family being disgusted with Penelope. Even if she was never going to stay, he couldn't accept their loathing. He realized it was one of the reasons he'd never spoken about her with them.

He took a deep breath. "The mage is Penelope Barclay, Heir to the Duchy of Eleusion."

The breath held in his chest, waiting for the shock to ripple through the room. But nothing happened.

"Barclay?" Fiadh asked. "I am not familiar with the name, though I do remember the name Eleusion from before the war. It's quite a distance from the capital, right? I did not know there was a duchy there now."

Aiden choked on that breath. "What? You haven't heard of House Barclay? The only family in all of Olympia that has power over plants and can bring them to life? There's only the two of them left in their entire family, Penelope and her mother, Duchess Dominique Barclay."

"Oh!" Shirina straightened. "I have heard of Dominique. She's the only female duchess at court and has such a high standing in Olympia's overly male council." Her brows drew together. "What is her daughter doing in Faerie? Their duchy was the one overtaken, was it not?"

Aiden blinked back his confusion. "Yes," he said, drawing the word out slowly.

Dair shook his head. "You have forgotten, cousin. We have not had real communication with the Olympians until King

Dion reached out to us only five years ago. Winter less so than everyone, considering we did not have a ruler at the time. There have been few regents over the years, and the laws concerning them are more limiting than what I believe they have in Olympia, specifically due to the nature of the calling. My parents have been doing all they can to keep things under control until you came of age, but there was not much they could do concerning the humans until you arrived."

"In fact," added Fiadh, "until the ambassadors attended the gathering at solstice, we had not had any contact with the Olympians since before the war."

"But there were Tuatha in Olympia before the treaty."

Shirina nodded. "Yes, those that had stayed on the other side of the Fuath and those that had the chance to portal there. I know Sgiath's family helped some move there for one reason or another, but that didn't really start happening until about twenty-five years ago when we started sending ambassadors to Olympia to treat with the king. We could feel the magic waning in Olympia all the way in Winter and we wanted to help." She shook her head. "But we are getting off track. What is Penelope Barclay doing here? Now?"

Aiden swallowed. "She's likely looking for me."

Dair frowned. "Why is a girl, an heir to a noble house with rare magic no less, traipsing around Faerie looking for you?"

"She's not only an heiress." He pushed out a breath. "She is —*was* also a spy, under my command as my brother's spymaster."

"And she came to take you home," Thaen stated. It was not a question.

Aiden dipped his head so they wouldn't see the tumult he could feel cracking through his expression. "Probably."

"But why only this mage girl?" Shirina asked. "Why did the king not send a team? Did he really have no one else to spare? Just a mage and a dog?"

"But it was not just a dog, was it?" Fiadh stepped forward and crouched in front of him. "Just as Penelope Barclay is not just a girl."

Aiden met his gaze and saw Fiadh's understanding written all over his face.

Fiadh reached out and placed a hand on Aiden's knee. "The two of you are in love."

The room thickened with silence until Aiden gave a small nod of his head. Oddly, relief flowed through him at his admission. He'd expected to mourn over the lost secret or become anxious over what his family would think. But peace swept through him instead.

Shirina stood from her chair. "I always wondered why you fought so hard to get back to Olympia those first few weeks. We kept in contact with some of our people across the border after the treaty was signed, asked for news about you and such, but a love match was never mentioned. Not even a hint of one." She rested a hand on her husband's shoulder. "I understood the desire to get back to your family, but I thought once you knew who we were, you would want to search out this other half of your lineage. I never thought to ask if you left behind another piece of your heart."

Dair leaped over the back of the couch. "So, our half mage king is in love with a mage girl. It's almost tragic."

"Why?" Aiden asked.

Shirina placed a hand on his arm. "Little Shadow, you two were doomed from the start."

"I know many of you look down on mages." He pulled away from her. "However, I don't see what that has to do with my feelings or my intentions toward her." Not that there were many intentions anymore. He knew she could never stay here, but someone forbidding it knotted his insides.

"It has everything to do with them," Fiadh said. "While we may be a bit more tolerant, the rest of Faerie would not allow such a thing. Most will overlook your mage side, calling it a novelty and brushing it aside considering your fae heritage, but a full mage in the Courts will bring more than just a little controversy. There would likely be calls for your head if it were ever known you'd fallen in love with one."

Aiden's chest ached and shadows zipped over his body. He'd known. He'd been telling himself for months that he needed to let Penelope go, but hearing it aloud was an entirely different beast.

He sighed and slouched back in his chair in a very un-kingly way. "It doesn't matter how I feel anyway. She cannot desert Olympia." He counted the reasons off on his fingers. "She's the only heir to her family's name, the only of two mages with the power over plants and her mother is notoriously domineering. I cannot even imagine what kind of havoc she's wreaking without Penelope at the moment."

Once he started listing the reasons, he couldn't seem to stop talking. The whole story came out in one big rush, starting from their first meeting the night of her debut. He recalled his deception as one of her employees, his saving her from the fire and leaving her to forget him. He told them about her talents as a spy and the way she felt free doing something for other people. About her injury by Durant's hand and the strength she maintained when facing off against her mother—regarding the rebellion and her marriage prospects.

There was so much. She was such a huge part of him now and for the past year she had slowly bound him to her, heart and soul.

The story ended with his retelling of the night of their engagement. His chest heaved with the exertion of his words but letting them out into the air lessened the strain of them in his chest.

Shirina stepped forward and cradled his face in her hands. "If you were to pursue that marriage, she would be the subject of ridicule from folk that would hate her because of what she is, and she would never be able to go home again because you cannot leave this place. It would be like making her a prisoner in two places rather than giving her the freedom she deserves in either of them."

Aiden's thrashing heart cracked. "I know. Trust me I know."

Dair gave a low whistle. "That is rough, cousin."

Aiden only nodded. He wanted nothing more than to go through with their engagement, to marry the girl he'd fallen so deeply for. But there was simply no way to do it and for her to be safe. For them to ever be happy here together.

"I am sorry, Little Shadow," Fiadh said. "You have already given so much because of the folk. I wish we could give you this."

"There will be more love to find," Shirina said. "I do not believe Danu wishes for you to reign alone. There is a queen out there, not a High Queen, mind you, but a queen that will rule over your heart."

Aiden didn't tell them that he'd already found her. Instead, he pushed a smirk to surface on his face and flashed it at Shirina. "But it most certainly won't be Lady Saranae. Honestly, Shirina, that female is terrifying."

Shirina pursed her lips, debating whether to let the subject of Penelope go. Her expression softened. "Perhaps Saranae was not the best candidate to throw at you."

Dair snorted. "The only thing you even got right was the plant magic."

Aiden winced at the memory of his reaction to that.

Shirina's eyes widened, likely remembering the same thing. "The revelation about Penelope is answering so many of my questions."

"Yes," grumbled Thaen, "but what are we going to do about her?"

They all turned to Thaen. "What do you mean?" Aiden asked.

"There is a mage girl wreaking havoc on our lands and

disrupting not only our citizens, but the enemies' forces as well. She's like a loose firework zipping about. She needs to be taken care of."

Aiden stood. "I hope you're not insinuating a threat right now," he practically growled. Even if he had to give her up, he would not allow any harm to come to her.

Thaen raised his hands placatingly. "While I do not like the fact we have a mage on our lands, it does not mean I will hurt her. I only do Danu's will."

"I hope that's true." Aiden stepped up to him until they were nose to nose. "Because if you ever harm her—if you ever *think* about harming her, I will make certain it's *your* death that comes about, whether Danu permits it or not."

"You can trust me, cousin," Thaen whispered. "I will not harm her unless I am told, and as long as she is not a threat to this kingdom, the Goddess will have no reason to bid me do so."

A hand settled on Aiden's shoulder. "If nothing else," said Shirina, "at least Thaen could probably find her if Sgiath comes back empty handed."

Aiden whirled to face her. "You think I would trust him to find her after what he just said?"

She gave him a serious look. "You have trusted him up until this point. Will this girl really turn you against him so quickly?"

He wanted to shout *yes*. Penelope meant everything to him. He would protect her from every possible threat he could. But Shirina was right. Thaen had proved his loyalty to Aiden. They had become family and Aiden should trust them.

He clapped a hand on Thaen's shoulder. "I do trust you, Thaen. I know you only seek to do the Goddess's will. I will not doubt you. If it comes to it, I'd appreciate you finding her for me. We need to return her to Olympia to help fight the rebels there."

Thaen nodded his acceptance of Aiden's apology and his request for aid.

Shirina began walking toward the door, Fiadh at her side, and turned back to face them. "I do not think it will even come to that. Sgiath was sent to find her. He is likely to bring her back—"

A knock rattled the door in front of them and a servant came barreling in. "Councilor Sgiath to see you, My Sovereign. He has brought guests as well."

Aiden jumped toward the door, but Fiadh held him back.

"What timing," Shirina remarked. "Yes, yes. Let them in."

The servant bowed and allowed the High Councilor to enter the room. He bowed to Aiden and swept aside to allow the others in behind him.

Devan came first, one hand held behind his back in a way that made him look respectable, but Aiden knew he was reaching for a blade. Following closely behind him was his wife, her torso swollen and a greenish pallor to her cheeks.

Aiden glanced behind them, but the servant shut the door.

His eyes met Devan's, then Angelica's wide ones. "Where's Penelope?"

Angelica turned to her husband, and she placed a hand over her mouth. "Devan…"

Devan jumped forward and grabbed a vase of flowers sitting on the table beside him. He dumped the bouquet out onto the floor and passed the dish to his wife. Angelica promptly bent over it.

Dair and Thaen stiffened where they stood next to Aiden. He stared up at the ceiling, his palms sweating as Angelica was sick into the presumably very old and expensive vase. He didn't know what the proper protocol was for such a situation. Should he leave the room? Or fetch a towel?

Shirina stepped forward when Angelica quieted. She took the used vase and set it outside the hall as Angelica was led to a chair by her husband.

Angelica waved off everyone's belated concern and took Devan's hand. "We were wrong."

"Yes, love," Devan replied. "I do believe we made an error in our assumptions."

Angelica's gaze moved to Aiden, and she furrowed her brow. "Curses."

32
ASSASSINS AND DAGGERS

Penny followed behind Farrah as they wove through the well-maintained streets. Banners hung across the roads, the colorful fabrics beckoning the crowds past the buildings. Boughs of flowering trees hung over the walkways, emitting a sweet scent that twirled with the food stalls and the earthy smell of the tree towering above them.

The fair folk had always brought vibrancy to Olympia, but Penny had never imagined how vibrant it could be on this side of the Mist. Her hand grazed a garland of flowers wrapped around one of the many tree trunks. The buds left to bloom over the next few days burst open at her touch.

Farrah pulled her toward the middle of the walkway. "We need to be more careful. Being human on this side of the Mist is enough of an oddity."

Devan had attested to that, his human contacts in Faerie numbering only a dozen or so. Penny tucked her hands into the folds of her cloak. She stood a full head shorter than Farrah, her skin not nearly as smooth and her ears nowhere near pointed. Not to mention the speed at which everyone moved about and the fact that they all looked like swans meandering through the streets. If she could compare Farrah to a willow, Penny herself was a shrub.

There had been little they could do about her human appearance without a full glamour—which everyone here would see right through. Fae could see through most glamours unless the concealments were cast with enough power to confuse even them. Those with enough power to do such a thing and live were rare.

Their path carried them around the tree's trunk. Farrah had portalled them on the Autumn side of the tree nearby, but the bridge over the Teine River stood on the other side of the massive tree. Penny and Farrah had stayed in an empty house owned by one of Farrah's friends, as that friend was currently trapped in Olympia. Farrah had returned to Angelica's last night to see if they'd made it through the day unscathed, but both Devan and Angelica had disappeared along with their packs for the trip. Penny could only pray they met her at the bridge.

Penny turned a street corner, and a band of street performers rallied the crowd around the square. Magic flew through the air, twining together with the music. A pair of satyrs pranced in a circle with a little dwarf girl. A quartet of sprites sang, accompanied by a one-man band, strumming a lute with spots of light while his fingers danced over a flute and his foot beat at a drum. Smiles creased every face.

The mesmerizing music caught Penny in its hold, and she felt herself take a step toward the performers.

Farrah's grip returned to her arm, and she pulled her down another side street. "There will be plenty of festivities to indulge in during the revel. We can't have you getting distracted now."

Penny shook the magic from her mind, the fog of the music lifting slowly until they were out of range. It was so strange to feel magic pour out of everything in this land. It was no wonder so many humans had found themselves at the mercy of the fae before the Faerie Wars.

The magic finally released her when they stopped under the awning of a cobbler's shop. Penny looked in the window and gasped at the variety of merchandise. There had to be a shoe for every occasion and every size displayed on the walls.

The rustling of paper drew Penny's attention. Farrah pulled out their map and squinted out at the street. "I think we're about two blocks from the bridge." She tilted her head a few times, listening, and then folded up the paper. "I can hear the water, but I don't think it wise to walk in blindly."

Penny looked about the street. It was too early in the day to be jumping around on rooftops, the sun glaring down over their heads. They only had until noon. Angelica had to be there. She had to. Penny's eyes continued to scan the street, but she could see no way to get up to scout out their destination. "I think we may have to chance it."

Farrah glanced back and forth down the street, contemplating. "All right, here's what we'll do." Farrah led Penny around the side of the building. Her hands opened wide and red-tinted shadow bled from her fingers and onto the wall of the cobbler's shop. Farrah clapped, signaling her finished design. "This portal leads back to the house. If something goes wrong, we can escape through here. We have to be careful though. Anyone can go through it while its open like this, so it would be best to get this done as quickly as we can."

Penny nodded and pulled up the hood of her cloak as they quickly vacated the small alleyway. She'd try for any anonymity she could get.

Farrah led her down the street, the morning traffic beginning to thicken as everyone went out to prepare for the celebrations that evening. Though Penny couldn't understand everything the folk said, she could easily read the excitement on their faces and feel the buzz of the celebratory air.

She looked up at the giant tree. They were celebrating their new king.

Penny's heart faltered even as her steps remained sure. He was so close. He'd been in this place for months. Did he feel trapped? He'd always been a slave to duty, but he'd always done it out of love for his family and his kingdom. Now, he had neither.

Now he was a king.

Her steps faltered then. What was she even doing? Farrah had said it would be impossible to take him home. Wasn't that the entire reason she'd come? The Hunt had delivered news of Adira's presence. Sure, she could give Faerie's new king more details about the rebels' plot, but the fae would obviously take precautions now that they knew about the rebels. They wouldn't need Penny's help, and frankly, there wasn't much she could truly do anyway.

But...

"Penny?" Farrah came back around the corner she'd just turned. "Where did you go?"

"What am I really doing here, Farrah?" She splayed her hands out at the foreign streets around them. "I'm so out of my depth it's ridiculous! You said it yourself, Aiden is being crowned today and there's nothing I can do to bring him back to Olympia with me. This is his home now and I don't belong here." She pulled back her hood. "Look at me! I look like a street urchin. It's been months since he arrived here, and he hasn't escaped. The Lord of the Underworld would have come back to me if he'd been able to." She swiped a stray tear as it fell down her cheek. "If he even wanted to."

"If he wanted to? Oh, Penny." Farrah swiped away more tears from Penny's traitorous eyes. "Do you remember when he was injured in Eleusia? When I found you dragging him through the streets, bleeding out, and you helped me get him to safety? That boy woke up in my shop and the first word out of his mouth was your name. He'd nearly died, and his waking thought was not of himself or his injury, but your safety. His glamour had fallen away in his fear of what might have happened to you, and he risked revealing who he was all because of his worry for you."

Her hands moved to Penny's shoulders. "We spoke about you in the couple of days he stayed with me." She threw a hand in the air. "Plump pumpkins, the boy spoke of little else but you! No one feels like that about a person and then forgets them."

Penny wiped at the trails on her cheeks. "I just don't know what to do, Farrah." She didn't want to ruin anything he'd begun to create here. She knew he couldn't leave. Would her going to him only make things harder for him? It already felt impossible to her.

"Well, I think we should see a girl on a bridge about a dress and then we can go from there. One step at a time."

Penny took a deep breath and let it out, nodding. She could handle this. If nothing else, she could simply get into the revel to check on Aiden and leave if she found he didn't need her anymore.

Farrah smiled and pulled her around the corner. "The bridge is just down the street. We should see Angelica arrive from here."

Penny looked up and saw the sun almost directly overhead. If Angelica had made it to Crann Mòr, she'd arrive on the bridge any moment.

A cafe sat a little way down the road, and Farrah directed them to a table outside with a perfect view of the bridge. A handful of púca splashed in the water under the bridge, their shapes changing as young ellylon—*ellyllon*—laughed from the stone platform above them.

The murderous beasts were almost... charming.

A band of redcaps came around another corner, their sharp smiles nearly childish as they chased after each other. Even in the air above there was play—the winged fae swooping through the air currents and diving between the branches of the great tree standing sentinel above them.

Penny turned her attention back to the light traffic on the bridge. Angelica would be there.

And like her thoughts had summoned her, Angelica crested the curve of the bridge. Penny stood as her friend stopped in the middle and leaned against the stone railing. Devan came a few steps behind her and joined her on the bridge.

Farrah pulled her back down with a hiss. "We can't go over there."

"What?" Penny asked, startled. "Why not?"

Farrah pointed at the other side of the bridge and Penny's eyes caught on the male standing where the children laughing at the púca had been moments earlier. The hilt of a large sword peeked over his shoulder and his head turned from one side of the bridge to the other, watching.

"He came in just behind Devan, though I wouldn't have noticed if Angelica hadn't looked at him."

"Who is that?"

"The Lòchran," Farrah whispered.

Hope whooshed out of Penny's body. The Council had set a trap for her. They'd taken Angelica and Devan and were using them to lure her to the waiting assassin.

"Will he hurt them?"

Farrah shook her head, keeping a tight hold on Penny's arm. "I don't know. He's only known for doing what needs to be done and doing it well."

Penny swallowed back the lump stuck in her throat as fire bloomed in her chest. If someone truly did want to keep her from getting to Aiden, they were certainly being thorough. She would not allow this fae to hurt her friends. She plopped herself back in her chair and wrapped her flickering arms in her cloak.

Her eyes closed as the magic took over. She reached out with her gift to feel for the many plants in the vicinity. She gasped as her magic's over enthusiasm reached out and caught on the tree. An entire ecosystem burst through Penny's mind. The tree itself was a whole other world. The entire thing was divided into four sections, just like the land. Penny could feel the sleepy Autumn piece, the snoozing Winter, the waking Spring, and the lively Summer. She saw the folk and the animals all living within the maze of hallways and branches.

The tree's magic overwhelmed Penny's, pulling it in as if it were its own. It even looked similar to hers, the green magic weaving with hers as if it was examining it. Her magic reacted to it, leaping at the opportunity to meet. Penny had only ever seen it do something similar once—with Aiden's magic.

"Penny!"

Her magic pulled back and she opened her eyes, panting. She met Farrah's terror filled eyes.

"Penny? What just happened? You started gasping and you wouldn't respond. Are you all right?"

Penny winced. "Sorry, I got distracted."

"Distracted by what?"

Penny closed her eyes and reached out with her magic again, this time shoving it toward the river rather than the tree. Her senses protested, her magic obviously wanting to go back, but she connected with the plants under the bridge.

"Penny!" Angelica's voice rang out over the street, distracting Penny for a moment.

Farrah muttered something and Penny heard her move, but she reconnected with the lily pads and river grasses beneath the bridge with fervor. She opened her eyes and saw the Lòchran turn toward her.

She grinned and pushed out with her gift.

A giant, plant-made hand broke out of the water and grabbed the male. His eyes went wide as he was yanked over the railing and into the river.

Angelica screamed and Devan threw himself in front of her as a shield. Penny ran to them, waving her arms.

"It's all right. It was just me!"

She made it to the foot of the bridge when a cloud of black burst into the air from the river. The Lòchran came soaring back over the side, sword drawn and dripping wet.

Farrah skidded to a stop beside her and grabbed her arm. *"Run!"*

The Lòchran growled, and Penny's feet found their rhythm, running in the opposite direction of the fearsome fae.

"Penny, wait!" Angelica called behind her.

But the murderous glint in the Lòchran's pale eyes overrode anything Angelica could say. By the Goddess, Penny had just dumped the assassin in the river. If Angelica held any notion that Penny would have made it out of there alive, she'd been sorely mistaken.

Farrah's lithe form zipped through the gathering crowd, all drawn by Angelica's shouts and the brute chasing after them.

"Clear the way!" the booming voice hollered over the crowd.

Penny tried to ignore how close he sounded and took the turn toward the cobbler's shop. She saw Farrah disappear into the alleyway and followed after.

She made it to the mouth of the alleyway and felt something snag the end of her cloak. She instantly released the clasp, throwing it behind her. She spun, drawing her knife from the sheath at her side.

The Lòchran readjusted his footing after she'd escaped the cloak. He looked at her, squinting as if looking into the sun.

Before he could take another step forward, Penny threw her dagger. He barely managed to avoid it, swinging to the side as the steel passed by his chest. She hadn't aimed to kill him, but the throw had done its job effectively. As he turned back to her, she'd already stuck one foot in the portal. He rushed toward her, a furious frown his face. Penny ducked fully into the portal and allowed it to pull her the rest of the way through.

A deep growl followed her into the darkness as she fell.

The portal spit her out onto the sitting room floor of Farrah's friend's house and the swirling black mass blinked out of existence.

Farrah pulled her to her feet and wrapped her in a fierce hug. "Great gourds, I thought he caught you. I was so scared. I nearly jumped back through, but you came stumbling out."

Penny slumped into one of the chairs situated about the miniature parlor. "It was a close one for sure. I didn't even get the dress!" Her fingers brushed the empty sheath at her hip. "And I lost one of my daggers."

Farrah slouched into the chair across from her. "By the Goddess, this has gotten out of control. What are we going to do now?"

A deep, obnoxious laugh erupted from Penny. "Improvise."

33
ANOINT

AIDEN FIDGETED AS THE SERVANT STRAIGHTENED THE SHOULDERS OF his jacket. Aiden stood as close to the window as he could, even if he couldn't view the bridge from that distance. Thaen had left with Devan and Angelica an hour ago to scout out the bridge and wait for Penelope. They would be meeting any minute.

She was so close to him he could almost feel her. If he closed his eyes, it was almost like her magic was reaching out and brushing up against his soul right there and then.

The door to his room burst open and Dair walked in. "I hope he is not late for the anointing."

"Who?"

Dair quirked a brow, but a knowing smile stretched over his face. "Thaen?"

Aiden shook his head and turned back to the mirror in front of him. Of course. "I have no doubt he will be here." He thanked the servant and dismissed him. The kind male slipped from the room, leaving Aiden and Dair in relative privacy.

Dair leapt and landed on the bed in the middle of the space. The High King's rooms were in the middle of a remodel, all the walls brought down by the Green Man—whom Aiden had the opportunity to meet briefly—and the space left completely open until Aiden decided how he wanted it laid out. The thought of figuring out a blueprint for his own rooms caused a whirlwind of feelings. There was a war coming to Faerie, so the idea of decorating didn't seem in good taste. He'd hoped to return to Eagallach after the equinox, but it seemed more apparent every day that wouldn't be the case.

"So," Dair yawned, "what do you think is taking so long?"

Aiden's pulse jumped, but Fiadh stepped into the room before he could respond. He had had his anointing as Winter King earlier that morning, to allow Aiden to be the spotlight for the evening, the High Councilors had said. Aiden almost begrudged his cousin the simple anointing, but his sour feelings washed away with Fiadh's presence. His smile radiated the joy he must have felt now holding the full power to rule over the Court he'd been steward over the last two decades. With Aiden's mother being the last queen, technically Aiden would've inherited Winter's crown. But as High Queen Rìanoch had had no children for the Land to even consider and no other heirs had been chosen, the faerie-glass throne had passed to him. Now that he was to be High King, Fiadh would officially rule over Winter.

"Bruadair, go torture someone else," Fiadh said, half-heartedly. "Your cousin does not need your prodding."

Dair grabbed a pillow and fluffed it before propping himself up on Aiden's gargantuan bed. "I am not prodding. I am only hoping to keep my cousin distracted from the upcoming ceremony."

Aiden felt his pulse in his throat now.

Fiadh glared at his son but turned a pitying look on Aiden. "Today is turning out to be a long one."

Aiden nodded and turned back to the mirror. The black jacket sat stiffly on his shoulders, silver trim glittering on the cuffs and curling around the shining brass buttons. He'd had someone cut his hair again, not yet willing to part with this particular hairstyle, no matter how many times Dair made fun of his "stubby hairs." Aiden still couldn't picture himself with hair down his back like the rest of his family. The only ellyllon he'd seen without an overabundance of hair was Auntie Taddie, who was completely bald.

Fiadh came up behind him. "Are you ready for today?"

Aiden tried to pull confidence into his expression but could feel himself failing. He turned to face Fiadh directly. "Am I allowed to say 'no?'"

Fiadh laughed. "Of course. I would take any other response as a sign of insanity."

"Or tyranny," supplied Dair.

"The point is," Fiadh said, "you do not have to be ready; you just have to be willing. Things happen in our lives that we are not in control of, but it is up to us to either face them or ignore them. We will not always believe we are ready, but Goddess willing, we will be able."

Aiden took a deep breath and let it out. He glanced back out the window and then turned back to Fiadh. "I am willing."

Fiadh clapped him on the shoulder. "Good."

"Excellent." Shirina swept through the doorway, obviously having heard the last bit of the conversation. "Now that we are all set, let us head toward the Throne Room."

Aiden looked out the window again and back to Shirina. "But what about Thaen?"

What about Penelope?

Shirina shook her head. "They haven't returned. I imagine there was quite a conversation considering the Elies and Sgiath's daughter assumed we were keeping things from you."

"Based on what you have told us of her," said Dair, "I bet she is giving Thaen a good thrashing."

"Maybe not a full thrashing," said a deep voice from the doorway, "but there was definitely a skirmish."

Aiden looked over Shirina's head to see Thaen standing in the doorway. Dripping wet.

Dair burst out laughing. "Did you go for a swim?"

Thaen growled. "More like our king's little mage dragged me into the river." He tossed something metal onto the table. One of Penelope's daggers.

Aiden was on him in the next instant. "Where is she?" The words came out quick and demanding. He grabbed at the front of Thaen's soggy tunic. "If you hurt a hair on her head, I swear—"

Thaen threw up his hands. "Easy, cousin. If anyone was hurting anyone, she was the culprit." He pointed at the dagger. "She nearly stuck me with that right before she jumped through a portal. I do not know where she went from there."

Aiden slowly released his hold. "I apologize." He turned back to the dagger, the one he'd had made for her, and picked it up. Where was she now?

Thaen shrugged. "No harm done."

Dair picked up the dagger. "Are you telling me a little mage girl almost got the best of the infamous Lòchran?"

Thaen growled. "Yes."

Even Aiden hadn't been able to get the upper hand on Thaen. Ever. "How?" Aiden asked.

Thaen frowned, his brows forming deep canyons on his brow. "I could not see her," he mumbled.

"What?" Shirina and Fiadh asked.

"I said I could not see her, all right? I almost lost her in the crowd because she looks just like Danu's magic. I could barely see her cloak and when I grabbed it, she practically disappeared. Penelope Barclay looks like every other piece of the Goddess's magic. If she were to lay herself down on the ground, I would likely mistake her for a patch of grass rather than a person." He pinched his nose between his fingers. "I could not grab her before she went into the portal."

"Why did she run?" Aiden asked. "You had Angelica with you. Didn't she explain?"

"I do not know. One moment, I was standing across from

the Elies on the bridge, the next I was in the water after she used plants to pull me under. I had to cut through the cursed stuff with my own sword."

Aiden raked a hand through his hair. "I knew I should have gone."

Shirina cut into the conversation. "We were not going to allow you to strut through the streets of the capital with a group of rebels running amok and the streets teeming with fae refugees and guests for your anointing." She glanced at a clock hanging on the wall. "Which will begin in five minutes."

His family ushered him out of the room, but he grabbed Thaen's arm to keep him at his side. "You said there was a portal and Angelica mentioned she'd been with Farrah. Could she have recognized you?"

Thaen nodded gravely. "It is possible. I have not had much interaction with Sgiath's daughter, but if she knew about me, we can assume she told Penelope. From what her father has said, the young female is notorious for knowing more than she should." Thaen pulled his sodden tunic from his chest. "I am sorry, Aedon. I wish I could have accomplished what you asked of me. I understand your worry about Penelope, even if I do not agree with it."

Aiden attempted to shake off his nervousness to give his cousin a smile. "If I know Penelope Barclay as well as I think I do, that will not be the last we see of her."

The group stopped Aiden at a tall set of double doors, much grander than the ones to the council room, but not nearly as intricate. Only a tall tree with wide roots stood carved across them.

Shirina turned, wincing at Thaen's soggy clothing before her gaze turned to Aiden. "All right, Little Shadow. This is it."

Locusts took flight in Aiden's chest, bouncing sporadically against his rib cage.

Fiadh chuckled and set his hands on Aiden's shoulders. "I

promise, there is nothing in that room as frightening as that thing you call a pet."

Aiden quirked a brow. "Spot is not frightening." They'd left him back in Eagallach, much to Aiden's dismay. He had seemed happy playing in the Winter Palace's extensive gardens.

Dair adjusted the cuffs of his fine, silver jacket. "If you say so."

Thaen flicked water from his tunic onto Dair, who shrieked in anger. Thaen smirked, but before Dair could retaliate, Shirina snapped "Boys!" and they straightened.

Fiadh shook his head. "We are about to send you off to be coronated High King of all of Faerie and still you have the indecency to act like children."

Aiden scuffed the toe of his boot on the ground. "Honestly, it makes this whole thing seem a little less dire."

"I suppose it would." Fiadh smiled. "Remember, this anointing is not anything like what you have in Olympia. There will not be long-winded ceremonies or speeches. All you have to do is say 'yes' one time and then allow the *èildear* to do the rest." They'd gone over what to expect a few times in the last couple of days, but Aiden still felt unprepared. Fiadh's grip on his shoulders tightened. "You are king, no matter how this ceremony goes. It is your calling, and no one can take that from you."

"Until I die."

Thaen stiffened and Shirina huffed, but Fiadh smirked. "And that will not be for another five centuries at least, if I have anything to say about it." His hand fell back, and he returned to his place beside Shirina. "We will be with you the whole way, and you can ask us anything afterward. Just remember, you only have to say 'yes.' Nothing too difficult."

Aiden took a deep breath and nodded. He could do this. He had his family gathered around him. There was little he couldn't face with them at his side.

Shirina gave him one last reassuring smile before sending a plume of shadow to open the doors.

Aiden clenched his jaw in an attempt not to gape. Faerie's Throne Room looked nothing like Olympia's.

No ceiling blocked the light from shining in, only thick boughs of greenish-blue leaves interlocked to form a semblance of a roof. Sunlight rained down through the branches, dappling the floor and the folk beginning to stand from their chairs. Instead of a long path up to a throne sitting at the back of the room, the faerie-glass throne sat in the middle, the chairs circling it instead of situated in front of it. The mythical throne sparkled in the sunlight, reflecting an array of rainbows onto the crowd around it.

An *èildear* stood at the front of the throne. The male stood, feet squared with his hands behind his back, dressed in a pair of black trousers and a pale-yellow tunic. Aiden wouldn't be able to tell him apart from the rest of the crowd if they hadn't spoken briefly that morning. He gave Aiden the same reassuring smile he had when they'd met and gestured for Aiden to join him at the base of the throne. Fiadh led Shirina past him to a row of empty chairs, followed closely by the twins, both more serious than they'd been only moments before. The *èildear* set a fist over his heart and bowed to Aiden. The rest of the room followed suit.

Aiden's insides squirmed at the attention, but his limbs remained still. The *èildear* straightened from his bow with the rest of the crowd and gestured for everyone to be seated. Shirina had told Aiden this was the one instance when he didn't have to be in charge. He only had to follow the holy man's orders.

The *èildear* cleared his throat, aquamarine eyes shining. "Welcome, Tuatha Dè Dannan, to the anointing of Aedon, Son of the Night Court and High King of Faerie." He led Aiden toward the throne and allowed him to sit before turning back to the crowd. "Just as in the past, we recognize that it is not us as the folk who decide who rules over us, but the Goddess Herself who chooses the guardian of our kingdom, blessed upon infancy by the previous ruler and once again blessed upon the age of thirty—or in this case, twenty—when they are taught the ways of the magic of the Land or take the Throne of Faerie if necessary."

He turned, speaking to another section of the room. "The last ruler, High Queen Rìanoch, was chosen by Danu to bring us into a new age. It is by Danu's own guidance that High Queen Rìanoch's crown be passed to her nephew, High King Aedon, who has already been chosen by the magic of Faerie as High King. Only by his death or his loss of Danu's favor can he lose such a title." He turned back and gave Aiden a wink. "Not that the second happens very often. As long as you do your best and try not to become an evil overlord, we should not have a problem."

A few in the crowd chuckled quietly, and Aiden returned the *èildear's* smile. The male's strong, sure hand cupped Aiden's shoulder and he felt magic buzzing under the *èildear's* skin. "I have spoken with High King Aedon," he said, facing the crowd once again, "and have found him of sound mind and pure heart. I believe he has a deep love of this land and that Danu has chosen him to rule over us for whatever time She deems him worthy to do so." He turned to Aiden, his keen, blue eyes somber. "Do you Aedon, accept the title of High King over all of Faerie and Her habitants until the Goddess, Danu, prepares the way for another, whether from your own seed or that of Her many children?"

Aiden swallowed. This was the moment. This was what his family had prepared him for all this time. This was what all these people had waited to hear since their queen had been taken from them.

But this wasn't the moment when he had decided to become High King. No, that had happened on the balcony overlooking the Grand Hall in the palace atop the snowy peaks.

This was not what made him High King. He'd been king long before he'd sat on this legendary throne.

"Yes."

Nothing miraculous happened. The sun didn't descend from the sky and the birds in the trees didn't break out into song. There was no flash of magic and no heavenly visitation. No one clapped, no one cheered. The only sound was his voice echoing his answer across the room.

But nothing could have taken away the feeling of peace that descended over him. This was what he'd been called to do. He'd simply never had the opportunity to see it until he'd stepped foot on Faerie's soil.

The *èildear* knelt at the foot of the dais and withdrew a vial from the pouch at his waist. "I anoint you with this oil, taken from Crann Mòr herself. There are many things we receive from the Great Tree and each of them has special significance. This oil is representative of the essence of the Tree, symbolizing the connection our ruler has with the Land and Her people, just as the *toradh na beatha* connects us individually." He stepped up in front of Aiden and sprinkled droplets of liquid on his head. "By the authority passed to me and gifted by our Great Mother, I bless you with a strong mind and a valiant heart. There will be many struggles you are faced with, and I bless you with the fortitude to hold fast to that which you know to be true, to protect your kingdom from those who would see its downfall. You must never forget who you are and must strive to always remember who you *truly* serve."

The *èildear* stepped back and reached his arm out toward the branches above them. One of the boughs descended and placed a ring of leafy branches in his hand. With a smile, he placed the crown on Aiden's head. "We do not have a crown of gold or jewels in our kingdom," he said quietly. "Only a ring of wood that represents the connection our ruler has to the magic of this Land and the blessing of our Goddess."

The male stepped down from the dais and once again

placed his fist over his heart and bowed his head. The rest of the crowd stood, and Aiden met Shirina and Fiadh's watery gazes as they mimicked the *èildear's* gesture with the rest of the attendees, their sons beside them with proud smiles stretching their cheeks.

"All hail High King Aedon," the *èildear* said.

Aiden settled his fist over his hand and bowed his head. He was not the only ruler here.

The rest of the crowd took up the call. "All hail High King Aedon."

34
BRIDGES AND BRANCHES

Penny glanced behind her again as she retrieved the small pouch from her pocket. The coat she'd borrowed from the house she and Farrah were using as their base of operations drooped over her hands, hiding her task completely from view of those on the street. Her fingers deftly untied the cord and the leather unrolled to expose the iron pins. She slid two out of their sleeves and set to work on the lock in front of her.

Farrah had left earlier in search of shoes, leaving Penny to the much harder job—the dress. Nearly all the shops had closed for the day, everyone preparing for the festivities taking place later that evening. The pins shifted in the lock, and she felt the mechanism inside click into place. She pocketed the pins and opened the door.

The crisp smell of fabric hit her nose. By the Goddess, when was the last time she'd been to a seamstress's shop? Mother used to take her at least once a month when they'd lived in Eleusion. Before everything had started falling apart. Penny took in another breath, the sharp aroma of the dyes hitting her firmly between the ribs.

She shut the door and drew the curtains together.

Focus.

Penny glided past the racks of fabrics to where a few dresses stood on display stands. It seemed like nearly every shop in town was catering to the parties for the equinox and coronation, but few dresses had been left to choose from. This was the first shop with one Penny could even manage to put on herself. The plain, black dress hung on the stand like a glittering mourner, the crepe skirt pooling on the floor around the base like ink. Penny would have to pin it up to accommodate her shorter legs. The bodice had some beaded embellishment, thin swirls wrapping around the bust and down the long sleeves.

It looked like a funeral dress.

"Happy birthday to me," Penny sighed. She stripped it from its stand, folding it neatly before setting it in the bag alongside the revel invitation. After tucking everything under the heavy coat, she withdrew a bag of coin and set it on the counter. If she had to steal, the least she could do was compensate the seamstress.

With the door once again locked behind her, she strode back toward the house. The invitation stated the guests would be admitted to the revel at sundown. She planned on arriving during the hubbub, hoping to get lost in the growing crowd of newcomers and into the tree without notice.

And then she'd find Aiden.

Her thoughts carried her around the street corner toward the safe house. The shock of orange standing at the door had her skittering back out of view.

Sgiath had already found them.

Cursing fae magic and all its fancy benefits, she peeked back around and saw Farrah leaning in the doorway, brow furrowed as her father spoke. Farrah's eyes widened and she began speaking, quickly, but her words were lost to the sounds of the city.

Penny's heart sank. Farrah was compromised. Penny pulled away from the street corner and sprinted the other way.

She would have to figure the rest out on her own. And curses, her sword was still in the safe house. The dagger in her boot would have to suffice for tonight.

First, Aiden. Then Devan and Angelica—and the dagger she'd thrown. Now Farrah and her sword. Everyone who could possibly help her was disappearing quicker than a cottonwood could shed its fluff. But if she was going to help any of them, she had to get into that revel. It was the only way she could warn everyone about Adira's schemes and plan their next move.

It was her only chance to see Aiden.

Tears sprang into her eyes as she looked up toward the giant tree shooting into the sky. He was king. He was stuck here. But what about her? Would she be able to return to Olympia when the one carrying her heart in his hands remained? Of course, she would stay until everything was finished, help Aiden like she did in Olympia and help him rid Faerie of Adira's scourge, but what about after?

A growl tore from her throat, and she shook her head, wiping the traitorous tears from her cheeks. That didn't matter right now. By the Goddess, they had a rebellion attacking two different kingdoms and attempting to overthrow both rulers. There would be time to sort through her feelings later. Right now, she needed to get to Aiden and figure out what they would do next. She had to uncover who else created the Mist and help keep Adira from finding them.

With determination at her back and a path forward, she turned her thoughts to her plans. The Winter Bridge was still the best option for her to get into the tree. She had a dress that covered her feet. Perhaps she could get away with wearing her boots. Dancing would be difficult, but she didn't have much hope of doing that anyway. This revel was a job, not a party.

The autumnal scenery shifted around her as she wove through the streets. The sun hid behind the trunk, giving the silvery bark a fiery aura. The shade of the tree spread over where she stood, casting the street into darkness while light still blazed everywhere else.

Penny's heartbeat picked up as she made her way to the Winter quarter of the city. Wooden cabins and barrow mounds made way for igloos and stone buildings. The temperature changed almost instantly, the crisp chill of Autumn giving way to the biting cold of Winter. It was strange, to say the least. If she were a plant, she'd have withered almost instantly.

In her mind, she recalled the map Devan had created for her and began trekking toward the tree. The light continued to fade as she stomped down the walkways. As she traveled nearer, more fair folk joined her on the street. The folk chattered excitedly, all dressed in their best as they made their way toward the great tree.

Perhaps it would be easier than she thought. She ducked down a small alleyway between a pair of quaint houses and pulled out her newly acquired dress. Quickly, she undressed, the cold wind nipping at her skin as she removed the layers of her disguise. The dress fell over her like water, puddling around her feet in ripples of black. Penny bit the inside of her cheek. Sweet Gaia, there was so much fabric.

She pulled her hair from the braid wrapped around her head. It fell in waves down her back, and she used the few pins she had to form a smaller crown of braids to keep it away from her face. If only she had a mirror. She couldn't imagine how terrible she looked. Mother would've gone purple seeing her in such a state.

Penny quickly turned her thoughts back to the long skirt. If she pulled it up, she could walk, but it would be difficult to hold up the whole time. She unraveled her belt from the trousers on the ground and used it to bunch up the excess fabric underneath. It gave the dress an odd fold where the bodice met the skirt, but thankfully her hips kept the belt from slipping. She hid her borrowed coat and the rest of her ensemble in a pile under a bush. If she had time, she would come back and grab it after the revel. It wasn't like she wouldn't be back before late tomorrow. With the dagger tucked back into her boot and the invitation tucked into the odd pocket she'd created around her waist, she stepped back out onto the street.

More fae streamed toward the tree as the sun finally descended, their voices heightened and faces grinning. The celebratory air thickened around her, buoying her steps. It felt like only days ago Dion had been crowned and she'd seen this same excitement sweep the streets of Olympia's own capital. Faerie's capital was a bit less populated, but the feeling nearly tripled what she'd witnessed when Dion had been crowned. Something about this night felt significant, as if the entire kingdom was taking a breath for the first time in a long while. She could see it in the way the fae spoke with one another. The ellyllon and the bwbachod mingled in the streets, mixes of shadow and light dancing in the air.

How is Aiden going to do with such a crowd?

Urgency gave her steps more speed as she thought of him. He was only a few blocks away, likely being harangued by all of the new folk coming to greet him. She'd felt the rumble in the streets when the announcement of his coronation went out. He really was High King now. Had he been willing? Olympia knew so little about the way things were done here. Was it similar to how it was done at home? Did Aiden have to be married? Penny balked at the idea, heat building in her chest. What if he'd had to agree to something he never wanted? From what Farrah had said, it seems like it had already been decided when the High Queen had died. When Adira had murdered her.

Was Adira already inside?

By the Goddess, she would bring that gargantuan tree to the ground if that cursed woman did anything to him. He already had enough on his plate, being High King after living his life thinking he'd always be nothing but a prince in name. If

Adira tried to pull anything tonight, Penny would kill her with her bare hands.

The crowd swelled as it neared the outer wall of the tree. It wasn't a true wall, the thing being made of smaller trees interwoven together to make a sort of see-through hedge. Between the trunks, she glimpsed the crowds flowing like a river toward the northwestern entrance to Crann Mòr. Penny lifted the edge of her skirt and broke away from the stream of fae. She had an actual river to find.

Snowy branches of the tree wall guided her around. Penny rubbed her hands together, attempting to banish the cold from her uncovered fingers. Having numb fingers while attempting a break in could become a liability. Devan's map was a tad blurry in her memory, but she recalled the bridge being almost exactly between the two main gates leading out into Winter and Spring. She turned her walk into a light jog to keep her body temperature up. Praise the Goddess she hadn't left her boots behind.

Her arms wrapped around her middle, attempting to keep her dress's haphazard alteration in place. The belt wiggled a bit on her waist, but the skirt didn't move too much before she finally spotted the glistening ice bridge.

Sweet Gaia, it looked like glass. Ice crusted the frozen river, gathering up into frosted steps and descending down the other side of the trees. The first hints of moonlight crept over the smooth arch into the wintery gardens of Crann Mòr.

Penny repeated the password Devan had given her over and over again. Her lips warmed with the exercise as she made it to the base of the bridge. Several steps stretched upward before the bridge flattened out over the branches of the wall. Penny gathered up her skirt and took a step up, her eyes and ears strained for the troll that manned the bridge. Devan had said it would be patrolling the top or sitting under the arch on the city side. She made it to the top of the steps without complication. Taking advantage of the vacancy, she quickly worked her way across the tops of the trees, wary of the slippery ice under her soles.

"Perhaps the troll got the night off," she whispered to herself. That would be more than lucky. It would make this impossible mission slightly more possible.

"You would be right."

Penny spun, slipping over the center of the bridge for a moment before catching herself on the frozen railing. She looked behind her and found a pair of pale eyes and a frown glaring back at her.

"Lòchran," she greeted. "I didn't realize 'troll' was another word for 'pest.'"

A grin slowly replaced the frown. "I might actually be able to see why my king likes you."

Penny's heart skipped a beat and she straightened. "Where is he?"

"Just inside." The Lòchran gestured to the tree behind her. "I will take you to him myself if you come quietly."

Penny's eyes narrowed and she pulled her hands behind her back. "And I'm to trust the word of a known assassin who tried to attack me earlier today?" He'd even used her friends as bait. Had he hurt Angelica? Devan? Farrah had said the assassin was known to get things done by whatever means necessary. Without knowing his true intentions, it was wiser to get past him and find Aiden for herself.

The Lòchran folded his arms over his chest. "It does not matter if you do not trust me. My job is to bring you inside where you will be safe and not cause a scene."

Penny nearly snorted and clenched her hands behind her back. "Says the fae with the giant sword to the unarmed mage." He didn't need to know about the second dagger in her boot. She was still angry she'd lost the first one.

"If I wanted you dead..." He squinted at her, shaking his head as if to refocus his gaze. "What are you doing, little mage?"

"Something you're definitely not going to enjoy." She splayed her glowing hands and the trees on either side of the bridge crashed against the ice. A trunk sheared through the bridge right between them. Penny didn't look back to watch the Lòchran fall, but instead turned to rush toward the Tree. Ice cracked beneath her feet and her hands flew out to steady her. In answer to her distress, the trees attempted to grab hold of her, cradling her in their branches.

"No! No, wait!" she cried out.

She heard a curse from behind her and looked down to see the Lòchran standing right where she'd been a moment before. The bridge below gave way as he sprinted across at a speed Penny would have never been able to match. He dove into the frosted grass on the other side right as the entire archway collapsed.

The branches hoisted her into the air of their own volition. The twiggy branches snagged on the skirt of her gown, leaving long tears and ruining the fine fabric. Her belt came loose from underneath her dress and dropped into the weaving net of tree limbs. A flash of silver caught her eye, and she watched the invitation flutter to the ground between the trunks.

The trees bent over, dangling her over the ground. She frantically searched for the shine of the invitation. Her chances of getting into the revel seemed to disappear every second.

The Lòchran got to his feet only a few dozen yards from her.

"Curses," she hissed as she ripped the last of her skirt from the branches and began running toward the trunk, the Lòchran closing the distance between them quickly. She reached the bark of the tree, the silvery skin smooth for several feet up from the roots. Her shining hand connected with the trunk, but she couldn't get the roots to move and trap the assassin gaining ground.

"Blast it all!" Penny growled between her teeth. She looked back to see the Lòchran only a dozen or so feet away, hand on his sword and shadows licking at his heels, with no escape in sight. At least if she could get into the tree, she could use the passages and crowds to somewhat slow him down.

He squinted at her as he drew close, shadows curling around his shoulders and rippling at his feet. After weeks of cheating it in this cursed land, death had finally come for her.

"Goddess, save me," she whispered, and turned to press her flickering hands against the trunk once again.

But her fingers only met air as she fell.

35
APPLAUSE

AIDEN PACED BACK AND FORTH IN FRONT OF THE MAGICAL FIREPLACE. He looked at it again, surprised they would allow such a thing in a tree, but then supposed it was a magical tree that could protect itself.

His fingers trailed over the leafy branches encircling his head. He hadn't changed out of his clothing or taken off the crown since the ceremony earlier that day. Shirina had told him it was tradition for the ruler to wear it until all of the celebrations were over. Then they would take it and put it in a chamber somewhere. The only crown Aiden needed was the one branded into his magic.

Shirina and Fiadh were already down in the ballroom, greeting guests and entertaining the crowd before Aiden made his kingly entrance. Apparently, the king was to arrive to his own party absolutely last. Faerie had the strangest customs, and it was still somewhat difficult to keep up with them.

Anxiety quickened his steps. Thaen still hadn't reported back. Devan had given them a full accounting of what Penelope had planned.

He touched his hand to the pocket of his jacket, the parcel

he'd sent Shirina out for tucked safely inside. Penelope was out there, practically alone and on her birthday. He'd been counting on celebrating with her in Olympia and this was nothing close to what he'd imagined for the occasion.

They had to get her somewhere safe before she got herself into trouble. She could obviously handle herself on the streets of Olympia, but Faerie was an entirely different world.

"Please stop!" Dair groaned. "Your constant pacing is making me nauseous."

Aiden slowed his steps but couldn't find it within him to completely cease the nervous tic. "This has grown completely out of control. How has no one stopped her?"

"Perhaps because the Tuatha underestimate every single other species on this planet?"

Aiden's brow furrowed and he finally ceased pacing to look at his cousin.

Dair rolled his eyes. "Pride is a powerful thing. There will always be those who look down on others for simply being different than them. The fae are children of Danu's own womb. Some believe that to mean we are entitled to more and that the things of this world are here simply for our benefit or pleasure."

"But that is not what your texts say. That is not what you teach."

"No, it is not. Every particle of life on this world was created—whether by birth or magic—by Danu's hand. She gave everything life and all of it purpose. We must respect the balance and remember how she cherished each one of Her creations. But there are still some—especially the ellyllon—who think they have a right over everyone else because they are more powerful, when instead they should be using that power to help others as Danu bade them to."

"They teach that in Olympia as well, that we are not to be rulers over men, but helpers to one another. But I feel like you all have so much more knowledge about the Goddess than we do."

Dair swung an arm over the back of his chair. "Isn't it interesting how quickly that can happen when one group separates from another? We used to all carry the same knowledge, the same access to magic, but because of our division, the humans are losing that."

"But they had to leave, "Aiden protested.

"I agree, but they also cut themselves off from anything to do with us, including the Goddess and Her gifts. Thaen and I weren't around, but our parents tell stories sometimes about the bloodbath the Faerie Wars were and the magic hunts for decades after. This rebellion is simply a repeat of the time after the Wars, when those without magic slaughtered those with it. This time, however, The Cartographer is attempting to reverse what happened and enslave the gifted in some sort of skewed form of justice."

"Skewed justice about sums her up."

Dair watched him for a moment, studying. Aiden attempted not to look away, though the scrutiny made the tips of his ears warm.

"I still cannot believe you were raised by her." Dair pursed his lips. "I remember the day *Athair* found out you had been sent to Olympia as a babe. When he heard about Auntie Morana's death. He was crushed. He had not left her side during the entirety of her bed rest, but he had to go back to Winter."

"Why did he leave?"

"Thaen's gift manifested only days before you were born," Dair answered, pain in his gaze. "One second, we were sparring, just fooling around and pushing our limits. The next, Thaen was on the ground, screaming. I've never seen him so terrified. *Màthair* came rushing in, trying to soothe him, but the amount of magic Thaen could feel from her overwhelmed him so much she could not even get near him.

"We had to call *Athair* back from Crann Mòr, where High Queen Rìanoch had put your mother up with the best healers we had. He thought he could help Thaen and make it back before Auntie Morana delivered. But you came weeks earlier than expected, the queen's body not able to handle the poison and carrying you. We did not even know you had been born until you were already gone, High Queen Rìanoch sending you to King Horace in the middle of the night."

He leaned forward. "We do not often see my *athair* cry, but he wept more during those days than any other time. I remember him holding that missive in his hand, telling him that High Queen Rìanoch had sent you across the border and that his best friend had died without him there." Dair's head drooped, and his lavender hair fell in a curtain around him. "I had never seen him so enraged either. He nearly went to get you, Fuath be cursed. *Màthair* talked him out of it, told him it would do more harm than good."

Aiden swallowed. "She was probably right." Father wouldn't have tolerated such a thing. He would have had Fiadh killed and Durant would have been more than willing to make it happen. "I am glad he didn't."

Dair stood and came up beside him, leaning an arm against the polished mantle. "We have always thought of you, cousin. You were constantly in our prayers and both my parents constantly petitioned the Goddess for your safety in the temple. Even now, we only have love for you." He clapped Aiden on the back, his sincere expression disappearing. "But enough of this dreary talk. I think it is time for us to make our way to the revel."

Aiden looked up at the clock on the wall. The revel had been going for little over half an hour already. Shirina told him to be at the grand staircase in another fifteen minutes.

He took a deep breath. "Any sage words of advice?"

"Find someone pretty to dance with and smile as if everything is exactly how you want it to be."

Aiden peeked through the small crack between the beautiful double doors. The music seeped between the songbirds frozen in flight against the wood. The sound grabbed his attention and pulled him forward until he could see the glittering lights and colorful costumes of the dancing guests.

By the Goddess, there were so many of them.

"My Sovereign, are you ready to go in?"

Aiden glanced over at the doorman. A trow stood waiting for Aiden to give him the command to open the door. A wide brimmed, red hat decorated with a gigantic, white plume sat askew on his overly large head. The trow flicked his star-shaped pupils toward the door and back to Aiden, obviously eager to get his job done. Aiden took a fortifying breath and took a step away from the door.

"All right. Open the door."

The trow grinned, showing two full rows of teeth and grabbed the giant handle to pull the tall doors open. Light flooded the hallway where Aiden stood, a level above the ballroom floor. He pushed his feet toward the end of the platform. No banister edged the balcony or the stairs along the wall.

Floating stars swirled along the cavernous ceiling above them. Wisps and pixies danced in the open air as the flightless Tuatha danced below. More colors than Aiden could even begin to absorb rippled over the floor. The fae did not have a singular style as the Olympians tended too. Instead, all different kinds of ensembles clothed the guests. Dresses made of gigantic leaves. Jackets shaped from the shells of large beetles. Full length robes and costumes not even the most daring of Olympians would wear. Some of the males went shirtless, some of the females in trousers. All looked resplendent, no matter what they were wearing.

The crowd all quieted, everyone's attention turning

upward without a cue. It was almost eerie until he realized the music had stopped. Perhaps there had been a signal he hadn't been aware of because everyone showed their deference.

The trow that had manned the door came up beside him. "All hail High King Aedon!" the trow called, and the crowd echoed it back. The words crashed over him; the sheer amount of voices thundering in the space vibrated in his diaphragm.

Aiden gulped and called for everyone to rise, his voice coming out more collected than he inwardly felt. He nodded his thanks to the doorman and made his way down the stairs. Perhaps he could get lost in the crowd and get through the night relatively unscathed.

The music started up again and his family met him at the bottom of the steps, Thaen still unaccounted for. Aiden patted his pocket again and opened his mouth to ask, but Shirina shook her head. No news. Aiden's heart thumped against his rib cage. If she was coming, she would have been there by now.

Shirina took his arm and led him toward the center of the room. "No news does not mean bad news. Even if she does not show up tonight, we will still find her and make sure to get her to safety." She smiled and greeted another member of the crowd.

Aiden attempted to mimic her calm and pressed an inviting smile onto his face. The folk set a fist to their chests when he got close or made eye contact, but that was all the interaction he received. He allowed Shirina to drag him to the buffet at the other side. A rainbow of delicacies stretched from one end of the wall to the other. Roasted meats, cheeses, and breads wove between fruits, raw meats, and what looked like punch bowls of actual blood. Aiden kept away from those, but his stomach rumbled as he set foods on his plate and grabbed a bowl of fruit with his empty hand. A variety of fruit mixed together, sprinkled with blue seeds.

He took his first bite of the fruit, praying the *toradh na beatha* would help center him. The magic at his core hummed. His thoughts cleared a little as the Land's magic aligned more firmly with his. He took another bite and smiled. He could almost feel the magic smile back at him.

Then it sent him a wave of excitement.

His brows pulled together. Excitement? What did the Land have to be excited about? He opened his eyes and looked about the room. His stomach buzzed. Perhaps he should have eaten something else before he'd eaten the *toradh na beatha.* He randomly selected something from his plate and stuffed it in his mouth, not caring what it was. He took a few more bites, but the crackle in his bones only increased.

A couple brushed past him, and he barely acknowledged their bows before they glided on. His eyes scanned the room, taking in the sweeping dancers, the colorful outfits and multitude of creatures. A female in a dress that looked like it was made of giant, orange butterfly wings slumped into a chair only a few seats away from him. She offered the same deference as the rest of the crowd and toyed with the food on her plate.

He grabbed the bowl of fruit once again and took another bite, but the excitement remained. Maybe he needed a distraction, something he had to focus on. Setting the bowl down he turned to the female. "Are you enjoying the festivities this evening?"

She turned, revealing a pair of keen green eyes under thick orange lashes. Aiden's heart skipped a beat, but they were nothing like Penelope's. She smiled, her black-painted lips revealing straight teeth. "I am enjoying the evening very much, Your Majesty. It is such an honor to be here to witness this momentous occasion."

"I appreciate your attendance. I hope your journey here was not too laborious." He knew the other cities could take days to travel from, most folk not having the luxury of portals from Sgiath as he did. She may even have been one of the residents of Summer and her travel would have been intense to say the least.

"Oh, I would not have missed this for the world," she claimed. "I believe your reign will be something spoken about in history books one day. Faerie will become something completely new with you as High King. I can just feel it."

Aiden held back a grimace. "Well, I hope for all our sakes it is a good change."

She gave him a confident smile and picked up a piece of cheese from her plate, raising it as if in toast. "I know it will be."

Aiden lifted his bowl in toast as well and they both took a bite. His soul settled, feeding off the confidence of the fae beside him and with the centering of the fruit. A hand settled on his shoulder, and he looked up to see Fiadh standing in front of him.

"It's time for you to ask a partner for the first dance."

He set down his food. "Please excuse me, apparently I'm..." He glanced over at the empty seat beside him.

Fiadh looked at him quizzically. "Who are you talking to?"

Aiden blinked at the now empty chair and then back up at Fiadh. "Someone was just sitting there." He looked around but couldn't spot any butterfly wings in the crowd.

"No matter. Shirina is waiting for you. She has a list of potential dance partners and wants to point them out."

Aiden groaned and Fiadh chuckled as he helped him to his feet.

"If I let her choose, do you think she'll let me get away with not dancing with anyone else for the rest of the revel."

"If you are all right marrying the only girl you dance with this evening."

Aiden grimaced then. He wouldn't be marrying anyone anytime soon.

They found Shirina and Dair at the edge of the dance floor,

whispering back and forth to one another. Aiden had to get up right behind them to even hear what they were saying.

"What is so wrong with Islay?" Shirina asked. "You liked dancing with her well enough last year."

"Yes, but now she is on the hunt for a mate," Dair said under his breath. "We do not want to entrap Aiden in a sticky situation, especially with the daughter of Spring's guard captain. Besides, Briar has been courting her in the background, but she will leave him for a bigger catch."

"Blizzards. He could ask Aisla."

"And have his toes broken."

"Morag?"

"He would be lucky to survive the encounter with his hearing intact."

Fiadh stepped up beside his wife to join the conversation. "She just came into another banshee gift."

"Caitir might be a good choice," Dair supplied.

"She just got betrothed," Shirina responded with a shake of her head.

Back and forth the three of them went. Aiden watched the twirl of fabrics and flashes of smiles as the dancers continued to circle the floor. The dances were nowhere near as stiff as the ones in Olympia, the movements here flowing and many of the dancers following their own rhythm rather than any choreographed steps.

His eyes roamed over the room. He could still see a division between the Courts, but the groups were woven in between one another. If he could just push them together—

He turned abruptly, his senses alerting him before his thoughts even registered what was happening. Thaen stepped up beside him, his eyes flashing and his brows furrowed.

Aiden clenched his hands, bracing for whatever he had to say. Thaen leaned down and spoke before the rest of his family even realized he was there.

"She is in the tree."

Aiden looked about. "Where? Is she safe? Did you take her to the study?" He took a step toward the exit. They had decided to bring her to the royal study first and gather Sgiath and Aiden's family to help explain everything.

Thaen grabbed his arm. "No, she is *in* the tree."

36
TRUNKS AND DRESSES

"LET ME OUT!" PENNY POUNDED HER FISTS AGAINST THE SMOOTH wood for what had to be the fiftieth time. Her arms glowed beneath the fabric of her torn dress as she pressed her palms to the trunk again, attempting to manipulate the tree that very much seemed to have a mind of its own.

Penny screeched in frustration and kicked the wall. The hit did little to the wooden barrier but did hurt her foot.

"You stupid tree!" The green on her arms blazed as she grabbed the dagger from her boot and went to stab at the wall in front of her. She would dig herself out, even if it would probably make her cry later just thinking about it. It was a beautiful tree, but it was very much in her way.

Before the blade could dig into the silvery flesh, the wood bucked beneath her, and she lost her footing. She fell on her rear, the green of her hands flickering in her shock.

"Did you seriously just knock me to the ground?" A chuckle of disbelief bubbled up. She set a softer hand to the ground beneath her. "What on Gaia's green earth?" She closed her eyes and connected with the tree rather than pushing herself on it. Penny heard herself gasp as her magic met the tree's, the magic that had lured her at the bridge earlier that day. It was immense, the depth of the tree's magic. It was rooted in everything around it, in the very Land itself. It connected with every creature, inside and out. Penny saw the folk dancing and celebrating above her. She saw the sparks of light and the wisps of shadow. They flashed in quick succession through her consciousness until landing on one so familiar it made her heart ache.

She opened her eyes, returning to the small hollow the tree had carved out. "Yes! Yes, I need to get to him. Please, I need to speak with him."

The floor gave a little shake under her hands. *Was that excitement?*

Penny shook her head and got to her feet. She thought this kingdom bizarre already, but sentient trees were definitely unexpected. Her arms still glowed faintly, the connection remaining even after she'd come back to herself. She set her green hands on her hips. "Will you please let me out?"

Instead of answering, light bloomed into the space. Penny spun and found a new hole growing in the wall across from where she'd entered, stairs forming as the entrance widened.

Penny let out a relieved breath. She took a step and then stopped. This was a Faerie tree—*the* Faerie tree. Who knew what kind of trouble awaited her if she followed where it led?

She touched the outer edge of the entrance. "I suppose it's better to take a chance on the magic tree than the grumpy looking assassin I nearly took out with a bridge." She stepped up the stairs and the room disappeared behind her, filling in with the wood it had probably been originally.

No going back now.

Penny continued up the trunk as it formed step after step, lighting the way. Was this how termites felt tunneling through the trees a thousand times their own size? Penny smiled at the odd thought and touched her hand to the wall. More light blossomed from where her fingers trailed against the wood, almost like a greeting.

Such a strange tree. Yes, the plants she'd connected with in the past had all possessed a semblance of life and magic within them, but nothing like this.

Penny's legs began to tire beneath her. Sweat beaded her brow and the back of her neck. She used the edge of her now ruined skirt to wipe away the moisture, attempting to keep herself from looking *too* frazzled when she saw Aiden. She tripped on her torn skirt, bashing her knee on the step in front of her. With her dagger, she cut the dragging fabric up to her calves and left the scraps behind her. *I suppose if I'm going to make an entrance, it ought to be a memorable one.* She just prayed Aiden wouldn't be embarrassed by her ragged appearance.

The growth of the steps slowed, reducing Penny's pace as well. Her chest rose with weary breaths, her magic finally taking its toll from the fight on the bridge and her rage at the tree. She would sleep like the dead later.

The steps stopped altogether, and a small hole formed once again, growing until Penny could slip through. The faint light the trunk had emitted disappeared as she stepped into a moonlit room. The ceiling of the circular room was open. Large branches arched over the space, allowing thin beams of moonlight to dapple the floor. Rows of chairs circled the room, like rings in a trunk, stopping at the base of a small dais where a crystalline chair sat in the center.

"The faerie-glass throne," Penny whispered, tucking her dagger back into her boot. She walked down the small aisle between the chairs until she stood at the foot of the throne— the one Aiden must have sat in only earlier that day. She took a step forward, her fingers reaching out to trail over the arm of the transparent seat.

She whirled, looking up into the branches. "Why did you bring me here?" The branches above her rustled, as if answering her, but Penny didn't know the language. She shook her head in frustration. "I thought we were going to see Aiden."

The branches above her head began to move.

More than a rustle.

Like an arm reaching out toward her.

Penny took a step back and the movement stopped, as if waiting for her permission.

Penny watched the branches for a moment. She'd faced the Gray Man, púca, goblins, trolls, and rebels in the last few months. Even the blasted Lòchran had made an appearance. Surely a tree was not the thing that would do her in. She gave a slow nod, not actually knowing if it could see her acquiescence, but not being able to speak if she wanted to anyway.

The tree must have understood, because the branch continued forward until it brushed past her side and slid around her waist. From there, thin tendrils crept out, forming the shape of a skirt. Dark blue leaves sprouted, covering the holes between the twigs and filling out the shape. Buds formed in rows down the length but remained closed. Penny felt a tug on her head and lifted her fingers to find more of the buds woven into the crown of braids around her head. A few flexible branches made their way down her arms, trailing the embellishments already woven into the sleeves of her dress.

"Sweet Gaia, this is amazing." She looked up at the branches as they retreated back into the sky. "Is dress making a regular hobby for a tree?"

The branches shook, almost like the tree was laughing.

Penny shook her head. *Laughing trees.* She really was losing her mind in this place.

A sliver of light peeked through along the wall, a pair of doors opening. She walked over, her boots sinking into the plush carpet beneath her feet. With a nudge, she pushed the doors open a bit further to peek into the hall. Not a soul stood on the other side. Penny crept out and shut the door behind her.

Her eyes soaked in the marvelous architecture, the open space having been grown into a hall rather than carved. *Amaz-*

ing. The tree itself was a marvel, a stunning palace morphed from the trunk. It was a feat of powerful magic, transforming something from its natural state into something new. Or perhaps it grew like this. The magic of this place was beyond her.

She really did feel like some sort of insect, scuttling about under the bark. Hopefully, nothing would come around to squash her.

Looking up and down both ends, she put her hands to her hips. "Would you be willing to offer me some direction here? I'd rather not run into the Lòchran skulking about the halls before I find Aiden."

A pinprick of light sharpened on the wall in front of her, growing to a circle no bigger than her hand. The light danced a bit against the wood before zipping down the hallway. Penny laughed as she gave chase down the corridor. She raced out of the center of the trunk, and windows materialized in the walls. The first one Penny came across afforded her a view of the Winter Court in all its glory. The frozen lake stretched out, glittering with starlight waltzing on its reflective surface. It almost looked like the sky itself had come down to rest on the earth.

Light flashed, urging her forward. The winding corridors descended, winding their way lazily down the trunk. The walk was far less rigorous than the hike up the magical stairs. Penny's stomach began to flutter as the sounds of life began to echo down the halls.

By the Goddess, she was so close.

The light guiding her stopped abruptly, spinning in a circle agitatedly and zipping back the way they'd come. Penny retraced her steps, following the beacon until it stopped next to a tapestry. It zipped back and forth from behind the large cloth.

"You want me to hide behind it?"

The light increased, as if in confirmation.

"Great, first I get a magical leaf dress and now the little

light is telling me to hide behind a tapestry." She sighed and moved forward to tuck herself behind the woven cloth. "I don't think Collista Seda herself could make something like this up."

The light flashed urgently before disappearing and Penny finally settled behind the cloth, a sliver of the hallway still in view from the side. She waited, hoping this wasn't some insane game of hide and seek.

The hairs on the back of her neck prickled. She squinted out into the hall, waiting for whatever had her nerves quaking. A shadow grew on the wall, someone coming around the corner. The male was a shadow himself, not even making a sound as his feet trod over the wooden floor.

The Lòchran.

If she was a termite, he was a spider. Hunting.

The Lòchran stopped in the hall, his eyes scanning the walls, flicking over her hiding place twice before he took another step forward.

Penny held her breath, fervently praying her skirts didn't make the tapestry bulge as much as she thought it would.

The Lòchran's silent steps took him out of view, and she let out the breath she'd been holding.

The tapestry flew away from the wall, completely revealing her and the Lòchran in front of her. She held in a gasp, shock rendering her completely still.

The Lòchran's pale eyes scanned the space, never once looking right at her, but more like through her. His eyes narrowed in confusion and Penny felt her own widen. He tilted his head back and forth, but the confusion only deepened on his face. His fingers lifted and began to reach toward her face.

Something clattered down the hall and the Lòchran's head snapped in that direction. A curse hissed between his lips and the tapestry fell from his hand, covering Penny once again.

The prickle of unease faded, but Penny remained where she was. She looked down at her skirts, seeing no glamour there and nothing to denote as to why the infamous assassin couldn't see her. She shook her head. She wouldn't ask why, but she'd take the blessing for what it was. A cursed miracle.

The little light returned, and Penny frowned at it. "And where did you run off to? I almost got caught."

The light zipped back down the hall, not the least concerned about their near catastrophe.

"I'm going to get killed in this place," Penny muttered. "I just know it." She followed behind all the same.

The light stopped at a set of intricate doors, where a red hat with a white feather sat on the ground. She heard footsteps fade off to the side, but her attention returned to the door. Songbirds engraved in the wood grain sat frozen in states of singing and soaring. Penny's fingers brushed over the design in awe. She could feel the vibrations of music and life on the other side. The revel. The guiding light fluttered through the wooden feathers of the birds' wings until it stopped around the polished handles.

Penny grasped the handles and pulled them open.

37
ADORE

Aiden held out his hand to the mint-haired girl. "Lady Saranae, could I trouble you for a dance?"

Shirina and Dair had finally agreed on the dance partner—much to Aiden's distress. Lady Saranae was the only female he'd been acquainted with, making his invitation somewhat natural. Her family's standing in Spring's Court only made it more so.

Lady Saranae grinned up at him, a predator attempting to act the demure prey. He'd seen the look flashed at his brothers enough times to recognize it for what it was. "Of course, My Sovereign. I would be honored." She placed her hand in his, her dry fingers like old twigs—or bones.

By the Goddess, he needed to stop being so morbid.

He led her out to the center of the dance floor, his other hand at his back as he faced her. The dance was one he'd practiced during what he called his "kingly lessons" with his cousins. The steps were similar to a cotillion, where the partners would switch as the dance went along. However, none of the dances here were anything like what he'd had to learn in Olympia. Between keeping a smile on his face and his panic at having Penelope running through the Tree at bay, he had to trust his instincts with the movements of the dance.

His family stood behind Lady Saranae, giving him looks of encouragement. He almost rolled his eyes but realized Lady Saranae had been speaking.

"Could you repeat that?"

She gave him a condescending smile as the music struck the opening chords and they began the first steps of the dance. "I asked if you were enjoying the evening so far."

Aiden bobbed his head. "Yes. I am humbled so many came to offer their support."

The dance separated them for a moment, delivering another partner into his arms for a turn, then switching back to Lady Saranae.

"I do not know why you are surprised. Everyone is excited to get to know you." She pulled him a step closer than the dance called for. "Especially me."

He retreated. Sweet Gaia, this female was bold. The dance took him away from her and gave him a brief reprieve before she sashayed in front of him again with her intense eyes and permanent pout. He took a fortifying breath and looked up toward the glittering ceiling above them. He didn't know if he was praying for deliverance or attempting to keep his face as far from hers as he could.

But it was only because he was looking up that he saw the doors to the balcony above swing open.

Aiden's heart stopped the moment his steps did, nearly sending Lady Saranae to the floor. He caught her before she could fall, but his eyes never left the vision at the top of the steps.

Penelope stopped at the edge of the balcony, her dress swaying around her as if the leaves making up her skirt were blowing in a magical breeze. Her hair caught the starlight above them, the red showing when the light caught it just right.

And then her eyes met his and that smile—that cursed, beautiful, brilliant smile—bloomed across her face. Her hands took on that greenish glow and her skirts rippled, blue flowers blooming down along her dress and in the crown of her hair. Without looking down at the flowery dress, she grabbed up her skirts and turned toward the stairs.

His steps moved of their own volition. He half-consciously passed Lady Saranae off to Dair, the people around them turning to see what he was looking at. The music trailed off as he almost sprinted to the stairs.

Penelope stopped three steps above the ballroom floor. Three steps from where he stood.

That glorious smile grew as she watched him. "Praise the Goddess. I finally found you." Her eyes moved to his hair and down to her skirts. "We seem to have coordinated outfits. Like true partners."

He reached up to touch the leafy crown at his head, finding the soft petals of flowers opening up.

Aiden had no words. Just speaking might break apart the dream he found himself in. He held out his hand to her and her fingers slid into his, warm and strong. As unyieldingly as she held his heart.

He pulled her behind him, leading her out to the center of the floor.

"Aiden, wait," she gasped.

Aiden nearly groaned. For months, he'd dreamed of her simply speaking his name. Of looking at him and seeing *him*. She was the only one who had ever done that. But he didn't stop as he brought her to the floor. He wrapped her in his arms and the musicians took it as a cue. They hesitantly took up a slow melody.

"What are you doing?" Penny whispered, mirroring his steps.

He'd almost forgotten how easy this was with her. How in sync they became when they were together.

"Aiden," she chuckled, a flash of frustration mingling with the stark relief and happiness on her face. "I need to speak with you."

Aiden shook his head. He didn't want to talk. He wanted to stay in this moment for as long as he possibly could, the rest of the world be cursed. He never took his eyes from her, not caring what the rest of the room thought or saw. This was probably his last chance to see her. He wasn't going to waste this one moment on worrying about everyone else.

Penelope reached up and touched his face. "I've missed you too."

He pulled her closer, resting his forehead against hers as their steps continued to glide with the music. She was here, in his arms. Her heart beat in time with his, their breaths mingling between them.

Words finally spilled from his mouth. "By the Goddess, I have never loved anything so deeply as I love you."

Tears sprung into her eyes, but her smile bloomed fuller, brighter than the moon outside or the lights suffusing the walls of Crann Mòr. "And I love you."

Nothing could have stopped the smile from stretching across his face. She laughed, a small laugh, but one that sent his stomach flipping and his heart soaring.

"Penelope..." He took a deep breath and reached for the small package in his pocket.

Before he could pull it out, the world came back into focus.

His eyes met Fiadh's, who watched them dance, heartbreak pulled across his face. Shirina wrapped an arm around her husband's, worry mingling with sadness there as well. Dair had disappeared, likely to find Thaen. Thaen, who was looking for Penelope so he could take her somewhere safe so they could figure out a way for her to go home.

Because that's what had to happen, and everyone knew it. She had to go.

He pulled back, keeping in step with the dance, but trying

to distance himself from her as much as he could—as much as it hurt to do so.

Confusion flickered in her eyes. "Aiden?"

"Oh, Penelope, you should not have come here."

Her smile melted into a frown, her brows furrowing. "And why not? I had to get to you, Aiden. There's so much you don't know. Adira is here and—"

"I know she is. She killed the queen. She's teamed up with the water folk and have attacked Summer."

Penelope stopped moving, their steps completely stalling as the rest of the dancers continued waltzing around them. "She did what?"

"We know you saw her in Spring. I met the child you were imprisoned with, and she told me everything." The memory of that child's retelling still burned in his mind. "I can't believe Durant had you chained to a cursed post."

Penelope tightened her hold on his hand. "That doesn't matter anymore. I finally found you and now we can work together to stop her."

"Together?" His heart tripped in his chest, but he cast away the possibility before it could take root. "Penelope, you have to go back to Olympia. It's not safe for you to stay here. The war has already begun on these shores. I can't keep you safe here."

"No. I'm not going anywhere. I'm here to help you. You can't do all of this alone. You need a team."

He looked up to his family still standing behind Penelope. Fiadh took a step forward, but Aiden gave an infinitesimal shake of his head. He didn't want his family getting involved and he needed to seem in control for the rest of the crowd. Everything had to appear as normal as he could make it— especially after he made the mistake of bringing her onto the dance floor, fool that he was. He pulled Penelope back into the last steps of the dance, praying he didn't look as foolish as he was beginning to feel. "I'm not alone. I have family here."

Penelope's eyes widened and began flicking around the room. "You found them? Your mother?"

Aiden felt his features soften. "I found my mother's family. I'm not alone here, but you are. You need to go back. What about *your* mother? What about Rissa and the others?"

"They need you too, Aiden. Why do you think I came all this way? I came to get you and bring you home."

Aiden shook his head. "I can't leave."

Penelope's shoulders drooped. "I know, but it doesn't matter." She straightened, assuming her perfect heiress face. The one she'd used that night when she'd practically black-mailed him into allowing her to learn the art of being a spy. "I'm not leaving, Aiden. Not until Adira is dealt with. We need to talk about what she has planned. I know what she's up to and it's nothing good. I came to warn you."

Aiden's eyes looked above her, watching the crowd. He saw the fury, the disgust as the crowd looked at her. There was no hiding what she was, and no one would tolerate a mage at the right hand of their half-mage king. It was an already difficult road ahead—for him and his kingdom. He wouldn't cause anyone more grief by keeping Penelope here, no matter how much he wanted to.

She had to leave. Even if his heart thrashed at the very idea of ever being separated from her again, she had to.

He met her eyes, pulling on his Lord of the Underworld mask for what he prayed was the last time. "I don't need your help, Penelope. For all our sakes, I need you to leave."

38
PROMISES AND SEEDS

He didn't *need* her help? He was going to make her leave? After everything she'd done to get to him, he was casting her aside.

Again.

He was going to disappear from her life.

Again.

Oh, blast it all! Penny yanked her hands free from his. "You think you don't need my help? You're wrong. I was trapped in that camp for weeks, Aiden. I spoke to Adira Durant every night while I was chained to a post. I know what she's going to do. She's likely already here." Her eyes flicked about the room, watching for those steely, green eyes or silver hair.

Aiden stepped forward, hands clenched at his sides, the Lord of the Underworld on full display. Yes, she'd seen this mask of his before and she could see right through it. He was afraid of something. But she would not allow his fear to dictate her actions.

"Penelope, you can't stay here any longer." He reached for her arm, but she dodged him.

"You can't make me leave." She took another step away

from him, watching the crowd from the corner of her eye. "The Mist is locked up, or so I've heard."

"Penelope, I am High King. I will have the Fuath open for as long as it takes to get you home."

Penny shook her head. "You can't do that." It was exactly what Adira wanted. The rebels only needed a moment.

Where is she?

Penny could only guess at what the cursed woman did in order to weasel her way into the revel without the invitation.

"I can do whatever I want," Aiden said through gritted teeth.

"No, you can't send me back. You can't unlock the Mist, Aiden. It's exactly what *she* wants." This whole thing had likely been a way to do just that. Adira knew Aiden better than anybody. What if Adira had allowed Penny to take the invitation? What if she'd planned to have Aiden reveal everything because Adira knew he'd do anything to protect her? If the Aigeans were already taking the coast, it would be simple for Adira to get men to come up the middle and essentially push the fae into a corner. It would be a massacre.

Aiden's hand almost grasped her sleeve then, but she blocked the attempt. "No, Aiden! You don't understand."

Shadow curled up along his shoulders. "No, *you* don't understand. You're not safe here."

"Neither are you!" she barked back. "You know her, Aiden. Do you really think she doesn't have everything figured out? A hundred different scenarios mapped out in her head. The only chance of defeating her is if we stay together, keep the Mist locked and track her down here where her power of influence is still limited."

"There is no more 'we!'" Aiden hissed. "Don't you see? We aren't a team anymore. We can't be partners! There's nothing you can do here, and I will drag you kicking and screaming to the border myself if I have to." His eyes flicked up behind her, widening.

That tingling sensation bit at the back of her neck. Penny crouched low, a pair of hands grasping the air where she'd just been. She rolled, grabbing her dagger from her boot in the process. The crowd closest to her stepped back as she stood, blade in hand.

The Lòchran grinned savagely. "Do you think your aim will be true this time?"

Penny matched his grin. "Why don't you come a little closer and find out?"

Aiden came between the two of them, his hand resting on the arm of the Lòchran.

"I've got this under control, Thaen." He held up his hand to another group of the crowd that had stepped forward. Penny saw the near perfect image of Aiden standing among them. The Lòchran—or rather Thaen—stepped back to join them. Penny could see the resemblance they all had to one another and the characteristics they shared with Aiden.

Her eyes widened and she looked back at Aiden. "Is this your family?"

Aiden nodded and took another step toward her. "Please, Penelope. Please let me take you home."

She gripped the blade tighter in her hand. The crowd around her began to murmur. Perhaps Aiden was right. Perhaps she did need to go. She obviously didn't belong here.

But looking into the amber eyes watching her now, with love and fear swirling in their depths, she decided she couldn't give him up. Even with the threats, he was worth it. It didn't matter if she was going to stay in a foreign world, or if Adira was traipsing around the kingdom. She couldn't have left him no matter the reason, and her reasons for staying were enough for anyone else to remain. The fact that Adira wanted to destroy him, the fact that he was in a new place with only a few allies, didn't come close to eclipsing the truth that she would feel empty without him. Life in Olympia would be colorless, lifeless, especially after everything they'd been through.

Yes, it was selfish. But for a man who held the world on his shoulders, for the boy who lived for everyone else and whose kindness knew no bounds, she would be selfish. For him, she would do anything.

Something tugged on her. No, not on her. *In* her. Her magic or the magic of the tree pulled her attention past where Aiden stood. Her eyes moved to where a table stood behind him, full of odd foods and familiar ones. At the very edge of the table, laid out in neat rows were bowls of fruit.

Sprinkled with vibrantly blue seeds.

A plan began to form in her mind. The mask of the Domineering Duchess's heir fell into place. He wanted to playact? She would join the troupe and give him the show of a lifetime. She turned her gaze back to Aiden, who in turn furrowed his brows.

"Penelope?"

"All right." She tucked the blade back into her boot. She didn't need *Thaen* pouncing on her for having a blade close to his king. "If you are so adamant about me leaving, I'll go."

Aiden's furrowed brow didn't ease an inch. "Just like that?"

Penelope pulled on her best courtly smile and turned to the room. "I apologize for ruining the fun of your evening. Please, carry on." She turned back to Aiden and walked past him but turned to keep her eyes on him in case he moved. "I'll just wait over here until you can conclude your night." The crowd parted around her, like wheat avoiding a flame so it wouldn't catch. "I wouldn't want to take you away from the party all of these nice folk threw for you." Her eyes flicked toward his family as well, watching to make sure the Lòchran didn't make a move either.

Aiden took a step forward. "What are you doing, Penelope?"

She gave him a smile as her hands began to shake. "I'm

attempting to be reasonable, Your Majesty. You are a king with many responsibilities. I'll simply have to wait my turn."

He took a few more steps toward her. "Why don't I believe you?"

Penny pushed out a light laugh. "Because you're paranoid?" She'd almost reached the table. She could feel the crowd lessen behind her. She purposefully bumped into the buffet. "Oh, pardon me." She turned and swept past the table, grabbing a bowl of fruit and tucking it against her side.

"Put that back *right now*, Penelope!"

Penny jumped and almost sent the bowl crashing to the ground at the sound of Aiden's booming words. He did not raise his voice often, but it thundered far louder than his older brothers' did.

Penny tried to exude innocence as she took another step from him. When he only matched her step, all sense fled, and she brought the bowl around and began lifting it to her mouth.

Aiden was on her in an instant.

She'd never seen him move so fast.

The bowl went flying, spraying fruit all over the floor.

Penelope watched the bowl land with a crash on the ground.

She turned back to meet Aiden's gaze and the absolute terror written all over his face. "Do you know what you almost just did? Do you know what could have happened if you'd eaten that?"

Penelope bowed her head. No, she didn't know what would happen. Six little beads of blue sparkled on the back of her hand. She used her other hand to cover them, placing them in her palm.

She looked back up, her gaze clashing with that of the man she loved, whom she would do anything for. Risk anything for.

"I'm sorry, my love. I can't let you open the Mist."

She brought her hand to her mouth and licked the six, blue seeds from her skin.

Aiden grabbed her face as if to pry them from her mouth himself, but watched in horror as she swallowed back the tiny capsules.

His family swept in, the lavender-haired one speaking quickly. "There were only a few seeds." He whipped his head toward the only female in the group. "It might not be enough."

The female's black eyes met hers and Penny saw the sorrow cracking through their depths, but there was also a hint of respect.

Aiden whirled toward the woman. "Shirina? Was it enough?"

Shirina opened her mouth when Penny felt a shudder rip through her core. Everyone turned. She gasped as she felt the well of her magic rip inside of her.

"No." Aiden grabbed hold of her waist. "No no no no no."

She tried to smile up at him, but another wave blackened the edges of her vision and her legs buckled beneath her. Someone close by gasped and an outraged screech followed after.

Aiden went to the ground with her. "No, Penelope, love, stay with me. Don't let the magic in."

She pushed a weak smile onto her face, hopefully expressing the surety she definitely didn't feel at the moment. "Don't open the Mist," she whispered. It took more strength than it should to speak. "Don't let her out. This is our only chance to get the upper hand."

Aiden pulled her to his chest. "Don't do this, Penelope. Don't let this place keep you from living."

She tried to reach for him, but she blacked out for a moment. "How can I keep living"—another rip of her magic pulled a gasp from her—"w-when the future I dreamed of is trapped somewhere I can't be."

She closed her eyes, the last bit of consciousness slipping from her grasp.

"Oh, Penelope," Aiden's voice followed her into the dark. "But now you're trapped here with me."

39
ATROCITY

AIDEN'S MAGIC RIPPED FROM HIM.

Screams rang in his ears, but he couldn't tell if they were from the crowd around him or simply inside his head. His chest ached with the strain of her pain and the magic flowing from him, but he couldn't make it stop.

She'd eaten the fruit.

No mage had ever eaten the fruit. No fae had ever allowed it. To even think of offering one was blasphemy.

But she'd eaten it.

Would it kill her? He felt her heart beat erratically against his own chest. Or maybe it was his own heart. It wouldn't slow down. What about her magic? Would this affect the gifts the Goddess had given her? Would she become as magicless as the bronties? Would the magic tear her apart from the inside out?

He pushed a tendril of his own magic with the Land's, attempting to find a connection. He'd seen them before. He knew what to look for. The warm magic melded with his, attempting to calm him and heal him of the tumult inside of him. He pushed it aside and found where it had bonded with Penelope. Not a single part of Penelope's magic was visible. It was as Thaen said. They looked identical. Aiden tried to pull it away. If he could separate them, perhaps Penelope could still go home.

But it was no use. There was no way to tell the difference between the two magics and the bond between Penelope and the Land grew deeper by the second. A little gasp passed through her lips, and he didn't know whether to be relieved or absolutely devastated.

"Aedon! You have to stop!"

He looked up to meet Fiadh's eyes, the gray swirls of his magic pushing against Aiden's shadows and forcing them up and away from the crowd. Aiden saw the splashes of silver and violet as well, the twins and Shirina restraining his magic while keeping the other fae away from the violent shadows he'd summoned. The rest of the room was in complete chaos, the ellyllon and bwbachod panicking around him.

But he couldn't stop. He didn't know how. He had to try to save her.

The terror and distress of the folk fed the shadows around him. It cut through him. Fae called for Penelope's head, spittle flying as they testified of the blasphemy they'd just witnessed. His arms tightened around her. No one would harm her. Not while he still drew breath.

"Aedon!" Fiadh's yell brought Aiden's eyes back to his cousin. Fiadh's face tightened with concentration. "Little Shadow, we need to get you both out."

Aiden felt the storm calm within him. Fiadh would help them. Fiadh loved Aiden and would help him figure this out. He was a lifeline, a safe place. If anyone could be trusted with this, it was Fiadh.

A flutter of orange appeared behind Aiden's cousin.

The skirt of giant butterfly wings melted away until only a pair of polished boots shined from under a black cloak. The painted face morphed into the familiar face of the woman he'd been raised by. A pair of green eyes flashed with unadulterated victory as she drew out her crossbow and aimed.

A shadow lunged in front of Aiden, a roar thundering against the winds of the storm around them. Thaen wrapped his body around Aiden's and shielded Penelope as well.

But Durant's aim had always been true.

Fiadh fell to the ground on his knees.

Then his hands.

Then he collapsed, the fletched end of the bolt sticking right out of his back.

"*No!*" Aiden screamed and the entire tree went dark. He looked up, ready to blast Adira Durant apart with every bit of magic he had.

But she was gone.

"We cannot find The Cartographer anywhere, My Sovereign."

The lights around them flickered and the guards at the door both jumped.

Aiden's fingernails dug into his palms. He had to control himself. After the absolute devastation left in the hall where they'd held the revel, he couldn't afford to let his emotions get away with him. He stopped his pacing at the foot of his bed. The bed where Penelope lay completely still.

"Search again."

The guards nodded and fled the room as fast as they could.

Aiden resumed his pacing, the sound of Penelope's breaths ringing out in the vast space of his chambers.

Three thousand eight hundred thirty-two. Three thousand eight hundred thirty-three.

The hairs on the back of Aiden's neck stood up and he looked to the left. Thaen stood in the shadowed corner, his eyes on Penelope.

"Anything?" Aiden asked.

Thaen shook his head. "Whatever magic that witch has stolen, it is more than I can uncover."

Exhaustion finally overtook him. Aiden slumped into the chair next to Penelope's still form. His fingers thread through his hair.

"I'm so sorry, Thaen."

A heavy hand landed on Aiden's shoulder. "This is not your fault. My father's death is not your fault."

"Durant was at that revel because of me. If I would have just—"

"If I would have been paying attention, I would have seen the mark of death on my father before I lunged for you. But after Penelope ate the fruit, I could focus on nothing but her."

"The magic?"

Thaen nodded, then turned to look at Penelope. "What are we going to do with her?"

A flicker of something hot and angry sparked in Aiden's chest. "What do you mean?"

"She cannot stay here, cousin. She does not belong in this land."

Aiden looked up to where she lay on the bed, her auburn waves cascading over the pillows and the crown of blossoms still bright against her hair. "But she cannot leave."

The door burst open, and Shirina lurched into the room. Tears still streamed down her face and sobs wracked her chest as she spoke.

"The Fuath." She took a shuddering breath. "The Fuath is gone."

EPILOGUE
AND THEY WERE TOGETHER AGAIN

ADIRA SIGHED. *BLISS. THIS MUST BE WHAT BLISS FEELS LIKE.*

She shed her disguise and cast the fake jewels the enchantment had been bonded to into the whirl of dunes under the flying carpet. Having to dress as the very beings she abhorred was no small task. She had been more than glad to get rid of that ridiculous butterfly costume. The undetectable glamour had cost a young púca all the magic in her little body, but it had been worth it to escape that revel.

And what a revel last night had been.

She'd almost lost her control when the little king had sat beside her only three days ago. Almost. But then his cousin, his near copy, had shown up. Praise the Goddess he had, or Adira might not have gained her real prize.

And the folk had seen their king's true colors. He'd allowed the mage girl to eat their sacred fruit. The confusion, disgust, and horror rippling over their features and the boy king's devastation...

Delicious.

Then the interrupting fae had shown his magic. It had been destiny and Adira had taken full advantage.

Having the boy king there to witness the death of his

reunited family member had been even better than she'd imagined. Actually witnessing the cracks spread across his heart brought a tranquility she hadn't felt in over five years.

The man riding beside her pointed ahead. Not a speck of fog dotted the horizon and Adira could see for miles and miles ahead of them. A smirk crept up onto her face.

Shadows began streaming out of the waves of sand, a mass of glittering armor and shining eyes. The commander with the salt-and-pepper hair arrived at Adira's side. A wide grin stretched across her face as she gestured toward the lines of soldiers she had led this far. There were a few who had been with them for the past few months, but many were new, eager faces, ready to release justice on this kingdom for the sins of their kind.

Adira spread her arms wide. "Welcome to Faerie! May you have the courage to rewrite your own destiny!"

The answering roar shook the ground and sand cascaded down the dunes.

Adira turned back toward the land she'd come to claim, a savage grin on her face. "I'm coming, Aiden."

Oh, wait! There's something else.
Have you been wondering what's going on over in Olympia?
Well, let me tell you...

Flip the page for a sneak peek of
The Seer's Assassin
A Cartographer's War Novel

PROLOGUE
AN UNFORTUNATE LETTER

Every lie I've ever told I made to get me to this very moment.

Paulo MacGregor set down the pen and ran a hand through his already unruly hair. The line was a bit melodramatic, even for him. He picked up the paper, ready to crumple it. Before he could toss it into the bin, he looked around him, finding dozens of balls of paper surrounding the bin. And his chair.

"Curses," he muttered. Of all the things not to receive visions about, this was what the Goddess chose? He set the paper down and smoothed out the crinkled edge. This was the single most important letter he had ever and would ever write, but he didn't know what words would help him. And he needed help.

With a sigh, he took up the pen once again.

I know this doesn't help my cause, but I pray our friendship will overcome any animosity you feel toward me after you finish this letter.

His chest tightened and he pushed away from the writing desk to look out the window. The first light of dawn grayed the horizon. He could make out the still crumbled stone of the outer wall of Iatrus Castle. If anyone found out what he'd done to make this happen, he could be hanged. *Treason* wasn't the worst of his crimes. He'd allowed war to come to his kingdom. His lands. His home.

He returned to the desk.

There are so many things that would have made everyone else's lives easier. So many things I could have prevented.

Sometimes, when the moon rose high in the sky and only the stars danced outside, he could hear Diana cry in the room across from his. Mater still looked at him with those wise eyes of hers, but the lines around her mouth had transformed from the history of her smiles to the evidence of her hidden frowns. Even Iatrus Castle itself felt the weight of Paulo's decisions. His deceit.

But if I'd changed the future, this future would not be possible.

He reached a hand into his pocket and once again squeezed the gift he'd been given. His last chance.

With a deep breath, he pressed the tip of his pen to the page.

Let me start from the beginning.

AUTHOR'S NOTE

When Persephone is taken to the Underworld, no one really looks at her again. Yes, we read about her mother, about Zeus, about Hermes and Helios and Hades, but what about Persephone? We don't even really see her again until she eats the pomegranate seeds. And I thought that was a tragedy.

And I think, so did Persephone.

When researching Persephone, I came across a lot of poetry about her. About the things she would say to her mother and to Hades. I found Penny's voice in those poems, and I realized there was so much more to Persephone's story than what we've been given. That there was a powerful, strong woman behind the myth, one who made her own choices and fought for what she wanted. That's what this book was. This was *her* story, just told with different lighting.

The scene in this book where Penny eats the fruit was the first scene I had planned in my head. It was the first true image I had of Penny even before I wrote about her and Aiden meeting at the debut ball. This piece of the story has been the catalyst for this entire series and I'm so happy to have gotten you to this point, to meet the Penelope Barclay who introduced herself to me when I started on this crazy writing journey. To meet the Persephone that I found.

This wasn't some simple maiden that had been caught by surprise and stolen from her home. This wasn't a woman that cowered in the dark caverns of the Underworld.

This was a goddess that looked death right in the face and said, "Take me."

ACKNOWLEDGMENTS

Another book and another slew of people to profusely thank. Seriously, you guys, there are so many people that have helped me get this book to where it is, and I would be as lost as Odysseus on the sea without them.

First, I need to thank my family. Eric, I love you. Thank you so much for everything that you do—even when I force you to create giant writing events (Authors in the Dungeon) so I can hang out with all of my cool author friends and talk about books with hundreds of people. Thank you my sweet, kind, patient kiddos for just being you and making all this crazy worth every headache and late night. I'm so glad I get to be on this adventure with you.

A huge thank you goes out to Jeff Wheeler! Jeff, you saved this book! You saved Aiden! I seriously could not be more grateful for your insights and for your continued support with these books. I seriously could not do this without your mentorship or your encouragement. Thank you to my amazing writing groups. To Dad, Ben Bailey, Aimee Hall, Marci Johnson, Robbie of the Beams of Stuffle, Jared Jensen, Tracy Tyler. Thank you for being my first writing group and for putting up with me for so long. You guys are seriously the best. To KayLynn Flanders, Lindsay Hiller, Bonnie Jo Pierson, HR Boyd, Marci Johnson, Kayla Beth Tillotson, Tarry Perry, Natalie Kraus, Sally O'Keef, and especially Kelsey Bryn Larson—because you see Penny and Aiden as I see them. Seriously, you ladies are my lifeline and I love our outrageous Zoom calls.

I need to give Tyleah Merino credit where credit is due. Tyleah, you have read all these books at their worst and have helped me in so many ways. From reading to listening to me rant about story on the phone while our kids are screaming in the background, thank you for all that you do.

Thank you to my wonderful publisher and for the team at OHB. Thank you, Tanya, for being so excited for these books. Here's to hoping it all pays off! Thank you, Kate Ward, for all the crazy things you make me do. This series is only getting better because of you. Thank you again to Sally O'Keef and her editing machete. You make these books shine.

And as always, thanks go to my Heavenly Father—my muse, my inspiration, my writing companion. With God, nothing is impossible.

ALSO BY ALLISON ANDERSON

Children of Ash

Children of Ash

Son of Steel

The Cartographer's War

The Spring Maiden

The Shadow Lord

The Unseen King

The Unwanted Queen

The Cartographer's War: A Necessary Tragedy

The Seer's Assassin

The Fated Mage

ABOUT THE AUTHOR

Allison Anderson lives her best life as a wife, a mom, a dedicated member of The Church of Jesus Christ of Latter-Day Saints, and a fantasy writer. As a lifelong fantasy nerd, she finds it natural to create stories of her own and you can often find her jotting down new story ideas or talking about dragons. She's spent most of her life across the southwestern United States.

https://www.allisonandersonauthor.com/